THE TROPIC
OF SERPENTS

THE TROPIC OF
SERPENTS

A MEMOIR BY LADY TRENT

Marie Brennan

TOR®

A TOM DOHERTY ASSOCIATES BOOK

NEW YORK

THE TROPIC OF SERPENTS

Copyright © 2014 by Bryn Neuenschwander

All rights reserved.

Interior illustrations by Todd Lockwood

Map by Rhys Davies

Designed by Greg Collins

A Tor Book
Published by Tom Doherty Associates, LLC
175 Fifth Avenue
New York, NY 10010

www.tor-forge.com

Tor® is a registered trademark of Tom Doherty Associates, LLC.

The Library of Congress has cataloged the hardcover edition as follows:

Brennan, Marie.
    The tropic of serpents / by Marie Brennan.—First edition.
        p. cm.
    "A Tom Doherty Associates book."
    ISBN 978-0-7653-3197-7 (hardcover)
    ISBN 978-1-4299-5635-2 (e-book)
    1. Women scientists—Fiction.   2. Dragons—Fiction.   I. Title.
    PS3602.R453T76 2014
    813'.6—dc23

                                                                2013026345

ISBN 978-0-7653-7508-7 (trade paperback)

Tor books may be purchased for educational, business, or promotional use. For information on bulk purchases, please contact the Macmillan Corporate and Premium Sales Department at 1-800-221-7945, extension 5442, or write to specialmarkets@macmillan.com.

First Edition: March 2014
First Trade Paperback Edition: February 2015

Printed in the United States of America

D 13

THE TROPIC
OF SERPENTS

PREFACE

Public opinion is a fickle thing. Nowadays I am hailed from one end of Scirland to the other as a testament to the intelligence and derring-do of our race; indeed, if I am not the most famous Scirling woman in the world, I daresay I give Her Majesty the Queen a good fight. I would not go so far as to presume I am universally loved, but if any news-sheet sees fit to mention me (as they do not so often anymore, on account of my signal failure to make any new shattering discoveries in the last decade, nor to nearly get myself killed in suitably gruesome fashion), chances are good that mention will be favorable in tone.

It was not always so. Though few are old enough to remember it, and even fewer rude enough to bring the topic up, I was once reviled in the scandal-sheets. But I have no compunctions about washing my dirty linen in public—not when the linen in question is so very old and wrinkled. Some of the errors I was accused of were entirely baseless; others, I confess, were entirely fair, at least insofar as my own opinion may be trusted.

As I have not yet finished composing my memoirs, I cannot say with certainty that this, the second volume in the series, will be the most gossip-ridden of them all. That honour may belong to a later period in my life, before my second marriage, when my interactions with my future husband were grist for a very energetic mill both at home and abroad. I am still considering how much of that I will share. But this volume will be a fair contender, as it was during these years that I found myself accused of fornication, high treason, and status as the worst mother in all of Scirland. It is rather more than most women manage in their lives, and I own that I take a perverse sort of pride in the achievement.

This is also, of course, the tale of my expedition to Eriga. The warnings delivered in my first foreword continue to apply: if you are likely to be deterred by descriptions of violence, disease, foods alien to the Scirling palate, strange religions, public nakedness, or pinheaded diplomatic blunders, then close the covers of this book and proceed to something more congenial.

But I assure you that I survived all these things; it is likely you will survive the reading of them, too.

Lady Trent
Amavi, Prania
23 Ventis, 5659

PART ONE

*In which the memoirist departs her homeland,
leaving behind a variety of problems
ranging from the familial to the criminal*

ONE

My life of solitude—My sister-in-law and my mother—
An unexpected visitor—Trouble at Kemble's

Not long before I embarked on my journey to Eriga, I girded my loins and set out for a destination I considered much more dangerous: Falchester.

The capital was not, in the ordinary way of things, a terribly adventurous place, except insofar as I might be rained upon there. I made the trip from Pasterway on a regular basis, as I had affairs to monitor in the city. Those trips, however, were not well-publicized—by which I mean I mentioned them to only a handful of people, all of them discreet. So far as most of Scirland knew (those few who cared to know), I was a recluse, and had been so since my return from Vystrana.

I was permitted reclusiveness on account of my personal troubles, though in reality I spent more of my time on work: first the publication of our Vystrani research, and then preparation for this Erigan expedition, which had been delayed and delayed again, by forces far beyond our control. On that Graminis morning, however, I could no longer escape the social obligations I assiduously buried beneath those other tasks. The best I could do was to discharge them both in quick succession: to visit first my blood relations, and then those bound to me by marriage.

My house in Pasterway was only a short drive from the fashionable district of Havistow, where my eldest brother Paul had settled the prior year. I usually escaped the necessity of visiting his house by the double gift of his frequent absence and his wife's utter disinterest in me, but on this occasion I had been invited, and it would have been more trouble to refuse.

Please understand, it is not that I disliked my family. Most of us got on cordially enough, and I was on quite good terms with Andrew, the brother most immediately senior to me. But the rest of my brothers found me baffling, to say the least, and my mother's censure of my behaviour had nudged their opinions toward disapproval. What Paul wanted with me that day I did not know— but on the whole, I would have preferred to face a disgruntled Vystrani rock-wyrm.

Alas, those were all quite far away, while my brother was too near to avoid. With a sensation of girding for battle, I lifted my skirt in ladylike delicacy, climbed the front steps, and rang the bell.

My sister-in-law was in the morning room when the footman escorted me in. Judith was a paragon of upper-class Scirling wifehood, in all the ways I was not: beautifully dressed, without crossing the line into gyver excess; a gracious hostess, facilitating her husband's work by social means; and a dedicated mother, with three children already, and no doubt more to come.

We had precisely one thing in common, which was Paul. "Have I called at the wrong time?" I inquired, after accepting a cup of tea.

"Not at all," Judith answered. "He is not at home just now—a meeting with Lord Melst—but you are welcome to stay until he returns."

Lord Melst? Paul *was* moving up in the world. "I presume this is Synedrion business," I said.

Judith nodded. "We had a short respite after he won his chair, but now the affairs of government have moved in to occupy his time. I hardly expect to see him between now and Gelis."

Which meant I might be cooling my heels here for a very long time. "If it is not too much trouble," I said, putting down my teacup and rising from my seat, "I think it might be better for me to leave and come back. I have promised to pay a visit to my brother-in-law Matthew today as well."

To my surprise, Judith put out her hand to stop me. "No, please stay. We have a guest right now, who was hoping to see you—"

I never had the chance to ask who the guest was, though I had my suspicions the moment Judith began to speak. The door to the sitting room opened, and my mother came in.

Now it all made sense. I had ceased to answer my mother's letters some time before, for my own peace of mind. She would not, even when asked, leave off criticizing my every move, and implying that my bad judgment had caused me to lose my husband in Vystrana. It was not courteous to ignore her, but the alternative would be worse. For her to see me, therefore, she must either show up unannounced at my house . . . or lure me to another's.

Such logic did little to sweeten my reaction. Unless my mother was there to offer reconciliation—which I doubted—this was a trap. I had rather pull my own teeth out than endure more of her recriminations. (And lest you think that a mere figure of speech, I should note that I *did* once pull my own tooth out, so I do not make the comparison lightly.)

As it transpired, though, her recriminations were at least drawing on fresh material. My mother said, "Isabella. What is this nonsense I hear about you going to Eriga?"

I have been known to bypass the niceties of small talk, and ordinarily I am grateful for it in others. In this instance, however, it had the effect of an arrow shot from cover, straight into my brain. "What?" I said, quite stupidly—not because I failed to understand her, but because I had no idea how she had come to hear of it.

"You know perfectly well what I mean," she went on, relentlessly. "It is *absurd*, Isabella. You cannot go abroad again, and *certainly* not to any part of Eriga. They are at war there!"

I sought my chair once more, using the delay to regain my composure. "That is an exaggeration, Mama, and you know it. Bayembe is not at war. The mansa of Talu dares not invade, not with Scirling soldiers helping to defend the borders."

My mother sniffed. "I imagine the man who drove the Akhians out of Elerqa—after two hundred years!—dares a great deal indeed. And even if *he* does not attack, what of those dreadful Ikwunde?"

"The entire jungle of Mouleen lies between them and Bayembe," I said, irritated. "Save at the rivers, of course, and Scirland stands guard there as well. Mama, the whole point of our military presence is to make the place safe."

The look she gave me was dire. "Soldiers do not make a place safe, Isabella. They only make it less dangerous."

What skill I have in rhetoric, I inherited from my mother. I was in no mood to admire her phrasing that day, though. Nor to be pleased at her political awareness, which was quite startling. Most Scirling women of her class, and a great many men, too, could barely name the two Erigan powers that had forced Bayembe to seek foreign—which is to say Scirling—aid. Gentlemen back then were interested only in the lopsided "trade agreement" that sent Bayembe iron to Scirland, along with other valuable resources, in exchange for them allowing us to station our soldiers all over their country, and build a colony in Nsebu. Ladies were not interested much at all.

Was this something she had attended to before, or had she educated herself upon hearing of my plans? Either way, this was not how I had intended to break the news to her. Just how I *had* intended to do it, I had not yet decided; I kept putting off the issue, out of what I now recognized as rank cowardice. And this was the consequence: an unpleasant confrontation in front of my sister-in-law, whose stiffly polite expression told me that she had known this was coming.

(A sudden worm of suspicion told me that Paul, too, had known. Meeting with Lord Melst, indeed. Such a *shame* he was out when I arrived.)

It meant, at least, that I only had to face my mother, without allies to support her in censure. I was not fool enough to think I would have had allies of my own. I said, "The Foreign Office would not allow people to travel there, let alone settle, if it were so dangerous as all that. And they *have* been allowing it, so there you are." She did not need to know that one of the recurrent delays in this expedition had involved trying to persuade the Foreign Office to grant us visas. "Truly, Mama, I shall be at far more risk from malaria than from any army."

What possessed me to say that, I do not know, but it was sheer idiocy on my part. My mother's glare sharpened. "Indeed," she said, and the word could have frosted glass. "Yet you propose to go to a place teeming with tropical diseases, without a single *thought* for your son."

Her accusation was both fair and not. It was true that I did not think as much of my son as one might expect. I gave very little milk after his birth and had to hire a wet-nurse, which suited me all too well; infant Jacob reminded me far too much of his late namesake. Now he was more than two years old, weaned, and in the care of a nanny. My marriage settlement had provided quite generously for me, but much of that money I had poured into scientific research, and the books of our Vystrani expedition— the scholarly work under my husband's name, and my own inane bit of travel writing—were not bringing in as much as one might hope. Out of what remained, however, I paid handsomely for someone to care for my son, and not because the widow of a bar-onet's second son ought not to stoop to such work herself. I simply did not know what to do with Jacob otherwise.

People often suppose that maternal wisdom is wholly instinc-tual: that however ignorant a woman may be of child rearing prior to giving birth, the mere fact of her sex will afterward en-dow her with perfect capability. This is not true even on the grossest biological level, as the failure of my milk had proved, and it is even less true in social terms. In later years I have come to understand children from the perspective of a natural histo-rian; I know their development, and have some appreciation for its marvellous progress. But at that point in time, little Jacob made less sense to me than a dragon.

Is the rearing of a child best performed by a woman who has done it before, who has honed her skills over the years and enjoys her work, or by a woman with no skill and scant enjoyment, whose sole qualification is a direct biological connection? My opinion fell decidedly on the former, and so I saw very little prac-tical reason why I should not go to Eriga. In *that* respect, I had given a great deal of thought to the matter of my son.

Saying such things to my mother was, however, out of the question. Instead I temporized. "Matthew Camherst and his wife have offered to take him in while I am gone. Bess has one of her own, very near the same age; it will be good for Jacob to have a companion."

"And if you die?"

The question dropped like a cleaver onto the conversation, sev-ering it short. I felt my cheeks burning: with anger, or with shame—likely both. I was outraged that my mother should say such a thing so bluntly . . . and yet my husband had died in Vys-trana. It was not impossible that I should do the same in Eriga.

Into this dead and bleeding silence came a knock on the

door, followed shortly by the butler, salver in hand, bowing to present a card to Judith, who lifted it, mechanically, as if she were a puppet and someone had pulled the string on her arm. Confusion carved a small line between her brows. "Who is Thomas Wilker?"

The name had the effect of a low, unnoticed kerb at the edge of a street, catching my mental foot and nearly causing me to fall on my face. "Thomas Wil—what is *he* doing here?" Comprehension followed, tardily, lifting me from my stumble. Judith did not know him, and neither did my mother, which left only one answer. "Ah. I think he must be here to see me."

Judith's posture snapped to a rigid, upright line, for this was *not* how social calls were conducted. A man should not inquire after a widow in a house that wasn't hers. I spared a moment to notice that the card, which Judith dropped back on the salver, was not a proper calling card; it appeared to be a piece of paper with Mr. Wilker's name written in by hand. Worse and worse. Mr. Wilker was not, properly speaking, a gentleman, and certainly not the sort of person who would call here in the normal course of things.

I did what I could to retrieve the moment. "I do apologize. Mr. Wilker is an assistant to the earl of Hilford—you recall him, of course; he is the one who arranged the Vystrani expedition." And was arranging the Erigan one, too, though his health precluded him from accompanying us. But what business of that could be so urgent that Lord Hilford would send Mr. Wilker after me at my brother's house? "I should speak with him, but there's no need to trouble you. I will take my leave."

My mother's outstretched hand stopped me before I could stand. "Not at all. I think we're all eager to hear what this Mr. Wilker has to say."

"Indeed," Judith said faintly, obeying the unspoken order woven through my mother's words. "Send him in, Londwin."

The butler bowed and retired. By the alacrity with which Mr. Wilker appeared, he must have sprang forward the instant he was welcomed in; agitation still showed in his movements. But he had long since taken pains to cultivate better manners than those he had grown up with, and so he presented himself first to Judith. "Good morning, Mrs. Hendemore. My name is Thomas Wilker. I'm sorry to trouble you, but I have a message for Mrs. Camherst. We must have passed one another on the road; I only just missed her at her house. And I'm afraid the news is unfortunate enough that it could not wait. I was told she would be visiting here."

The curt, disjointed way in which he delivered these words made my hands tighten in apprehension. Mr. Wilker was, quite rightly, looking only at Judith, save a brief nod when he spoke my name; with no hint forthcoming from him, I found myself exchanging a glance instead with my mother.

What I saw there startled me. *We're all eager to hear what this Mr. Wilker has to say*—she thought he was my lover! An overstatement, perhaps, but she had the expression of a woman looking for signs of inappropriate attachment, and coming up empty-handed.

As well she should. Mr. Wilker and I might no longer be at loggerheads the way we had been in Vystrana, but I felt no romantic affection for him, nor he for me. Our relationship was purely one of business.

I wanted to set my mother down in no uncertain terms for harboring such thoughts, but forbore. Not so much because of the sheer inappropriateness of having that conversation in public, but because it occurred to me that Mr. Wilker and I were engaged in *two* matters of business, of which the Erigan expedition was only one.

Judith, fortunately, waved Mr. Wilker on before I could burst out with my questions unbidden. "By all means, Mr. Wilker. Or is your message private?"

I would not have taken the message privately for a hundred sovereigns, not with such suspicions in my mother's mind. "Please," I said. "What has happened?"

Mr. Wilker blew out a long breath, and the urgency drained from him in a sudden rush, leaving him sagging and defeated. "There's been a break-in at Kemble's."

"Kemble's . . . oh, no." My own shoulders sagged, a mirror to his. "What did they destroy? Or—"

He nodded, grimly. "Took. His notes."

Theft, not destruction. Someone knew what Kemble was working on, and was determined to steal it for their own.

I slumped back in my chair, ladylike dignity the furthest thing from my mind. Frederick Kemble was the chemist Mr. Wilker had hired—or rather *I* had hired; the money was mine, although the choice of recipient was his—to continue the research we ourselves had stolen in the mountains of Vystrana, three years ago. Research that documented a method for preserving dragonbone: an amazing substance, strong and light, but one that decayed quickly outside a living body.

The Chiavoran who developed that method was not the first one to try. What had begun as a mere challenge of taxidermy—born from the desire of hunters to preserve trophies from the dragons they killed, and the desire of natural historians to preserve specimens for study—had become a great point of curiosity for chemists. Several were racing to be the first (or so they thought) to solve that puzzle. Despite our best efforts to maintain secrecy around Kemble's work, it seemed someone had learned of it.

"When?" I asked, then waved the question away as foolish. "Last night, and I doubt we'll get any time more specific than that." Mr. Wilker shook his head. He lived in the city, and visited Kemble first thing in the morning every Selemer. This news was as fresh as it could be, short of Kemble having heard the intruder and come downstairs in his nightclothes to see.

I wondered, suddenly cold, what would have happened if he had. Would the intruder have fled? Or would Mr. Wilker have found our chemist dead this morning?

Such thoughts were unnecessarily dramatic—or so I chided myself. Whether they were or not, I did not have the leisure to dwell on them, for my mother's sharp voice roused me from my thoughts. "Isabella. What in heaven is this man talking about?"

I took a measure of comfort in the irreverent thought that at least she could not read any hint of personal indiscretion in the message Mr. Wilker had brought. "Research, Mama," I said, pulling myself straight in my chair, and thence to my feet. "Nothing that need concern you. But I'm afraid I must cut this visit short; it is vital that I speak to Mr. Kemble at once. If you will excuse me—"

My mother, too, rose to her feet, one hand outstretched. "Please, Isabella. I'm dreadfully concerned for you. This expedition you intend . . ."

She must be concerned indeed, to broach such a personal matter before a stranger like Mr. Wilker. "We will speak of it later, Mama," I said, intending no such thing. "This truly is a pressing matter. I've invested a great deal of money in Mr. Kemble's work, and must find out how much I have lost."

TWO

B eing a recluse is not good for one's conversational agility. I was accustomed to thinking over my words, revising them, and writing fair copy before sending the final draft of my letter to its recipient. My comment accomplished its intended purpose—she let me go at last, with Judith's polite farewells to fill in the awkward gaps—but my satisfaction faded rapidly as I went out into the street. "I fear I will regret that," I admitted to Mr. Wilker, pulling on my gloves.

"I don't think you've lost much of your money," he said, raising his hand to signal a hansom on its way to the nearest cab stand.

Sighing, I drew his arm down. "My carriage is across the street. No, I don't mean the investment; I don't regret that in the least. Only that I said anything of it to my mother. She is determined to see bad judgment in everything I do nowadays."

Mr. Wilker did not respond to that. Although we were on more cordial terms by then, we were not in the habit of sharing our personal troubles with one another. He said, "All is not lost, though. Kemble took his current notebook upstairs with him last night, so that he could read over his thoughts as he prepared for bed. His wife may deplore the habit, but in this instance it's been a godsend."

(To those of my readers who flinch at minor blasphemies of this sort: I must warn you that there will be more ahead. Mr. Wilker restrained his language around me in our Vystrani days, but as we grew more comfortable with one another, he revealed a casual habit of naming the Lord. If I edited his language here, it would misrepresent his character, and so I pray you pardon his frankness, and mine. We were neither of us very religious.)

Mrs. Kemble was no resentful housewife; she worked alongside her husband, handling the practical matters of ordering and measuring chemicals, while he spent hours staring at the wall and chewing on the battered tail of his pen, mind lost in theoretical matters. But she believed in a separation of work from daily life, and I—who, you may have noticed, am more of Frederick Kemble's mind—blessed her failure to break him of his habits.

I said as much to her when we arrived at Kemble's house and laboratory in Tanner Fields, and got a dry look that did not entirely hide the nervous aftereffects of the intrusion. "I appreciate that, Mrs. Camherst, but I'm afraid it didn't save the glassware."

"May I see?" I asked. Mrs. Kemble led us into the cellar, presently in a state of half gloom, the only light coming in by the street-level windows. It was enough to show the destruction: shattered glass everywhere, measuring instruments bent and smashed. A chemical stink flooded the air, despite the open windows and a boy outside cranking a device to ventilate the room. They had not merely taken Kemble's notes; they had also done what they could to delay his further progress.

I held my handkerchief over my nose and said, "Mrs. Kemble, I am so very sorry. If you send a letter to my accountant, I'll see to it that you're reimbursed for what you've lost. It can't restore your peace of mind, but—" I gestured helplessly. "It can at least replace the glassware."

"That's very good of you, Mrs. Camherst," she said, mollified. "Kemble is upstairs; I needed him out from under my feet while I sort out what's broken and missing. Lucy will make you some tea."

Mr. Wilker and I went obediently up to the parlour, where we found Frederick Kemble scribing furiously onto a loose sheet of foolscap. Others like it were scattered across the table and the floor, and Lucy, the Kembles' remaining unmarried daughter, was trying to find a clear space to set down a tray containing not only tea but a stack of blank paper. She saw us come in and touched her father's elbow. "Papa—"

"Not now—let me—" He jerked his head in a motion I thought was meant to stand for a wave of his hand, his actual hands being occupied in note-taking.

Lucy retreated to our side. "What is he doing?" I asked, not daring raise my voice above a murmur.

"Writing down as much as he can remember," she said. "From the notebooks that were taken."

After three years' work, the process for preserving dragon-bone must have been engraved on the inside of his eyelids; *I* had it memorized, and I was not even chemist enough to understand what most of it meant. As for the rest—"Mr. Wilker said the most recent notebook was not taken, yes? So long as we have that, the older notes do not matter half so much." Most of them were obsolete by now, documenting failed experiments.

Lucy spread her hands. "He says even the old notes are important—that he likes to look over them from time to time."

She went off to fetch more teacups, and then Mr. Wilker and I settled in at the far end of the parlour to hear Lucy's account of the break-in and the investigation thus far. By the time she finished, Kemble was ready to pause in his work and acknowledge the rest of the world.

"If they'd come before the Sabbath . . ." he said, clearly grateful they had not. His daughter presented him with a cup of tea, which he took and drained absently. "I was looking back through the old notebooks during lunch on Eromer, and something there caught my attention. Last year, I—"

Mr. Wilker, who had long since learned to recognize the warning signs, cut him off before he could descend into a thicket of scientific language I would not understand in the slightest. The body of our collective knowledge has grown so rapidly in my lifetime that although I am accounted an extremely learned woman, there are whole fields I know very little of; chemistry is one such. It was not a part of young ladies' curricula in my youth, and my self-education had gone in other directions. Mr. Wilker therefore diverted our chemist to the points he knew I would care about. "You said something about that this morning, yes. It gave you an idea?"

"I think so," Kemble said. "It's only a thought so far; it will take a great deal of testing. But I may have an idea for synthesis at last."

Had that not been the fifth time I heard those words from his mouth, I would have been more excited. It was, after all, the purpose for which we had hired Kemble. We knew how to preserve dragonbone; that was no longer a challenge. But Mr. Wilker and I, discussing the matter three years ago, had seen the peril in that knowledge.

Quite apart from the desire of hunters to preserve their trophies, and the desire of natural historians to study their subject at leisure *post mortem*, the qualities of dragonbone made it attractive to other kinds of person. Its mechanical properties were far superior to those of iron and steel, being both lighter and stronger—and as the easily accessible iron deposits in Anthiope and other parts of the world began to run dry, the value of any alternative grew by the year.

I could enumerate at length the drawbacks to the industrial use of dragonbone. Indeed, I had an article already prepared on the subject, ready to send at a moment's notice to all the reputable publications. Dragons were even rarer than iron, and while it was true that they reproduced (which ore was not known to do), any widespread demand for their bones would lead to mass slaughter, perhaps even to extinction. The irregular shape of many bones rendered them less than ideal for the construction of machines, which would result in a great deal of waste. The expense and hassle of harvesting them from dead dragons (many of whom lived in locales as foreign and distant as those still rich in iron) rendered the prospect less than entirely profitable. It went on for pages, but the entire thing was flawed in its basic assumption, which was that people would consider the matter rationally before making their decisions.

The truth was that the idea would bring speculators flocking like vultures to a dead horse, ready to pick the bones clean. And if I tried to persuade myself that I was exaggerating—that such a doom-filled scenario would never come to pass—I had only to consider the Erigan continent, where the lure of iron had led several Anthiopean states to involve themselves in the affairs of the nations there. If Thiessin was willing to conquer Djapa, and Chiavora to encourage revolution in Agwi, and Scirland to insert itself between the Talu Union and the military might of the Ik-wunde, for the sake of being able to build new steam engines, we would not hesitate to sacrifice a few dumb beasts.

I sighed and drained the last of my tea. "With all due respect, Mr. Kemble, I would almost welcome another set of eyes on the matter. I have every confidence that you can solve this riddle, given sufficient time—but that, we may not have. Sooner or later *someone* will figure out Rossi's method, even without your notes. If we are to avert chaos, we need a way to satisfy the demand for this substance that does not involve butchering dragons."

"I doubt we'll be that lucky," Mr. Wilker said, sounding bleak. "With the eyes, that is. How many people will go to the amount of effort you and I have, just to spare animals? We already butcher elephants for their ivory and tigers for their skins, and those are only decorative."

He was likely right. Sighing, I said, "Then we had best hope the police recover the notebook—small hope that it is. Do we have any notion who took it?"

By the grim silence that fell, the answer started with "yes" and got worse from there. Mr. Wilker replied obliquely. "You know about the symposium, I think."

A gathering of scholars, hosted by the Philosophers' Colloquium, the preeminent scientific body in Scirland. Mr. Wilker had not been invited to attend, because he was not a gentleman. I had not been invited to attend either, because although my birth was gentle, I was not a man.

But we knew someone who met both of those requirements. "If it was one of the visitors, Lord Hilford might be able to find out."

"He won't have much time," Kemble said, coming out of the reverie into which he so frequently lapsed. "Doesn't that end this week?"

It did, and the scholars would be returning to their homelands. "Indeed. Then I suppose I know what I am doing with my afternoon."

I was at the door to Lord Hilford's townhouse before I remembered that I had promised to pay a visit to my relatives by marriage. I knocked on the door anyway, thinking to ask the earl whether I might send them a note. As it transpired, he was not yet home from a lecture, and so I had more than enough time while I waited for him in the drawing room.

If you find yourself thinking that I had enough time to make good on that promise, you would be more or less correct. The Camhersts lived not far from Lord Hilford, in Mornetty Square, and it would not have taken me above twenty minutes to get there and back. But I did not know how long they would keep me, and it was of the utmost importance that I warn Lord Hilford about the intruders at Mr. Kemble's as soon as possible. If any of the visitors to the symposium were behind this outrage, we had limited time in which to find out—even more limited time in which to do anything about it.

So I told myself, at least. The truth is that, although I had told my mother that Matthew, my brother-in-law, had agreed to take in little Jacob while I was gone, I had neglected to mention his lack of enthusiasm for the entire plan. His wife did not mind the addition of a temporary child, but Matthew minded very much the possibility of keeping him permanently. He might have even been the one who spilled the secret of the Erigan expedition where my mother could hear. Drained by my morning confrontation and by the dreadful news of the break-in, I was not minded to face anyone I did not consider a good friend.

I therefore wrote out an excuse and had Lord Hilford's boot-boy run it to Mornetty Square. Then I linked my gloved hands together and paced, and worried, and made a hundred different (and useless) plans, until Lord Hilford came home.

When I heard his booming voice in the front hall, I did not trouble to wait in the drawing room. He saw me as I came to the door, and the white tufts of his eyebrows rose. "Not that it is anything but a pleasure to see you, Mrs. Camherst—but I judge by your expression that whatever has sent you here is not good."

"It is not," I confirmed, and explained while he divested himself of overcoat and hat. His cane he kept; over the years it had become less of an affectation, more of a necessity, as his rheumatism worsened. Lord Hilford followed me into the drawing room and lowered himself into a chair with a sigh.

"Mmmm," he said when I was done. "Makes me wonder if

someone has been to Vystrana. I've heard nothing from Iljish in Drustanev, but you know what the post is like. And someone might have slipped past them."

The villagers were supposed to protect the nearby cavern from curiosity-seekers. It was the preserved dragonbone in that great cemetery which had given the first clues to the role of acid in that process. "We said nothing of it in the book," I reminded Lord Hilford, referring to the monograph we had published after our expedition. "Only that the dragons tore apart their deceased kin and took the pieces to a certain cave. No one could assume preservation from that—nor could they find the cave."

The flapping of the earl's hand reminded me I was saying nothing he did not already know. "Still, it's a possibility, and one we have to consider. Another possibility: Kemble talked."

"If he had talked, would they have smashed up his laboratory?" I said indignantly. Then I saw the flaw in my own logic. "Ah. You are not accusing him of selling the secret—only of letting slip some hint that might have allowed another to guess what he's doing."

"Any of us might have done it," Lord Hilford admitted. "Including me. I'd like to think I'm discreet, but—well. Scholars drink a great deal more than anyone thinks, and I don't hold my liquor as well as I once did."

I thought that I, at least, was unlikely to have betrayed our secret. Not out of any particular virtue; only from lack of opportunity. I hardly spoke to anyone who didn't already know. But it would do no good to say that, and so I said only, "Is there anyone among the Colloquium's visitors that you would suspect? Or among its members, I suppose."

Lord Hilford grunted. "Several, unfortunately. There's a ratty Marñeo fellow I don't trust in the slightest; he's been accused of passing other people's research off as his own. Guhathalakar openly admits he's working on the issue of preservation. No one in the Bulskoi delegation is, but they have more opportunity than most to go poking around in Vystrana. The Hingese . . . I'm sorry, Mrs. Camherst, but without more to go on, all I can do is guess."

"Well, Mr. Wilker is still at Kemble's, and they've spoken with the police; we can hope for some kind of lead." I got up and paced again, fingers twisting about one another. "I *wish* I could do something to hurry the research along. Money is only helpful to a point; it cannot make Frederick Kemble's brain work faster."

"Attend to your own research," Lord Hilford said, very reasonably. "You may find something of use there; or if you do not, then every bit we know about dragons is one more bit we can use to protect them. But, ah—if I may shift us from one nerve-wracking topic to another—"

It was enough to stop me pacing. I tried to remember the last time I had heard the earl so wary, and could not think of a single time. When I turned to look, he was chewing on the drooping end of his moustache. I waited, but he did not speak. "Oh, out with it," I said at last, quite sharply. "My nerves are no less wracked for being forced to wait."

"Natalie," he said, reluctantly. "Or rather, her family."

His granddaughter was not ordinarily a topic of any tension at all. Nor were her family, but—"Let me guess," I said with a sigh. "They have decided I am not fit company for her. Well, everyone else in Scirland has come to the same opinion; I am not fit company for *anyone*."

"That isn't precisely it. They think you eccentric, yes, but for the most part harmlessly so. The trouble is that an eccentric is not good company for an unmarried young lady—not if she wishes to change that state."

I frowned at him in surprise. "But Natalie is only—" My

arithmetic caught up with my words, and stopped them. "Nearly twenty," I finished heavily. "I see."

"Quite." Lord Hilford sighed, too, studying the head of his cane far more closely than it warranted. "And so her family is quite adamant that she should not accompany you on this expedition. You are likely to be gone for six months at least, likely more; it would be ruinous to her marital prospects. Old maids and all that. I've argued, truly I have."

I believed him. Lord Hilford had progressive notions of what ladies might do, and he doted on Natalie besides; but in the end he was not his granddaughter's guardian. "Have you spoken with her?"

"She knows how her family feels. I was hoping you might approach her—woman to woman, you know—and see if you can't reconcile her to the situation. They aren't intending to shackle her to some brute."

If she did not look herself out a husband soon, though, she might have trouble finding anyone other than a brute. "I will see what I can do."

Lord Hilford sounded relieved. "Thank you. You'll have to be quick about it, though. I was intending to write this afternoon, but now I can tell you in person: the schedule has moved up. Can you and Wilker be ready to depart in two weeks?"

Had I been holding anything, I would have dropped it. "*Two weeks?*"

"If you can't, then say so. But it may be another delay otherwise. There's going to be a changeover at the Foreign Office, and the incoming fellow is not very keen on travellers going to Nsebu, not with the unrest in the area."

"Unrest?" I echoed, my mother's comments rising to mind.

"Ah, yes—that hasn't reached the papers yet," Lord Hilford said. "I had it from our man in the Foreign Office. A group of

Royal Engineers were ambushed while surveying the south bank of the Girama, which is territory that is supposed to be firmly in our control. It seems Eremmo has quieted sufficiently under the Ikwunde yoke for the inkosi to start looking outward once more. It has certain people rather worried."

As well it should, given the military success the Ikwunde had enjoyed in the last fifty years, under one warlike inkosi after another. Still, I had faith in our soldiers there; and besides which, the river region between Bayembe and Eremmo was clear on the other side of the country from Nsebu. "One scare after another," I sighed. "I am beginning to think this expedition will never happen."

"It will, Mrs. Camherst, if we move quickly enough. Otherwise we'll have to argue the new fellow around."

We had already spent months arguing the previous fellow around. I reviewed the state of my affairs, and suppressed the unladylike desire to curse. I had counted on Natalie to be my companion on this journey. Would it be worse to travel alone—with an unmarried man, no less—or to find some other woman on short notice? Or rather, would suffering the latter be worse than suffering the consequences of the former?

Either way, I could not let it change my answer to Lord Hilford. "I can be ready, yes. You will have to ask Mr. Wilker yourself."

"I know what Tom will say." The earl levered himself up out of his chair. "Two weeks it is, then. I'm sure you need to prepare. And in the meanwhile, I will look into the matter of this break-in."

THREE

Natalie's wings—The merits of a husband—Keeping promises—
Ladies at supper—Lord Canlan

"Miss Oscott is here," the footman informed me when I returned home. "I believe she is in your study, ma'am."

Natalie. I would have preferred to delay my promise to Lord Hilford, but if I was to leave in two weeks, I simply could not spare the time. "Thank you," I said, distracted, and went upstairs.

My study had been my husband's study, once. The servants had called it *the* study for a good two years after his death; it was not the sort of room women normally laid claim to. But eventually their speech had shifted. No doubt that owed a great deal to the amount of time I spent there, often in the company of Natalie Oscott.

She was indeed there, tacking a sheet of paper onto the piece of corkboard we had hung for the purpose. "Oh, good heavens, Natalie," I said when I saw the figure drawn on it. "*That* again?"

"I've improved it," she said, flashing a grin at me over one shoulder. "On advice from an enthusiast in Lopperton. He thinks I'm a lad named Nathaniel—I do a very good boy's hand, when I put my mind to it. On account of falsifying my brothers' workbooks, when they had not written the exercises our tutor had set. What do you think?"

The sheet of paper bore a large diagram, whose predecessors I had seen several times before. A wing spread across the page, with measurements carefully marked out, and annotations I could not read from where I stood. Even at range, though, one difference was apparent. "Are the wings curved?" I asked, curious despite myself.

"Yes, he thinks that would work better than a straight line. And he suggested an alteration to the harness, too, which he is going to try for himself as soon as he can get it built."

To be perfectly honest, I thought they were both mad. True, as I said in the previous volume of my memoirs, I had been obsessed with dragon wings since I was a small child, and the idea of being able to join them in the sky was attractive. But a human being cannot possibly achieve the pectoral strength necessary to fly by flapping artificial wings—that having been Natalie's first notion. The best he (or she) can hope for is to glide, and even then, I had my doubts.

But Natalie found the notion an intriguing challenge. For her, the puzzle was intellectual: was it possible to engineer such a thing? In pursuit of that question, she had taught herself a great deal of mathematics, most of which I understood not at all. She had also entered into correspondence with others, for she was not the only one with an interest in the matter.

Natalie had not yet attempted to construct or test any of her designs, for which I was grateful. Although my husband had called me the queen of deranged practicality, putting into practice ideas others would never think to attempt, even I have my limits. Those limits may, as this narrative will show, lie further out than I claim (and honestly believe)—but I never know that until I pass them. And that, I invariably do under circumstances in which going further seems to be the only feasible course of action. It is only afterward that the "deranged" part of "deranged practicality" becomes apparent to me.

Besides, I was less sanguine about others' foolishness, and I should not like to lose my closest companion to a broken neck. Natalie had been a great source of comfort to me since Jacob died. It made my heart all the lower, thinking that I could not bring her with me to Nsebu.

She saw my fallen countenance, but mistook the cause. "I promise you, Isabella—I have no intention of committing my own bones to the tender mercies of physics. At least not until after Mr. Garsell has conducted enough tests of his own to assure me the design is sound."

"That isn't it." I sighed and went to my desk—Jacob's desk, once—in front of the broad windows overlooking the back garden. The surface was cluttered with books and stray pages, my preserved sparkling Greenie standing guard over them all; I had forbidden the maid to touch anything there, even to dust. Maps of Eriga, travellers' reports, a draft of an article I was considering asking Lord Hilford to submit for me, under his own name. The Colloquium would not accept a paper from a woman.

Perhaps it was the reminder of the Colloquium's requirements that made my voice more bitter than I intended. "I spoke with your grandfather today. About your family."

"Oh." That one word might have been a valve, letting out all the air and vitality that had made her so animated.

I lowered myself into the familiar leather of my chair. "You know, then. That they don't want you to go to Eriga."

"They want me to stay here and find a husband. Yes." Natalie turned and paced a few steps away.

Her deficit of enthusiasm was plain enough that I could read it without seeing her face. "It needn't be bad, Natalie. You have your grandfather on your side, and from what you tell me, your family has at least some understanding of your interests. My father consulted a matchmaker to obtain a list of unmarried men who might share their libraries with me. I am sure you can go

Miss Natalie Oscott

further, and find yourself a husband who will support you in your work."

"Perhaps."

She did not sound convinced. Before I could muster the words to develop my argument, however, Natalie spoke again. "It is an untenable situation, and I know it. One way or another, I must be dependent upon *someone*. If not a husband, then one of my brothers, or—" She caught herself. "I cannot ask that of them. But how much less can I ask it of some stranger?"

I had not missed that *or*. She had been about to list a third option, and had stopped herself. I could guess why. Rather than approach it directly, though, I said, "Do you not *want* a husband? Presuming you could get a good one."

She stood very still; I think she was considering my words. Then she turned to face me, and answered in the tone of one who had never realized her true reply until this moment. "No," Natalie said. "I don't."

"Not for security," I said. At that time the Independent Virtue movement had not yet taken shape, but its arguments were beginning to be spoken, in hushed, half-scandalized whispers. If a woman traded her marital favors for financial support, did that not make marriage a form of prostitution? "But for companionship, or love, or—" Now it was my turn to stop shy of my final words.

Natalie blushed, but answered me. "Not for any of those. I welcome the friendship of men, of course. But childbirth is dangerous, and motherhood would demand too much of my time; and I have no interest in the, ah, *activity* for its own sake. What is left?"

Very little, really. Except, perhaps, for an end to her family's nagging—and that could be gotten in more than one way.

It would have been wiser for me to wait until I had examined the state of my own finances. But I was to leave for Nsebu in two weeks, and had no desire to waste my time or Natalie's on the wrong preparations. "If you must be dependent on someone," I said, "and if your conscience will permit it, then be dependent upon me. Widows often take on companions, and you have very nearly been mine these past few years; certainly you have been a dear friend. We might make it official."

The hitch in her breath told me I had struck my mark precisely. Still, she protested. "I could not do that to you, Isabella. If I do not marry, I will be a burden forever. What if you change your mind, two or ten or twenty years down the road? It might poison our friendship, and I would never wish for that."

I laughed, lightly, trying to ease the desperate tension in her eyes. "A burden forever? Piffle. Stay with me, and I will qualify you for a life of independent and eccentric spinsterhood, supported as you choose by your learning and your pen. Other ladies have done it before."

Not many, and few in the sorts of fields that Natalie had proven herself drawn to. Historical scholarship was more permitted to women than the designing of crazed glider-wings. But I had formed the resolution to live my own life as my inclinations demanded, and furthermore to do so with such zeal that society could not refuse me; it would be the height of hypocrisy for me to preach feminine obedience to Natalie now. She knew the obstacles and the cost: she had seen how I lived.

By the growing light in her eyes, the obstacles were trivial and the cost not even worth mentioning. Her mouth still spoke protest, but only because of her commitment to logic. "My family will take some convincing, I fear. Possibly a great deal of it."

"Then you have two choices," I said, rising from my desk. At this time of day, the light through the windows at my back would frame me with a kind of halo; I was not above using that for dramatic effect. "You may stay in Scirland and work on convincing them, and I will welcome you at my side once that is done. Or you can inform them of your intentions, leave for Nsebu with me in two weeks, and let them work through it on their own."

"Two weeks?" Natalie said, her voice going faint. "You are leaving in—oh, but—"

I waited. My words were sincere; I would welcome her company whether she had to join me later, or wait for my return to Scirland. It would not be fair to importune her with my preference.

Besides, I knew her well enough to guess her answer. Natalie's shoulders went back, and her chin rose. "I had promised to come with you to Eriga," she said. "A lady should keep her promises. I will inform my family at once."

I had never thought Maxwell Oscott, the earl of Hilford, to be a sadist. His chosen method for smoking out the thief, however, had me reconsidering the matter, with conclusions not favourable to him.

The symposium whose attendees comprised our most likely suspects was, as Mr. Wilker had said, scheduled to end that week. With the police turning up nothing of use in their examination of Mr. Kemble's laboratory, Lord Hilford settled upon a more direct method of looking for the guilty party, which was to invite everybody to supper and see if anyone flinched.

To this end, he arranged, on vanishingly short notice, to rent out the upper hall at the Yates Hotel, and made certain that all those we suspected would attend. His excuse for this event was that the Colloquium, which would be hosting a formal banquet the following night to mark the end of the symposium, did not permit women within their hallowed walls, and he was most determined that the gentlemen attending should meet various ladies of education and merit—chief among them, though he did not advertise this fact, the widowed Mrs. Camherst.

I suffered Lord Hilford to put me in the limelight because it would aid in our efforts, but under my mask of cooperation, I was petrified. At that time, the only monograph attributed to my name was *A Journey to the Mountains of Vystrana*, which was hardly a scholarly work; I had laid no claim to *Concerning the Rock-Wyrms of Vystrana*, being concealed in the small print line "and Others" that followed Jacob's name. The few articles I had published regarding my research on sparklings had not gone to scholarly journals. Furthermore, I had been a confirmed recluse for going on three years. The prospect of attending a dinner party with a crowd of intelligent strangers made me so ill, I could hardly eat.

But if my spine weakened, I had only to think of the dragons who risked slaughter if the secret of dragonbone preservation became widely known, and my resolve returned to me on the spot.

The upper hall at the Yates blazed with candles that night, their light reflecting from polished wall sconces, crystal chandeliers and glasses, and the silver cutlery laid in precise ranks along the table. The men who filled the room were a mixed lot: northern Anthiopeans in their black-and-white suits, southern Anthiopeans in calf-length caftans, Yelangese in embroidered silk robes, Vidwathi with gems pinned to the fronts of their turbans.

It was not a proper dinner party, such as Mrs. Gatherty would approve of; the gentlemen outnumbered us ladies by more than three to one. But Lord Hilford had done an admirable job, given the short timeline, of organizing female guests, so that Natalie and I were not the only women present. The noted ornithologist Miriam Farnswood was there, as was the mathematician Rebecca Norman; the others, regrettably, would mean little to a modern audience, as their work has not survived history's forgetting.

I pasted a smile on my face, took Lord Hilford's arm, and sallied forth to see who flinched.

He introduced me, one by one, to the individuals we considered to be possible culprits. Nicanor de Androjas y Reón (the "ratty Marñeo fellow," whose nose did give him an unfortunately rodentlike profile), Bhelu Guhathalakar, Cuong Giun Vanh, Foma Ivanovich Ozerin. Mr. Wilker was with us throughout. None of us expected our interlocutors to have broken into Kemble's laboratory themselves—that was undoubtedly the work of some hired criminal—but surely the thief would, by now, have glanced through Kemble's notes. Both Mr. Wilker and I were mentioned in abundance. The connection between that work and our names could not be missed.

Cuong dismissed me immediately as beneath his notice, directing all his conversation to Lord Hilford and Mr. Wilker. Ozerin gave me more attention than I wanted, but entirely of the wrong kind; I extracted myself from that situation as soon as possible. De Androjas y Reón did indeed flinch, but he flinched at everything. (I daresay that man was even less comfortable in such a crowd than I was.)

By far my best experience was with the Vidwathi chemist Guhathalakar, though not, at least initially, for any reason useful to our investigation. He was a younger man than the others, thirty at most, and of a type I have met countless times in my life, which I confess is one of my favourites: so powerfully interested in his subject that trivial considerations such as the sex of his conversational partner are quickly forgotten. I might have been an orang-outang, for all he cared; what mattered was that I showed an interest in chemistry, and could respond to his statements with intelligent questions (even if I did not understand the answers). It took no encouragement at all to get him expounding at length, his voice growing louder in his enthusiasm.

It took only slightly more encouragement to steer his exposition in the desired direction. "Dragonbone, yes," he said, his Vidwathi accent thickening as his mind raced ahead of his Scirling. "I think it is on the anvil. With so many working on the problem, and the new equipments we have now, we will have answers soon."

He showed no sign of secret knowledge, no coy hint that he knew more than he said. Even as I responded, I transferred my attention to the milling guests around us. Guhathalakar's voice carried well enough that soon the entire room would know we were discussing the preservation of dragonbone. "It would be a tremendous breakthrough, if so. But I confess myself troubled as to the potential consequences, once the problem has been solved. My own interest being in natural history, I cannot be easy with anything that might encourage men to butcher dragons."

An indulgent chuckle from my left heralded the arrival of Peter Gilmartin, marquess of Canlan and vice president of the Philosophers' Colloquium. "But did your own party not butcher a dragon for study in Vystrana, Mrs. Camherst? Indeed, I believe the drawings of that carcass were your own work. Surely it would be beneficial if natural historians could keep dragon skeletons for study, rather than having to obtain a fresh specimen each time they have a new question."

His words were sensible, but his patronizing tone ruffled my feathers the wrong way. Still, deference for his rank forced me to moderate the reply I wanted to make. "It is not natural historians who concern me, my lord, but others, who would likely not be satisfied with a handful of skeletons. Humanity is not known for its moderation."

"And yet, think of the advances that might come from this discovery. Should we put the well-being of savage beasts above our own?"

I had an entire article's worth of reply ready for that, but Lord

Canlan gave me no chance to begin. He turned instead to Guha-thalakar, leaning forward with a friendly and conspiratorial air. "I should like to talk with you tomorrow, when we are in more scholarly surroundings. Your work interests me a great deal, and I believe I may be in a position to help it along."

Had a Vystrani rock-wyrm breathed on me in that moment, I would not have been more frozen. While Guhathalakar made his reply, my gaze was pinned to Lord Canlan, unblinking, as if by sheer intensity of stare I could prove or disprove the sudden suspicion in my mind.

The marquess was in no position to exploit Kemble's research himself; his primary interest was in astronomy. But that did not mean he could not benefit in other ways. For example, by selling Kemble's notes to the highest bidder.

Did I imagine it? Was the smile he directed at me before moving onward merely more patronizing courtesy, or did it send a private, gloating message that he had what I had lost, and intended to profit thereby?

He was a marquess, above even Lord Hilford's elevated station. I could hardly accuse him where he stood—though shock nearly overrode my better judgment and sent the words flying out by reflex. And he had said nothing I could even begin to construe as evidence, let alone expect anyone else to accept.

I fulminated on this through dinner, for there was no opportunity to step aside with any of my own friends and give them my suspicions. Afterward, though, while Lord Hilford was bidding his guests farewell, I pulled Mr. Wilker into a corner and delivered the tale in a rush.

"It's a thin reed," he said when I was done, and frowned across the room at where Lord Canlan stood.

Although the words of his reply were scarcely encouraging, I took heart from them nevertheless. There was a time when Thomas

Wilker would have scoffed at my fears and chalked them up to an overactive imagination. Now he gave them due thought—even if that thought did not lead him to agree.

"I don't know how he would have learned about Kemble's research," I admitted. "But you have met him before—is he the sort of man who would flaunt his coup in front of me like that?"

Mr. Wilker's grimace gave me my answer. "When it is the project of a woman and a man like me . . . then yes. He loves nothing more than to put his lessers in their place."

An unpleasant personality hardly constituted proof, though. "Will you be at the dinner tomorrow night?" Mr. Wilker shook his head, mouth set in a hard line. Of course not: his sex might grant him entrance to the Colloquium's premises, but the son of a Niddey quarryman would not be invited to their celebratory meal. "Lord Hilford will have to watch, then. Lord Canlan may be offering the notes for sale, or at least sounding out his prospective buyers. Given how chatty Guhathalakar is, it won't be difficult to encourage him to say."

A muscle tensed in Mr. Wilker's jaw. "It doesn't offer very good odds for stopping him, though. We can't ask Lord Hilford to make a scene."

"It's the best we can do for now," I said. And left unspoken the rest of my thought: that we might not have any chance to do better.

FOUR

*Farewell to Jacob — My brother-in-law — Lord Denbow
is distraught — Natalie's escape — Scene at the
docks — A woman's wishes*

I can only blame myself for the incident that occurred prior to my departure from Scirland.

The rush to depart left me with several dozen matters to take care of, ranging from soothing family to receiving Lord Hilford's report on the final dinner of the symposium. (He did indeed question Guhathalakar, but to no avail; Lord Canlan had ignored the man all night, much to Guhathalakar's disappointment.) One matter in particular had me more distracted than most.

On the afternoon before my departure, Mrs. Hunstin, the nanny, brought my son downstairs to await his uncle and his aunt, who would be caring for him in my absence. Jacob was dressed in a toddler's tunic, but his hair, a sandy shade that had not yet darkened to his father's rich brown, was presently bare of the cap clutched in his free hand. The other was clinging tightly to the nanny's thumb, his eyes fixed on the staircase, which he descended one careful step at a time.

My mother had accused me of heartlessness, abandoning him to go gallivanting (her word) off to foreign parts. Her accusation was only the first of many, as that judgment eventually spread not only to others in our social circle, but to complete strangers and even the news-sheets. There is no reason anyone should believe me, justifying my behaviour at so late a date, but since I cannot move on without addressing this subject, let me say: a pang went through my heart at the sight of my son.

I had not been close to him during his rearing; he was not a fixture of my life the way children are for more involved mothers. I found more satisfaction in scholarly work than in the day-to-day tasks of feeding, cleaning, and comforting him. In hindsight, a part of me does regret missing such events—but even then, my regret is an intellectual one. The development of children from soft, formless infants into adults is a complex process, and one I have come to appreciate on account of my dragon studies. (If you read that comparison as demeaning, please understand that, for me, it is not. We, too, are animals: the most wondrous and fascinating animals of all.)

Despite that distance, however, I was not without feelings for my child. Indeed, I imposed that distance in part *because* of my feelings. Jacob's serious expression, focused on the challenge of navigating the stairs, reminded me profoundly of his namesake. As people had told me, again and again, he was in some sense a piece of my husband, something left behind by Jacob the elder. I was not always prepared to deal with the reminder of that connection. And so a part of me chose instead to flee.

But it does a disservice to my own life to claim the Erigan expedition was motivated by fear. It is equally true, if not more so, to say that I was running *toward* something, as well as away. Jacob and I had shared a love of dragons, and if leaving his child behind was a betrayal of his memory (as so many people assured me it was), staying home would have been a betrayal as well. We had agreed, on a mountaintop in Vystrana, that caging me in the life expected of a Scirling gentlewoman would be the death of me: spiritually, if not physically. I had been caged for three years, caught in a trap of my grief and obligations as well as society's expectation, and the work I did on paper granted me only partial freedom. Enough to make me long for more, but not enough to satisfy.

And yet I *was* leaving behind a child. An innocent toddler, bereft even before his birth of one parent; now I proposed to subject myself to any number of potential calamities that might rob him of the second.

I cannot say whether, given the chance to revisit that choice, I would change my mind. I know now, to a very precise measurement, how great the dangers would be, and how narrowly I escaped them. But I also know that I survived. Little Jacob was not left orphaned, as so many had direly predicted.

Did I have the right to undertake such risk? I can only give the same answer I gave then: that I have, and had, as much right as any widower in the same situation. Few question the widower's decision, but everyone questions the widow's.

On that day, I buried all such thoughts beneath the press of business. (Almost all of them. The aforementioned pang was real, nor was it alone.) When little Jacob had finished his conquest of the stairs, I knelt on the cool stone of our front hall, putting myself closer to his eye level, and held out my hands. He came to them, hesitantly, after a nudge from Mrs. Hunstin.

"You must be very good," I told him, trying and failing to affect the tone I had heard others use with toddlers. "Nanny H will be coming with you, so you must mind her as you always do, even if you are in a different house. I shall write to you often, and she will read you my letters; she will write to me of how you are doing. And I shall be home before you know it."

He nodded obediently, but I doubt he grasped the import of my words. That I should go away for a few days was a thing he had experienced many times; that I should go away for months or a year was beyond his comprehension.

I heard the crunch of gravel before the ringing of the bell. My brother-in-law Matthew had arrived, and his wife, Elizabeth, with him. They came into the hall, and I gently shooed Jacob toward Bess, with Mrs. Hunstin close behind.

Matthew sighed, looking at Jacob, and shook his head. "I know it's too late to talk you out of this. But still—"

"You're right," I said, before he could finish that thought. "It *is* too late. I am profoundly grateful for your assistance, Matthew; never doubt that. But I am going to Eriga."

His jaw shifted, briefly giving his face the air of a bulldog facing an unwelcome target. "I never would have predicted that Jacob would marry so obstinate a woman."

I wanted to say, *then you did not know him very well.* But in truth, I'm not certain Jacob himself would have predicted our match, in the years before we met. Antagonizing Matthew would accomplish very little, and so instead I said nothing; I merely kissed my son on the head, admonished him once more to be good, and waved them off down the drive.

Their carriage, departing, passed another on its way in. The coat of arms painted on the door was familiar; it was the white stag's head on a blue field of Hilford. The carriage, however, was not the earl's. I stood in the entrance, frowning, and so had no chance to hide when the door flung open (almost before the carriage had stopped) and emitted the angry form of Lewis Oscott, the Baron of Denbow—and the earl of Hilford's eldest son.

"Where is she?" he demanded, striding across the gravel to confront me. "Bring her out here at *once.*"

"She?" I repeated dumbly, for my tongue had not yet caught up with my brain.

"*Natalie!*" His bellow made my ears ring. "I have tolerated her association with you; until now it did little harm. But this is beyond the pale. You will give her up this *instant.*"

My brain had only got as far as knowing who "she" was. Why else would Natalie's father be here, if not because of his daughter? But the rest still escaped me. I had not seen Natalie in several days—a fact which, in retrospect, should have concerned me. We left for Eriga on the morrow, after all. I had been too distracted to think of it, though, assuming (when I considered it at all) that she must be with her grandfather.

A foolish assumption, and one that was now having some very unfortunate consequences.

"My lord," I said, collecting my thoughts, "I cannot give you what I do not have. Natalie is not here."

"Don't lie to me. Where else would she be, if not here?"

The accusation set my back up. "With her grandfather, perhaps? I take it she spoke to you about her intentions."

He snorted in disgust. "*Intentions*. It is madness, and you know it. A position as a companion is all well and good for women who cannot do better, but Natalie has perfectly good prospects, so long as she is here to take advantage of them. And you will not want her with you forever. When you tire of her—or get yourself killed, which is entirely possible—what will become of her? No, Mrs. Camherst, I will not allow you to ruin my daughter's future for your own benefit." Setting his shoulders, he strode forward.

I slapped my hand against the doorjamb, barring his way with my arm. "Your pardon, Lord Denbow," I said, with icy politeness. "I do not recall inviting you in."

This sudden and brazen resistance startled him, but he did not let it slow his tongue. "I am here to collect my daughter, Mrs. Camherst, with your permission or without it."

"If she were here, I would be glad to broker some kind of negotiation between the two of you. As she is not, you will have to seek her elsewhere. I will not suffer you to rampage through my house regardless."

He was not so far gone as to try and shove me aside, though he very easily could have done so. His fury thwarted for the nonce, he resorted to persuasion. "Mrs. Camherst, please, see reason. You are determined to put yourself in danger, regardless of the consequence to your family; very well. I have no authority to command you to better sense. But I *can* protect my daughter, and I will."

"Lord Denbow," I said, moderating my own tone to suit his. "I have told you, she is not here. I have not seen Natalie in days. Should I see her before I leave, I will tell her you came, and advise her of your concerns. That is all I can promise."

He deflated visibly, like the punctured bag of a caeliger. "I am sure she is coming here. Please, might I—"

"I will tell her you came," I said firmly. Had he not attempted to thrust his way into my house, I might have been more tolerant; as it was, I wanted him gone. "If I see her."

With that, he had to be content. By then the footman was hovering behind my shoulder, looking distressed at the prospect of having to forcibly evict a baron from the premises, but determined to do so if necessary. (Clomers was a very good footman, the best I ever had.) Half-fuming, half-dejected, Lord Denbow returned to his carriage, and so away.

Once he was well down the drive, I deflated a bit myself. "If he comes back, do not let him in," I said wearily to Clomers; and, having received his stout agreement, I went upstairs to my study.

Natalie was sitting in front of my desk.

I very nearly swallowed my own tongue at the sight of her. While one part of my brain sorted out the contradictory impulses of gasping, shrieking, and demanding an explanation of her, the rest noted certain details: the open window on the side wall, overlooking a fine (and easily climbed) oak tree; the fierce and frightened look in Natalie's eyes; the small valise on the floor at her feet.

"He locked me up," she said, sounding almost as if she could not believe it. "We argued for days, and when I told him I was going whatever he said, he locked me up. Him and Mama. I am sorry to have made you a liar."

"She only lies who tells a falsehood knowingly," I said, as if such distinctions were at all the most relevant thing at hand.

Natalie drew in a breath, and the unsteadiness of it advertised her distress. "I fear I have made a great deal of trouble for you. I came here intending to go with you tomorrow—but if I do, Papa will be infuriated."

If she did not, then she would have little choice but to return to her family. And while they might have what they perceived as her best interests at heart, the disjunct there was severe enough to send Natalie up my tree and through my window, and who knows what else before that. Her actions, more than any words, told me that return was simply not to be borne.

Her grandfather might protect her against the worst of it—but a better protection would be to go beyond her family's reach. "Your father will have to be infuriated in Scirland," I said, the dryness of my tone covering for any temporary quailing of spirit. "He doesn't have a visa for Nsebu, and isn't likely to get one anytime soon."

Hope kindled new life in her posture. "Do you mean—"

"The ship leaves tomorrow," I said. "We must think of how to get you on it."

We smuggled her on board by way of the workers' gangway, where her father would never think to look. With Natalie dressed in the clothes of a laborer (yes, trousers and all) and a sack of potatoes on her shoulder, Lord Denbow never had the slightest chance of spotting her.

He was there, of course, and made a great protest, insisting to the gathered members of my family (Paul and Judith; my mother and father; my favourite brother, Andrew; Matthew and Sir Joseph, who was my father-in-law) that I had kidnapped Natalie.

"I have *not* kidnapped her, my lord," I said, covering my nervousness with irritation. In his distress, he had not yet thought to ask me outright whether I had seen his daughter. If he did, I would have to make up my mind whether to lie, and a sleepless night of pondering that very question had failed to supply me with an answer.

I had kept my word, if only halfheartedly, talking with Natalie of his concerns. The conversation had failed to divert either of us from our course. My one source of apprehension was that I had no opportunity to speak privately with certain individuals, namely, Mr. Wilker and Lord Hilford. The former would be coming with me on this expedition, and the ear not occupied by Lord Denbow's furious expostulations was being filled with my mother's insistence that in addition to it being madness for me to go abroad, it was even *more* mad to do so without any kind of female companion. Marriage had provided me with a mystical shield against impropriety, one not entirely lost with widowhood, but she still feared rumour. (In fairness to her, I must say she was right to do so. But I get ahead of myself.)

Lord Hilford, I thought, had guessed something of what was going on, though whether he knew I was actively helping Natalie, I could not say. I did, however, see him draw Mr. Wilker aside upon his arrival, and whatever he said turned Mr. Wilker's face to stone. That done, Lord Hilford set himself to diverting his son as best he could. They went together to examine my cabin, to satisfy Lord Denbow that Natalie was not there; I hoped she had found a good place to conceal herself until we were well away from shore.

Andrew, to my pleasure and relief, set himself the same task with our mother, and accompanied me on board when the time came, as he had done when I departed for Vystrana. "So, where are you hiding her?" he asked as we crossed the deck.

A heavy step brought my head around. Mr. Wilker had joined us, pacing to my right, leaving me feeling trapped between them. But Andrew was grinning as if it were all a tremendous lark, and the grim set of Mr. Wilker's jaw told me he would not be surprised by anything I might say.

"She is hiding herself," I said. "I honestly don't know where. This was her decision, you know, though I support her in it."

"Miss Oscott is even less sane than you are," Mr. Wilker said.

"Then she's in good company," I said lightly. That would not be the end of it, I knew; but Mr. Wilker would not go against Lord Hilford's clear wish, that his granddaughter be permitted her escape. He was too loyal to the earl, and owed him far too much. What arguments we would have—and oh, did we have them—would come later.

Our ship was the *Progress*, the famed steamship that for many years formed the primary link in the Scirling-Erigan trade. Built from Erigan steel and fueled with Scirling coal, it was a symbol of the partnership inaugurated by the Nsebu colony—at least, it was seen as a partnership on our side of the ocean, though the truth was less balanced than that word implies. The bulk of its capacity was given over to cargo, some of which would be scattered through various ports like seeds as we made our journey, the rest traded in Nsebu before the holds were filled once more with iron, gold, ivory, and more. But the *Progress* was the jewel of that sea route, and so it also had passenger cabins, well equipped for the comfort of the dignitaries who occupied them. The three of us were hardly dignitaries, but Lord Hilford qualified, and had arranged for us to travel in style.

We met him emerging from my cabin with Lord Denbow behind him. Or rather, Lord Hilford emerged; his son charged,
backing me against a wall. "Enough of this, Mrs. Camherst! You
will tell me where my daughter is, or—"

My brother was already stepping to defend me. I was very glad
that Lord Hilford intervened, before I had to discover what
Andrew would do. "Lewis! Control yourself. Or do you *want* the
crew to drag you bodily off this ship? You are making a scene."

All hail that bane of the upper class, *a scene*. The spectre of being publicly shamed was enough to check Lord Denbow. It was
not enough to calm him, but with his momentum broken, the
baron knew he could not prevent the ship from departing. And if
he attempted to detain me, he would face any number of consequences. He could not decide what to do before his father took
him firmly by the arm and dragged him away, not quite by force.

Still, he indulged in one final accusation, shot over his shoulder. "You will ruin her life."

"I have not ruined my own, Lord Denbow," I called after him.
"Trust your daughter to find her own way."

Natalie emerged when we were out of Sennsmouth harbor, and
once she was properly attired, I called Mr. Wilker in.

He shook his head at the sight of her. "I would ask whether you
have any notion what you've just done. But you're the earl's
granddaughter, and I know you've inherited at least a portion of
his intelligence. So I will only ask you, in God's name, *why*."

"Because I had to," Natalie said.

I understood her meaning, but Mr. Wilker clearly did not. Yet
we required some degree of comity, or this expedition would be
doomed before we arrived in Nsebu. "Mr. Wilker. I am sure you
endured hardships of your own, gaining your education, forcing

those of higher station to accept you as their intellectual peer. Why did *you* do it?"

"This will rebound on her family," he said, ignoring my question.

"And were there no consequences for your own family, when you left Niddey for university?"

It was a guess, but not a blind one; I knew Mr. Wilker was the eldest son of his line. His indrawn breath told me I had struck my mark. Belatedly—as usual for me, I regret to say—I wondered whether his sensitivity on this matter was *because* of his own experience, rather than in spite of it.

"When you came to Vystrana, it was different," he said, as if appealing to me for reason. "You came with Jacob, and with his blessing."

"Are a woman's wishes only fit to be considered when blessed by a male relative?" I asked sharply. "If so, then take Lord Hilford's for Natalie, and let us be done with it."

He flushed, and left soon after. It was not the last time we argued the matter, but my words had lodged under his skin like a barb, and their effect became apparent in due course.

PART TWO

In which we arrive in Eriga,
where we achieve both success and scandal,
and embroil ourselves in various conflicts

FIVE

Sea-snakes—The port of Nsebu—Faj Rawango—
Half-naked men—Nsebu and Atuyem—We are no threat

E ven at the reliable pace of a steamer, the journey to Nsebu
was not short. We stopped in various ports for trade; we
battled foul weather; once three boilers broke down in
concert, and the *Progress* made no progress at all until
they were repaired. We were at sea for a month altogether, and to
alleviate my boredom (for we soon completed the plans for our
research, and there are only so many hands of whist one can play
without going mad) I began observing the sea life.

Fish and whales, sharks and seabirds; the latter held the most
interest for me, as I had not lost my childhood partiality toward
wings. But despite its lack in that regard, I was most captivated by
the great sea-snake we saw one afternoon near the end of our
voyage.

We were entering Erigan waters, crossing the latitude known
as the Tropic of Serpents, so named for the large numbers of sea-
snakes found there. This was the only one we got a good view of,
and all the passengers (and half the crew) crowded to the rails to
observe it. "People argue about whether they should be considered dragons," I said to Natalie, watching the great coils rise above
the water's surface and slip away once more. "Your grandfather
doesn't believe the Prania sea-snakes should be, but I wonder
about these beasts. There are so many creatures around the world
that seem partially draconic in nature, but they lack wings, or

forelimbs, or extraordinary breath. I think sometimes that Sir Richard Edgeworth's criteria may be wrong—or rather, too strict."

"Another thing to study," Natalie said, amused. "Will you ever be done?"

I smiled into the sun, one hand holding my bonnet against the firm grasp of the wind. "I should hope not. How dreadfully tedious that would be."

Four days later, with all the passengers lined up at the rail once more, the *Progress* steamed past the rocky outcrop of Point Miriam and into the deep harbor of Nsebu.

Because the geography of this region will be of great relevance later, I should take a moment to describe it now. The land of Bayembe lies on the northern side of the Bay of Mouleen, mostly along a plateau lifted above sea level, but beneath the mountains that form their northern border with the Talu Union. Their eastern border and part of the southern are ocean; the rest was, at the time, the disputed territory between the Girama and Hembi rivers, and the edge of the great, sunken swamp of Mouleen, whose streams spill into the bay at a thousand points.

Mouleen is born from an eccentric quirk of geology. It would, in the normal way of things, be a great river delta, as the Girama, the Gaomomo, and the Hembi converge only a few hundred kilometers inland, the culmination of their long rush to the sea. But a fault in the underlying rock dropped the region nearly to sea level at what should have been the confluence, with the result that all three rivers tumble over a cliff and drown the land below. Furthermore, the prevailing winds at that latitude blow from the east, funneling much of the atmospheric moisture into the low channel formed by that geologic fault, and therefore much of the rain. The resulting morass is the impenetrable jungle of Mouleen—more colloquially known as the Green Hell.

But that was not yet my destination. Although I spared a few glances for the emerald band that marked the western edge of the bay, the bulk of my attention was on the town perched just off its corner, over which the fort at Point Miriam stood guard.

Neither words nor images suffice to communicate what greeted me as we came into port, for even the best artwork is a static thing of the eye alone, and words are by their nature linear. I can tell you of the smells that assaulted my nose: the salt sea, the coal smoke of other steamers, the fish and shellfish that even today make up a brisk part of the port's local trade, the spices whose aromatic vibrancy is all out of proportion to their quantity. Unwashed bodies and tar, fresh-cut tropical lumber, the greasy stench of lunch being fried for dockworkers and hungry travellers alike. But I can only tell you of one scent at a time, and I cannot present those to you at the same time as I give you the sounds and the sights, the mad clamour that was my first experience of Eriga.

With the knowledge I have now, I can give the proper names to what I saw then only as a bewildering array of peoples. There were Scirlings among them, of course, merchants and soldiers, there to protect our interests in iron production. Nor were we the only Anthiopeans, despite tensions with our rivals over their involvement elsewhere in Eriga; there were Thiessois, Chiavorans, a cluster of Bulskoi looking exceedingly uncomfortable in the heat. Pigtailed Yelangese bustled around their ships, and Akhians were nearly as common as Scirlings.

But it was the Erigans who dazzled my eye, for they were new to me, and formed the bulk of the crowds.

Amongst themselves, they displayed a hundred different modes of dress and adornment, a hundred different details of physiognomy that mark one people as distinct from another. I saw complexions ranging from inky blue-black to bronze, mahogany, and dark amber, sharp chins and square jaws, high foreheads and low, full lips and wide mouths and cheekbones that rode flat or stood out like the arches of a bow. The people wore their hair in loose braids or braids close to the scalp, in beads or strips of fabric, in soft clouds and corkscrew curls and sharp ridges held in place by white or red clay. There were Agwin veiled from head to toe and Menke in little more than loincloths, Sasoro in silver and Erbenno in embroidery, Mebenye and Ouwebi and Sagao and Gabborid in variations on the folded wrap, whose subtleties of color and arrangement communicate a great deal to the knowledgeable eye, but escaped my understanding entirely that first day. And, of course, there were countless Yembe, the dominant people of that land.

I had studied the Yembe language (from a reference grammar, which is an abominable teaching tool), but it had in no way prepared me for the social language before me now. Staring out at the docks, I understood, for the first time, that I had left behind the familiar commonalities of Anthiope, and crossed the oceans to a different continent.

Mr. Wilker put his hand under my elbow, which tells me I must have reeled. "It will be a little while before we can go ashore," he said. "You might want to go below until we do. The sun can be brutal, for those not used to it."

Once he would have phrased it as "you *should* go below." Disagreements over Natalie's presence aside, we had indeed made great strides in our relationship with one another. "The sun does not bother me," I said absently, digging in my satchel for my sketchbook. I'd done little drawing since leaving Scirland, the pitch and roll of the ship wreaking havoc on my ability to place a precise line, but I could not pass up this opportunity to sketch the docks.

Point Miriam

I could feel him wrestling with the answer he wanted to make to that, before finally swallowing it—for the sake of harmony, I suspect. "I will make certain our trunks are being seen to," he said, and went away.

I had only put the broadest outlines of the scene down on paper when a popping noise sounded behind me, and then my page was in shadow. "Natalie," I said, annoyed.

"You'll burn otherwise," she said, all practicality as usual. "Grandpapa warned me. About the sun, *and* about you—that you wouldn't take sufficient precautions."

"The sun here is strong, yes. It was strong in the mountains of Vystrana, too, and I had little trouble there." I had suffered more from dryness of skin than from sunburn.

Natalie laughed. "Yes, because you were cold all the time. You covered up and spent much of your time indoors to get away from the wind. But carry on with your work; this parasol is shading us both."

I hadn't needed her exhortation to continue. Line by line, the people were taking shape beneath my pencil, surrounded by crates and ropes and warehouses and shops, with little boats bobbing in the water at the lower edge of the scene. Drawing at speed was something I'd practiced these past few years; the images I produced lacked the polished elegance of my youthful art, but I'd improved greatly in my ability to capture the subject accurately in a short span of time.

By the time Mr. Wilker returned, I had enough of it down that I could fill in the remainder without trouble later on. "Is it very far to our hotel?" I asked, tucking my pencil away and closing my sketchbook. Certainly there would be other sights worth seeing beyond the docks, but I hoped to manage some individual portraits. Sailors the world over are a visually fascinating lot.

"Actually," Mr. Wilker said, "it seems our plans may have

changed. See that fellow at the corner there, beneath the yellow awning? The short one, with the band of gold around his forehead? He's a messenger from the palace, sent to watch for our arrival. The oba has invited us to be his guests."

I blinked at him in startlement. "At the palace? Surely not."

"It seems so," Mr. Wilker said. "And we're expected to come straight on. The messenger brought horses, and he says we needn't worry about our trunks."

No doubt the gesture was intended to be helpful, but in my travel-frayed state, it struck me as faintly sinister. "What is this messenger's name?"

"Faj Rawango," Mr. Wilker said, with the careful air of one who doesn't trust his tongue not to trip over the unfamiliar syllables. He too had studied the language, but Faj Rawango was not a Yembe name. Was the man a foreigner, or did he hail from one of the other peoples that made up the nation of Bayembe?

I didn't realize Mr. Wilker and I had both fallen into a brief silence until Natalie broke it by saying, "Well, we cannot refuse such an honour."

"No, of course not." I replaced my sketchbook and drew the satchel up onto my shoulder. "And I suppose there isn't much to be gained by delaying. Come, let us go meet this Faj Rawango."

We descended to the ship's longboat and were taken in to shore, disembarking on the salt-stained wood of the docks near where Faj Rawango stood. He was, as Mr. Wilker had spotted, a small fellow by the standards of those around him; in fact, he was a bit shorter than I. His skin, though still dark, was lighter and more reddish in tone than many of those around him.

Lacking a better option, I greeted him in the Yembe manner, touching my heart, and received the same in return. Natalie and Mr. Wilker echoed us both. But once the formal greetings were done—a rather lengthier process among the peoples of that

region than among Scirlings—Faj Rawango spoke in our own
tongue. "The oba regrets putting you to the trouble of a further
journey, but you will rest in more comfort in the royal palace, in
Atuyem."

"That's very kind of him," Mr. Wilker said. "Our arrangements are for rooms in a hotel near Point Miriam. We had hoped
to perhaps gain an introduction on some future date, but had no
thought of imposing on his time and generosity so soon after our
arrival."

Faj Rawango dismissed this with a wave. "It is no imposition.
He has met many Scirling merchants and soldiers, but no scholars. He is very curious about your work."

The last time a foreigner with a title had taken an interest in
our work, it had not ended well. That, more than anything in the
messenger's words, put apprehension in my heart. But what could
we do? As Natalie said, we could not refuse this invitation. I
cursed the politicking that preceded our journey. Necessary
though it had been to procure our entrance to Nsebu, it had ap-
parently drawn rather more of the oba's attention than I wanted.

Our horses waited beneath a striped canopy not far away, in
company with enough others that I understood the place to be
some kind of waiting room for equines. Ours, however, stood out
from the crowd, not only for their quality, but for the grandness
of their equipage, beaded and gilt. No fewer than four soldiers
stood watch over this wealth, who clearly would form our escort.

I call them soldiers, but at the time I had difficulty attaching
the term to them, despite the Scirling rifles they bore. To my
mind, a soldier was a man in uniform. I thought of these men instead as warriors, for their garb looked nothing like the uniforms
I was accustomed to—stiff wool in solid colors—being drapes of
cotton tied about their waists and dyed in some intricate pattern,
with leopard skins hanging down their back like cloaks. Wool, I

suppose, does little to protect one against a rifle ball or a cavalry sword, but such logic did not prevent me from fearing for the men's bare and unprotected flesh.

As I turned to mount, I saw Natalie blushing. Until that moment, it had not even occurred to me, in more than an intellectual sense, that the men were half-naked. Then, unfortunately, I could think of nothing else. My own cheeks heated, and I fumbled my rise to the saddle, catching my shoe in the hem of my divided skirts. (My self-conscious embarrassment was somewhat mitigated by seeing Mr. Wilker a bit pink in the ears himself—likely more for ladies being exposed to such a thing than for his own sake, as gentlemen see one another bare in many contexts. We had all known this would happen, the climate of the region being what it is, but knowing and experiencing were separate things.)

To cover for my loss of composure, I questioned Faj Rawango as we rode out of the dockside district and through Nsebu proper. Or rather, that was my intention; it soon devolved into a polite argument wherein each of us tried to insist upon using the other's native tongue, with the result that he spoke to me in Scirling and I responded in Yembe. Languages have never been my *métier*, so I fear he had the better of me in the comparison of skill, but my experience in Vystrana had taught me that there is nothing like using a language on a regular basis to better one's skill. I therefore persevered until Faj Rawango bowed in the face of my stubbornness and began answering me in Yembe.

We conversed on a variety of topics then, exploring as widely as my limited vocabulary and Faj Rawango's instructions from his royal master would allow. The former was more of a restriction than the latter, but I soon discovered (through my customary curiosity and lack of discretion) that the political climate of Bayembe was not a suitable subject. The man did not chastise me for asking, but he showed a marked disinclination to speak about the movement of Ikwunde troops that had so spooked the new man at the Foreign Office, or even more generally about the expansionist ambitions of the inkosi, their ruler. Nor would he speak of the Talu, the "union" to the north that was, in truth, an empire by another name, assimilating its neighbours one by one. Clearly such matters were not for the likes of him to share with Scirling outsiders—even outsiders here for non-political purposes.

(Yes, I thought my stay in the region would be non-political. When you have finished laughing, you may proceed.)

We spoke instead of the men and women we passed, Faj Rawango giving me my first education in distinguishing one people from another, which in retrospect was at least as valuable to me as his political opinions would have been. Physical distinctions are, of course, often muddied by intermarriage, but enough patterns persist in that region to be of moderate use, and of course the apparel and ornament of each people has its variations. Nowhere, however, did I see anyone resembling Faj Rawango himself, and he deflected me when I asked. My suspicion that he was of foreign birth grew, but I did not press.

In this manner did we ride through the fortified gates of Nsebu and into the grass beyond.

These days the two places have run together into one indistinguishable city, but back then Nsebu and Atuyem were quite separate. The former had a small port district that had, up until fifty years ago, been all there was of the town. Increased trade had spurred its growth, and then the alliance between Scirland and Bayembe had seen the construction of the fort at Point Miriam, with the colony following soon after. Now Nsebu was a strangely hybrid place, creeping across the open ground toward the more aristocratic precincts of Atuyem.

These sit above Nsebu both socially and physically, on a plateau high enough to enjoy cooling winds, but near enough to the port to benefit from the trade; which is why Bundey n Mawo Nsori, the reigning oba a century before, had moved his primary residence there. Atuyem is further stratified between the lower town and the upper, which perches atop a rocky, flat-topped hill, the better to command a view of the surrounding countryside. The walls of the oba's fortified residence rose higher still, a crown surmounting that stony head, and they shone gold in the afternoon light.

Much of that gold was metaphorical, an illusion created by the color of the soil used in building the walls and the warm glow of the sun. The highest tower within the complex, however, gleamed too brightly for mere dirt. The stories were untrue, that the oba of Bayembe lived in a palace of solid gold; but one tower, at least, had been plated in the substance.

It was a suitably impressive display of wealth—though one the oba perhaps regretted in a time of such conflict and greed. Then again, Bayembe's gold was not what attracted interest from Satalu, Ikwunde, and Scirling alike. Iron was the prize those three lands sought to claim.

Around that central fortress spread the courtyards and compounds of his chief nobles, patriarchs of the various lineages that made up the aristocracy of Bayembe. These had, over the years, grown too numerous and extensive, crowding all others off the small hilltop, exiling the common folk to houses and shops gathered around the rocky skirts of the hill. Our little party attracted a great deal of attention as we rode through, for our escorts were clearly royal warriors, and Faj Rawango a high official; nor had Scirlings become so common here as to be unworthy of remark, as they were in Nsebu. Natalie and I drew particular commentary, Scirling *ladies* being very uncommon in any part of Bayembe.

I rode self-consciously, feeling the burden upon me of representing my race and my sex to these people. My clothing—travel wear that was simple to the point of tedium by Scirling standards—seemed fussy and overcomplicated here, designed for sensibilities and a climate foreign to this place. I knew my face was flushed and damp with sweat, and likely sunburnt despite the protection of my bonnet, and the gritty dust of these grasslands clung to me all over. As representatives went, I felt like a shabby one indeed.

We circled the base of the hill along what was clearly the main road, until we came to a gate built in the style of these lands: hard-pounded earth, decorated with bright tiles, and studded regularly with wooden struts that were, as I understood it, both internal supports and climbing aids for when the exterior needed repair. Here Faj Rawango conversed briefly and incomprehensibly with a guard, making it apparent just how much he had slowed and clarified his speech for my sake. Thus interviewed, we rode onward, and began our ascent of the hill at its gentlest point.

The Atuyem we traveled through now was entirely different. Instead of the clamour and crowds of the base, we passed the near-faceless walls of the lineage compounds, whose decorative tiles communicated a message beyond my skill to translate. Guards stood at the gates, and servants traversed the roadway, some of them bearing the shaded palanquins of their masters. Where the curtains were gauzy, I could glimpse dark shadows within, that sometimes stretched out gold-laden hands to twitch the fabric aside and study us directly. These stares were different from the ones before: to the nobles of the heights, we were not mere curiosities, but new variables in the political equation of their land. Whether our effect would be positive or negative had yet to be determined.

It was both a relief and a fresh source of tension to ride through the mighty gates of the oba's own fortress, away from those measuring eyes. We dismounted in a front courtyard and were met by kneeling servants who offered up bowls of fresh, cool water with which to cleanse our faces and hands. Our escort stood at attention while we conducted our ablutions, then saluted and jogged once more out the gates.

In their place came a pair of what I guessed to be upper servants, one male and one female. "Rooms have been prepared," our guide said. "These two will show you."

The presence of *two* servants gave me a hint as to what we might expect. "Are our quarters separate?" I asked.

Faj Rawango nodded, with an impassivity I read to mean he had anticipated the question, but still thought me a simpleton for asking. "Men and women do not lodge together in the royal palace."

I wondered what they would have done had Jacob been alive, and here with me. Were married couples given joint quarters, or did husbands have to arrange to call upon their wives? But that was hardly the sort of question I had come here to ask. "We intend to spend much of our time together," I said instead. "Our work requires it."

"Of course," Faj Rawango said, all courtesy. "There are public areas."

Where we could be watched, I supposed, for any hint of improper behaviour. I had hoped to leave that sort of thing behind in Scirland.

We suffered ourselves to be led away, Mr. Wilker in one direction, Natalie and I in another. Our new guide was an older woman, her hair faded to an iron-grey that reminded me of Scirland's interests in this region. She led us through a honeycomb of courtyards and colonnades, until at last we climbed a set of stairs to a cool and airy room tiled in blue.

By now I was tired enough that my brain had become sulky about handling a foreign tongue, but I understood from the woman's words that this was to be a shared residence for Natalie and myself. It was sparsely furnished by Scirling standards, with a few padded benches and stools of the kind that can be folded out of the way when not in use, and chests for our belongings. The bed was draped with gauzy curtains, the better to keep out troublesome insects while still allowing cooling breezes through. After the cramped conditions of the ship and the rigor of a long ride, it seemed to me like a small corner of heaven.

While Natalie asked after the bathing arrangement, I explored. One set of windows, covered with wooden laths hung on string, faced west, and looked out over a section of the palace that, by what I could see of the bustle therein, was a working area for servants. We had not, it seemed, been given terribly desirable quarters, however elegant the tiling.

The windows on the opposite side overlooked another of the myriad of courtyards that made up this palace. (Indeed, I was not far wrong in thinking of the place as a honeycomb; it was composed as much of open space as enclosed, and virtually everything of substance seemed to take place in the former. In a country as hot as Bayembe, fresh air is not only pleasant but necessary for survival.)

Our servant departed, and Natalie collapsed with a sigh on the bed—the benches there being far less suitable for collapsing upon than sophas and divans. "I promise I will say this only once," she remarked, "but good *Lord*, the heat."

(With all due respect to Natalie, whom I love as my own self, she lied. If I took a sip of gin every time she said that during the expedition, my liver would be *foie gras*.)

I gave in to temptation, sitting down on a bench and unlacing my boots. The coolness of the tiles beneath my bare feet was a blessing. "I can't decide whether this is a good development or a bad one," I said. "Has the oba brought us here to offer his assistance, or is he going to interfere?"

"Why would he interfere?" Natalie asked, reasonably. "I can't see what he would gain by it, and he would risk antagonizing our fellow countrymen."

"That might be reason enough. It would be minor antagonism at worst—I doubt the military and industrial gentlemen have much concern for our research—and so it would be a relatively safe way for the oba to show that he won't be pushed around by Scirlings." I scratched my fingers vigorously along my scalp. "One thing is certain; he has quite neatly separated us from most of our countrymen. Perhaps he thinks we'll be less of a danger that way." My fingers came away covered in sweat and grit, and I grimaced at them.

Natalie rolled over to regard me directly. "But we aren't any kind of threat, are we?"

"No," I said. "I don't see how we could be."

Later I would recall those words with a great deal of irony.

SIX

Meeting the olori—M. Velloin—My views on hunting—
The uses of M. Velloin—Dinner at Point Miriam—
Sheluhim—The worship of dragons

True to Faj Rawango's words, there were public areas in which we could socialize with the opposite sex. Before we found them, however, we had to run a gauntlet of women.

The next morning (having dined alone and retired early the night before), Natalie and I sponged ourselves off, dressed in fresh clothing, and went downstairs in search of Mr. Wilker. Trying to follow what we thought was the proper path, we found ourselves in a courtyard full of ladies, all of whom fell silent at the sight of us.

We were, I own, shockingly out of place. Everyone else in the courtyard was Erigan, and dressed in patterned cotton wraps that looked a good deal more comfortable in that weather than our own stays and long-sleeved dresses. Such exotic creatures as a pair of Anthiopean women must, of course, draw attention. But there was, I felt, more to it than that: we had now entered waters not only foreign but political. We were not merely strangers; we were, as I had thought before, new variables.

It soon became apparent whose responsiblity it was to address the change in the local calculus. A woman sat on a low stool at the far end of the courtyard, watching us, and by the disposition of the people around her, she was clearly the most important in the group. Her features were of the sort Faj Rawango had identified to me as characteristically Mebenye: a low forehead and rounded jaw that gave her broad face an almost circular appearance. It was a friendlier shape than a more angular face might have been, but the set of her full mouth and the sharp regard of her eyes warned me not to read personality into physiognomy.

She gestured, and another woman approached us. Speaking in Yembe, she said, "Olori Denyu n Kpama Waleyim bids you come speak with her."

Then I knew who had snared us. "Olori" was the title given to the oba's lesser wives; we might translate it as "princess consort," the position ranking below that of his principal wife or queen, who had the title ayaba. The current oba had three wives, I knew, but that was where my knowledge ended. Information on them had been hard to come by in Scirland, and what little I'd gleaned had to do with Idowi n Gemo Tagwi, the queen.

The only way to learn was to proceed. Natalie and I approached, until the olori held up one hand for us to stop, about four paces from her. She sat beneath a canopy of beaded and embroidered fabric, and her hair was braided with gold, a match for the jewelry that burdened her every limb.

I curtseyed to her as I might to the queen of Scirland, hoping either that other Anthiopean women had been here before me, or that the olori would independently recognize it as a gesture of respect. Scarcely had I risen from this, and Natalie beside me, when the woman spoke. "You are here alone?"

"No, olori," I said, hoping I was unlikely to go wrong if I addressed her by her title. "Miss Natalie Oscott here is my companion, and we also came with a gentleman named Mr. Thomas Wilker."

The pursing of her lips did not look impressed by this answer. "Your name. It is Isabella Camherst."

"Yes, olori." We must have been a topic of gossip before our arrival.

"Women of your people take the lineage name of their husband, yes? Then this man is not your husband. You came here alone."

Too late, I understood. "I'm afraid my husband is dead."

Her gaze flickered across my body. Looking for signals of mourning or widowhood, I supposed. "And his brother did not marry you?"

I thought of Matthew, and narrowly avoided laughing at the thought. "That is not our way, olori." Tardily, the recollection came that Bayitists in some countries faithful to the Temple still followed such practices—often the ones who also took multiple wives—but I did not trust my command of the language to address so complicated a topic, nor was it particularly relevant. Scirlings did not do such things; that was enough.

"Mmmmm." The olori showed no sign what she thought of this. She was, I suspected, a deeply political creature, who never showed much of anything unless it might bring her gain. I did not like her, but whether that was because her reserve hid any impulses I should fear, I could not tell.

Then she asked the question—the same question I have gotten dozens, nay, *hundreds* of times in my life, always with that same air of faint disbelief. "You are here for . . . dragons?"

"Yes." She could be reserved all she liked; I made no effort to hide my enthusiasm. "We are scholars of dragons." It was the closest I could come to saying "natural historian" in Yembe.

"What is there to study? They are not gods or great heroes. They are not even livestock, or beasts of war. You cannot train them to be useful. Are you hunters?"

"Gracious, no!" The words burst from me. "That is—we *have* hunted dragons, Mr. Wilker and I have, though I suppose it would be more precise to say he did the hunting. I only drew the body afterward. But we are not hunters as I think you mean it, olori, killing them for sport or for trophies. We seek to understand them: their nature, their behaviour."

Ordinarily this is the thread my conversational partners pursue, the (to them) incomprehensible question of why understanding the nature and behaviour of dragons is worth so much effort, if not for the purpose of killing them. Olori Denyu n Kpama Waleyim had other things on her mind. "Draw them? Then you are an artist?"

"I suppose so," I answered, taken aback. "I'm much more of a scholar, really, but I do draw and paint. For my work."

For some reason, this appeared to please the olori, though I could not imagine why. She put her hands on her knees with a self-satisfied air, nodding. It seemed to be a signal that our interrogation was done: other women began to speak then, and Natalie and I passed a pleasant (if mentally taxing) half hour conversing in Yembe. We only escaped by pleading the necessity of finding Mr. Wilker.

This gained us a guide, who showed us through the royal honeycomb to a more public courtyard. We found Mr. Wilker there, beneath the shade of a spreading tree, deep in conversation with another man.

I was not sure whether I should be surprised that his companion was Anthiopean. Foreigners were not all confined to the colonial districts of Nsebu, of course, but I had not expected them to seek us out so quickly. Or had Mr. Wilker sought him out?

He did not appear to be a military man. Blond of hair and reddish of whisker, he wore loose, practical clothing made out of the fabric the Isnatsi call *khaki*, not a woolen uniform. His fair skin was weathered to a solid brown, much seamed with lines, though I judged him not to be above forty. He had the fit look of an athlete, and I had no idea who he was.

Mr. Wilker did not leave me long in suspense, of course. Rising from his stool, the other man a heartbeat behind him, he said, "Ah, Mrs. Camherst, Miss Oscott. I'm glad you could join us. May I introduce M. Gregoire Velloin?"

M. Velloin's hand was solidly calloused, with thick, blunt nails. A working man's hand, I thought. When he spoke, I was surprised to find his voice tinged with an Eiversch accent, instead of Thiessois. "Mrs. Camherst, a pleasure. Miss Oscott, very nice to meet you. There has been much gossip in advance of your arrival. You are not what I expected."

"Oh?" I said, mildly nettled for no reason I could discern. Perhaps my audience with the olori had put me out of sorts. "What did you expect?"

"Someone older and plainer," he answered, with bluntness that was likewise much more Eiversch than Thiessois. "I had heard you were a widow."

Now, at least, I had reason to be nettled. "I am, sir. But my late husband's passing has no bearing on my age or appearance."

Rather than taking offense, he laughed. "Oh, indeed. But that is rumour, is it not? Making assumptions with no basis, just to fill the time. I am sure gossip will be more accurate, now that you are here."

Based on my experiences thus far, I sincerely hoped I would not be there for long. I had far rather be out in the bush, pursuing dragons, than dealing with the people in Atuyem, be they Erigan or Anthiopean. "What brings you here, M. Velloin? You cannot be with any Scirling delegation, and I note your accent—and yet you affect a Thiessois title of courtesy."

"And a Thiessois name, too. My father was of that land; he was born in Fonsmartre. You know of it? Quite near the border, yes. He emigrated in his youth, and married an Eiversch woman. But I am *monsieur* instead of *Herr* because I have made my home in Thiessin for ten years now, and it is owing to the generosity of a Thiessois patron that I am here."

I frowned. "You have not yet answered my question, *monsieur.*"

"M. Velloin is a hunter," Mr. Wilker said, intervening.

Thinking back over my words, I winced; the hostility I was showing to our Anthiopean companion held some echoes of my early behaviour toward Mr. Wilker himself. I made an effort to moderate my tone. "I see. Is it the elephants you are here for, or the leopards?"

Velloin smiled, as if our conversation had been friendly all along. "I do not discriminate, Mrs. Camherst, except to choose only the most dangerous of prey. There is no challenge, without risk. I have hunted tigers in Rematha, bears in Kaatsedu, and mammoths in Siaure. Here I will hunt the elephant and the leopard and the dragon."

So much, I thought, for friendliness.

Natalie laid a restraining hand on my arm; she knew what the stiffening of my posture meant. It did not stop me from speaking. "The dragon. Indeed. In that case, I cannot honestly wish you luck in your endeavours. I have little fondness for sport hunting in the first place, and less in the case of dragons. You may not be aware, sir—unless you make a habit of reading scientific monographs, which I doubt—but on our Vystrani expedition—"

"You discovered mourning behaviour among Vystrani rock-wyrms." Velloin's mouth had compressed, though he maintained a good approximation of his amiable tone. "I do read monographs, Mrs. Camherst, where they concern the great beasts. A good hunter must know his prey."

"They are more than prey," I said, biting the words off. "That you should see them so, for the mere prize of teeth and claws, is a very great pity."

Pity fell far short of what I truly meant, but Scirling politeness restrained my tongue. Now, years after the fact, I have no compunctions about telling you what I truly felt.

It is true, yes, that my companions and I have killed dragons in the course of our research, and sometimes even for the purpose *of* that research. But even before I developed reservations about such practices, I had an utter loathing for trophy hunting, which was (and in many places still is) considered a wonderful expression of masculine virtue. Rarely do such men hunt verminous creatures, of the sort that truly plagues the common people; if they foxhunt, it is with a fox captured for the purpose and released in a pleasant park, not the one eating the chickens of the peasant outside that park.

No, the beasts they hunt are the splendid ones, the majestic kings and queens of the wild, and they do so for no better reason than because a splendid trophy is far more glamorous than a scrubby one. The occasional hunter will test his courage by going after a hippopotamus, which is as dangerous as it is comical looking, but most prefer those with pelts or hides they can display after the fact. To kill a creature simply to decorate one's study is repellent to me, and I cannot help but be repelled by those who engage in such activity.

And that abhorrence is redoubled when the hunter's target is a dragon, for I, as all the world knows, am partisan to their kind.

Velloin seemed unconcerned by my disapproval. Why should he be? I could do nothing but seethe. "Teeth and claws are prizes, yes, but hardly the only ones. I have captured animals, too—even a dragon, once. You may have seen it yourself."

"What dragon?" I asked. The question came out sharp, for a dreadful suspicion had taken shape in my mind.

"A Moulish swamp-wyrm," he said. "Took it from near the coast; only safe place to go, really, and hardly even then. The creature was a runt, but it made its way into the menagerie at Falchester."

He was watching me as he spoke, and I could not hide my re-action. I had indeed seen that dragon, along with two other runts, on the very day that I met my husband. Without those dragons, I might never have married Jacob, with all the consequences, both good and bad, attendant upon that decision. The thought of ow-ing even a fraction of my happiness to a man like Velloin was in-furiating.

Casually, he added, "I hope to try again, in the jungle or out in the savannah. Buyers are much harder to find for full-grown dragons—too difficult to keep them caged—but still, the chal-lenge is the thing."

It would be hypocritical for me to wish him luck in that endeavour. It would also, however, be hypocritical for me to condemn him, given the joy I had derived from seeing those cap-tive dragons. In the end, I clamped my jaw shut and let others take the conversation onward.

Unfortunately, it transpired that Mr. Wilker had engaged us to dine with the bloodthirsty M. Velloin that afternoon. He was on good terms with a number of people at Point Miriam, which served not only as a defensive fortification but also as the home of Nsebu's colonial government. Given that we were newcomers to the royal palace, unfamiliar with the rhythms of life there and (thus far) ignored by the oba who had invited us in the first place, it made all the sense in the world that we should accept Velloin's invitation. But I did not like the idea, and regretted that I saw no acceptable way to beg off.

On the contrary, our plans rapidly expanded from a single meal to a full day in the man's company, exploring the lower town of Atuyem before riding back down to Nsebu. As we left the royal compound, Natalie making light conversation with M. Velloin, I seized hold of Mr. Wilker's sleeve and dragged him back, so that I might hiss my words without being overheard.

"How could you put us in the company of such a man? And with no warning? You know quite well my feelings on the matter." I glared at M. Velloin's broad back.

Mr. Wilker freed his sleeve from my grasp with an irritated jerk. "I did so because he can be useful to us. Or would you rather kill *more* dragons, for the purpose of our tests?"

We had passed under the arch of an unfamiliar gate and out into a street, whose surface was not so well maintained as the one that led us in. At Mr. Wilker's words, I stumbled over an uneven bit of stone. We had agreed, when this expedition was first planned, that one of our tasks must be to test Rossi's preservation process on the bones of an Erigan dragon, to determine whether it was effective only on Vystrani rock-wyrms, or for a broader selection of species. And for that purpose, indeed, we required a dead dragon.

"Then—" M. Velloin's back had taken on an entirely different cast in my eyes. "You mean to steal his kills."

"Once he has his trophies, there's no reason for him to deny us the rest. We can tell him we're trying to make plaster casts of the bones; it's a reasonable enough excuse for us to take them."

Plaster casts had, before the preservation method, been the only means of keeping dragon bones for study. It did not work very well—encased in plaster, the bones deteriorated more rapidly than usual—but Elia Paradino had improved the process a bit. Mr. Wilker was right; it made a very good cover.

Still, I sighed. "It will require us to be in his company. Quite apart from his hobby, I do not like the man."

"No one is asking you to marry him, Mrs. Camherst."

Three years had passed; my grief for Jacob was no longer an open wound. Or so I had thought. But I was tired, and vexed with M. Velloin, and above all, I was on an expedition to study dragons. Bayembe was a vastly different place from Vystrana, but the fact remained that it had been on such an expedition that Jacob died.

This time I did not stumble. I stopped entirely. Only for a moment—then I forced my legs into motion once more—but it was enough to tell Mr. Wilker he had erred. He stopped, too, and turned to face me, so that I had to halt again.

"I'm sorry," he said, and I think it was not the heat alone that had flushed his face red. "I—I didn't mean that as a jab. It was supposed to be facetious, but I didn't think before I said it. Please, forgive me."

I wondered, irrelevantly, how long our relative harmony would have to last before I stopped reflecting on the change from our early interactions. But for that harmony to last, I had to do my part, which did not consist of standing in the middle of a street reflecting on such things, while Mr. Wilker's apology hung in the air. "Forgiven," I said. "I did not take it as an insult; it simply— well. You understand."

We had, of course, attracted the attention of the other two, who had paused in the street up ahead. "Is everything all right?" M. Velloin called.

"Yes, quite," I called back, and offered Mr. Wilker a reassuring smile before going to join the others.

Dinner at Point Miriam was oddly disorienting. The heat and scent of the air were inescapably Erigan, but the house in which we dined had been built according to the standards of my people. The table was laid as if it stood in some lady's country house, and beforehand we enjoyed *hors d'œuvre* in a drawing room that might have been a small piece of Scirland transplanted onto foreign soil. The effect might have been intended to reassure, but it made for a sweltering evening; our architecture is not suited to the climate.

The composition of the group was quite as unbalanced as Lord Hilford's snare-setting meal had been. There were only three ladies in attendance: myself, Natalie, and a married woman from Uaine named Erynn Anne Kerwin, who was there with her husband.

"Such a relief it is to have other women here," she said upon our introduction. Her accent was much like Mr. Wilker's, but stronger. Uaine, lying as it does to the north of Niddey, is the most isolated of the large Scirling Isles; it is isolated even now, and was more so then.

"I take it you don't find much company among the Yembe," I said, which was perhaps not the most politic response.

Mrs. Kerwin did not take offense. "Oh, I spend a mort of time with them—but that's work, not leisure."

Despite my having come to Eriga for work of my own, I had assumed Mrs. Kerwin was here as an adjunct to her husband, whose profession I had not yet determined. Embarrassment leashed my tongue, and so it fell to Natalie to say, "What work is it that you do?"

"We're sheluhim," Mrs. Kerwin said.

Embarrassment had put a leash on my tongue; startlement took it off again. "What—do you mean to say that you're proselytizing to the *Yembe?*"

"That is precisely what we're doing," Mrs. Kerwin said. If her warm smile had cooled somewhat, I could not blame her. "We have brought the sacred fire of the Temple to this land, and will carry it to all peoples. Already a number of men and women here have chosen to become the Chosen of the Lord, following His laws. Sure I am that number will only grow."

It was unfair of me to be so startled. Sheluhim have been traveling all over the world since men invented ships safe enough not to drown their passengers in the ocean; it was only that I had never encountered any myself. There were a few Bayitist sheluhim in Scirland, trying in vain to convert Magisterials back to the old ways, but the proselytizers of both major sects devoted the bulk of their efforts to lands where Segulism held no sway in any form.

Mrs. Kerwin was almost certainly a Temple-worshipper herself, being from Uaine. The Magisterial reforms in Scirland never penetrated that island very deeply. I had dealt with her co-religionists in Vystrana, but theirs was a rural theology, not the sort that sought to convert others to its way. And no Magisterial sheluhim had yet taken it into their heads to convert the Vystrani.

This, however, was a land of heathens, and with the Scirling presence, prime territory for such efforts. I should have expected to find her kind here.

"Erigans worship their ancestors, do they not?" Natalie asked. She and I had both done a certain amount of reading during the preparation for this expedition, but very little of it had been devoted to religion.

"Together with idols of nature, yes," Mrs. Kerwin said primly. "They are entirely lacking in scriptures of any sort, and of course what few of the laws they follow, they follow by accident."

Had I known more about Erigan religion at the time, I would have pointed out to her that what they lacked were scriptures of *our* sort. At the time, however, I was both ignorant of such matters and distracted by a different thought. "Have you gone down into the swamp at all?"

Mrs. Kerwin looked horrified. "You mean into Mouleen? Certainly not. We wouldn't survive two days there. Wild beasts, fevers, not to mention the natives—"

"I take it they don't welcome visitors?"

"They have the Ikwunde on one side and the Yembe on the other." M. Velloin had overheard our conversation. "And the Satalu lurking in the wings, hoping to snatch up Bayembe for themselves—though to what extent the Moulish are aware of that, who can say? They trade occasionally with the peasants along their borders, forest ivory for food, that sort of thing. But those who go deeper into the swamp never return."

I wanted to shift away from Velloin, but he was clearly somewhat informed about the region, and I could not pass up the chance to ask. "There are stories about the Moulish, that say they worship dragons as the Draconeans once did."

We were gathering quite the audience now: not only Mr. Wilker, but Sir Adam Tarwin-Bannithot (who was then the governor of the Nsebu colony) and a man whose sober dress and Uaine accent marked him as Mr. Kerwin. The latter said to me, "I take it you've read the work of Yves de Maucheret."

By M. Velloin's expression, so had he. "Yes," I said, "though he was writing two hundred years ago, and not everything he put to paper has proved to be true. Still, it's enough to intrigue the mind, isn't it? Dragons rarely tolerate human company well, and Moulish swamp-wyrms are not known to be the most approachable of breeds. If the Moulish do indeed worship them, do they do so from afar? Or are they able to partially tame them, as the Draconeans are said to have done?"

"They are nothing like the Draconeans," Mr. Kerwin said, dismissing the notion with a wave of his hand. "That ancient civilization—well, it was a *civilization*. They built great temples, developed art, administered territory across multiple continents. The Moulish bang on drums and run about naked. They may worship dragons, but there is no reason to suppose their manner of doing so bears any resemblance to Draconean religion."

"And yet, it would be closer to Draconean religion than any other example we have before us today," I said. "Do not ethnologists use modern evidence to analogize to the past? We might learn a great deal from the Moulish, regardless of their musical traditions and sartorial habits."

I spoke with the assurance of a young woman who thought her experience with natural history and *ad hoc* education in other subjects more than qualified her to hold forth on topics she knew nothing about at all. The truth is that any such comparison is far more complicated and doubtful than I presented it that evening; but it is also true that no one in my audience knew any more about it than I did, and most of them knew less. My assertion was therefore allowed to stand unchallenged.

For those who wonder why I showed such interest in the Draconeans, whose works I dismissed in the previous volume of my memoirs, do not think this meant I had undergone any great change of heart in the intervening years. I still at that time cared little for their ruined temples and stylized art; my interest was in living things, not dead civilizations. But as I said to Mr. Kerwin, the Draconeans were said to have tamed dragons. *That* was of great interest to me indeed, and so if Moulish religion was able to shed any light on the matter, then it, too, fell within the sphere of my attention.

Of course, there was the minor problem of the Green Hell being one of the deadliest regions on earth. But my interest was, that evening, still academic; my purpose in coming to Bayembe was to study the dragons of their arid plains. Moulish swamp-wyrms were a minor note—in much the same way that a fisherman's lure is a minor note in the world of a fish.

Sir Adam said, "I wouldn't waste much time or thought on the Moulish, if I were you. Whatever you might learn regarding dragons cannot possibly be worth the risk, and as for learning anything about humans—feh. That swamp is a backwater, in every sense of the word."

"A backwater which is presently protecting this country, is it not?" I said.

He shrugged. "For now."

A brief silence fell, broken a moment later by Sir Adam's uncomfortable cough and too-loud amendment. "Besides, you won't get into the swamp, not without the oba's permission. And he won't give it."

There is nothing in the world so enticing as that which you have been told you may not have. "Whyever not?" I asked. "Or rather, why should I need his leave in the first place? Mouleen is an independent state, is it not?"

Mr. Kerwin muttered something about not dignifying that festering pit with the name of "state," but my attention was on Sir Adam. He said, "At times like these, with the Ikwunde interfering with our work at the rivers, we must keep a careful eye on our borders."

Which was not much of an answer, but it was all that I could get from him, in the wake of that momentary lapse. Sir Adam had taken a bit too enthusiastically to the prescribed regimen of gin and tonic, with which we all held the malarial fevers at bay, and had said something he should not. Why would the Green Hell cease to protect Bayembe? Were the Moulish looking to ally themselves with the Ikwunde on the other side?

I did not know, but Sir Adam's slip had made me wary. I wanted only to study dragons, but first I had to get past the humans, and I feared they might be a greater danger to me than all the fevers of the tropics combined.

SEVEN

A certain taboo—The agban—*Galinke—Matters of lineage—*
Natalie joins me—Making use of M. Velloin

I must warn my male readers that I am about to address a topic which may be deeply discomfiting to them, taboo as it is for their sex.

When I awoke a few mornings later, I found my bedding stained with traces of blood. I clicked my tongue in annoyance; caught up in our affairs, I had not monitored the days as closely as I should, and my menses have never been the most reliable besides. But this was, I thought, only a minor irritation. I wet a cloth, washed myself clean, changed into a fresh chemise, and called for a servant.

When she came, I gestured at the stained bedding, washcloth, and chemise, indicating that she should take them away to be laundered. "And I will need rags," I said—as yet blissfully unaware that in many parts of the world, rags are not employed, but other, less comfortable alternatives.

(Indeed, for those young ladies who wish to follow in my footsteps, I must warn you that this inconvenient fact of our sex is one of the most vexatious aspects of being a lady adventurer. Unless you contrive to suppress your courses through pregnancy—which, of course, imposes its own limitations—or through strenuous exercise and privation, you will have to handle this necessity in many circumstances that are far from ideal. Including some, I fear, where the smell of fresh blood is a positive danger.)

Returning to the moment at hand: the serving girl's eyes widened at the sight of the stains, and she darted out of the room almost before I had finished speaking. So rapidly, in fact, that she left the laundry behind. I sighed, wondering if the fault was with my imperfect command of the language, or whether she—being prepubescent—was the sort of silly nit who bolted at the sight of blood. Well, I thought, if it came to that, I could sacrifice the rest of the stained chemise for rags.

The girl returned with equal speed, though, this time accompanied by a much older woman, who went to gather up the bedding and other articles. The girl herself approached me and draped an undyed robe over a bench, indicating shyly that I should wear it.

I saw no rags. "Thank you," I said, "but I have my own clothing; I only need something to stanch the bleeding."

The older woman—who was, by the look of her, well past the age of bearing herself—said, "Put it on; Lebuya will take you to the *agban.*"

This was not a word I had encountered, either in my studies or my time there. "*Agban?*" I repeated.

She indicated the soiled items. "Until you are clean."

My first thought was that she meant a bath. But I knew the word for "bath"—that was where Natalie had gone, while I worked on rousing myself to wakefulness—and had she meant such a thing, would she not have said "where you can wash yourself"? Suspicious, I asked, "How long will that be?"

By her reaction, I might have been as young and ignorant as Lebuya, needing an older female relative to explain the basic matters of womanhood to me. "Seven days."

I recoiled. She did not mean blood on my skin; she meant *impurity.* It was not a topic that concerned us much in the relaxed Magisterial traditions of Scirland, and although I had encountered traces of it in the Temple-worshipping environs of Vystrana, many of the finer points of religious doctrine there had been whittled down to accommodate local practicality. The women of Drustanev could not afford to seclude themselves for the duration of their "impurity."

But I had not expected to find evidence of the Kerwins' success here in the oba's own palace. Startled, I said, "I didn't realize you were Bayitist."

She frowned at me. "What is Bayitist? You are unclean; you cannot stay out here, where you will pollute others. Go with Lebuya. She will show you."

No, this was not the work of the sheluhim; it had the sound of a standard practice, and surely I would have heard if the entire ruling class of Bayembe had converted to Segulism. But I could no more afford to lose a week of my life than the women of Drustanev could. (Or at least I was not willing to; that, I think, is the more accurate statement, though it benefits from hindsight.) I planted my hands on my hips, drew myself up like a proper Scirling lady—taking Judith and my mother as models—and said, "Nonsense. I have gone about in this condition once a month for my entire adult life, and never polluted anyone."

The old woman made a gesture I thought was probably a ward against evil and said, "Then the oba will throw you into the Green Hell—if he does not have you executed for witchcraft." She picked up her bundle and left.

My certainty that the oba would do no such thing faded when I looked at Lebuya, who would not meet my eyes. She had avoided them, as she avoided touching me, placing the robe on a bench rather than handing it to me directly. She had brought an old woman to take away the stained fabric—someone past her own bearing days. The implications I saw there might be my own invention, but I did not doubt that *some* manner of significance clung to those actions. Whether the oba punished me or not, I would not be able to carry on my work as usual; it would be all around the palace before lunchtime that I was unclean, polluting everything around me. The consequences would damage us far more than a week of enforced idleness would.

Had we stayed at our hotel down in Nsebu, or better still among the Scirlings at Point Miriam, I might have avoided this difficulty. Since I had yet to see any particular benefit from being housed in the royal palace instead, it was with no little annoyance that I picked up the robe and put it on. The thing was shapeless cotton, draping to the floor, the sleeves long enough to cover my hands; there was even a hood for me to draw up over my impure face. Lebuya produced a pair of rough sandals and set them on the floor for me to don. I wondered if someone would come into the room after I was gone to purify it, and thought they probably would.

Natalie chose that moment to return, saving me the confrontation of insisting that, impure or not, I would go nowhere until I spoke with her. Her eyebrows rose at my explanation, and when I was done, she sighed. "Unless there's an exemption for unmarried women—which I doubt—then I'll be taking your place in this *agban* of theirs just as you're ready to leave. How can we be expected to get any work done, if one or the other of us is locked away two weeks out of every four?"

It would not be that much time—as I said before, my courses have never been fully regular—but I brooded upon Natalie's question as I followed Lebuya out. We might escape the restriction by going into the bush for an extended period of time; even then, though, we would need porters to assist us, and what if they rebelled against serving impure women? Perhaps we could hire foreigners from the docks. But they would not know the bush as the locals did, and lack of experience on that front might prove very dangerous.

With the hood blocking the edges of my vision, I could not see our path clearly, but it was not one I had traced before. We left the women's wing by what I suspected was a back entrance, passed through a low wall—not leaving the palace, but entering a new region of it—and came at last to a modest building that seemed almost like an ordinary house.

I did not need Lebuya's pointing arm to tell me where I was to go. This, obviously, was the *agban*: the prison for menstruating women. And I was to remain here for seven days? I should have brought my notebooks—presuming, of course, that they would not be irredeemably contaminated by such use.

Sighing, I muttered a thank-you to Lebuya that was not very heartfelt, and went inside.

The interior was pleasant and not at all prisonlike. It was, after all, where palace women spent one week out of every four; I suspect servants had their own *agban* elsewhere, as neither Natalie nor I ever saw one there. The front room had benches and hooks along the walls, one of which held a robe like mine, with the sandals beneath. I took this as a sign that I could discard my own. Thus freed, I ventured onward to a small courtyard, where a woman I judged to be around my age lay on a carpet beneath a tree, reading a book.

She looked up as I entered and smiled, showing only a little surprise. "I have not seen you before. You must be one of the new guests, those who came to study dragons."

"Isabella Camherst," I said. "I'm afraid you have the advantage of me."

The woman rose, laying her book aside, and touched her heart in respect. "Galinke n Oforiro Dara. I'm glad you came. It's pleasant to have time to read, but after a day or two I find myself eager for company."

"We're allowed to have things with us, then?" I said, gesturing at her book. "I was afraid they would burn my notes if I brought them here."

Galinke laughed. "No, no. We would go out of our minds if we couldn't have distraction! But why would you work, when you could relax?"

I joined her under the tree and discovered that, to Yembe women, and those of other Erigan peoples who engaged in similar practices, seclusion was not an exile, but more in the nature of a holiday. The other three weeks out of the month, they were obligated to work at various tasks—not the backbreaking labor of the peasant in the field, certainly, but weaving, child rearing, and other duties suitable to highborn women. When their impurity sent them to the *agban*, they could enjoy complete leisure. (They could also enjoy a respite from their husbands, which for some of them was even more valuable.)

Galinke herself was not married. "For now," she said with a sigh. "My brother would make a match for me, but he has to wait, in case it ends up being necessary for me to wed the mansa."

"The *mansa?*" I repeated, sure I had misunderstood the Yembe sentence. That was the title given to the Talu leader.

She nodded. "He has one wife from each of his subject peoples— as our ancestors had to do, when Bayembe was young. Even now, my brother has a Mebenye wife and a Sagao one, to keep the different peoples happy."

Had she been Scirling, I never would have blundered in such fashion. We trace descent through the paternal line, and pass on family names in the same manner; the Satalu do likewise, as do societies in many parts of the world. But the Yembe and the other peoples of their country are matrilineal: individuals belong to their mother's lineage, not their father's, and inheritance therefore passes from a man to his sister's son.

Galinke's lineage name was Oforiro Dara, which is to say she came from the Oforiro branch of the Dara line, as her mother had before her. Her mother, clearly, had been a lesser wife of the man who wed the mother of the current oba of Bayembe—whose lineage was Rumeme Gbori—and Galinke herself was the oba's half sister.

(I say "clearly" as if understanding came to me in an elegant flash. It didn't; I sat openmouthed for a solid minute while my brain struggled to bend itself around a system of kinship and inheritance utterly foreign to my way of thinking.)

"But—" I said, still working through the implications. "If you wed the mansa, would that not mean your children would have a claim on Bayembe?" The feud between Talu and Bayembe was an old one, as old and as bitter as that between Thiessin and Eiverheim, and it had only grown worse in recent decades. Anthiopean influence to the north had encouraged several Erigan kingdoms to band together against them, though their Union had swiftly transformed into something much more like an empire, with the others in a client-state role to the mansa of Talu.

Over time the Union had begun to intimidate their neighbours into joining them: a less violent approach to conquest than the Ikwunde used, but still not very appealing. Getting a claim on the rule of Bayembe would be exactly the sort of tactic the mansa might use, and I did not think the oba would be so foolish as to allow it.

"How could he have a claim?" Galinke asked, politely baffled at the wrongheadedness of my question. "I'm not Rumeme Gbori. Only our sister Nsami's sons can inherit."

Nsami, presumably, being the oba's full sister. Give me dragons any day; I understand their ways far better than those of my fellow human beings. We make our world much too complicated.

"I thought your brother detested the mansa," I said, then winced. "Forgive me. This is turning into gossip, and I have no business talking of such things."

Galinke waved my apology away. "What else does anyone in this place talk about, other than politics? You are right. But a wise ruler must be prepared to do what is necessary for the well-being of his people. Even if that means giving his sister to a man he detests."

Or inviting foreign soldiers to come defend his land—but I kept a better leash on my tongue this time, and did not say it. Still, the entire point of Bayembe's alliance with Scirland was to make sure this land would not have to give in to Talu pressure, just to defend themselves against the Ikwunde. If the oba was keeping Galinke in reserve, it suggested that he was less than entirely confident in our aid . . . or less than entirely pleased with it.

Galinke seemed matter-of-fact about the possibility of marrying the enemy, which is more than I could have managed in her place. I said as much to her, and she shrugged, looking philosophical. "Such trades are common. Not with the Satalu, perhaps, but others, to join one lineage to another. I have always known my marriage would be arranged."

I squelched the urge to tell her I had helped Natalie flee Scirland, that she might avoid any marriage at all. "I hope the good efforts of our soldiers can at least spare you *that* particular fate," I said. "I have heard rumours that the Ikwunde are moving their forces toward the rivers, which means we may have a chance to prove our use quite soon."

The words were as much a test as conversation, and I think Galinke knew it. Her full mouth curved in a hint of a smile. "The Ikwunde can never stay still for long," she said. "No sooner do they digest one meal than they go in search of another."

So she, unlike Faj Rawango, was permitted to discuss politics with me. I pressed the advantage. "You are fortunate to have Mouleen defending most of your southern border. I am told that anyone who tries to venture beyond the edge of the swamp is never seen again. Is that why the oba restricts travel there? To protect his people from the Moulish?"

Galinke laughed. "Few people wish to go there in the first place, except for hunters, sometimes. But my brother must keep a close eye on his borders in these troubled times, until we can build better defenses for them."

The only defense we had built thus far was Point Miriam. Were we planning another, or more than one, for points along the border? I had no chance to ask her; a servant entered then with food, and in the course of dealing with that, Galinke turned the conversation so deftly that I did not even notice until hours later.

I came to know her rather well over the four days we were in the *agban* together, and liked what I saw. Although we never returned to the specific matter of the Ikwunde, I learned a great deal about Bayembe politics from our conversations. This I absorbed more out of duty than anything else, for while Galinke seemed to view such things as a puzzle, an engaging challenge for her intellect, I could not bring myself to enjoy them in the same way. I had not been raised to such a life, and was grateful indeed for my freedom.

In retrospect, I wonder about those conversations. Galinke had not been forbidden to discuss politics; had she been *instructed* to do so? Certainly my time with her changed my view of the alliance between Scirland and Bayembe, which until that point had largely been shaped by the news-sheets of Falchester. Those sheets spoke glowingly of economic opportunity, and disapprovingly of the rapacious behaviour of Bayembe's neighbours, from which we were nobly protecting them.

This was not inaccurate, but it lacked nuance. From Galinke, I began to understand the unequal nature of the "alliance"—which is why I scar it with quotation marks—and the extent to which that economic opportunity favored Scirland. She spoke obliquely, of course; at no point did she tell me outright that her half brother resented the dependent condition of Bayembe, which he had inherited from his predecessor, the last oba of the previous royal lineage (and a less than competent ruler). Nor did she spill details of our government's plans, though I think she knew them. She did not even say that the aggressive movements of the Ikwunde and the Talu Union were driven by a desire to build strength against Anthiopean influence; that, I think, is something she did not think of consciously, as both nations were the enemy to her, and she was uninclined to view their behaviour in a tolerant light. Galinke merely talked, in the delicate and subtle manner of a well-trained courtier, and the ship of my thinking heeled slowly over to a new course.

Despite all the trouble that came of it, I thank her for that work, whether it was carried out on her brother's orders or not. Had she not laid those foundations in my mind, I might have failed to grasp the significance of later hints, and the course of history might have been very different.

After Galinke departed, I had two days in which I shared the *agban* with three women I did not know, with whom I made polite but uninteresting conversation, and otherwise devoted myself to my work. The leisure time might have been pleasant if I had been tremendously busy prior to my seclusion, but by the time Natalie arrived on my final day, I was more than ready to get back to my affairs.

"Mr. Wilker was less than pleased to hear where you'd gone," she said with a wry smile. "And even less pleased when he realized this would be a regular occurrence."

She had arrived at lunchtime, and joined me for the plain but nourishing food that in Bayembe was considered suitable for impure women: eggs and fufu (a doughy mass made from yams). "I imagine Mr. Wilker was unhappy to be discussing the subject at all," I said; he was unmarried, and so had never yet been forced by domestic necessity to consider that aspect of women's lives. "I'll see him straightaway tomorrow. What has happened, while I languished in here?"

"In terms of work, very little. I have met more of the palace ladies, and Mr. Wilker has spent much of his time at Point Miriam, talking to the Royal Engineers stationed here. They've been surveying the countryside, which may be of use in helping us chase dragons—though of course that is not why they're doing it. They are planning a railway, and a dam in the west, too, if the Ikwunde can be pushed back. Did you know that someone has developed a turbine which can use water to generate power? Like a waterwheel, but far more efficient."

I laughed. "*Which* one of you has been speaking to the engineers?"

Natalie ducked her head in sheepish acknowledgment. "I have more to converse about with them than with the palace ladies."

Given that the Royal Engineers are the unit responsible for building and/or destroying anything the army needs or wishes removed, I doubted they were accustomed to young women quizzing them on their work. "What of M. Velloin?" I asked. "Is he still in Atuyem?"

"Yes, though he intends to go out hunting soon."

This was precisely what I wanted to hear. The next morning I presented myself to the old priestess who oversaw the *agban*; she purified me by means of prayer and rolling an unbroken egg down my arms and legs and back, and then I was on my way. (No, I do not know the significance of the egg, except that it is a symbol of fertility, and therefore considered to be good luck.)

Mr. Wilker was not in the palace. I sought him down in the lower town, where some kind of festival was under way, with a boisterous parade wending through the narrow streets. Many of the people I attempted to question were drunk; I could discern only that the festival was religious in nature, as evidenced by the finely carved masks worn by the dancers at the heart of the parade. After days of quiet in the *agban*, the noise and movement were jarring; I was on the point of abandoning my search when I finally saw a handful of Scirling soldiers at the side of the road, and Mr. Wilker among them.

"There you are," he said when I arrived. "It's going to be damned inconvenient, Mrs. Camherst—pardon my language—if you and Miss Oscott must be locked away like this."

"I will see if anything can be done," I said. "In the meantime—is there any chance we could join M. Velloin's hunting party?"

"If we can persuade him to wait until Miss Oscott is free, then yes. Or if we are willing to leave her behind."

I was not willing to leave Natalie, but Velloin agreed to postpone his departure, and so we made plans to join him, combining our research with his hunt for trophies. Credit where credit is due; Mr. Wilker was right in suggesting it. Indeed, without M. Velloin to assist, we might have had more difficulty in beginning our work.

EIGHT

*Into the bush—Okweme and his interest in me—The watering
hole—My first savannah snake—Hunting tactics—We study
the carcass—Chemicals and plaster—An awkward
conversation—An even more awkward interruption—Rumours*

We made quite a cavalcade as we headed out into the
grasslands the following week. In addition to the usual
necessities of food, water, tents, and so on, plus the
guns and ammunition for the hunters, our scientific
expedition, which had attached itself to M. Velloin's group like a
barnacle, carried a great deal of equipment. There were no fewer
than four pack mules devoted to our notebooks, scalpels, measuring devices, plaster, tubs, and so on, along with a tent to do all
the work in—not to mention, of course, the chemicals for preserving bone, which was our true purpose in coming.

It was by then the first week of Gelis—a fact which I consis-
tently forgot, despite my assiduous care in recording the date in
my journal every day. It did not feel like Gelis. The Days of Light
were drawing near; the weather, my instincts insisted, should have
been settling into the kind of damp, aching cold that made one
glad even for a candle's flame. Instead it was as hot as a Scirling
summer day, with not a cloud in the sky. Bayembe was firmly in
the grip of its long dry season; the intermittent wind kicked up
veils of dust from the hard ground, and the stiff grasses rattled as
our horses and mules moved through them.

I have not been to Bayembe in nearly twenty years, but my

memory of it remains as fresh as yesterday. Not the factual details, but the experience of the place: the enormous quality the sky seemed to take on, and the vast stretches of dry grass rustling in the breeze. Scattered umbrella thorns spread their branches like flat clouds above the ground; I caught occasional movement in the grass that told me small creatures had taken advantage of the shade beneath.

I had put on a bonnet for the ride, of course. My shipboard argument with Natalie aside, I knew better than to ride all day in the tropical sun with a bare head. But compared with the damp chill that had greeted me in Vystrana, this warmth seemed a friendly welcome, a promise of good things to come. I did not yet realize how brutal the heat would become—though even then, I would choose that heat above an equal or even lesser degree of chill. The evidence of natural history points to a tropical origin for our species, and I believe it to be true.

M. Velloin rode with a rifle tucked into one arm, its barrel lying across the pommel of his saddle. I nudged my mare up to join him and asked, "Do you expect to have need of that, this close to Atuyem? I would think there are too many people about for your sort of game to show their heads."

He laughed easily, teeth flashing predatorily in his tanned face. "One never knows, Mrs. Camherst. Besides, in these troubled times, it isn't only beasts we need to watch for."

"The Ikwunde?" I asked, skeptical. "I have heard they are threatening, but even if they overran our troops at the rivers, we would know of it long before they got this far."

"Single men can be as dangerous as armies, Mrs. Camherst, in the right place. But no, the truth is only that I like to keep my hand in. There are small beasts about that make good target practice— and good eating, too, some of them."

He was not wrong about the small beasts. I had field glasses with me, and put them to frequent use as we rode; it allowed me to see the creatures keeping a wary distance from our noisy herd. Low disturbances in the grass were occasionally visible as rock hyraxes, while larger ones were the rangy, rust-furred wild dogs endemic to the area. A cloud of dust marked the passage of a herd of zebra. An odd lump on a distant tree proved, upon examination, to be the recumbent body of a leopard, draped elegantly along a branch with its tail curving below. "Keep your distance," I murmured under my breath, as much for the leopard's safety as our own.

I had spoken in Scirling, and did not expect to have an audience. But from behind me, a voice said in Yembe, "I would like to learn your language."

Turning in my saddle, I found my interlocutor was a tall, well-made young man, one of the Yembe who had joined us for this excursion. Not a porter; the richness of the cloth wrapped about his hips and the gold braided into his hair made his status clear. He rode with easy grace, and his horse was, if I did not miss my guess, an Akhian stallion of breeding as good as his own.

"I would be a poor teacher, my lord," I said, defaulting, in the absence of his name, to a generically polite address. "I have struggled three years to acquire any ability in your language. Such things do not come easily to me, I fear."

He smiled broadly and touched his hand to his heart. "I am Okweme."

"Of what lineage?" I inquired. "If it is not impolite to ask."

"It is not impolite. I belong to the Kpama Waleyim."

My mare danced beneath me at my involuntary start of surprise. After meeting Galinke, I had vowed to learn more about the various lineages, and now that vow was bearing fruit. "You are the olori's son!"

"I am," he said, still smiling. "But here, in the bush, I am only Okweme."

Only a prince, as we would consider such things. A prince, and the son of the woman who had examined me on my first day in Atuyem as if I were a beetle under a magnifying glass.

But he had nothing of his mother's calculating manner. Okweme was a font of information about the savannah and its creatures, which he did not hesitate to share with me as we rode. His familiarity came from long experience as a hunter, but he did not put me off as Velloin had, for he seemed little concerned with the glory of his trophies. Or perhaps it was merely that he was a far more personable man.

Okweme took our plain supper with us when we stopped for the night, and traded delicate corrections to our Yembe grammar for some basic instruction in Scirling. Afterward, while Natalie and I helped one another dress for bed inside our tent, I said, "He seems a friendly sort. I'm surprised he's taken an interest in us, though. Aren't we far beneath his station?" Galinke had talked to me, but that was because we were locked in the *agban* together.

Natalie laughed. "An interest in *us?* I only saw interest in one person." She poked me in the side.

"Me?" I said, twisting to face her. "What? Why?"

"Oh, let me think," she said, turning so I could undo her buttons. "A handsome young man, an available young woman . . ."

Her description took me aback. I was not accustomed to thinking of myself as young, for all that I was barely twenty-three. I had been married; I was a widow, and had a son. In the eyes of society, all those things put me firmly into the category of "mature," and not the sort of woman with whom handsome young princes would trouble to flirt.

But what were Yembe views of widows and their marriageability? It was not something I had thought to research before coming, and now I felt the lack most acutely.

Fortunately, I soon had other things to occupy my attention. The following day we moved into a region too arid for agriculture, and here flourished the kind of game that attracted M. Velloin's eye.

In terrain of that sort—an arid mosaic of grassland and savannah, which is a kind of loose woodland—watering holes are everything. Their number is few, and a wide array of creatures must come there to drink; but the predators know this, and lie in wait for their prey. The approach to a watering hole is therefore perilous, and the beasts remain in a state of heightened alertness while there.

M. Velloin had not come this way before, but Okweme and the other Yembe with us knew the area well. They directed our group to a stony hillock, lesser cousin to the one upon which Atuyem stood. It lay downwind from the watering hole, which was as great a benefit as its elevation; if we did not make very noisy spectacles of ourselves, we could observe the area at our leisure, and make plans for further work.

I dismounted on the lee side of the hillock and immediately began scrambling up its slope. M. Velloin would be not far behind me, I was sure, and I wanted the chance to see this for myself, without his presence spoiling the moment. Nearing the top, I dropped into the grass and (silently cursing the long skirt of my dress) crawled the remainder of the way, until at last I could see what we had come for.

My gaze went first to the elephants. They were simply too large to overlook. A group of six had come to the far side of the watering hole; the rest of their herd stood a little more distant, perhaps keeping guard. The largest of those at the pond's edge, whom I judged to be an old cow, was showering a juvenile with water while he splashed in the shallows. For all that I am partisan to creatures with wings, a delighted smile spread across my face

The Watering Hole

at the sight. The playfulness of the pair was undeniable, and charming. (I may also say that their large, flapping ears would very nearly serve as wings—an exaggeration, but one that crossed my mind whenever I saw the beasts.)

The watering hole itself was a kidney-shaped pond, muddy and reflective under the bright sun. It was, I later learned, fed by a tiny spring, which kept it present year-round; others wither to a tiny puddle or vanish entirely during the dry season. Even with the spring, I could see the hard-packed dirt where the waterline had receded; it would withdraw farther still before the rains came again.

A herd of gazelles had arrayed themselves not far from the elephants, presumably seeing their fellow herbivores as no threat, despite their great size (against which the gazelles seemed positively tiny). Frogs spotted the water's edge like brown, restless lumps, and flies and other insects made a haze a little distance above. Several pairs of Erigan geese floated near the middle of the pond, muttering amongst themselves and occasionally setting up a great ruckus with their wings, the shading of whose red and grey feathers at rest resembled nothing so much as the scaled back of a Hakkoto carp.

Out of both wariness and eagerness, I looked about for predators, but saw none. Lions, of course, prefer to hunt at dusk and at night; leopards and hyenas are the same. Cheetahs will hunt during the day, but they are less common in that region—their niche being occupied by a Certain Other Beast.

My eye, I am not ashamed to admit, was simply inadequate to the task.

Their business at the watering hole done, the gazelles were loping away, their delicate legs flickering through the grass. Then something else flickered, too, that was most decidedly *not* a gazelle.

It came low and fast through the cover, at an angle to the herd that caused them to startle and veer in their course. Then, with a surge that caused my heart to give a great leap, it sprang into the air: an Erigan savannah snake.

The dragon's wings seemed to go on forever. Long and narrow, they are incapable of sustained flight, but they work excellently well for the species' chosen method of hunting. On the ground, with their wings folded in tight to their bodies, savannah snakes can very nearly equal the speed of a cheetah. Once they come within range, though, they leap upward and spread their wings, gliding above the panicked herd until a suitable target presents itself. Then they swoop down, long necks extended, and bite down hard upon the spine of their prey. If the dragon has gauged his attack well, he retains enough momentum to drag the beast sideways out of the main herd, whereupon the rest thunder off and he may enjoy his meal in peace.

So it was on that occasion. The entire incident was over with shocking speed: a few seconds of the dragon in gliding flight, followed by a bellow and a confusion in the rushing mass of gazelles. Then they were gone, leaving their dead brother or sister behind.

In repose, the savannah snake is not the most prepossessing of dragons. Compared with the Vystrani rock-wyrms I had known before, it seems almost laughably small; the largest specimen on record today weighs ninety-eight kilograms. Its scales are dull, shading to green during the rainy season and dun in the dry, and the elongated structure of its body, along with the contrast between its deep chest and narrow waist, conspire to give it the appearance of a serpent that has recently swallowed a very large meal. But its wings are a glory: slender and maneuverable, their translucent membrane glowing gold when the sun shines through them. (A sight most commonly available to their prey, who do not much appreciate the aesthetics. But I once had the pleasure of seeing a savannah snake airing its wings after being tumbled into water.)

"Ah, she's a beauty."

I had a smile on my face and words of agreement on my lips before I realized the remark had come from M. Velloin. At some point—I did not know when—he had crawled up to join me on the hilltop. He had brought field glasses, and raised them to better study the feasting dragon. Beneath that, his expression was not one of wonder, but rather of calculation, and I could guess what equations were in his mind.

On the other hand, I *had* come here to take advantage of the fruits of his hunt, and could hardly fault him for doing that job. I merely disliked him praising the beauty of the savannah snake with such a purpose in mind.

"They are solitary hunters, yes?" I asked, determined to make use of his knowledge.

"The females are, like that one there. Males will hunt together sometimes, in pairs or trios, occasionally quartets. Especially if they're brothers. If you hunt males, you must be *certain* how many there are, or that last one will be on your head while you're taking aim at the others."

(I must confess my imagination presented me with a picture of M. Velloin shrieking and running about with a dragon attached to his scalp. The reality, of course, would have been bloody and not at all amusing, but the image entertained me.)

I tugged my hat forward to better shade my eyes. "How do you hunt them? With a rifle, I presume—but do you chase them, or lie in wait?"

M. Velloin snorted. "Good luck chasing them; they can outpace an Akhian without trying. If the terrain allows it, lying in wait works very well. Unfortunately this hill is too distant to be of any use, unless the snake drives its prey right past us." He put down his field glasses and gave me a predatory smile. "Let me show you how it is done."

The showing took several days. Even an experienced hunter like M. Velloin is not successful on every outing—not in bagging dragons, at least, though there was not an afternoon in which he failed to bring back *some* kind of carcass. We dined that first night on roast waterbuck, and he took two zebra the following day, whose striped hides our servants were set to defend from scavengers attracted to the smell. Okweme and his companions went out at dusk in pursuit of lions, but had no luck.

M. Velloin's tactic for dragon hunting was this: He would watch from the hilltop until he saw a cloud of dust advertising the approach of some group of medium-sized herbivores (antelope or other such ungulates—never anything so large as an elephant). Then he and the others would ride to intercept it, close enough to the watering hole to be within a savannah snake's likely orbit. The arrival of men on horseback would invariably spook the herbivores, which in turn could sometimes be relied upon to provoke the snake, if present, into striking. Then M. Velloin, galloping along with the herd, would attempt to shoot the dragon from the sky.

This is, of course, a hazardous undertaking. Like all species then considered to be "true dragons," the savannah snake possesses extraordinary breath, in this case a corrosive mist. On the first instance of M. Velloin successfully flushing a dragon, he failed to shoot the beast, and one of the other men took the retaliatory spray across his right arm and shoulder, even up to his face. This immediately raised painful blisters, which soon after burst; and in a tropical environment such as Bayembe's, open wounds of that sort are extremely dangerous. They attracted midges and flies, and despite our best care, soon became infected. The man ultimately survived, but he was scarred thereafter, and much weakened in body.

Yet such perils do not deter hunters from their goal. M. Velloin was not the only one to ride out again after the man was wounded, and two days later, he met at last with success. And, as per our arrangement, he immediately quit the field and dragged the body back to where we had set up camp.

Almost immediately. He had, I saw, taken the time to claim his trophies, prising the teeth and claws free. I scowled at him. "I should like to have seen those in place, M. Velloin. We are not *only* going to make casts of the bones; there is a great deal to be learned by studying the specimen as a whole. How am I to understand its swift running, when you have taken away the claws?"

He looked abashed, and also like he was trying to use his abashment to mollify me. I refused to be mollified, and ordered him out of the way as we got to work.

The routine will be familiar to those who read the previous volume of my memoirs. My words to M. Velloin were true; I had every intention of extracting as much data from this carcass as possible. I therefore set to work sketching, while Mr. Wilker and Natalie took measurements, which I would use to correct my anatomical drawings when I produced the finished images.

We had quite an audience at first, some of whom were even willing to assist rather than getting in the way. M. Velloin, I must grant, was among those who chose to help. But our work is not exciting to watch, and so before long most of the observers drifted away. I was on my knees in the dirt beside the snake, flexing and twisting its hind foot to consider how it ran, when I realized that one was still present and watching very closely: Okweme, the oba's son.

"Can I help you?" I asked, too distracted by my task to address him as politely as I should have.

He slid one of my sketches from beneath the rock pinning it down and studied it. "You are indeed an artist."

"Had you any reason to doubt it?"

Okweme shrugged, returning the paper to its place. "Women sometimes exaggerate their skill, to attract a better husband."

It was very fortunate that Mr. Wilker was undertaking the task of butchery, severing and defleshing a wing on the far side of the carcass. Had the knife been in my hand, I might have cut myself. Was Natalie right? Was he evaluating me as a potential marriage prospect?

Among the Mebenye and the Yembe alike, creativity and artistic talent are considered great virtues in a wife: well, I was an artist. I was also a widow with many fertile years ahead of her, and that is not a thing they tend to leave at loose ends in their society. And this might explain the olori's interest, when I told her of my work. But surely a prince like Okweme was not so bereft of prospects that he needed to court the first unmarried woman who wandered by, artistic talents notwithstanding. Why should he be interested in a Scirling, anyway?

I had to answer him. "I am hardly a professional," I said, realizing too late that a disclaimer of skill is a sign of modesty, and also attractive. Was there nothing I could say that would not dig me in deeper? In desperation, I rose up to lean over the snake's body. "Mr. Wilker, is the wing ready? Ah, excellent. We should take the casts now, if Natalie has mixed the plaster."

She had indeed, along with other materials none of us mentioned aloud. We retired into our tent with the wing bones: long things, so slender it seemed they must snap beneath their own weight. But of course they did not, for that is the virtue of dragonbone. "The solution is under the cot there," Natalie said in a low voice, then went out, pulling the flaps shut behind her.

Mr. Wilker took the bones over to the cot. Between the two of us, he was the superior chemist (I being not much of a chemist at all), and better qualified to run the process that should, at least in theory, preserve savannah snake bones as well as those of rock-wyrms. I busied myself with the plaster, which would suffer an unfortunate miscarriage of procedure in the next few hours, resulting in no usable casts at all. The prospect of mockery for my error hardly pleased me, but we had agreed that it would arouse less suspicion than if Mr. Wilker were blamed for the loss. And we did not want anyone giving much consideration to the question of why we had no casts—not when we would, we hoped, be busy hiding the actual preserved bones.

We worked in silence for about a minute. Then Mr. Wilker cleared his throat. "He has one wife already."

Savannah snakes, as I have said, are not large beasts. Of course Mr. Wilker, on the other side of the carcass, had heard every word. I flushed and answered him sharply. "Is that meant to deter me? I am not looking to make him my new husband."

"I didn't think you were," he said. Then he fell silent: perhaps because he was attending to the task of dripping one chemical solution into another at a steady pace, or perhaps because he was thinking. Either way, when the dripping was done, he went on. "But you haven't exactly been dissuading him."

"Instruct me in how to dissuade a prince in a fashion that will not offend him and cause us trouble soon after," I said, "and I will do it with a glad heart. Until then, I must go on trying to be polite, for the sake of our expedition."

Mr. Wilker laid the last of the bones in their chemical bath and sealed the top, to protect them from both dust and prying eyes. We would need to remain here for at least three more days before they could be moved; I hoped M. Velloin would not take it into his head to shift his camp. Then my companion stood, looking at me. "Do you *want* to remarry?"

My hand on the edge of a plaster-filled tub almost overturned it, which would have made a very nice answer for why the casts had failed. "I fail to see how this has any relevance for our work, Mr. Wilker."

"I should think it's obvious, when you attract marital interest wherever we go."

"One princeling hardly justifies that description."

It would have been wiser for me to leave the matter there. But I made the mistake of looking at Mr. Wilker, whose expression I could not read. With the flaps closed, it was stiflingly hot inside the tent, and I was all too conscious of the need to keep our voices low. Natalie was supposed to be keeping watch outside, but canvas makes a very poor barrier to sound. All these factors and more combined to make me leave my plaster tubs and cross to Mr. Wilker, who, with the cot and the box it hid behind him, could not retreat. "Do you have a personal reason for broaching this topic, Mr. Wilker? Because if so, I would thank you to do me the courtesy of admitting it."

His face had been reddened by days in the sun, but I think he flushed still further. "Mrs. Camherst—"

I will never know what he would have said. I suspect, looking back, that he would have pointed out to me what the roaring of my heartbeat in my ears had obscured: Natalie's voice outside, greeting the man approaching our tent, warning us that we were about to have a visitor. But I did not hear it, and Mr. Wilker did not find his tongue quickly enough, and so when light burst upon our dim little scene, M. Velloin found me standing scant inches from my companion, face tilted up toward him, and both of us red as beets.

We could only have looked more guilty had he caught us in an embrace. We sprang apart with exclamations of surprise, me retreating to my plaster. With Velloin silhouetted against the brightness outside, I could not see his expression, but the way his head turned from me to Mr. Wilker and back again said more than enough. "I thought I would see how you're getting on," he said, and I could have slapped him for the amusement in his tone.

"Quite well, thank you," I said, failing to sound at all polite. "Thank you for the specimens."

He approached me and held out a sack. "The claws. I assumed you would like to examine them."

Velloin offered them to me, not to Mr. Wilker, which under the circumstances was not only decent of him but surprising. He had to have been questioning my scientific purposes—men like him generally do—and would question them even more now. "Thank you," I said, this time with more sincerity. "I will draw these this afternoon, while the plaster dries, and return them to you."

"No need to hurry," he said. "I'll be going out with the prince in an hour or so, to see if we can't bring down a few lions. You're welcome to join us, Wilker."

Mr. Wilker was not a hunting enthusiast, but I was hardly surprised when he accepted. It would separate the two of us for a time, which was good both for our own peace of mind, and for quelling suspicion.

Or so I hoped—quite naively. As you may have guessed, this was the beginning of the long-lived rumour that Mr. Wilker and I were on intimate terms. At least, this is the point at which such whispers became common currency in Bayembe; it is possible that the simple fact of my departing on the expedition with him, especially in combination with the to-do over Natalie, began those rumours at home even before more specific word arrived from Eriga. A widow, by virtue of having been married, is protected from a degree of scandal that would ruin a maiden, but it does not mean that she can carry on in whatever manner she pleases without anyone taking notice.

I would like to say that I cared not a whit for the whispers. It would suit my dashing reputation for me to shrug off the concerns that burden more ordinary women. I was younger then, however, and apart from the damage to my own esteem, I cared a great deal for the effect the rumours had on those around me. It undermined Mr. Wilker, to have his scientific work overshadowed by impropriety; it reflected badly on Lord Hilford, to have given his patronage to two such scandalous people. But what enraged me the most was the foul elaboration of the rumour that said our indiscretions had begun in Vystrana, and that Jacob had either winked at it, or died because he did not.

All of that lay in the future that Gelis afternoon. The first stirrings of it, however, began during the hunt that night, when Okweme was (so I later heard) jocular with Mr. Wilker in a way that did not seem friendly at all. It continued for the remainder of the trip, and when we returned at last to Atuyem, the seed nurtured in water found fertile soil in which to grow.

NINE

*The rumours continue — Galinke's theory — Two months
in the bush — Reconsidering Edgeworth — Malaria —
Witchcraft — A letter from Lord Denbow*

One might have expected Okweme's interest in me to cool, with rumour saying I was already involved elsewhere. On the contrary, he pursued me more closely after that— but I did not like his reasons for doing so.

He said nothing directly, of course. But his manner shifted: friendliness taking on an oily sheen, warmth bringing him closer than I wished him to stand. I tried to describe this to Natalie, and could not find anything specific to point to; the problem was in the aggregate. "I cannot help but feel," I said in frustration, "as if my supposed misbehaviour with Mr. Wilker has, in his eyes, made me available to any man who chooses to claim me. One expects this sort of thing from a rake at a masquerade ball in Vickery Gardens, not from the son of a king."

"Some of those rakes at Vickery *are* the sons of kings," Natalie said dryly. "But I know what you mean. Well, I shall cease telling him where you are; perhaps that will help."

It did, but not enough. In desperation, I turned to Galinke. My irregularity meant I did not rejoin her in the *agban*, but I saw her after she emerged, and she invited me to stroll with her in the oba's gardens. As soon as I thought it reasonable, I directed our conversation to that particular knot. "There is nothing between myself and Mr. Wilker but professional matters," I told her, when the tale was done. "But I cannot see how to convince anyone of that."

"Sometimes women keep themselves to our side of the palace for a long time, and after that the rumours fall quiet," Galinke said. "But only sometimes. And you cannot do that, not without abandoning your work."

Which I would never do—though sometimes I had cause to be glad for the segregation the palace imposed. "Tell me," I said. "Okweme is your brother's son; have you any notion why he might be pursuing me? He did so even before I sullied my reputation. My skill with a pencil is hardly enough to make me a desirable catch, and I do not flatter myself that my beauty or charming manner has anything to do with his intentions. What political benefit might he gain, that I do not see?" Or what benefit his mother might gain, though I did not say it. I was beginning to think she had set her son on me, like a hunter putting a hound after a rabbit.

"Your people are currently very important in Bayembe," Galinke pointed out. "If they gain more territory and influence here, it could be to Okweme's advantage to have a connection."

"But *I* lack connections. My family, if they were Yembe, would not even rate chambers in someone else's compound up on this hill. My late husband's family would, but only barely. Unless—" The hypothetical I had described, the Hendemores and Camhersts as Erigan families, gave me a new idea. "Is it possible he thinks my children—*our* children, if he married me—would inherit something of value? We pass down such things in the father's line, not the mother's. My brothers' wealth, such as it is, will go to *their* sons, not mine."

Galinke had been shaking her head as I spoke, but the way in which she stopped told me a thought had come to her. She cast a surreptitious glance around and then, seeing no one, still took the precaution of drawing me down onto a bench, where we would be half-concealed by a stand of flowering reeds.

"It would be very strange," she said. "But—to your people, children belong to their father's lineage. Here, it is the mother's. *Your* people would expect Okweme's sons to inherit from *him*."

I began to see what she aimed at. "Is there something of value he has, that he cannot pass down to his own children?"

Galinke nodded. "Certain honours and property from his uncle, yes. And Okweme has no full sisters; all of Denyu's other children have died, so his heirs are more distant—cousins he does not like. He has two daughters from his wife, but that means nothing. They belong to her lineage, not his. But your children would belong to *your* lineage—and he could try to argue that, by the customs of your people, what is his should become theirs. To do otherwise would be to leave them with nothing."

It was almost enough to make me laugh. Okweme n Kpama Waleyim wanted me for my country's inheritance laws—or at least that was our speculation, though we had no proof as yet. But putting even a possible explanation on his behaviour renewed my incentive to escape it. "I shall have to contrive to be in the field more often," I said. "*Without* him, this time. Tell me, what happens if a woman becomes, ah, impure, while out in the bush?"

I will not say it was my desire to avoid Okweme and the *agban* that led to our second excursion, but they were among the relevant factors. He was not so shameless as to contrive a reason to join us again—not when there would be no hunting on our trip—and Galinke assured me that rural people were more flexible in matters of impurity, so long as we had ourselves cleansed appropriately.

Other factors included our first preservation attempt, which, while not a failure, had been less than perfectly successful. Mr. Wilker (who was exceedingly stiff with me, on account of our as-yet-unfinished confrontation) said the acidity of savannah snake blood differed from that of rock-wyrms, but thought he might adjust the process and achieve better results. And apart from the anatomical study of dragons, we had a great deal to learn about their behaviour and movement, which would require observation under conditions that did not involve Velloin shooting everything that moved.

We spent more time in the bush over the following two months than we did enjoying the comforts of Atuyem, which was exactly as I preferred. Mind you, I cannot pretend the environment of Bayembe is entirely pleasant: as in the previous volume of my memoirs, there is a great deal I am omitting regarding the heat, the dust, and the ever-present flies, whose buzzing I learned to hate beyond all reason. (One night a fly became trapped in our tent, and its aimless wandering in search of an exit brought me to the very end of my tether; only Natalie's intervention kept me from turning up the oil lamp and lighting the canvas on fire.) But on the whole, I find the hardships I suffer in warm climes vastly preferable to those of the cold—flies being the exception.

What pleased me was the understanding, for the first time in my life, that I was indeed a *naturalist*. Not the wife of a naturalist, brought along for her artistic and secretarial skills; not a hobbyist, collecting sparklings in her garden shed; but a scholar in my own right, engaging fully in my work. The tasks we set ourselves—to document the prey of savannah snakes, their breeding habits, their sexual differentiation, and so on—gave myself and Mr. Wilker sufficient distraction to pretend our unfortunate conversation had never occurred, and we fell into a rapport (at least for the purposes of our work) that was deeply and satisfyingly professional. I will not bore you with the minutiae of that work; anyone interested may refer to *Dragon Breeds of the Bayembe Region*, *Draconic Taxonomy Reconsidered*, or the articles eventually published in *Proceedings of the Philosophers' Colloquium* over the years following our expedition. As the second of those titles indicates, however, it was during my time in Eriga that I began to consider the question of what, precisely, constitutes a dragon.

At the time, of course, we were all still operating on Sir Richard Edgeworth's criteria, which were six in number:

1) Quadrupedalism
2) Wings capable of flight
3) A ruff or fan behind the skull
4) Bones frangible *post-mortem*
5) Egg laying
6) Extraordinary breath

Our voyage to Eriga had reminded me of the disputes over the great sea-snakes, which at the time constituted the main challenge to Edgeworth's model; I also thought about "draconic cousins" such as wolf-drakes, wyverns, and even my old sparklings. Furthermore, there were various theories regarding dragons in the Bayembe region, with some arguing for three breeds—savannah snakes, arboreal snakes, and swamp-wyrms—and others for as many as seven. (The latter came closer to the mark, though as it later turned out, for entirely the wrong reasons.) We could not see the swamp-wyrms without permission to visit Mouleen, but we applied ourselves to examining the distinctions between the grass-dwelling savannah snakes and tree-dwelling arboreal snakes, and found them to be entirely opportunistic: there is no meaningful difference between the two, beyond the simple matter of what territory each beast takes for its own.

Dry work to tell of, but it pleased me deeply—all the more so because it took me away from the strict and unfamiliar customs of Atuyem (of which the *agban* was only one), as it had previously taken me away from the strict and familiar customs of my own land. It was therefore a grave disappointment, as well as a cause for alarm, when Natalie fell ill.

I cannot say it was a *surprise*. Tropical diseases are legion, and we Scirlings are terribly susceptible to them. We all drank our gin and tonics as advised (I grew to like them, which of course made me a scandal when I drank them for pleasure back home), but one cannot haunt the bug-infested environs of watering holes without risking malaria.

We knew the signs to watch for. For Natalie to develop a headache was nothing of significance—we all suffered them, from the brutal strength of the sun and our appalling excuses for field pillows—but when she began to shiver, on a day when I was having to exercise care lest the sweat dripping from my face mar the page on which I sketched, there was no question as to the cause. And Natalie, to her credit, did *not* attempt the foolishness I have seen from others (men and women alike), which is to insist that it was nothing, she could go on working, it would pass. Malaria is nothing to trifle with, and we all knew it.

As soon as the porters we had hired could pack our camp, our guide (a chatty Mebenye fellow named Welolo n Akpari Memu, who knew the bush as well as I know my own library) led us to the nearest village, where Natalie could rest in greater comfort. That much, at least, went smoothly.

We ran into difficulty, however, when it came time to treat her illness. I cannot fault the medical assistance she received; they gave her water and herbs for the fever and the pain, which is all we could expect from a small cattle-raising village in the Bayembe bush. Erigans may be less vulnerable to such afflictions than Scirlings and other foreigners, but their people still suffer malaria often enough for it to be a familiar foe.

The assistance they offered, however, did not end at the medical.

Natalie's treatment was being overseen by an old woman—the oldest in the village, I think—whose name I never did get; they only called her Grandmother. Between her rural accent and missing teeth, I had difficulty understanding her speech, but I soon picked a repeated word out of her explanation: *witchcraft*.

You will hear more of this later. For now, it will suffice to say that there is a view common across Eriga which attributes most or all trouble to the malevolent action of witches. These are not necessarily the figures of intentional and blasphemous evil my Anthiopean readers associate with the word; witchcraft can, as I understand it, be accidental, the result of ill will or unresolved conflict in someone's heart. Nor would Grandmother or her neighbours have claimed Natalie's problem consisted *solely* of witchcraft, and had nothing to do with our bizarre fondness for spending time in fever-ridden areas. But what sent us to such places, or weakened Natalie so that she fell ill? Witchcraft, clearly. And Grandmother, it transpired, wanted to bring a man from another village to treat Natalie's spiritual ills.

"Nonsense," Mr. Wilker said when I told him. "It won't do Miss Oscott one bit of good, and may upset her."

We were outside the house in which she rested, so she would not overhear our conversation. Beyond the edges of the small village, which hunkered down as if hoping the sun would cease beating on it so fiercely, the tree-spotted grass stretched forever. I felt very small and very insignificant: any one of us could cease breathing and this place would not care. "Grandmother believes she has one of the worse forms of malaria," I told him. "The sort that most frequently kills."

"Then we must get her back to Atuyem, if she can be moved. Sir Adam's doctor can treat her best."

This required us to time our journey very carefully. Most forms of malaria afflict the subject with periodic fevers (the interval of which is the primary means of distinguishing them), and during the respite the patient may be more capable of activity. That is not, however, the same thing as being well. Natalie suffered terrible joint pain, and this she *did* endure with admirable stoicism; she knew as well as we did that there would be no relief for her out in the bush. When her fever returned, we stopped until she could ride again. And so, by agonizing stages, we made our way back to Atuyem.

I expected our quarters there to have been given to another during our absence. (Those of you with good memories may recall we had been invited into the royal palace itself by the oba, supposedly because of his great interest in us; the man had ignored us completely since our arrival. There was every reason to think his interest had vanished.) To my surprise, they had not, and furthermore his own royal physician came with Dr. Garrett to examine Natalie and treat her. I was, in the meanwhile, given my own room, so that I might not have to share a bed with a sick woman.

Sir Adam, however, did not even do me the courtesy of allowing me a chance to sleep in that bed before he sent a message demanding my immediate presence at Point Miriam. I defied him long enough to bathe; you could have grown strawberries in the dirt caked on my skin. Then, wearing one of my non-bush dresses—which is to say, one of the only clean items of clothing I had left—I rode wearily down to Nsebu in answer to his summons.

Our resident ambassador had a fine office set up in one of the rooms, with heavy oak furniture totally at odds with their Yembe surroundings. The tired and therefore cynical part of me wondered if he had imported it so that he might plant his fists on the desk and loom at me across its polished surface in proper Scirling fashion.

"I have received," he said, biting each word off, "a letter from Lord Denbow."

My head was full of malaria and draconic taxonomy; it took longer than it should have to place the name. "Natalie's father."

"Yes. Miss Oscott's father. He is demanding I send his daughter home at once. Mrs. Camherst, what the devil have you done?"

"Nothing like you are thinking," I said, wishing desperately that I had ignored his summons until the following morning. A night of sleep would have been more precious than dragonbone, right then. "Unless you are thinking that I did as Miss Oscott wished, in which case you are correct."

Sir Adam slapped his hand atop his desk. "This is no subject for jokes, Mrs. Camherst. Lord Denbow is very angry."

I wondered how long ago his letter had arrived. Not that it mattered; Sir Adam would hardly be persuaded by the argument that leaving a baron to stew for a few more months would improve his temper. "Lord Denbow may be angry, but I will lay pebbles to iron that Lord Hilford is not. Or have you forgotten that the earl is our patron? He knows his granddaughter is here, and does not mind."

Acknowledging my sponsor's complicity may not have been my wisest move; I apologized to him for it later. It did no good in either case. Sir Adam launched into a diatribe about Lord Denbow, not Lord Hilford, being the legal guardian of Natalie Oscott, and furthermore the girl's own wishes not being of the slightest relevance. I suffered this in silence, but when he expanded his theme and brought up Natalie's illness, I lost my temper utterly.

"So you will blame me for her malaria? As others blame me for my husband's death—how very familiar. I cannot be permitted to make my own choices, as Natalie cannot either, but I am somehow to blame for the choices of others. What tremendous power I seem to have! But certain things are out of my hands, Sir Adam, and one of them is whether Natalie will even live to be *sent* home.

I suggest you search your heart and find the decency to leave the matter of her disposition until *after* we know the answer to that question."

I had risen from my chair during this tirade, and by the look on Sir Adam's face, the last thing he had anticipated was for me to shout right back at him. (I think he expected me to break down crying—which only goes to show how little he understood this entire situation.) What he thought of the rest of my words I cannot say, but one part at least had clearly penetrated his mind, for he said, "Yes, well, everything of course depends on whether the girl recovers."

"Indeed," I said, mimicking the biting manner in which he had begun our meeting. "And if you should breathe even one word of this where she can hear, you and I will speak again." Whereupon I pivoted sharply and walked out of his office.

I must grant Sir Adam this: he had sufficient discretion that he had not said anything of Lord Denbow's letter prior to our return. (He would not want our internal troubles known among the Yembe.) He also was sufficiently chastened to leave the matter in peace during the weeks it took Natalie to overcome her malaria and regain a modicum of strength.

Before he had an opportunity to raise the matter again, someone else stepped in and, in the manner of one who takes a chessboard and flings its contents into the air, changed the game entirely.

TEN

The oba's interest—Ankumata's history—Legs of iron—
Royal greetings—Guard dragons—A mission to Mouleen—
The carrot and the stick

I said before that the oba of Bayembe had first invited us to the palace, then ignored us. I have never been a political creature, and so I can only guess at his motivation, but I believe he was testing our ostensible purpose in coming to his land. In short, he brought us under his eye, then left us to our own devices, in order to see what we would do.

The Scirlings who visited Bayembe came for a very narrow list of reasons. First there were the merchants, trading through the port of Nsebu even before it was established as a Scirling colony. After them came the diplomats, to represent our interest in Erigan iron, and they made arrangements for the soldiers (who equipped and trained the Yembe with Anthiopean guns against the Satalu and Ikwunde) and the engineers (who would build railways and dams, from which Scirland would subsequently profit). Beyond them were a handful of sheluhim and hunters like Velloin, and very few others.

My little group was therefore an aberration—and one that, as I came to understand, held particular interest for the oba. When it became apparent that Natalie would live, but while she was still recovering in her bed, he sent messengers to summon myself and Mr. Wilker to meet him at last.

This summons put a nervous chill in my heart. Given his

previous neglect, I could only assume Sir Adam had spoken to him, and he was going to order Natalie at a minimum and possibly all three of us out of the country, lest Lord Denbow speak out in the Synedrion and cause diplomatic trouble. If he did, I could not think of a single thing I might say that would retrieve the situation.

Good grooming was unlikely to sway him, but I attended to my toilet with the finest care I could manage—much finer than I had ever troubled with before. (My Season does not count; Mama and the maids took care of it then.) Then, my heart fluttering with nervousness, I went to meet the ruler of Bayembe, in a courtyard before the golden tower of Atuyem.

Given the man in question, I must provide a certain amount of context first. Ankumata n Rumeme Gbori has been the subject of so much mythologizing during the course of his life that I feel it necessary to set the record something closer to straight before I proceed with any account of my dealings with him.

It is true that he was born to his father's fourth wife (putting him out of what was then the royal lineage), and that he was born deformed. The exact medical nature of his deformity I do not know, but it left his legs unable to bear his weight; though healthy in other respects, he was not able to walk until well into his childhood. Some sources claim he was seven when this changed, and others ten. The exact number does not matter.

What matters is that his mother died, and there is credible evidence to say that she was murdered by one of her co-wives. Ankumata would likely have died, too, except that a man of his father's court took him and raised him away from Atuyem, as his own son. And this man happened to be a blacksmith.

I cannot adequately convey the importance of that to a non-

Erigan audience. For my Scirling readers, blacksmiths are a feature of village life: strong men, but not expected to be particularly
bright. Their reputation in Eriga, and particularly in the eastern
part of the continent, is a good deal more impressive. More
than a few peoples there trace their origins back to a legendary
blacksmith-king, and many more attribute magical powers to
men who work in iron. It is part of the reverence they give in general to artisans, but it goes beyond that. An ethnologist could
theorize for you whether this has something to do with the abundance of iron in Erigan soil, or whether it arises from some other
aspect of Erigan existence; I can only report the fact of it. For
Ankumata's subjects, it was as if he had been taken to be raised
by a particularly wise magister, the sort who knows the secret of
bringing golems to life.

And that is nearly what this blacksmith did. When Sunda n
Halelu Gama took Ankumata into his home, the boy still could
not walk; he rode there on his rescuer's back. But once there,
Sunda—who, in the more dramatic version of this tale, is said to
be Adu himself, the Yembe god of blacksmithing—set about
crafting for him a set of iron leg braces that would do what the
boy's own muscles and bones could not. So wondrously did he
craft them, the story goes, that they weighed nothing at all, and
no sooner did Ankumata don them than he leapt over the blacksmith's house to show his joy.

The truth is rather more prosaic, I am sure, for I never saw the
oba leap any distance at all. But the braces do exist, and I believe
he could not walk without them, which means Sunda deserves
every bit of the credit he receives. He, perhaps more than any
other save Ankumata's own father and mother, made the man
who came back and claimed the rulership of Bayembe (a tale in
its own right), and held it for so many years.

And what of the man himself? I found his age hard to judge;

history told me he was fifty or thereabouts, though (as I have said) mythologizing has obscured some of the finer points of his life. He was broad of feature, as Yembe often are, and I think his shaved head was a disguise for natural hair loss (a bald scalp being more regal than a patchy one). He gave a sense of being both shrewd and good-hearted, which is an impressive combination, and not one many people of either sex can easily convey.

He greeted us sitting on a stool that made up in splendor for the deliberately simple appearance of his braces. The stool, as some may know, is an element of Sagao regalia adopted by the Yembe from their riverine subjects centuries ago, and although it is often likened to an Anthiopean throne, the truth is that its significance more closely parallels that of the crown. Yembe rulers are invested in their office by being seated upon the stool—and not just the oba, but the lineage chiefs as well, each with their own ancestral stool. This one was of sufficient size that I might have called it a bench instead, and moreover was crafted of solid gold, but it had its origins in the smaller and more humble wooden stool found in every home in the region.

Beyond that, much of the scene was a common one. I have, at this point in my life, met enough heads of state to know they are almost always seated in some kind of frame—before a tapestry or painting or coat of arms, atop a dais, or, in this case, beneath a splendid awning—and surrounded by ministers, servants, and assorted hangers-on. How else is one to know that they are important? His wives were there, and various youths bearing enough resemblance to one of those women or to the oba himself for me to guess them to be his children; the olori Denyu n Kpama Waleyim and her son Okweme were in the group, and I was not glad to see them.

Nor was I glad to see Sir Adam and several of the army men. To my heightened nerves, this seemed like proof that we were all

ANKUMATA N RUMEME GBORI

to be ordered back to Scirland. (The truly irrational part of me tried to combine this with one of my other problems, and invent a scenario in which Natalie and Mr. Wilker would be sent back, but I would be forced to marry Okweme.) But they could not command my attention now; it must all go to the oba of Bayembe.

A court functionary had instructed me beforehand that I would be permitted to show respect in the Scirling way (by curtseying) rather than the Erigan way (by kneeling and, before a personage as august as the oba, lowering my face to the ground). I have never been especially graceful at curtseying, and my knees have a regrettable tendency to go tremulous and unreliable when I am nervous; I almost wished they would let me kneel instead. It is difficult to fall over when one is already on the ground. But it might have looked a mockery if I tried, and so curtseying it was, with Mr. Wilker bowing at my side.

Our progress was marked by sonorous words from the *griot* at the oba's side. These learned men and women are sometimes called bards, but more often we use the Thiessin word, which serves as a synonym for a full dozen terms in different Erigan languages. I might equally use a dozen terms to describe them in Scirling: historians, storytellers, poets, musicians, praise-singers, and more. They are attached to aristocratic and royal families, and are often aristocrats in their own right, with all the power and wealth that implies.

I could not make out what the *griot* was saying; he spoke in the highly stylized form of Yembe used for his work, which bears as much resemblance to ordinary Yembe as Akhian or Yelangese calligraphy does to ordinary text, and is even less comprehensible to me. (Calligraphy at least will sit still and give you a chance to puzzle it out.) Knowing what I do now of their customs, however, I expect the bulk of it was a recitation of the oba's praise-names, his ancestors, his ancestors' praise-names, and other things meant to impress us with our insignificance in comparison to him.

One of those praise-names, rendered into Scirling, is "he whose legs are made of iron"—or "Iron-legs," I suppose, though that lacks elegance, sounding more like the nickname sailors might give to a particularly salty captain. Certainly the braces, at least in their most recent iteration, deserved a degree of elegance. Gold had been inlaid along their sides in the characteristically geometric patterns of Yembe art, for it would not do to clothe the country's ruler in anything ordinary. But no effort had been made to gild the steel completely; to do so would defeat the purpose. Nor did he wear the lower-body wrap affected by many in his court that might have concealed the braces. Instead he wore an elaborate loincloth, for Ankumata n Rumeme Gbori understood the role of his own infirmity and its cure in his legend, and used them to his advantage.

This was a man who had taken weakness and made it strength. If you understand only one thing about him, that would be enough.

We minced our way through the opening formalities and the inquiries into Natalie's health. I half-expected this to lead into Sir Adam's demands, but no; the ambassador stayed silent (looking, if truth be told, a trifle bored), and the oba said nothing of Lord Denbow.

Instead he waved back the youth cooling him with a large fan and stood. I heard a quiet hiss as he did so: the braces contained cunningly engineered hydraulics. In a mild voice that did not obscure the weight of command, he said to myself and Mr. Wilker, "You will walk with me."

"Yes, *chele*," we chorused. I suppose I might render the word as "Your Majesty," since an oba is the sovereign ruler of his nation (though in a different manner than a Scirling king); this, however, would obscure its derivation from *eche*, the Yembe word for "gold." Polite address for the oba meant something closer to "Golden One."

To my startlement, the invitation appeared to extend only as far as the two of us and his *griot*. By subtle signals Ankumata indicated to his wives and his servants that they would stay behind; the servants were less subtle in communicating this to our fellow Scirlings. Sir Adam's protest faded behind me as we followed the oba through a shadowed archway into a garden—the same garden in which I had walked with Galinke a few months before.

The oba walked slowly, though how much of that was his braces and how much the dignity of his rank, I cannot say. After we were well through the arch and out of earshot of the others (though not out of bow or rifle shot from the guards on the high walls), he addressed Mr. Wilker. "You have studied dragons. What have you learned?"

Unlike the boyar of Drustanev, who had once asked a similar question of Lord Hilford, Ankumata seemed genuinely interested in the answer. Mr. Wilker collected his thoughts and delivered a good précis of our findings thus far, adding—unwisely, from the perspective of my still-twitching nerves—the regretful coda that "Miss Oscott's illness forced us to suspend our work for the time being."

The oba nodded. Then, without warning, he spoke to me. "You have a desire to study the dragons of the swamp."

My heart gave a great thump in my chest. It was not precisely a secret, but I had only spoken of it to a very small number of people, and did not like the reminder of how easily gossip spread. But I could hardly lie to the man, and so I said, "Yes, *chele*. There is more we could learn about the dragons here—there will be more for years to come, I imagine—but comparison is useful; we might in some ways learn more about savannah snakes and other breeds by looking at Moulish swamp-wyrms than by studying the others alone."

We had reached the end of the garden, where a staircase led up the wall. One hissing, mechanical step at a time, Ankumata climbed; we followed, though not before exchanging a look of puzzlement.

At the top, with the guards standing respectfully aside, the oba gestured downward. "I have captured savannah snakes. But only their breath is of use; they cannot run with chains on, and if I remove the chains they escape."

I found myself looking down into a dry, sandy moat, at the bottom of which two discontented dragons paced at the ends of their iron tethers. "You use them as guards?" I said.

"They impress people," the oba said. "They are not useful." He took a piece of dried meat from his *griot*'s hand and threw it to the sand below, where one of the snakes looked at it with resignation. (They will eat carrion, but prefer their meals to be juicy and running away.)

Offering advice to the sovereign of a country is a touchy affair, but his silence seemed to invite my thoughts. Cautiously, I said, "Were these captured as juveniles, or adults?" He indicated it was the former, and I rubbed one finger across my chin. "Hmmm. Perhaps if you raised them from the egg . . . some birds will imprint on the creature they see first. I do not know if it is the case with dragons."

Ankumata smiled. It should have been encouraging—a sign that I had not offended him. His expression, though, was not exactly one of pleasure; if anything, I would call it *satisfaction*. As if I had played into his hands.

He said, "You will go into Mouleen and get me swamp-wyrm eggs."

"I beg your pardon?" I said, echoed closely by Mr. Wilker.

"We have tried raising savannah snakes from eggs. It does not work. But the Mouri, the farmers on the edges of the forest, say the Moulish raise their dragons from eggs, and this is why swamp-wyrms eat anyone who tries to go into the swamp. You will bring me eggs, so that I may try it myself."

As royal orders went, this was a tall one. "*Chele* . . . who is to say *we* will not be eaten by the dragons? Or fall prey to disease, or to the Moulish. I am told they kill anyone who comes into their forest."

He dismissed this with a flick of his hand. "The forest kills people, not the Moulish. They dislike hunters, but you are different. And I will send Faj Rawango with you."

I had not forgotten the messenger who came to collect us on the docks. A short man, compared to the Yembe, and more ruddy of skin, nor was his name a Yembe one. He was Moulish? I briefly damned Yves de Maucheret for spending all his words on tall tales of the Green Hell, and none on describing that place's inhabitants.

Even with a guide, however, our survival was far from assured. Our success was even more so. "If you will pardon me for saying so, *chele*, your kingdom's climate is very different from that of Mouleen. I doubt whether any hatchlings would thrive here. And even if they did, this is quite a lot of work simply for a few palace guard dragons—" I stopped, my words cut short by understanding.

An understanding which, as it so often does, trotted out of my mouth without asking leave of my brain. "Ah. It isn't your palace you intend to guard, or not only. You are hoping to use them against the Ikwunde. Or the Satalu."

The oba's face hardened. In conversation with a sovereign, or anyone else of power, it is not generally advisable to say what they have chosen to keep unspoken, especially when it pertains to matters of state. But after a pause, he laughed: a long, hearty chuckle that called an involuntary smile from me. "You see? I am not wrong to send you. Your mind is sharp; you see things well."

I was also an outsider, not only to the Moulish, but to the Yembe. Such a person might die, and it would be no great loss to his nation.

Mr. Wilker and I exchanged looks. On the one hand, it was a research opportunity, and one we both desired; nor were the physical risks appreciably worse than they would have been without the oba's involvement. On the other hand, it placed a burden on us, one we might not be able to fulfill. What if he was wrong about Moulish control of the dragons? Or what if they did indeed tame them, but we were not able to learn how? The warmth of our reception when we emerged from the Green Hell might depend heavily on what we brought with us.

I wondered how useful the eggs could possibly be. No large species of dragon reaches maturity in less than two years, and some take longer. Did Ankumata expect to still be at war two years from now? With enemies on both sides, I supposed he might. And even if he were not, it would be no bad thing to improve his country's ability to defend itself. I doubted this man, heir to centuries of Bayembe sovereignty, enjoyed his present dependence on Scirland.

Carefully, Mr. Wilker said, "What if we decline?"

One dark, gold-ringed hand waved this question away. "Is this not something you want? And your assistant, the young woman. You would want her with you, of course, once her strength returns."

This time I kept my thoughts behind my teeth. It was bribery, or perhaps I might more charitably call it payment: if we agreed, then he would block Sir Adam's attempts to claim Natalie. "But if we do not go . . ."

"Then I imagine the girl's father will retrieve her. Your ambassador says he is an important lord. I would not want to offend him."

First the carrot; now the stick. If we did *not* agree, Ankumata would do nothing to stop Sir Adam. It might even go further than that: if I protested or caused too much trouble, I might find myself evicted from the country as well.

"Might we have time to consider your generous offer?" Mr. Wilker said. "We would have to speak with Miss Oscott before we could make any decision."

"Of course, of course. Such choices should not be made rashly."

We descended the stairs. I saw Galinke in a far corner of the garden; she sat with three other women, but I knew from the angle of her head that she had been watching us on the wall. It confirmed my suspicion that her interest in me had not been entirely casual, and that her royal brother knew some of what we had discussed. Which operated to my benefit, at least in part; whether I would thank her for it or not remained to be seen.

ELEVEN

A nice idea—Consulting Natalie—Companions in my
madness—More preparations—The long rainy season

T here was no privacy to be had in the palace. Mr. Wilker and I went into the lower town, ostensibly to visit the market, but in truth to talk away from interested ears.

"You are going to tell me I should not have brought Natalie," I said with a sigh after we had cleared the gate at the base of the hill.

Mr. Wilker shook his head, looking resigned. "That ship sailed from Sennsmouth months ago—and if it were not Miss Oscott, it would be something else. He did not quickly volunteer the threat, but he wanted and expected us to press for it."

"If I had enemies on my borders and allies only too eager to take advantage of my weakness, I suppose that I too might be ruthless in my use of tools." I sighed again. "Empathy, however, does not make the tool any happier about her use."

We entered the market. It was not the chaos of dockside Nsebu; this was laid out in an orderly fashion, though not the grid of streets common in many Anthiopean cities. The merchants and artisans organized themselves instead by lineage, each of which formed round clusters through which Mr. Wilker and myself wound. On all sides we were besieged by vocal and determined hawkers, selling everything from copper pots to religious charms.

Under the cover of this clamour, Mr. Wilker said, "What do you think?"

I shared with him my wall-top evaluation of the risks, and concluded by saying, "I won't deny that I've been trying to think of how we might convince the oba to allow us into Mouleen. I thought I might approach him through Galinke, his sister. To become involved in the affairs of Bayembe, though . . . not to mention that it may not be fair to the dragons. They did not ask to participate in this war."

Mr. Wilker's laughter briefly lightened the concern that weighted his expression. "I might have guessed you would fear for the dragons' well-being." Sobering, he went on. "It's a nice idea, conducting our work without getting tangled in local affairs. Maybe in twenty or fifty years it would be possible. But we chose to come here now, and having done so, I don't think we can escape politics."

We were talking ourselves into accepting. I wanted to see the swamp-wyrms of Mouleen; I had wanted to see them since I saw that runt in the king's menagerie. They were ugly beasts, and not known for their charming personalities—but they were dragons, and that meant I loved them.

I could not in good conscience make that decision, however, without first taking a certain precaution. "We shall have to talk to Natalie. Whether the oba would have found another lever or not, she is the lever he has chosen to use, and I imagine she will have an opinion on the matter."

At the beginning of our journey, I had thrown some sharp words in Mr. Wilker's direction regarding the validity of Natalie's wishes. Now their effect, and that of our trio's months of partnership, began to show. He nodded, with no hint of surprise or reluctance. "Indeed. Malaria may have dulled her taste for adventure—but if not, then I think we know our course."

* * *

Malaria had not, in fact, dulled Natalie's taste for adventure. "I knew it was a risk when I came here," she said cheerfully, despite the pallor that had overtaken her in the aftermath of the fever. "Pity it isn't one of those diseases where, after you've had it, you never need fear it again. But what is this you say about Mouleen?"

I explained the oba's requirements to her, and his halfheartedly veiled threat. She made a face. "I shan't ask you to go into the swamp for me. If my impending deportation is the only thing making you consider it, then don't worry about me; I'll find some other way to deal with my family. Hide behind Grandpapa's skirts, perhaps, or run away to join the circus."

She spoke lightly, but I could see that she meant it. Her resolve comforted me. It is one thing to decide that you are willing to risk leeches and fever; it is another entirely to drag someone else along with you.

What showed on my face in that moment, I do not know, but Natalie's smile faded and she reached out to take my hand. "Isabella, what is it?"

I could feel my answering smile waver. "Only reflecting on how fortunate I am, that I should not be alone in my madness."

It sounds like a platitude, but it is the honest truth. I found myself nearly overwhelmed with gratitude more than once over the subsequent days, as we prepared for our descent into the Green Hell. I was grateful for Natalie's companionship and enthusiasm; for Mr. Wilker's reliability and professional cooperation; for Lord Hilford, my patron, whose money made my presence in Bayembe possible; for Faj Rawango, without whom this escapade would have stood at best a minuscule chance of success. I was even grateful to Ankumata. Undoubtedly he was using us for his own ends—but he had also permitted us into his country, provided us with quarters in his own palace, and given us both the permission and the guide that made the next stage of our research possible.

The preparations were extensive, and unlike any I had made before. On our previous trips into the bush, we had been able to bring pack animals for our gear, but Faj Rawango warned us that horses, donkeys, and mules all tended to sicken in the swamp. Our supplies must be minimal, or we would find ourselves overburdened when the animals died.

The economies we made, however, were in peculiar places. Two tents (very small) and a minimum of clothing, but seemingly endless quantities of gin and tonic water, which would be our main protection against not only malaria but the parasitic infestations caused by foul water. (On no trip before or since have I carried more alcohol than undergarments.)

We also agreed, in a hurried conversation, to bring with us not only our chemical materials, but also the preserved bones we had gathered. Leaving them anywhere in Atuyem was not feasible; someone would be sure to find them. Destroying them would have been difficult, as the main feature of preserved dragonbone is its remarkable durability. If they became too burdensome to carry—in bulk, not mass, as savannah snake bones were even lighter than those of rock-wyrms—then we would bury them, with the hope of retrieving them later, but until then we would keep them under our watch.

One of the necessary tasks has become an oddly routine part of my life over the decades. I wrote letters to Lord Hilford, my parents, my brother Andrew, and my brother-in-law Matthew Camherst, explaining the alteration in our plans, with the unspoken understanding that this might be the last communication they received from me. Certainly it would be the last for a while; there was no postal service in the swamp, and even these letters would not go out until the next Scirling steamer came into port. I did not

have to lay out instructions for what should be done if I perished—
that, I had taken care of before my departure—but the implication
whispered ominously between every line. I was only grateful that
I would not be within my mother's reach when she read her letter.

Even that missive, however, was easier to write than the one to
my son. I was painfully aware, with each line I scribed, that it might
be the last he would ever hear from me. That had been the case
with each letter, of course, but I felt it now more keenly than before. His brief note took me longer than all the others put together.

It was Seminis before we were ready to go. The calendar used
in Bayembe, of course, is not the common Anthiopean one, and
most of my Anthiopean readers will have no sense of what that
means for the region. I will therefore make clear the significance, so that you may all appreciate our folly:

The long rainy season had begun.

At first the change was refreshing. Bayembe had been parched
since our arrival; it was a positive delight to breathe air washed
clean of dust, to see flowers bloom and gold things turn green.
But the humidity in that season is dreadful—it is true what they
say, that dry heat is more tolerable than wet—and, as you may
recall, we were about to descend into a region known for its
abundant rainfall.

Faj Rawango warned us. But he was a servant of the oba, and
the oba wanted us to go; he did not warn us very strenuously. We,
for our own part, were fools. None of us had experienced a rainy
season in Eriga, let alone in the swamps of Mouleen, and Yves de
Maucheret, the great Thiessois traveller whose writings were one
of our only sources regarding the Green Hell, had not said much
about the rain. We shrugged off Faj Rawango's warnings, loaded
our pack donkeys (with a twinge of conscience for the fate to
which we were about to subject them), and bade farewell—though
we did not know it—to our last dry moments for a long, long time.

PART THREE

*In which we suffer many privations
for the sake of our research, and
risk death by a variety of routes*

TWELVE

An introduction to the swamp—The drakefly—
Moulish notions of property—Five visitors—We are tested

Words, I fear, will again fail me as I attempt to describe the environment into which we now entered. But words are what I have, along with my humble line drawings, and so I must employ my tools as best I can. For it is important that you have a clear sense in your mind of the world I inhabited for the better part of the next seven months, and keep it always in your thoughts as you read of the events that transpired there.

The first thing and the last, the thing that was there at dawn and still with me at dusk and present all through the day and the night, the thing that, it seemed, could not be escaped for even the briefest moment, was the heat. Even for a creature such as I, who passionately favors warmth over cold, it was oppressive and often foul. The high plateau that makes up much of Bayembe is arid and windy; these factors mitigate the tropical heat. But in the airless, low-lying swamp so aptly called the Green Hell, there was no such happy aid. In a region that humid, sweating brings no relief, for the air is as wet as your skin. You drip with sweat; it pours from your body; if you wipe it away then more comes to replace it in mere seconds, and all you achieve is to dehydrate yourself. So you endure the sweat, long past the point where you would give your left arm for a cool bath, and this becomes your new reality, until you cannot remember what it felt like to be dry, let alone cold.

I learned to survive it. I cannot tell you how. It is a trick of the mind, one I chanced upon when I reached my absolute limit of endurance and knew there was nothing I could do to relieve my state. Somehow I accepted the situation; I acknowledged it, then laid it to one side and went on with my work. I was still filthy with sweat and longed for a cool breeze, but these things no longer consumed my thoughts. (Natalie and Mr. Wilker, I presume, must have made their own peace with the heat, for neither of them ran mad with a shotgun or tore off their clothes in a futile quest to lessen their suffering.)

Other matters, however, could not be disposed of through tricks of the mind.

After the heat, there are the insects. Gnats, mosquitoes, dragonflies, butterflies, black flies, beetles, moths. Ants and spiders; my temperate-dwelling readers cannot *imagine* the spiders. They are every size, from too small to see to larger than my outstretched hand, and some of them are quite horribly poisonous. Others will lay their eggs below your skin, with predictable and gruesome consequences. The ants, at least, have the courtesy to advertise their hazard; there are some, fully three centimeters in length, that are the most amazing shade of electrical blue. They warn you, very clearly, that you will not be happy if you provoke their bite.

So your skin crawls not only with sweat but with insects and their effects. In the meanwhile, you stab yourself with thorns and spines if you are so careless as to lay your hand upon a tree; and you *will* lay your hand, because you will lose your balance on the rough ground, or slip in mud, or tangle your foot with an unseen branch or root. The wounds inflicted by flora and fauna alike risk infection, plus even the slightest hint of blood (and yes, my female readers will be thinking now of the occurrence that sent Natalie and myself to the *agban*) brings all manner of creepy-crawlies flocking to gorge themselves upon it. Leeches are not even the worst; I came to be quite sanguine about leeches, if I may be forgiven the dreadful pun. Once you overcome your disgust, it is easy to pull them off and cast them away—and this I did more times than I can count.

But not all the denizens of the forest are unpleasant. Such an environment teems with life not only on the small scale but the large: guenons and mangabeys and colobus monkeys, gorillas and chimpanzees, bongos and duiker and okapi, pygmy hippopotami and forest elephants and night vipers and more birds than a hundred naturalists could hope to catalogue in a year.

And, of course, dragons—but I will come to them in time.

Amidst this panoply of life, humans are not easy to find. Had I given in to the impulse I entertained from time to time and gone blundering into the Green Hell without proper guidance—and if I had, through divine Providence or sheer blind luck, managed to survive a month, which I doubt—I still might never have found the Moulish. There are fewer than ten thousand of them in an area more than fifty thousand kilometers square, and they shift camp regularly; it is like looking for a migratory needle in a haystack the likes of which you have never explored.

With Faj Rawango guiding us, we still could not find the Moulish. We could, however, go to a place where *they* might find *us*.

After leaving Atuyem, we traveled along the Bayembe border a hundred kilometers or so inland, keeping to the savannah, where our progress was easier. But we drew steadily closer to the broken land that fell from the plateau into the swamp, and the Green Hell loomed ever larger to my left; I stared frequently at it while we rode, even to the point of neglecting my other observations.

Was it my imagination that supplied a distant sound of drum-beats? That emerald sea seemed an abyss to me, full of dragons and fevers, from which I might never emerge. Perhaps the sound I heard was only the pounding of my own heart.

But I had committed to this purpose. When at last we came to the region Faj Rawango sought, we bade farewell to the land-scape that had been our home these four months, and which had grown almost comfortably familiar, and addressed ourselves to the forest below.

Our descent from the plateau was swift, but we were still some way above the swamp floor when we came upon a clearing. It had obviously been hacked out of the jungle more than once, but as swiftly as men cut the vegetation away, it grew back. "It is a place of trade," Faj Rawango said when we asked. "We—the villagers bring their harvest here, and the Moulish bring meat and ivory."

"How long will it be until they come?" Mr. Wilker asked.

Faj Rawango only shrugged. They would come when they came. It was not a formal market, to be held every four days.

We set up our tents. There is a hazard to having a party with multiple naturalists in it; we occasionally shirk our camp chores in our rush to observe the world around us. (I fear Mr. Wilker and I left Natalie to do much of that work herself.) Myself, I be-came distracted with only two tent pegs in the ground, because a buzzing, fluttering sound drew my eye to the trees.

The creature I observed was birdlike but, with my recent taxo-nomical efforts fresh in my mind, I hesitated to classify it as such. In size it was comparable to a bird, with feathers of a luminescent blue-green, and a drooping bifurcated tail. Its head, however, was distinctly draconic, with a muzzle in place of a beak.

I had only a moment to observe it; then it spread its wings to fly across the clearing, and I saw the reason for the buzzing sound.

Like a dragonfly, it had *two* long pairs of wings.

A Drakefly

I exclaimed in delight, and then had to explain the cause to my companions, who had not seen the creature. Natalie is the one who coined the term "drakefly," on account of their insectoid wing configuration; Mr. Wilker objected to it, as the animals were clearly not insects of any sort, but it is the common designation even today.

We were still arguing this point the next morning, when Faj Rawango returned from the forest around our camp. His appearance stopped us short, and set both Natalie and myself to blushing, for he had discarded the wrapped garment of the Yembe, and in its place wore nothing more than the briefest of loincloths, held on his hips by a thin cord.

Dressed that way—I might better term it "undressed"—he seemed an entirely different man. With his Yembe trappings shed, those details which marked him as separate could no longer be overlooked: the smaller stature, the reddish cast to his skin, the leaner facial structure. He did not look like the other peoples who had surrounded us since our arrival.

Mr. Wilker broke the silence first, clearing his throat. "The iron knives we brought. We'll be bargaining with those for their assistance?"

Faj Rawango shook his head. "No bargain. We will give them the knives. They will help us."

It sounded like sophistry, but he appeared to believe there was a genuine difference. "Why would they help us," I asked, "if not in trade? Is there something else we will be offering?"

He squatted down near us and picked up the pot that had contained our morning porridge. He had, I think, spent his time out in the forest not only changing his apparel, but considering how to explain the situation to us. "This," he said, holding up the pot, "isn't yours anymore. Not *only* yours. It belongs to the camp.

Everything you have, you'll share. And they'll share with you. This is how they do things. It's how they survive."

I quote him as exactly as I can; if his meaning is not clear, that is because the kind of society he described is foreign beyond the ability of mere words to explain, at least for all who are likely to read this account. The Moulish have few material possessions, and little concern for personal property as most of us see it. Their way of living neither permits it nor derives much benefit from it. To own more than you can carry is folly; you will have to abandon it when the camp moves. But most of the things you own—if the "you" in this instance is Moulish—are easily replaced anyway, so their abandonment is no great loss. To try and hoard more than those around you have is a grave insult to social harmony and, I think, to the spirits; it invites ridicule from your fellows and, if that fails, more aggressive methods of forcing you to share. From this the Moulish get their reputation as thieves, but that word belongs to a different world.

Faj Rawango explained it as best he could, but we had little basis on which to understand him; and besides which, he was not Moulish—not precisely.

"My father came from the forest," he said, when Natalie pressed him for his story. "My mother was a villager in Obichuri. I went into the forest for a time when I was a boy, but came back and studied, and went to Atuyem."

He was an intensely private man; it took us months to expand that brief summary into something more like a story, one fleeting detail at a time. I will share the whole of it now, though—as much of it as I ever learned.

His mother had belonged to one of the Sagao lineages whose traditional role is that of the *griot*. To this day, I cannot tell you that lineage's name; Faj Rawango never shared it. Despite the matrilineal nature of Sagao society, he was not welcomed by his mother's people—likely out of distaste for his Moulish blood—and so he did not claim kinship to them. It was, I think, this same estrangement that sent him into the forest. But he declined to stay there, and upon returning to Bayembe, laid claim to the education that was his right. It did not suffice to make him a *griot*, but it won him a place in the civil service, and thus he came to us.

What lineage did his mother's family serve? Not the royal one, that much I knew. How did he end up with his name? It was neither Sagao nor Moulish; I found out much later that it came from the Mouri, the people dwelling at the northern edge of the forest, who are close kin to the Moulish. I had only fragments of story, never the full tale. He was a man who did not properly exist in any single world, but he seemed to have found a place between them, and that, more than his past, was who he was.

This, of course, is the judgment of later years. At the time, those fragments made my curiosity itch like mad. We thought we had discovered more, though, the day that a group of five Moulish—two men, one old woman, and two male youths—showed up in our clearing.

We heard them coming well in advance of their appearance. It is no advantage to be silent when traveling in the Green Hell; animals will attack silent creatures. The Moulish sing and stomp as they go, making themselves sound a far larger party than they are, to scare off beasts that might otherwise trouble them. We were therefore ready when they emerged from the trees.

All were dressed in the manner of Faj Rawango, in brief strips of barkcloth hung from their hips, and (apart from the occasional ornament) nothing more. The old woman was bare-breasted like the men—a sight that startled me a great deal at first, but soon became routine. (Nudity, I find, rapidly becomes boring when it is not treated as scandalous.) They looked at us with open curiosity, and listened with interest as Faj Rawango explained our purpose there.

Philologists say that there used to be a Moulish language unrelated to the Sachimbi family, that today only survives in some of their songs and chants. It was fortunate for our purposes, though perhaps tragic in other ways, that it has since been replaced with a language derived, through the Mouri villagers, from Yembe and other Sachimbi tongues native to the region. Because of this, while I had difficulty understanding Faj Rawango, the task of learning this new language was akin to learning Chiavoran when one has studied Thiessois. I could, by extrapolating from that common foundation, expand my vocabulary with good speed, although grammar took more time. For one such as I, with average skill at best on that front, this was a vital advantage.

I was therefore able to determine that Faj Rawango greeted the two adult men as "Brother," and the old woman as "Mother." "I thought he said his mother was a villager," Natalie whispered to me, confused.

"It may just be a title of respect," I whispered back. "The men, though . . . Mr. Wilker, can you understand him? It sounds like he's actually claiming to be their relative."

Mr. Wilker waved me to silence, the better to listen in, then nodded. "That's why he wants to join them in their camp. Because he's their brother. Half brothers, perhaps? They don't look much alike."

Indeed they did not, beyond the simplest resemblance arising from their shared heritage. Faj Rawango gestured at our camp, and as if that were a signal, one of the men and both of the youths began to prowl around, examining our tents and equipment. One of the boys approached the three of us and asked a question I could not understand.

"Your names," Faj Rawango said. We obediently gave them, which led to much merriment on all sides; the Moulish had great difficulty pronouncing them, as we did we with theirs. The old woman was Apuesiso; the men were Natchekavu and Eguamiche; the youths were Kisamilewa and Walakpara.

It was Kisamilewa who had approached us, and his attention soon alighted on the notebook I held. He extended one hand for it, in a manner that struck me as peremptory; but, mindful of Faj Rawango's comments on property, I handed it over. Not without misgivings: it was a fresh book, not the one in which I had recorded my savannah observations, but it did have my sketch of and notes on the drakefly, as well as sundry less memorable creatures. I did not want to lose them.

And lose them I did. Kisamilewa smiled broadly and walked off, notebook still in hand. (I did not regain it until nearly a month later.) It was, of course, a test: would we share as we were expected to? My notebook was not the only thing the Moulish claimed that day. Much of it, I realized in time, was not even "sharing" by their own standards; they pushed as far as they could think to go, beyond the boundaries of their usual sense of propriety. We were strangers to them, more so even than the "villagers" (a category encompassing not only Mouri, but every Erigan who is not Moulish), and it was necessary to see what we would do.

We handed over pots and pans, notebooks and compasses, an entire crate of gin. (A drink they returned as soon as they tried it; the taste was not at all to their liking.) I began to wonder where it would end, and no sooner had the thought but found my answer: Walakpara pointed at my blouse.

I almost did it. The heat was intense—I understood why the Moulish wore so little clothing—and I had been insisting to myself so vehemently that I must cooperate that I almost began to undo my buttons. Mr. Wilker's gaping stare stopped me, though, as did the understanding that I would be eaten alive by insects if I stripped. (And although I had an undershirt beneath the blouse, would they not ask for that next? Would it end before I was naked?)

"I'm afraid not," I said firmly, in Yembe, and vowed to take the consequences.

My refusal was met, not with anger, but with laughter. Apuesiso said something to the boys; it had the sound of calling them off from the hunt. My blouse stayed on; some of our belongings were restored; and so we packed up and went to join their camp.

THIRTEEN

Entering the Green Hell—Moulish society—Hunting and other tasks of daily life—Geguem—Trousers—We go deeper

aj Rawango had given us other warnings on the ride to that clearing, chief among which was to show no fear of the forest. The villagers fear it—with good reason; they do not know how to survive in it—and the Moulish scorn them for this; to show fear, therefore, is to mark oneself as a villager, and not welcome.

Is the swamp frightening? In some ways, yes. I have mentioned the great variety of creatures that live within it; what I have not yet said is that they are invisible to the untrained eye. You hear them on all sides, but the dense growth conceals them, sometimes even when they are scarcely two meters away. It is also as near to trackless as makes no difference. The clearing in which we had camped persists only because the nearby villagers maintain it; Moulish camps vanish almost as soon as their inhabitants depart. I never did acquire the skill by which they find their way, and so following our quintet of guides felt like plunging into an abyss from which I might never return. I had been far from home before, but never had I felt so strongly that I was in a different world entirely. I could only trust to those around me, and hope it would be enough.

Contrary to some of the more foolish reports that have been made about my time in the Green Hell, facing the swamp with courage does not make one an "honorary member of the tribe."

It may suffice to win acceptance in a camp, and from time to time I did wonder whether the Moulish around me recalled any noteworthy difference between us, apart from my childlike incompetence with various tasks. ("Childlike" is a generous term. I might better be compared to the victim of a head injury. Moulish children are astonishingly competent, on account of not being coddled, as offspring in Scirling society are.) But the basic assumptions of life in the swamp are not those of life outside it, and although I reached the point of being able to navigate them with a degree of ease, they never became habit, much less unthinking reflex. I misstepped time and time again, and was tolerated only because of my willingness to learn from my mistakes.

As an example of this: when we came to the Moulish camp, perhaps two hours' walk from our clearing, I assumed we would be taken before some kind of chief or headman. It took me days to understand how erroneous this assumption was. The elders of their people are looked to for wisdom and advice, and their youths for judgment in times of conflict (a fact which startles me deeply even now, depending as it does on a view of the cosmos I do not share), but there is no single leader, nor even a formal council.

How could there be? If there are eight elders in camp today, there may be only six tomorrow, two having wandered off to spend time in another camp. This, also, is a source of the odd acceptance we encountered: membership in a camp is not at all a formalized thing, like the lineages of the Bayembe region. A member is someone who eats and sleeps near the others, and contributes to their work. As soon as that person leaves—and they do leave, very often, while others show up—that membership ends, until the next time.

This, we came to understand, was the source of our confusion over Faj Rawango's greeting to the others. Natchekavu and

Eguamiche were his "brothers" in the sense that they were men of his own generation, nothing more. Claims that the Moulish have no concept of "family" are not true; they acknowledge that some people are the sons and daughters of the same parents, and such relatives often work together when they are in the same camp. But all those of a given age group within the camp are brothers and sisters, as all those above them are mothers and fathers, or (if older still) the camp's elders. Faj Rawango calling those two his brothers was simply a way of claiming the right to join their camp, and to bring the three of us with him.

It sufficed to get us in the door, metaphorically speaking. Those presently belonging to the camp—about fifty altogether—gathered on the open ground at the center, where Kisamilewa and Walakpara, the youths who had brought us in, explained our situation. We distributed the iron knives and a few more things besides, and assured them, through Faj Rawango, that we did not at all mind doing our share of the work. There was a stretch of time during which he was drawn in for further questioning, and the rest of us shooed to the edge of the camp. This was nerve-wracking on two accounts, the first being that we worried about the closer examination they were giving him, and the second being our inability to cope in more than the most atrociously broken Moulish with the questions we still received during that time.

I cannot give you a full report of why the camp chose to accept our presence that day, any more than I can recount who said what and to whom. At the time they were all strangers to us, apart from our quintet of guides, and even those five I could only understand in snatches. I felt, indeed, as if I had suffered a head injury, and lost all comprehension of the world around me. Curiosity had a great deal to do with it, I know; the Moulish were largely unfamiliar with pale-skinned Anthiopeans. But there were deeper reasons I never fully uncovered. The decision having been made, the Moulish frowned upon us questioning it, as that might disturb the harmony created by their agreement—and they prize harmony to a high degree.

What I can tell you is that we were allowed to stamp out our own bit of forest, not quite a part of the camp but near to it, rather like the clearing in which their children played. Instead of building temporary leaf-walled huts as the Moulish did, we pitched our tents in that space, stacking the supplies and equipment between them and using a few crates for seats and tables. After some discussion with Faj Rawango, the Moulish slaughtered the donkeys who had carried our belongings from Atuyem (our horses having remained in a nearby village). Both creatures were mild-tempered enough that I did regret their fate, but as Mr. Wilker pointed out, the alternative was to wake up some morning and find nothing but a bloodstain where they had been. Better that our hosts should get the benefit of their meat, rather than some nocturnal predator.

His logic was sound, but I could not help seeing the poor donkeys as our last link with the world outside the Green Hell. With their deaths, we were committed to this course, for good or for ill.

If we wished to be successful in the mission Ankumata had given us, then we could not pursue it immediately.

We could not even pursue our broader agenda of research. If we went gallivanting after swamp-wyrms straightaway, the Moulish would have dismissed us as antisocial lunatics, more concerned with our own inexplicable desires than with the well-being of the camp. At best they would have lectured us on our lack of consideration; at worst they would have abandoned us, solving an intractable conflict in their usual manner, which is to simply walk away from it. A group as small as ours does not survive well on its own in the swamp, even with guns to help. We had to prove our worth to the camp first.

Fortunately, proving our worth was far from incompatible with the work of naturalism. The morning after our arrival, a deafening chorus of cicadas and other insects roused us from our sleep, followed shortly by Faj Rawango. "Today is a hunt," he said, and nodded at Mr. Wilker. "They'll expect you to come and help with the nets."

"What of Natalie and myself?" I asked.

He shrugged. "Here with the children, or making noise to drive the game into the nets. They will tell you."

It was a near thing that morning; the children were fascinated by everything from my clothing to my hair, and wanted the chance to study me. But I, of course, preferred to study the swamp, and so we compromised: Natalie remained behind, and I came to do my part in the hunt.

This entailed walking past what I later learned to identify as the sacred hunting fire, whose odorous smoke—nearly as foul as a swamp-wyrm's breath—must touch all those who go out for that task, and then navigating the intricate maze that is the natural environment of Mouleen. We were still close enough then to the swamp's edge that the land was mostly dry; farther in, one seemingly cannot go ten feet without crossing a waterway. Here I only had to wade through two narrow streams before we came to the area chosen for our day's work.

It was as Faj Rawango had said. The men (with Mr. Wilker among them) strung nets between the trees in a broad arc; then the women (myself among them) beat sticks together and shouted at the top of our lungs to frighten the game from us into that arc. Now I began to see all the creatures only my ears had detected before: tree hyraxes, talapoin monkeys, delicate little duikers. Where larger animals charged, the nets were pulled aside to let them through; the Moulish will hunt such beasts, but by different means than we used that day. The smaller ones, once caught, were clubbed or stabbed with fire-hardened spears.

I had not brought my notebook, but I recorded all that I could in my memory, for commitment to paper that evening. This became the standard mode of my work for much of my time in the swamp; although we did have excursions wholly for the purpose of observation, a great deal of our data was gathered in the course of participating in the daily labors of our Moulish hosts. It is excellent training for the memory, if not quite as good for scholarly progress, which prefers to commit things to paper straightaway.

I could not, however, resist asking questions. (Nor could I resist paying attention to things the Moulish considered entirely uninteresting. They are fond of giving nicknames to people; mine was soon Reguamin, which translates to something like "woman who stares at things." Natalie was Geelo—"builder"—for her good assistance with huts and other such structures, and Mr. Wilker was ignominiously dubbed Epou, "red," for his permanently flushed face.)

On our way back to the camp, when we reached the first of the streams, I gestured at the water. Grammar was beyond me as yet, but I knew from Faj Rawango the word I wanted. *"Legambwa?"*

The girl leading me laughed. She was no more than sixteen, I judged; her name was Akinimanbi, and in all my time with her I rarely saw her other than cheerful. Her answer meant nothing to me, but she was quickly adapting to my ineptitude, and bent to splash her hand in the water, indicating its shallowness. By way of similar motions and a few Yembe words I inquired as to the depth a swamp-wyrm would require, and got a shrug; her explanatory gesture seemed to indicate a variety of possibilities, from little more than half a meter to a channel that would merit the name of river.

I pantomimed jaws latching onto my leg, and pretended to scream. Akinimanbi laughed again. That much I understood; she thought me foolish for worrying about such a thing. The significance of her waving arm, however, was opaque to me, as it seemed to indicate the trees. I had thought swamp-wyrms aquatic, but I had not forgotten the so-called arboreal snakes of Bayembe; were their lowland cousins similarly opportunistic, and known to climb? I might be eager to see dragons of any sort, but the prospect of having one drop on my head was alarming.

No dragons fell on my head during our return to the camp, nor in the days that followed. We were about three weeks in that location, with hunts every few days, and smaller excursions to gather food every morning: nuts, berries, roots, frogs, whom the Moulish ate in vast quantities, without ever seeming to dent the supply.

(Because someone always asks: yes, I ate termites. Also ants, beetles, caterpillars, and the cicadas whose cacophony woke me every morning. If one is to live without the benefits of agriculture beyond sporadic trade with villagers, every source of food becomes vital. I will not, however, pretend I ever became fond of the practice. Insects are too crunchy for my taste.)

During those three weeks, we applied ourselves assiduously to being good members of the camp—a task made easier by the absence of dragons, at least that we saw. Moulish came and went, some of them drawn from other camps after word reached them of our presence; others moved to visit kin, or to get away from neighbours who vexed them. It meant constantly learning new names and, as our command of the language improved, explaining ourselves again and again; I began to feel we would never truly settle in, but be trapped forever in this limbo of novelty. But in time the questions stopped.

With the fluctuation of the camp (most of which I will gloss over here, except where it becomes pertinent), you might rightly ask whether we stayed with the same people our entire time in Mouleen. For sufficiently small values of "the same people," the answer is yes. Akinimanbi, I discovered, was newly married, and she and her husband Mekeesawa shared a fire with her grandparents, Apuesiso and Daboumen. At all times except a few I will note in due course, we were always in camp with one or the other of those two couples, and often both.

As in the previous volume of my memoirs, I will not force you to toil through broken sentences that would more accurately represent my early lack of skill with the Moulish tongue. You may simply imagine that when I said to Akinimanbi, "I've heard that the dragons here are rather bad-tempered," one morning shortly before we left that campsite, my phrasing was not nearly so fluent.

She shrugged, cracking nuts with great efficiency and throwing the shells into the fire. "A hippopotamus is worse. The dragons usually won't chase you."

I had less faith than I might in that "usually," owing to my experiences with the "usually" approachable rock-wyrms of Vystrana. "Do you ever hunt them?"

Akinimanbi stared at me as if I'd suggested throwing a baby into the fire along with the shells. "*Hunt* them? That would be"—and she finished with a word whose meaning I could not guess. (*Geguem*, which I suspect is a term left over from the older language.)

"I don't understand *geguem*," I said, apologetically.

She looked to her grandmother, Apuesiso, who was squatting on the other side of the fire. I could not imitate their posture; a lifetime of chairs has trained me out of the position. I sat on one of our crates, having discovered that sitting cross-legged on the ground meant unpleasant visitors crawling up my skirts.

Apuesiso was braiding a rope from some fiber I had not identified. Without pausing in her work, she sang a song, at least half of
which was in the older tongue. I could not understand a word of
it, and prepared to say so. But Apuesiso knew that; I think she
began with the song for reasons of tradition or propriety. When
it was done, she shifted without pause from music to speech. "A
long time ago, a man killed a dragon. He was ashamed of what
he'd done, so he tried to hide it by getting rid of the body. He ate
the meat, used the skin, and turned the teeth and claws into tools.
But it was no good: the spirits knew what he had done. *Geguem.*"

Murder, then; or perhaps sin. "Did they punish the man?"

By her snort, I might have asked whether rain fell from the
clouds. "Because of him, we die."

The broken quality of our conversation meant I had to ask
several more questions before I properly understood what Apuesiso meant. The death of the dragon was, in their view, the reason
human beings are mortal.

I am more a natural historian than an ethnologist; my immediate thought was to wonder how hungry that man must have
been to resort to eating foul-smelling and fouler-tasting dragon
meat. But of course such myths change over time; the exact
phrasing owed more to the usual hunting practices of the Moulish than to the actual disposition of a dragon's body. (Indeed, I
later heard another rendition of the story wherein the bones were
also said to have become tools. I was far too excited about that one,
until it became apparent that, no, the Moulish ancestors did not
have their own method for preserving dragonbone.)

But if I have relatively little interest in the religious practices
of other people, there is no surer way to draw my attention than
to bring up dragons. "Why did he kill it? Was it for food, or did
the dragon attack him?"

They laughed my questions off, as well they might. It was a

myth; such narratives are not known for their exploration of the human psyche and its motivations. As well ask why Chaltaph refused the gifts of Raganit in the Book of Schisms: scholars may think up interpretations, and those are enlightening in their own fashion, but in the end the story itself gives no clear answer. But the taboo against further dragon killing was clear.

I brought this up with Natalie and Mr. Wilker that afternoon, as we went through the tedious routine of washing our clothes in buckets of water collected for the purpose. (We could not use groundwater, as it was too often muddy. Fortunately, the storms that came every afternoon as regularly as clockwork made it easy to collect rain.)

"So they won't look kindly on us killing a dragon," Mr. Wilker said, wringing out one of his shirts. It is a credit to the man that he never once asked Natalie or myself to do his laundry for him— though on reflection, it may be more a discredit to our own clothes-washing skills, or lack thereof. We were both too gently reared to have firsthand experience with such matters; Mr. Wilker, with his working-class childhood on Niddey, knew more than we.

"About as kindly as we would look on someone pulling an-other fig from the Tree of Knowledge," I said, trying, with less than total success, to scrub mud from the hem of one of my skirts.

Natalie was hanging the clean articles from a line to dry (inas-much as they could, in the eternally damp air of that place). "No tests on bone, then, unless you want to try and do it in secret."

Mr. Wilker and I exchanged glances, then both shook our heads. "Not yet, anyway," he said. "Too much risk of being found out and losing their goodwill."

"Besides," I added, "it works, with modification, on both rock-wyrms and savannah snakes, who cannot possibly be related except in the most distant sense. I think we can assume it would work on swamp-wyrms as well. And as much as I would like to be able to study samples for reasons other than preservation, Mr. Wilker is right; it would lose us their goodwill, which would do more harm to our work in the long run."

I had gone on with my skirt-washing efforts while I spoke, but my thoughts had drifted from that task; it startled me when a pair of hands appeared and took the skirt away. Mr. Wilker set it against the crate lid he was using for a washing board and began to scrub it, doing in mere seconds what would take me minutes to achieve, if indeed I could at all.

"Thank you," I said, blushing. "Would it scandalize you terribly if I cut that apart after it dries and turned it into trousers?"

"Oh, *please* do," Natalie said, with vast relief. "Then I won't feel guilty for doing the same. Skirts in this place are sheer madness."

Mr. Wilker had seen me in trousers before, in Vystrana. He had not liked it at the time—but then, we had not liked each other at the time, either. He said, only a little stiffly, "It seems the practical choice, yes."

Natalie and I accordingly spent the evening cutting up and restitching our clothing, much to the amusement of our hosts the following morning. The only differentiation they observe in clothing the two sexes lies in how they hang their loincloths; skirts versus trousers meant little to them in that regard. But Natalie and I both felt awkward in such masculine garb, and it showed. We soon adjusted, however, and this is the origin of my practice of wearing trousers whenever I am on an expedition, which has been such an article of gossip over the years. (Whatever the scandal-sheets may claim, I do not wear them at home, though I have considered it once or twice.) (The incident at Booker's Club should not be counted; I was *extremely* drunk at the time.)

Our decision was timely, as we moved camp the very next day.

I have spoken already of the tendency for the Moulish to come and go from a camp; there is also the migration of a camp wholesale, when they have been long enough in an area to exhaust the nearby sources of food, and must move elsewhere to find game and wild fruits.

This created a spot of difficulty for our expedition, as we had known it must when they slaughtered the donkeys. With no beasts of burden, the Moulish carry all of their belongings with them, in baskets strung from tumplines on their heads. Although this is quite an effective method for those whose neck muscles are conditioned to it, the four of us (Faj Rawango included) could not be so described, and also had more equipment than we could carry in such fashion.

Our best guess at conversion from "distance a Moulish man carrying a burden can walk before noon" to Scirling units told us they intended to move about fifteen kilometers farther into the swamp. Some of our things we could abandon, having discovered we had no real need of them. (A proper Moulish sentiment, and one that has become habit for me over the years.) Others we could get rid of, so to speak, by encouraging members of the camp to take them; they rarely resented us borrowing things back when we needed them. But some items—foremost among them the crate of gin and the box containing our preserved dragonbone—posed a genuine problem.

"Well," Mr. Wilker said with a sigh, "I suppose we could conduct another experiment. Bury the bones, and see how they fare in this muck." He kicked at the wet soil.

That box was nailed firmly shut; the Moulish did not know what was in it, and I preferred to keep matters that way. "Will we be able to find it again? I feel I've come to know this area quite well, but I'm sure that a week from now it will look like every other bit of swamp to me."

"They know the spot," Natalie said, fishing a machete from among our baggage. "And I think Faj Rawango could find it again. We'll just have to ask for help. I fear, though, this is the closest thing we have to a shovel."

We dug the hole with two machetes and our bare hands, which would not have gone very well in more solid earth. In that terrain, however, it was more a matter of hacking through a mat of roots, then scooping away what muddy dirt remained. (And then pausing with every handful to shake off the small creatures crawling up one's arms.) This, of course, attracted an audience, but we were able to satisfy their curiosity by saying we only wanted to spare ourselves the effort of carrying the box's contents with us.

Everything else went into packs and baskets and so on. Akinimanbi talked her husband Mekeesawa into taking our bottles of gin, removed from their crate and wrapped in clothing for protection; he grumbled at carrying a tumpline-hung basket "like a youth"—grown men carried their nets and spears, not other burdens—but agreed without much rancor, as the rest of us were taking on substantial loads of our own. And so, shouldering our loads, we went with our hosts to their next camp.

FOURTEEN

*The heart of the swamp—Leeches—Egg-hatching season—
Hunters of knowledge*

I thought I had seen the Green Hell during our weeks in that
first camp, but I was wrong.

Compared to the swamp proper, those upper reaches are
dry and scrubby, with dwarfish vegetation (however much it
may tower above the trees and brush of the savannah). Once you
descend into the heart of the Green Hell, you find yourself in a
land of water and giants.

The trees there soar forty or fifty meters high, as if they were
the pillars of some great temple. Their roots form great bladelike
walls, bracing the trunks in the soil, sometimes growing closely
enough that earth accumulates in between and a smaller tree
begins growing in the cup thus formed. The space beneath is
emerald and dim, save for where a stray beam of sunlight breaks
through the many layers of vegetation to strike the ground.
There the swamp grows even warmer, but at the same time the
light is a glorious thing, as if it carried the voices of angels.

Most of the light is to be found where the waterways grow
wide enough that branches cannot fully bridge the gap. But these
are rare; storms and floods along the three rivers that feed the
swamp can change the landscape enough that what last year was
a minor stream has now become a main artery of the delta.
"Rivers" in Mouleen therefore have trees growing in them like
islands, and are patched with sunlight like a piebald horse.

When we came to a waterway deep and broad enough to be troublesome, or (more often) turned to follow one for a substantial distance, the Moulish paused to make simple rafts, on which they floated their belongings for ease of transport. "Tuck the hems of your trousers into your stockings," Mr. Wilker said, suiting action to words. "It will reduce the chance of you finding a leech on your leg."

"I think trousers just became my favourite thing in all the world," Natalie said.

We tucked our hems into our stockings and half-waded, half-swam downstream. When we came out again, our hosts picked leeches off their limbs with an unconcerned air. We Scirlings examined ourselves and one another; Natalie circled behind me, and I felt her tug on the fabric of my shirt. Then she made a most peculiar noise—a sort of strangled moan.

"Ah, Isabella?" she said. "You, ah—your shirt—"

My shirt had come loose from my waistband during our exertions. I put my hand to my back, very unwisely, and felt the soft, disgusting mass of a leech just above my right kidney.

I fear it may damage my reputation to admit this, but I yelped and promptly began to dance in a circle like a cat chasing her tail, trying to see the leech and also to get away from it. The latter was futile; it had fastened onto me, and slapping at it with my hand was hardly persuading it to let go.

The Moulish were no help, as they found my antics utterly hilarious. Finally Akinimanbi took pity on me; while Mr. Wilker held me by the shoulders, stopping my dance, she lifted my shirt and pried the thing off. I shuddered at the sight of it, and kept shuddering for a good while afterward, obsessively running my hands over various parts of my body to make sure I had no more bloodsucking passengers, at least none of any size larger than a mosquito. (I did, as I have said, eventually become accustomed to leeches, but this being my first encounter with them, it did not proceed so calmly.)

On we went, until we came to the place the camp had agreed upon for its next site. How they identified it, I do not know; with the landscape as changeable as the shifting waters, there seemed no guarantee a location would still be where one remembered it, even if one could find it again.

With what remained of the day (and our energy), we helped the others cut away brush and saplings from the new site, trimming the detritus to make huts for them to sleep in. Pitching our own tents took longer, and when it was done, I had no will even to eat. But Natalie insisted we feed ourselves, so I swallowed a plantain and some starchy root whose name I had not yet learned, then collapsed face-first into my pillow.

This was the basis of our routine for the next several months. The camp—or rather, the portion of it that consisted of us and Akinimanbi's family—never stayed more than three or four weeks in any one place. We were in the depths of the rainy season now, which meant a daily deluge each afternoon, and often showers at other times of day; it is not the near-constant rainfall seen elsewhere in the world, but it is more than enough. The mountains farther inland had melted their snowcaps by now, feeding the three rivers; it began to seem that the swamp was eighty percent water and twenty percent land. Campsites were wherever the ground rose high enough to have a chance of staying above the flood. Nor were such places accidental: Mekeesawa told Mr. Wilker that they piled branches and planted certain vegetation in what passed for their "dry" season to ensure these miniature hillocks would persist.

There was, I began to realize, more organization to their society than met the eye—though it is still nothing like as structured as those which develop in less ecologically hostile regions.

The Moulish cannot afford stratification by class, nor even much in the way of gender roles; all must do what they can. But they not only understood their environment, they shaped it in small ways to suit their purposes. They also maintained a surprising degree of connection between camps, firstly through the constant migration of people, and secondly through the use of talking drums.

Natalie was fascinated by these. For a people with so few material possessions, and most of those temporary, the drums were treasures: carved with elaborate designs, and carried with reverence each time the camp moved. Their use is too complex for me to explain, but the Moulish have a way of translating their language into drumbeats, which can then be used to send messages between camps. By passing a message from one camp to the next, they are able to communicate from one end of the swamp to the other, much faster than any human could carry a message. The drums therefore permit them to stay in touch with kin far away, and are often used to ask or tell where someone is, so that another may find them.

Mekeesawa explained this to me one afternoon, while Natalie was questioning the current drum bearer about the method of translation. He added, "It is very useful during this season. No one wants to wander for too long."

By now my command of the language had improved substantially, such that I could converse with him in more than my early mixture of nouns and mime. I laughed and said, "Because of the rain? I can understand that."

"The rain," Mekeesawa said, "and the dragons."

We were not busy with any task for the camp; I judged it safe to question him, without fear that my interest would seem selfish. "What makes them more dangerous in this season than another? Do they object to this much water?"

He grinned. "They love it. Full of things to eat. But this is when the eggs hatch."

I attempted not to perk up like a scent hound that has come upon the trail of a fat, juicy rabbit, but I fear my success was middling at best. It was easy to forget that a world existed outside the Green Hell: a world, and perhaps a war. Had the Ikwunde backed off from the rivers, or were Scirling soldiers and Bayembe warriors fighting them as we spoke? I had no way of knowing.

Even if open conflict had broken out, nothing I did here could affect it—or so I thought. Eggs would not help Ankumata immediately. Even so, Mekeesawa's words reminded me that the oba would be waiting for us to deliver on our promise.

If the eggs were in the process of hatching, though, he would have to wait a while longer, until there was a fresh set. "Do the dragons lay them in the water?" I asked. "Or on dry land, and they hatch when they become submerged?"

It was not, I thought, an alarming question. Mekeesawa, however, clapped his hands together, which I recognized as a sign to ward off bad luck or evil spirits. "I don't know about such things," he said.

The peculiarity of his response arrested me. The key factor distinguishing the Moulish from their neighbours—even the closely related Mouri—is not physiognomy or language; it is their relationship to the swamp they call home. They know every plant that is useful and every one that is hazardous, every insect that can poison you and every one that can be eaten for lunch. They hunt a wide variety of creatures, even hippopotami and forest elephants (against whom they use some of those poisonous insects), and are as well versed in the behaviour and life cycle of those beasts as any naturalist could hope for.

Now a Moulish hunter claimed to me that he did not know

where swamp-wyrms laid their eggs. You may understand, gentle reader, when I tell you this made me suspicious.

I considered several possible responses and settled on, "Many animals become quite violent if they believe you might threaten their young. I should like at least to know what to watch out for, so as not to stumble upon swamp-wyrm eggs." Of course I would go *looking* for them eventually, but this made for a more discreet way of questioning him.

Much good it did me. "They've all hatched by now," Mekeesawa said.

"Yes, but if we are still here when the next set are laid—"

I should have known better. Yves de Maucheret had claimed the Moulish worshipped dragons; I had seen no sign of it thus far beyond that one myth, the tale of how humans became mortal, but I should have known that *something* gave rise to that claim. I had clearly stumbled upon a taboo subject, and it is my fault for letting my intellectual curiosity drive me into pursuing it too directly.

No more would Mekeesawa say on the topic, and I had to restrain the urge to question others in the camp, in the hopes of finding someone more willing to speak. Instead I passed this along to the others, and we discussed how we might proceed.

"We have a fair bit of time to spare," Mr. Wilker said. The rainy season meant the Moulish had only to drop a net in the water to get their supper; they spent much of their day at leisure, singing and dancing, when they were not occupied with household tasks like pounding out fresh barkcloth or weaving baskets. "We've gathered useful information for the general purpose of naturalism, but perhaps it's time we devoted ourselves more strictly to dragons."

I nodded in agreement. We had caught distant glimpses of a few, and likely been closer to more; a swamp-wyrm who wishes to remain concealed is not easily spotted. But those glimpses had taught us very little so far. I said, "Not pursuing eggs, of course; not immediately. But we know virtually nothing of what swamp-wyrms eat, or how they hunt, where they sleep, the differences between male and female, their mating habits . . ." I ticked each item off on my fingers, and stopped when I ran out on that hand. I could have kept going. My understanding of what a naturalist *did* had greatly deepened in the years since Vystrana.

"We don't even know how one might safely observe them," Natalie pointed out; and that became our first question to answer.

For some time we had been agreeable if moderately inept members of the camp, mostly going along with the day-to-day activities of our hosts. Now that we reared our heads as natural-ists, however, we met with more difficulty. Not hostility, per se, but simple confusion.

"This is the lazy season," Akinimanbi said, suiting inaction to words. At her side, Mekeesawa was stripping the bark from a branch to make a new spear, but his movements were desultory. He might have been a Scirling farmer, whittling wood to give his hands something to do. "Why would you go out when you don't have to?"

"We *do* have to," I said, and then stopped. Most of the reasons I could give her were so foreign to the world in which she lived, I might spend the next hour explaining them and still not convey my point. There was nothing like the Philosophers' Colloquium here, nor journals in which one might publish, nor acclaim given for that sort of thing. And simple scientific curiosity, as I had learned in Vystrana, rarely meant much to the people for whom my object of curiosity was their daily and sometimes disagree-able reality. (One need look no further than Scirland for proof of that: while we have naturalists who study local birds and bugs, they are far outnumbered by those whose interest lies in more distant lands—myself chief among them.)

Akinimanbi waited patiently while I considered how to explain myself without seeming like a madwoman. At last I said, "If you consider the three of us to be hunters of a sort, then what we are hunting is knowledge."

Her eyebrows went up at this, and I realized my error. "Except it's not like your story, where the man did wrong by killing the dragon! We don't want to kill anything. Forget what I said about hunting; we *gather* knowledge, as you gather food. To, ah, feed our minds. Or—"

At this I stopped, because Akinimanbi and Mekeesawa both were laughing at me, slapping their thighs and rolling back where they sat. I deserved it, for the way my words had tumbled over one another; I might have explained myself, but the part about not seeming like a madwoman had been a resounding failure.

Belatedly, I thought of a better way to make my point. "Your people understand the forest: how the animals behave, where to find them, and so on. I want something similar—but instead of the forest as a whole, I want to understand dragons. They are not only here, you know; there are dragons in the savannah—" Mekeesawa nodded. "Well, there are more than that, all over the world. They live in the mountains and on the plains and maybe even in the ocean. I want to know them as you know the creatures of this forest."

"But why?" Mekeesawa asked. His eyes were still merry with laughter, but his question was serious. "You don't live in all those places."

With the amount of time I have spent traveling in my life, one might make the argument that I *do* live in all those places, if only temporarily. But Mekeesawa's point was a good one, and not easily dismissed. The Moulish understood the creatures of the Green Hell because their survival depended on it; my survival did not depend on my traveling the globe to find dragons. (Indeed, it has on more than one occasion nearly been detrimental to my life expectancy.) How could I answer him?

Thinking back on the matter now, it is possible my only true answer to that question is now in its second volume, with more to come. These memoirs are not only an accounting of my life; they are an accounting *for* it.

But that day in the Green Hell, I could hardly present these books to Mekeesawa. I gave the matter my final try. "There is a man—an elder of my camp, in a manner of speaking. He has asked me to do this for him." That was the best explanation I could give for Lord Hilford's role as my patron. "And if *that* does not make sense to you, then I can only ask you to tolerate the mad-woman."

I suspect that last suggestion was the one they accepted in the end. One way or another, we got the freedom to continue with our work—and, at long last, an explanation for Akinimanbi's over-head gesture so many days before.

FIFTEEN

Traversing the flood—Moulish engineering—
Swamp-wyrms on the hunt—I miss my footing—
My misfortunes—Witchcraft, again

I have described to you how the inundation of the Green Hell made the place almost more lake than land. We had gained two newcomers to the camp since settling there, and lost five others; I had assumed they went by raft while I was otherwise occupied. But travel by raft is too dangerous during that season: apart from the usual predators, swamp-wyrms not excepted, the water swarms with small, eel-like creatures we had dubbed fangfish, which are rapacious carnivores. To avoid these hazards, the Moulish traveled by other, more exciting means.

Three of us went out with Mekeesawa; Faj Rawango elected to stay in camp, I think to mitigate any sense that we were being antisocial by pursuing our own ends. Mekeesawa took us to the end of the long spit of land on which we had pitched our camp, and we waded across a shallow stretch to another spot that was not so much island as tree. It was one of the great forest giants, tangled about with smaller parasitic trees, and he indicated to us that we should climb.

Tamshire's rocky soil does not support much in the way of good climbing trees; nor do Tamshire's gentry support much tree-climbing in girls. Mekeesawa clambered up with no trouble, and Natalie followed him with surprisingly little, but I required Mr. Wilker's assistance. My face, I am sure, was flamingly red by the time we reached the others; in part because of the heat, but much more because of the indelicate physical contact his aid required. We had swept aside our conversation on the hunt—or rather, swept it under the rug—but it is difficult to ignore questions of propriety when a man places his hand on your posterior to help you up a tree.

He, at least, could blame the redness of his skin on his Niddey ancestry. (I am not sure Mr. Wilker had stopped being red since we arrived in Nsebu.) And we were both soon distracted by what Mekeesawa had brought us up there to see.

The giant tree soared higher still, but here the parasites that clung to its trunk branched outward. In front of us those branches tangled with others from another tree; then I looked more closely, and saw the tangle was no accident at all.

It may have begun that way. But just as the island on which we camped had been built up by human action, so too had this tangle been fostered, with creeping vines binding the branches together and shaping them into—

"A bridge!" Natalie said, grinning from ear to ear.

In Scirling, I said to her, "You truly have the soul of an engineer." I did not mean it as a slight, though. Nor did I mean to denigrate the bridge, especially once I discovered it was part of a semiformal network extending across various parts of the swamp. During most times of the year this elevated system is more trouble than it's worth to use, but when the waters rise high, it allows the Moulish to traverse the places where dragons and other predators are likely to lurk.

As works of building go, it may not be as obviously impressive as a Nichaean aqueduct or a Yelangese highway. But I defy anyone to stand at the end of a Moulish tree-bridge and not be impressed.

I also defy them not to be the slightest bit nervous about

committing their weight to such a structure. Mekeesawa went first, examining the bridge and pausing occasionally to weave a branch in where it would grow to reinforce the whole. While the process was fascinating to observe, it did not exactly foster confidence.

We three Scirlings exchanged dubious looks. "There are two ways to approach this," Natalie said. "Mr. Wilker, you are the heaviest of us. If you go first, the bridge will be the least damaged and most able to support your weight; however, that may increase the risk for Isabella and myself. If *we* go first, you will have some warning as to its structural integrity . . . but it may also be damaged, and therefore unsafe, by the time you cross."

Mekeesawa was by then on the other side, and waving impatiently for us to come. "It must be quite safe," I said, and made myself approach the end of the bridge. "The Moulish cross these things all the time."

"The Moulish," Mr. Wilker muttered, "weigh half what I do"— which was only a minor exaggeration.

I drew in a deep breath and set my foot on the branch, gripping a nearby vine as if my life depended upon it (which I hoped it would not shortly do). The structure I faced was to what I would call a "bridge" what a rope ladder is to a staircase: it might support my weight, but that did not make it reassuring. Sparing a moment to bless once more the decision to dress in trousers, I slid my other foot past my ankle, settling it just beyond the point where another branch crossed my main support. Bare feet, I realized, would be much better for this task, being able to bend and grip the surface—but only if those feet belonged to a Moulish woman, mine being far too tender for the task. The branches and vines I gripped were, at least, blessedly thorn-free; at this height, they had much less to fear from passing herbivores. Step by step, I proceeded.

It is inevitable, I suppose, that halfway through such an undertaking, one *will* commit the error of looking down.

Beneath me lay a lacework of branches and vines too thin to support my weight if I fell; beneath *that*—vertiginously far below—the water was a murky, green-brown plate, broken only by the wake of something swimming just beneath the surface.

I forced myself to look away and breathe through my nose, preventing the hyperventilation that would have made me dizzy. When I finally forced myself to take the next step, my shoe slipped a few centimeters: not enough to imperil me, but more than enough to set my heart racing. The half-dozen steps it took to reach Mekeesawa seemed to take forever—but then, at last, I was safe.

Whether Natalie and Mr. Wilker had similar difficulties, I cannot tell you, for I was busy restoring strength to my now jellylike limbs. Once we had recovered, Mekeesawa led us onward to a place where he said we could likely observe the dragons—including some of their young.

This was an area low-lying enough that it had been thoroughly drowned by the flood, with only the tips of underbrush poking up here and there in the water to show there was anything between the trees. Swamp-wyrms love such territory; it is full of fish, frogs, and other bite-size snacks. Much of their diet comes from these sources, but they do also pursue more substantial targets; and here, as in the savannah, we did not have to wait long before we saw this demonstrated before our eyes.

The manner of it was quite similar; only the environment differed. In the trees across the way from where we sat, a troupe of colobus monkeys had begun a chattering argument amongst themselves. One of them so offended another that the second took to flight, branch to branch across an overhanging tree; and so it met its end.

A ripple of disturbance made a traveling V along the water's surface, our only warning of the dragon. And scant warning at that; an instant later, the swamp-wyrm burst above the surface, lunging into the air with jaws extended—snap! And the monkey was gone. A great wave spread as the wyrm splashed down. The colobus troupe fled in a panic, but one of them missed his grip upon the next branch and fell. He floundered only briefly in the water before the lithe, mud-green body eeled over to him and sent him to join his brother.

This is not the only way swamp-wyrms hunt, of course. They will, like crocodiles, snap up creatures that wander too close to the water's edge, as well as those in the water with them. In the drier reaches of the forest, they will behave more like arboreal snakes, concealing themselves beneath brush or twining around a tree. This semi-aerial hunting, however, is their most striking characteristic. When they swim, they fold their wings up into something like a fin that helps them steer at speed; then, when they are ready to strike, they extend their wings and use them rather like the arms of a ballista to propel themselves into the air. Sometimes one will lurk beneath his prey and bring his mouth just to the surface of the water; then he will patiently expel his extraordinary breath (which readers of the first volume may recall is a noxious fume) until the creatures above are so overcome that they drop. The result is rather like manna from heaven—at least if you are a swamp-wyrm.

"It's very like a savannah snake," Mr. Wilker said when the dragon had subsided once more. "They may be more closely related than we thought."

Natalie's mind was on more immediately physical matters. "I've never seen a wing *fold* like that. How on earth are those joints structured?"

Without killing and dissecting one, answering that question

would be difficult. But we had more than enough to occupy us, trying to estimate the size of the beast (from our brief glimpse of it), querying Mekeesawa about how that compared to the usual run of swamp-wyrms, and guessing at the number of colobus monkeys a dragon would have to eat each day in order to keep itself in good health.

Mr. Wilker climbed a tree to study the water, calling down observations regarding the movement patterns of the creature, while Natalie exhorted him to be careful he was not eaten himself. I took my sketchbook from the small bundle I had lashed to my back and put down a loose collection of lines, but what I had observed thus far was grossly insufficient to let me make a good drawing. I had seen the one Velloin captured, but it was a malformed runt, and much inclined to curl into a sullen ball. I remembered well enough that the legs were set more like a crocodile's than those of a terrestrial dragon, but not their exact disposition, and of the jointing of the wings I had little idea, on account of the runt's deformities.

Indeed, it took many observational trips before we had good data on such matters. But those trips took longer than they should have, because of the difficulties we—or more precisely, *I*—encountered.

It began on the journey back to camp, when I fell into the swamp.

We had crossed two tree bridges on the way to that spot; those traverses had been enough to reassure me that the structures would bear our weight. Perhaps that reassurance made me careless; I cannot say. I believe I was still as cautious as any woman might be who is trusting her life to a few branches woven together with vines. But on the second bridge, not far at all from camp, I misstepped, and found myself off balance. I reached for a vine—it tore—I windmilled my arms, trying to recover—I struck a nearby branch—and then I was falling.

A Swamp-Wyrm

The instinct to flail for support was still active, and it saved my life. My right hand caught a lower branch, and if its bark tore half the skin from my fingers and palm, it slowed my descent. Slowed, not stopped: when the limb finished bowing beneath my weight, my arm was nearly yanked from its socket, and I lost what grip I had. Like that second monkey, I fell into the water, and you may recall that the purpose of these bridges is to lead the Moulish safely past the areas where dragons and other perils may lurk.

I hit the water with a slap, driving down hard enough that I sank almost to my knees in the soft mud below. That came as near to killing me as the fall or any predator did; had I not managed to pull myself free, I might have drowned in short order. But pull I did, with all the strength that a good dose of panic can bestow. Then I kicked to the surface and sucked in a great gulp of air, and at that point I was home and dry, apart from being in the middle of some dragon's possible hunting pool.

A commotion off to one side was the two men hurling themselves down the tree as fast as they could go. I struck out toward that sound, trying not to splash too much. My thoughts kept returning to that smooth ripple across the water, and the swift death that had followed. Would a swamp-wyrm attack something as large as a human woman?

The general answer to my question is yes. But as it turned out, that was the least of my worries.

My fall had sent everything in the water darting away, but now they were returning. I felt movement past my limbs, and then a sharp pain on my left arm: one of the eel-like fangfish had found me, and buried its sharp teeth in my flesh.

It had already been imperative that I get out of the water, but with this, my situation became dire. Fangfish will come to the scent of blood, and a school of them could tear me to pieces, leaving nothing but a skeleton behind.

As with the leech, I reacted on terrified instinct, seizing the fangfish and ripping it free. My blood made a dark ribbon in the muddy water. I retained sufficient presence of mind to shout for Mr. Wilker to stay out; he had reached the shore, and was plainly about to throw himself in, but it would help not at all for both of us to be chewed on. Heedless now of splashing, I redoubled my efforts, and soon came within reach of his arm; he gripped my wrist and hauled me from the water.

My breath sobbed in my chest, from exertion and fear alike. But I was safe now—or so I thought, until I heard Mekeesawa shouting in alarm. Heart pounding, I turned to look over my shoulder, expecting that narrow and graceful V.

What I saw instead was the charging thunder of a pygmy hippopotamus.

You may laugh; hippos are absurd-looking creatures, and the term "pygmy" suggests a pocket-size version. But your average pygmy hippo weighs more than two hundred kilograms and will beat the living daylight out of anything that trespasses in its waters. It is smaller and less vicious than its savannah-dwelling cousin, but this is like saying that a tornado is smaller and less destructive than a hurricane. While true, that does not mean it cannot wreak havoc.

Mr. Wilker and I prepared to run. But Mekeesawa, knowing what we did not, urged us back up into the branches instead.

Which is how I came to be treed by a furious, porky creature that would have cheerfully employed its silly little legs to stomp me into the mud. Once roused, hippos cannot be trusted to stop at defending their waters; they will chase the intruder, and can often outrun him. The one benefit of the entire debacle was that the creature's bellows of rage drew the attention of the nearby camp, and some of the hunters came and killed it; we dined upon hippo meat that night.

* * *

(This, you may be interested to know, is the incident which persuaded me to wear trousers at all times while in the field. I no longer cared what others thought proper; I was all too aware that I never knew when I might have to swim, run, or climb a tree to escape an angry beast. I may risk my life on a regular basis—or I did in my youth—but I will not do so in the name of mere propriety.)

I had torn a great deal of skin from my hand, wrenched my shoulder, and thoroughly jammed my legs with my landing in the mud. This slowed our progress, and as I indicated above, it was only the first of many setbacks.

To this day, I maintain that the difficulties we suffered were only the natural consequence of doing strenuous work in a hazardous environment. I have been in other hazardous places before and since—Vystrana; the Akhian desert; anywhere politicians may be found—but I think only the Mrtyahaima peaks equal the Green Hell for sheer lethality. Even the Moulish, who know the region better than any, suffer a great deal of hardship as a result of living there. Had we *not* encountered difficulties, it would have been a clear sign of supernatural blessing.

But I cannot deny that the dragon's share of those problems fell upon my head. It was I, not Mr. Wilker or Natalie, who fell from that bridge. I am the one who, on a subsequent day, was bitten by a venemous snake; I am the one who fell inglorious victim to an intestinal parasite, which had to be purged with a careful dose of strychnine. I broke two fingers on two separate occasions, attracted leeches like iron filings to a magnet, and knocked one of my sketchbooks into the campfire one night. I was, in short, a recurrent disaster.

The effect of this upon my mood was if anything worse than the incidents themselves. In Vystrana I had ostensibly been my husband's companion and secretary to the expedition; here I was supposed to be an equal partner with Mr. Wilker, yet I felt incompetent in comparison. It raised the spectre of our old strife— less, I should say, through any fault of his, and more through my own self-doubt. I tried harder to prove my worth (which led to things like the broken fingers), bore an unjustified grudge against Mr. Wilker for seeming proof against all perils, and generally made an utter shrew of myself. (How the two of them never gave in to the urge to chuck me into the swamp, I will never know.)

The most detrimental effect, however, was upon our pursuit of a certain goal.

I had not forgotten the matter of dragon eggs. Remembering Mekeesawa's reticence on the subject, I tried asking Akinimanbi; Natalie's theory was that the Moulish had a gender taboo, and such things were considered the proper province of women.

As theories go, it was not a bad one, but in this case it was incorrect. It might have been a seasonal taboo—eggs not to be spoken of in the season of their hatching—but I did not know enough to suspect such a thing, and in any event that was not it either. This frustrated me enough that I began to press more sharply than was polite.

Which did not earn me an answer, but did give me something else. Akinimanbi rounded on me at the edge of camp and said, "Why should I tell you? You're cursed!"

By then the "camp" had dwindled to Akinimanbi, her husband, her grandparents, and our crew of four. This was usual for the season; later they would come back together in larger groups. I had cause to be grateful for the smallness of the camp, as it meant the embarrassment of our argument was seen only by a few. "What do you mean, I am cursed?"

"All these accidents," Akinimanbi said, gesturing at my splinted finger. "A witch has put an evil spell on you, Reguamin. Everyone knows it. No one will tell you anything until you deal with it."

Before the last division of the camp, some of the youths had been telling stories in my presence—quite loudly—about people under the influence of witches. I had not realized their stories were meant as a coded message to me. It was the same notion I had gotten from the grandmother in that village, when Natalie became ill with malaria; and I had as little patience for it now as I did then.

"No one has put a spell on me," I said, "evil or otherwise. It's simply bad luck. Or who are you saying has done this? Your husband? Your mother? One of the people who has been with us in camp?"

"The witch doesn't have to be here," she countered. "It could be a villager. Or someone in the land you come from."

That struck me as very convenient. Blame misfortune on someone not even present: it was the same as saying the Lord did it, with an extra helping of blame. "No one in my land practices witchcraft," I said. "If anyone does such things, it's your own people."

"*Everyone* practices witchcraft," Akinimanbi said forcefully, stepping closer. With my advantage of height, she should not have been able to glare *down* at me, but somehow she gave the impression of doing so. "They practice it in their hearts, when they become angry or upset. Maybe your brother here in camp lusts after you, but you won't marry him, so his heart works witchcraft against you. Maybe you have a child who wasn't mourned properly, and so its spirit has cursed you. Who have you wronged?"

I thought of the tension between myself and Mr. Wilker, my mother's disapproval, Lord Denbow's fury at Natalie's disappearance. But if he were working witchcraft, would it not target his daughter instead?

It was all nonsense, just like the legend of Zhagrit Mat. I even wondered for a moment if one of the Moulish might be responsible for my misfortunes. But no; it was simply bad luck, and I said so.

"Bad luck has a cause, Reguamin," Akinimanbi told me darkly. "If you spent your time staring at the right things, you would understand. Until you take care of it, the bad luck will not go away."

And she would not tell me what I wanted to know. Controlling my impatience and frustration as best I could, I said, "Assuming for a moment I believe a word of this . . . how would I take care of it?"

Even the hypothetical possibility of my cooperation made her look relieved. "Find the cause. Think who you've wronged, and make peace with them. Undo the witchcraft."

I could hardly go back to Scirland for a tearful reconciliation with my mother. "I will think about what you've said," I told Akinimanbi, and hoped that would be the end of it.

But the worst, of course, was yet to come.

SIXTEEN

*Yellow jack—The dragon roars—Akinimanbi's argument—
The ritual—Natalie and Mr. Wilker—My confession*

You may recall that I praised Natalie Oscott in an earlier segment of this narrative, for not being so foolish as to attempt to press on with her work when she suspected that she might have contracted malaria.

I was less sensible than she.

My excuse—and it is a poor one—is that I already felt a keen sense of my insufficiency, owing to the string of misfortunes I had suffered. My broken fingers had healed enough for me to be of use once again; I did not want to delay us more, or put my share of the burden on Mr. Wilker and Natalie. (No, that phrasing is too noble, though I shall leave it for posterity. I did not want to surrender to others' hands what contributions I might now make.)

When I felt the first stirrings of a headache, therefore, I shrugged them off. The ache in my body I attributed to the ongoing lack of a proper bed; stiff muscles were a familiar problem, and if they pained me more now than before, surely that did not mean anything. Nor did my lack of appetite, which could be attributed to weariness with a diet of hippo meat, honey, and termites, and a craving for the familiar comforts of home—never mind that I felt no such craving, not even for foods that were ordinarily a pleasure. Part of me recognized the peril in these signs, but I was not yet ready to admit their significance, not even to myself.

That stage of my denial may, perhaps, be excused. But as the day wore on, I began to shiver, and then I acted like a proper fool: I strove to conceal my shudders from the others, knowing they would insist we return to camp at once. The three of us had found a swamp-wyrm wrapped around a tree, lying in wait for unwary prey, and I had at last a good opportunity to draw it; I told myself that the opportunity should not be wasted, and that evening would be soon enough for me to lie down and rest.

But soon my hand began to shake badly enough that it affected my work. And Natalie, who had been crouched where she could study the jointing of the dragon's wing, noticed.

"Isabella," she whispered, in a tone of concern.

Before she could say anything further, my lack of appetite abruptly asserted itself in the other direction. I dropped my sketchbook and vomited into the underbrush, and from there matters only got worse.

The dragon fled, which brought Mr. Wilker back to us, and he wasted no time in lecturing me as I deserved (though at the time I was bitterly angry with him for it). He insisted we return to camp on the spot, and I was no longer in any condition to argue; indeed, I was in no condition to walk. Before long he resorted to carrying me, and by such ignominious means did I find myself back in my tent.

Once laid on my pallet, I moaned and curled into a ball. Mr. Wilker, about to depart, stopped and turned back. "What is it?" he asked.

"My back," I said. "It *aches*."

He dropped to his knees and rolled me over against my protests, peeling back my eyelids with careful fingers. Whatever he saw there made him recoil. "God almighty. This isn't malaria."

"What?"

I will never forget the look of abject fear in his eyes. "I think you have yellow fever."

And so I did. The early stage is much like malaria; the back pain and sometimes a yellowing of the sclera in the eyes are what distinguish the two. For the next three days I shuddered and sweated on my pallet, alternately attempting to take sustenance and refunding it a short while later. It was like a dreadful case of the 'flu—dreadful first because it was so physically unpleasant, and second because I knew the peril I was in. Yellow jack rarely kills Erigans; they most often contract it in childhood, and afterward are immune, as we Scirlings are with measles or the pox. But for those of us not exposed to it from an early age, it can be very hazardous indeed.

I knew all this, and yet when my fever abated, I still fell prey to the unfounded optimism that accompanies the course of the disease. "I feel quite better," I insisted, and ate a hearty meal to prove it. "We shall be back at work tomorrow."

But Mr. Wilker would not let me take refuge in hope. "If you remain healthy for a week," he said, "then we may consider it. Until then, you rest."

He was, of course, correct. Some people escape yellow fever that easily, but I was not among them. Shortly after my apparent recovery, I entered the second, and far worse, stage of the disease.

I can tell you very little of what happened during those days, at least from my own perspective. I was delirious with fever and pain, which rendered my memories little more than a hallucinatory smear of impressions. Natalie told me afterward that Akinimanbi's grandmother Apuesiso stripped me bare and coated me in cool mud, changing it as necessary to bring my fever down; this explains why, when I came to my senses, I was filthy and naked even by the minimalist standards of the Moulish. She also told me I vomited black bile, which is a terrible sign and heralds death more often than not. I dreamt of the talking drums, pounding out my doom. I shook and I raved; I sweated blood out my pores, and where the mud did not cover me my skin was gold with jaundice. In short, I nearly died—a phrase I can write with equanimity only because it was so long ago, and because I have the reassurance of knowing I survived. (As you can plainly tell, for I am not writing this memoir from beyond the grave.)

But at the time, it was nothing short of terrifying, even once the worst was past. Knowing that, having recovered, I was thereafter proof against further infections comforted me little; I had thought myself recovered before, only to be dragged under once more by the second stage of the fever. I lived in fear that this new reprieve was likewise temporary, and I would soon succumb entirely.

My will to live was sufficient to make me bathe, so that I could dress once more in something other than mud. But my enthusiasm for our research was shattered by the conviction that the Green Hell was going to kill me.

In this fragile state did the dragon find me.

If you have never been seriously ill, you cannot understand how sensitive your mind is afterward, how easily jarred by the world around you. But remember that state, if you have experienced it, and imagine it if you have not.

Now imagine that a sound begins in the forest, beyond range of your sight. It is a snarling, roaring sound, which your tired, sensitive mind immediately tries to identify, fitting it to one beast or another you have seen. You fail, because this is nothing like any animal call you have heard before, and this failure makes you afraid. Is the creature something new, or is your mind going to pieces?

Before you can answer that question, the sound changes. It draws closer, in a trampling rush that paralyzes you where you sit. And then *something* comes bursting between the trees, a beast like none in all the world, with a terrible maw and a seething, many-legged body behind it, which snarls and rages in a swift circle around you, then turns its fury upon your camp. It knocks down tents, flings your belongings into the dirt, scatters the fire and stomps your clothing into the ashes. It is chaos and noise incarnate, and if you were healthy and well rested you would recognize it as nothing more than someone wearing a wooden dragon mask, with others trailing behind it under cover like a Yelangese festival puppet.

I was not healthy, nor well rested, and I had never seen such a puppet. I shrieked and cowered, the noise and destruction too much for me to encompass. The dragon saw my fear and fed it, rushing at me again and again—and then, with one final snarl, vanished back into the forest.

Silence fell, more complete than any I had heard since coming to the Green Hell. The display had shocked even the natural beasts of the swamp into quiet.

Just as I began to regain my breath, Mr. Wilker broke the silence. Red with rage, he stormed forward, to where Apuesiso was picking herself up from the dirt. He swore the air blue in Scirling, then mastered his tongue enough to speak in a language she would understand. "What is the meaning of this? Your people have just destroyed half our things! They've terrorized Isabella—is this how you treat a woman only barely recovered?"

"It is how we warn those who do not listen."

The voice was not Apuesiso's. I turned, still trembling, and saw Akinimanbi standing a little way behind us. She and Mekeesawa had not been with our camp in some time—not since before I fell ill. When had she returned?

Only just now, by the surprise with which Mr. Wilker and
Natalie faced her. Akinimanbi nodded to her grandmother. "She
sent word of what happened, through the drums. We brought the
legambwa bomu. It is a thing we do, when people ignore the advice
of those around them."

That gave me the strength to rise to my feet. "You are saying I
brought this upon *myself*? How? And what is this—this *destruction*
supposed to teach me?"

"It teaches us all," Akinimanbi said, gesturing around the
camp. Following her hand, I saw that Apuesiso and her husband
Daboumen had not been spared the pseudo-dragon's wrath: it
had torn leaves from the roof of their hut, smashed their meat-
drying rack, broken the new spear Daboumen had been working on. "We have made noise in the world, and so it comes back
to us. We are all to blame for letting it reach this point." Her
gaze came back to me, its weight almost palpable. "You know
what the noise is, Reguamin. You must root it out, before it kills
you."

Noise, to the Moulish, was not simply unpleasant sound. It was
a disruption to social harmony. And Akinimanbi directed her
words to me, as the pseudo-dragon, the *legambwa bomu*, had directed its roars.

Even with my body and spirit exhausted by fever, I did not believe in witchcraft. But I had submitted before to foreign rites, in
order to reassure those around me—could I not do the same here?

It depended on the rites in question. The Vystrani might have
been Temple-worshippers, but at least they were Segulist. I did
not know what might be required of me here.

There was a simple way to find out. I drew in a deep breath,
stiffening my weak knees, then went forward so I could talk to
Akinimanbi without others listening in. "What would I have to
do, to rid myself of this ill?"

She said, "Witchcraft is caused by the evil in people's hearts. It unbalances the world and makes problems for everyone. Whatever evil is in your heart, you have to let it go."

I could not contain a weary snort. "It's that simple? I decide to let go of whatever troubles me, and all will be well?"

Akinimanbi shook her head. "Maybe others resent you. Maybe your brother and sister"—by which she meant Mr. Wilker and Natalie—"or people who aren't here. Have you done something to offend them?"

"I can hardly mend bridges with people all the way back in my homeland."

"Apologize to them anyway," she said. "Here, in camp. We will hear you, and so will the spirits."

Her advice struck me as oddly Segulist. The New Year lay several months off as yet, but she was urging me to repent of and atone for my errors. Had I not known better, I would have wondered whether sheluhim had come to the Green Hell after all, or some shred of our religion filtered through into the Moulish world. I think, however, that such practices are simply a basic human impulse. If we cannot ask for and receive forgiveness, how can any society survive?

I have never been a very good Segulist, though, and I still did not accept the notion that following Akinimanbi's counsel would end my misfortune. With all the dreary pessimism of my half-dead state, I told her as much.

Her reply was pragmatic and eye-opening. "Is that a reason to stay silent?"

There was no good answer to that. All the things I feared— giving in to superstition, humiliating myself in front of others, tearing the scabs off wounds I was happier ignoring—did not outweigh Akinimanbi's point. My spirit was *not* easy; it ached under the weight of all the things I had not said, even to myself. Even if that was not the cause of my woes, would it not be better to lay that burden down?

And—lest you think my motives were purely noble—I suspected that going along with her plan would also remove the barrier that stood in the way of my research.

(Admitting to such mercenary thinking will not reflect well on me, but I do not want anyone thinking I am one of the Righteous. The driving force in my life has always been my passion for draconic research, and although I have tried to be fair in my dealings with others as I pursue that goal, my motivations are not what you could call selfless.)

"Very well," I said, resigning myself to this fate. "Show me what to do."

I did not speak of what followed for many years after the fact. It was too personal, not only for myself, but for Natalie and Mr. Wilker, and while I may choose to expose my every flaw here in this text, I have no right to decide the same for them. Before he passed away, however, Mr. Wilker gave me permission to tell others what he said that day, and everything Natalie said became public eventually, in its own fashion. What Faj Rawango and our Moulish hosts said was, to their way of thinking, behind them as soon as the event ended; they do not object to others mentioning it later, so long as it is not done to encourage further discord. Furthermore, it feels contrary to the spirit of the event itself to dishonestly recount what we said. I will therefore set it down with as much precision as memory permits.

The Moulish, of course, have ceremonies for such things. The youths who had made up the *legambwa bomu* rejoined us, as did Mekeesawa, and we all seated ourselves around the central fire of the camp—a significant place, as it is both literally and metaphorically where they come together as kin. Certain leaves were thrown into the fire, creating fragrant smoke, and we scooped this smoke with our hands as if we were hunters departing with our nets. The leaves may have soporific qualities; I cannot say for sure. It is possible that the feeling of quiet contemplation that settled over me was simply the consequence of my choice.

I began by making my apologies to the camp. "We came here not to aid you and act as kin, but to learn about dragons. We want this knowledge for our own people—" I caught my phrasing, stopped, and began again. "*I* want this knowledge for *my* people. They will respect me more if I learn things they do not know. But they will not respect you for knowing it, because you are of a different people. I was going to present the knowledge as my own, even though you helped me gain it. That is not fair to you, and I am sorry."

Our hosts clapped their hands, to banish the evil in my words. Then Akinimanbi said, "I have been impatient with your ignorance, Reguamin. You try, but you are like a child; I have to spend much of my time telling you what to do or what is going to hurt you. It makes for more work." She cupped one hand over the bare skin of her belly. "But I carry a child now, and teaching you has prepared me to teach my son or daughter. I should not have resented you."

Dutifully I clapped my hands, but my cheeks heated with embarrassment. I was a world traveller, a natural historian, and beginning to think of myself as intrepid, even if that sense had taken a beating of late. Being called an ignorant child put me quite neatly in my place.

Mekeesawa spoke next. "My brother left to join another camp because he did not like having you among us. I had not seen him since before the floodwaters rose. I thought about going to visit him, but I did not want to leave Akinimanbi, and she did not want to leave you. Finally I insisted we go, and she agreed—but while we were gone, your troubles grew worse. She might have stopped it, if she had been here. I took that from you; and I was angry at you for being the reason I have not seen my brother, and for claiming so much of my wife's attention. Forgive me."

On it went, through Akinimanbi's grandparents and the others in camp. It was an eye-opening experience; despite living among them all these months, we had not seen the effects of our presence very clearly. Our willingness to do our part, however ineptly, had won us a degree of tolerance; but our ineptitude, and the burden it imposed on those around us, was greater than we had realized. I saw that understanding dawn on Natalie and Mr. Wilker, even as it did on me. They were not the focus of this undertaking, being not the ones supposedly targeted by witchcraft, but the arrangement of it was such that we could not help but all be made aware of some of our errors.

Faj Rawango kept his words simple, because of our Moulish audience. "You made a promise," he said. "You have not yet carried it out. If you are set on keeping your word, then I do not believe witchcraft will come on you—but if you are reluctant in your heart, it will."

My promise to the oba. Was I set on keeping my word? I honestly did not know. I should not have made that promise so blindly; I had sworn to give Ankumata something that belonged to another people, without understanding its value to them. I still hoped that, when I learned more, a solution would reveal itself—but what if it did not? Which obligation would I honour: my promise, or the debt I owed to the people around us now?

When it came time for Natalie to speak, she hesitated and looked around the fire. "I—I don't think I can say this in your language. Not easily."

Daboumen flapped one hand at her. "Your words are for your sister and for the spirits. They will understand you."

I confess I felt relief at that. The Moulish might be watching, but what we Scirlings had to say, we would say only to one another. Natalie looked equally glad. In our language she said, "The truth is that I'm not sure *what* to say. I think you were an idiot not to admit you were unwell, but apart from that, there's very little I resent you for, and far more to make me grateful."

"Your father would not agree," I said ironically. "If there is anyone minded to curse me, I think it may be him."

Natalie shrugged. "Apologize to him if you will, but not to me. While I do not think this is the life for me—I miss my bed too much—it has given me the courage, and I think the freedom, to pursue the life I *do* want."

"What is that?" I asked, curious.

She blushed and glanced sidelong at Mr. Wilker. "I—do you remember what I said to you before we left Scirland? About things I was not interested in?"

Her reddened cheeks directed my memory. She did not want the touch of a man. "Yes, I remember."

"While we were in Atuyem, I found out that sometimes co-wives will . . . provide one another with affection. I have wondered, from time to time, whether *that* is what I want. But I—well. Suffice it to say that I have tested my theory, and proved it false. I enjoy the company of women a great deal, but I honestly do not think I want anything, ah, *more*."

By now her blush was fierce, despite her oblique phrasing, and Mr. Wilker's expression far too stiff to pretend he had not caught her meaning. Sometimes a widow's companion provided her with more than just a friend, though such arrangements were not spoken of in polite society. I wondered with resignation whether *those* rumours had begun making the rounds as well.

"I understand, Natalie," I said. "And you are welcome to stay with me for as long as you please. If you do not want to join me on expeditions—"

"I honestly think I would like to work," she said. "At a proper career, I mean. But that is something we can talk of later."

Given a choice, I would have preferred to go on talking about whatever career she had in mind, rather than continuing with this ceremony. But the Moulish were waiting, and Mr. Wilker had not yet had his turn. Natalie and I clapped; the others followed suit; and now I had nothing left with which to delay.

He sighed. "Where to start."

"Oh dear," I said involuntarily, glad all over again that we were speaking Scirling. "That bad, is it?"

Mr. Wilker scrubbed one hand across his face. "No, not *that* bad. But we have never been very good at saying things to one another, have we?"

I had to grant the point. "We resented one another in Vystrana, for certain. I thought you low-class—which was entirely arrogant of me, and I'm sorry for that. But I also resented you for being a man, and not having to justify your presence on the expedition. You were skilled, and that was enough. *I* had to ride my husband's coat-tails."

"No coat-tail could have brought you in if Lord Hilford did not think you qualified," Mr. Wilker said. "Which I did not see at first. But even once you had proved yourself . . . I mean no slight against the earl, who has been exceedingly generous to me. But my position is far from secure. I feel the necessity, every day, of proving myself to him and to the world, and I have spent far too much time worrying that . . ." He trailed off, and I could tell he had gone further into the truth than he meant to. But having gone that far, he could not retreat, and so he finished what he had begun. "Worrying that I would lose my place to you."

Startled, I said, "But you have so much knowledge I lack!"

"Yes—but *you* amuse him. I don't mean to belittle you by saying that, either. Lord Hilford likes to shock people, and he likes other people who do the same. Getting as far as I have, though, has depended on caution, on never offending those whose toleration and aid I need. I may be a good assistant for him, but I am not what he looks for in a protégé."

We were indeed headed for territory through which our command of the Moulish language could not have borne us. I said, "I have wondered from time to time which of us faces the more difficult obstacles. A lady can be taken as an exception to the rules, if her breeding is good enough; mine will carry me this far, at least. You cannot escape your own breeding as easily. But I think that, in time, the quality of your work will win you a place in the Philosophers' Colloquium; they have taken men of your class before, if not often. They have never taken a woman. So there are doors that will open for you, which remain firmly nailed shut for me."

For the first time, I saw Thomas Wilker unbend enough to grin at me. "Shall we storm them together?"

"That sounds like a splendid plan," I said, and extended my hand. He took it in a firm grip, the way he might have taken a man's hand, not a lady's. The very frankness of the gesture made me say, "You—do not have an interest in marrying me, do you?"

A laugh exploded out of him. "For God's sake, no. No insult intended—"

"None taken. To be perfectly honest, I have little interest in remarrying." I sighed and released his hand, returning my own to my lap and studying it as if it were of great interest. "I would give a great deal for Jacob to still be alive. But with him gone . . . a widow has freedoms a wife does not. I could wish for greater financial security, but apart from that, what would I gain from having another husband?"

"It would provide a father for your son," he said.

That swiftly, the scab was torn off. Little Jacob: he did not deserve to be thought of as a wound, but there it was, and with my defenses lowered by illness and this ritual, I could no longer pretend otherwise. A sudden jolt rattled my shoulders, as if something—a laugh, a sob, a shout—wanted to burst free. "My son. Oh, God. What am I to do with him?"

"What do you mean?"

The words came forth, slowly at first, then increasing until they formed a flood. "How could I risk coming here, when I have a son? Of course, few people ask that question of men who leave *their* sons behind to go abroad—because those sons have mothers to care for them. But even if the man is a widower, he does not face a tenth the censure I have received. Should his child be orphaned, everyone will pat the boy on the head and praise his father's courage. Should *I* die, Jacob will grow up knowing his mother was an unfeeling madwoman who got what she deserved."

I could not bear to look at anyone, whether they spoke my language or not. I fixed my gaze on the fire, as if its flames could burn this tangle out of me, and leave me free of such conflicts. "I *resent* my son. There—I have said it. I resent him because he shackles me; I cannot live the life I want, not without feeling guilty for devoting my heart to the thing that makes me happy. Surely it is selfish of me to care so much about the contributions I could make with my intellect; surely the greatest contribution to society a woman can hope to make lies in raising her children. No sacrifice she might make is too small, in service to that great cause.

"And all the while I have people telling me, *at least you still have something of your husband.* Do they mean the book chronicling our work in Vystrana? No, of course not—never mind that we undertook that work together, with intent. That cannot *possibly* be as valuable as the accidental consequence of biology."

Very quietly, Tom said, "Is not a child worth more than a book?"

"Yes," I said violently. "But then for God's sake let us value my son for *himself,* and not as some relic of his father. When he is grown enough to read, I will be delighted to share his father's legacy with him; it is my legacy as well, and I hope he has inherited our curiosity enough to appreciate it. I would not mind a motherhood where *that* was my purpose—to foster my son's mind and teach him the intellectual values of his parents. But no; society tells me my role is to change his napkins and coo over the faces he makes, and in so doing abandon the things I want him to treasure when he is grown."

At long last I brought my gaze away from the fire. Akinimanbi sat with one hand on her belly; she was bearing, and seemed glad of it. I was happy for her—but I had never particularly wanted that for myself, and at least half of my disinterest in remarrying stemmed from that fact.

"'Would that I were a man,'" I said, quoting Sarpalyce's legend. "Except that I do not wish I were a man. I only wish that being a woman did not limit me so."

The fire crackled quietly. Then, nodding—in understanding or acceptance, perhaps both—Tom Wilker brought his hands together in a clap.

The others followed suit. I did not cry; I have rarely been prone to tears. But I felt purified. There is a word I learned later, a term from Nichaean drama: *catharsis.* I had, at long last, said what was bottled up tight in my heart, and while I still did not believe in evil spirits, I felt infinitely more free for having spoken.

Of course, others believed in evil spirits. Daboumen gestured me out of the way. I obeyed and watched, mystified, as he dug in the soil beneath where I had been sitting. I had chosen the spot of my own free will—no one directed me there—but a few inches below the surface, he found a twisted, ugly piece of wood. (Cynic that I am, I believe he placed it there by sleight of hand, though I am uncertain how he managed that when his only garment was a loincloth.)

"The witch put this there," he said, and gave it to me. I did not need his gesture to guess my part in the script: I threw the twisted thing into the fire.

"Now," Akinimanbi said, "you are free."

PART FOUR

*In which I make several discoveries,
not all of them related to dragons*

SEVENTEEN

*Improved fortune—A newcomer in camp—The "pure"—
The Great Cataract—Yeyuama's challenge*

When I have related an abbreviated version of this tale to others, every last one of them has asked the same question: did the ritual work?

I am not sure how to answer that. Did we suffer no more mishaps in our research? Of course not; we were still in the Green Hell, which had not transformed itself into the Garden of Paradise simply because my companions and I voiced our woes. Furthermore, I doubt there is a single person reading this account who is not aware of the even larger problems I was to encounter before long.

But it is true that I no longer felt myself jinxed. In part, I attribute this to the improvement of my mood and my concentration; I no longer made the sorts of careless errors that had caused me trouble before. The rapport between myself and my companions improved, and so did the coordination of our efforts, with concomitant good effects. And since human minds are very good at finding patterns, and ours had recently shifted from looking for bad luck to looking for good, we wrote off setbacks as expected, rather than proof of misfortune. This is how I explain it, at any rate; our Moulish hosts, of course, viewed the matter differently.

What mattered was that both groups were in better spirits, and as a result my companions and I soon found ourselves offered the very opportunity we had been looking for.

* * *

It began with the arrival of a newcomer into camp, a man I had never met before. Mekeesawa introduced the man as his brother Yeyuama, and I soon realized he was an *actual* brother: related by blood, not merely by age, as the Moulish measure such things.

Yeyuama was not like the other Moulish men we had known, in any age group. "Did he go out hunting with you yesterday?" I asked one morning, about three weeks after I had purged myself of the witchcraft taint.

The intimacy of the ritual had changed matters between Thomas Wilker and myself; he was Tom to me now, and I was Isabella. (Natalie remained "Miss Oscott" to him, I think because of his situation with her grandfather. I found myself much more aware now of his little deferences, the ways in which he acknowledged his lower-class origins and made certain no one would think him trying to rise above them.) Tom said, "Not that I saw. Was he here in camp?"

"Not that *we* saw," Natalie said. And that was peculiar indeed, for it did not fit any of the patterns we knew for Moulish responsibilities.

Yeyuama did not keep us wondering for long. He came over to the fire we had built in front of our much-bedraggled tents and squatted on his haunches with the ease of a man who has sat thus his entire life. "You follow the dragons, Reguamin," he said.

Followed, and stared at. "With caution, yes," I said, hoping my humourous tone would come through. Yeyuama had an air about him that intrigued me: both gentle and watchful, as if he could spring into action at a moment's notice. He was *extremely* fit; the Moulish are not a fat people, as a consequence of diet, behaviour, and natural physique, but Yeyuama had the compact muscula-ture of a man who both eats well and exercises often.

He cocked his head at me. "Have you killed?"

"A dragon? No, of course not. I know the story."

Yeyuama waved that away. "Not only dragons. Anything."

My thoughts raced back to the savannah snakes we had hunted, the rock-wyrm in Vystrana, the wolf-drake I had shot (but not killed) when I was fourteen. "With my own hands?" He nodded. I was about to say no—I *wanted* to say no, as it was clear which answer Yeyuama was looking for—when I remembered the Great Sparkling Inquiry.

Both ethics and pragmatism prevented me from lying to him, the latter because my face fell before I could stop it. "Yes. In my homeland, there are these creatures . . ." I held out my fingers to indicate the size of a sparkling. "Like insects."

(Lest anyone accuse me of dishonesty, I must assure you that my taxonomic speculations had not yet gone so far as to change my thinking about sparklings. Would I have admitted it to Yeyuama, had I begun to think of them as members of the draconic lineage? I do not know. The honourable answer, of course, is yes— but I am not certain my ethics would have carried me that far.)

Yeyuama brushed this off as being of no consequence. Everyone in Moulish society killed things like insects, but only grown men were hunters. He looked next at Natalie, who denied killing anything, and Tom, who confessed it. Yeyuama nodded, as if he had expected that. "What I have to say is not for you," he told Tom. "Only the pure may hear it."

The pure: those who had never hunted and killed. Yeyuama was pure; he never went with the other men. He was, I realized, the closest thing to a priest one might find in Moulish society. This must be what Yves de Maucheret had meant.

With our recent conversation so fresh in my mind, I could easily read Tom's expression. Here, where there was no stratification of wealth or birth, he had expected to be able to participate in full; to be refused, as the Colloquium refused him, cut deeply. On impulse, I said to him in Scirling, "You've shot animals with a gun. Perhaps that doesn't count as 'with your own hands'?"

That provoked a rueful, bitter laugh. "No, I imagine it counts. And besides, when I was fifteen I cut the throat of my family's carthorse after he broke his leg. Don't offer," he said, forestalling the next words out of my mouth. "It may upset them if you share what he says afterward. If this is a research opportunity, then you two should make the best of it." He got up and left.

As it transpired, the core of what Yeyuama told us was not so secret that I feel obliged to leave it out of this narrative. (There would be a great gaping hole if I did, as if you walked in at the tail end of some tremendous anecdote being told over drinks. Everyone in the room would be goggling and laughing and you would wonder where the elephant came from.) I may elide some details, but the bulk of it should be clear to you.

"There is a test," Yeyuama said, once Tom was gone. "Before you can touch the dragons. This test is dangerous; sometimes it kills those who try."

A Moulish man—a lifelong resident of the Green Hell—was telling me something was dangerous. I said before that the Moulish do not fear their home, because they know how to survive it; this does not mean, however, that they fail to respect its perils. I asked, "Do we have to say now whether we will try? Or may we decide after we know what the test is?"

Yeyuama laughed, breaking the atmosphere of hushed secrecy. "Only a fool would agree without knowing. I will show you. There is no shame in refusing; most boys do."

For there to be men like Yeyuama, who have abstained from killing in order to remain pure, this test must be offered while they are still young—before they, as youths, join the men on the hunt. I use male terms; virtually all of those who "touch the dragons" (a phrase whose meaning will become apparent later on) are men, though the Moulish denied any prohibition against women when I asked. It is simply that the challenge is a strenuous one, and few women choose to undertake it. But there was no resistance to Natalie and I trying. Merely a great deal of curiosity, to see how the Scirling women would do.

This challenge required us to go with Yeyuama on a lengthy journey. He would not name our destination, but we knew it lay west, toward the cliff from which the three rivers fall. It would take us the better part of a month to get there and return, he estimated, and no one could go with us who was not also pure.

Which meant leaving behind both Tom and Faj Rawango. The latter said, "After this, you will get eggs for the oba."

The way he phrased it, I wasn't sure whether it was a statement or a command. "After this, I may finally have some notion of how to *do* that. But much will depend on when the egg-laying season is." I thought about how long we had already been gone, and added, "Would you like to go back and report to him? He must be wondering."

"No," Faj Rawango said. "I will stay here." (A decision which I chalked up mostly to his unwillingness to report so little progress. He did not seem to be enjoying his sojourn among his father's kindred.)

Tom was another matter. "You'll be going from camp to camp," he said, having queried Yeyuama for details. "Not going entirely on your own. Still . . ."

"You do not like it," I said.

"First that business with witchcraft, now this test of theirs. I didn't expect you to embrace so many of their ways."

I had not *embraced* anything. In the case of the witchcraft ceremony, it was more "shoved unwillingly," and as for this—"We require doctors to obtain certification before they can practice, and lawyers must sit examinations before they can pass the bar. Whatever this test may be, think of it in that light. It is a matter of qualification, nothing more."

"Passing the bar," he said dryly, "rarely threatens one's life. But you're right about one thing: it appears to be necessary. We can observe dragons all we like, but there are some secrets we won't know unless you go through with this. I'm not trying to stop you. I only wish we had another way."

For my own part, I wished he could come with us, though I had wit enough not to pain him by saying so. Natalie and I packed up what we could; it was not much, as neither of us had the strength of neck to carry a basket on a tumpline. Then we made our farewells to Tom and Faj Rawango, Akinimanbi and Mekeesawa, Apuesiso and Daboumen, and ventured deeper into the swamp.

I will gloss over the process of our journey, in favor of coming more quickly to its end. Suffice it to say that we did, as Tom had predicted, go from camp to camp, meeting both strangers and people who had formerly been part of our own camp, and enduring a thousand questions when they discovered that Yeyuama was taking us on this pilgrimage. I soon realized our destination was not secret; it was merely taboo, a thing not spoken of except when the occasion arose. Those we passed seemed to have at least a general understanding of what Natalie and I faced, and few of them seemed to think we stood much chance.

There is no faster way to harden my determination to do a thing than to assume I will fail at it. But when I saw at last the challenge Yeyuama intended, the revelation shook even my self-confidence and will.

We had left the last camp behind two days before. My sense of geography was sorely addled by the tracklessness of the swamp, but Natalie and I, making estimates of the distance we had traveled, could guess where Yeyuama was taking us. We were drawing near to the western border of the Green Hell.

The noise grew by subtle degrees as we traveled onward, at first remaining faint enough that my conscious mind did not notice it. Then it rose high enough to attract my attention: the steady, rushing thunder of falling water. "We must be near," I said, and got a bright grin from Yeyuama in response.

This I took to be agreement, only realizing my error after we had slogged at least another mile onward. We were not yet near at all. I had simply underestimated the magnitude of what we had come to see.

The Great Cataract of Mouleen.

As I have said before, the three rivers of Girama, Gaomomo, and Hembi come together west of the Moulish swamp, a confluence of the sort that happens in many parts of the world. But here, as nowhere else, the rivers are stopped shy of their peaceful meeting by a fault in the earth that dropped the land of Mouleen not quite a hundred meters below the rivers' previous beds. Along this curving and irregular edge, the three rivers spread out and break up their flow, plunging downward in a roar of countless waterfalls.

Yeyuama brought us to the very edge of the great lake which forms the base of these falls, an expanse of water large enough to give me an unobstructed view of much of the Great Cataract. Even at this range, I could feel the force of it: the constant thunder of the water, torrents of it crashing endlessly down, threatening to drive the air from my lungs. Everywhere I looked I saw rainbows, light refracting from the mist thrown off by the falls. I might have stepped through some portal into a magical place—the homeland of wild-hearted faerie creatures grander and more terrible than any human could hope to understand.

My face opened with exhilaration, in an expression that was not quite a laugh. I could not help myself; the madness I felt at the mere sight of this place could not be held in. Natalie looked much the same. Yeyuama was solemn by comparison; but then, of course, he had been here before. And this place, clearly, was sacred to his people.

I could not imagine a place less like the sober Assembly Houses I associated with religion; but I could, with no difficulty at all, understand why one might attach such a word to this place. Such sublime grandeur seemed very much like a thing of the gods.

The cataract itself was too breathtaking to behold for long, even though the height of the floods had passed and the waters of the swamp were beginning to subside. My eye sought out more restful sights. I saw that the lake was the hollow pounded out by the falling water, and surmised that it must be quite deep. From there the mingled contents of the three rivers spread out through the low-lying region we called Mouleen, and thus gave rise to the swamp; indeed, from here we could no longer speak of it in a meaningful sense as a river, whether singular or multiple, for the waterways branched and recombined into the mazelike delta which I had been inhabiting for the last five months.

But for what purpose had Yeyuama brought us all this way?

Such was the noise that I had to raise my voice almost to a shout in order to be heard. "Is this the place of the test?" I asked, gesturing at the entire stunning scene: cataract, lake, and all.

Yeyuama grinned again. "*That*, Reguamin, is your test!" And he pointed.

The broken curve of the Great Cataract was not a single fall, but many. Here and there along its length, islands persisted on the edge, dividing the whole into its parts. It was not, however, to one of these that Yeyuama directed my attention, but rather to an island *within* the cascade itself.

It jutted out from the white thunder perhaps two-thirds of the way between us and the plateau above. It was framed by falling water all around: the rivers tumbling down one stage behind, then parting to plummet the remaining distance on either side. Thinner trickles, some of which might have been respectable falls in other parts of the world, ran through the island and emerged from its front like strings of diamonds. And the whole of the island was thickly covered in verdant growth, trees finding purchase on the stone, vines falling in elegant curtains below.

"You must visit that island," Yeyuama said, his voice strong over the roar of the water. "Then you will be ready to touch the dragons."

I understood why many boys refused, and few women tried. Visit the island? How was one to get up there, or for that matter to come back? It stood in the midst of the falls, nowhere near the border of the lake. To go over the first edge in a boat (or the more stereotypical barrel) would only result in missing the island, or being dashed to pieces if one did not. Swimming the lake would be both hazardous and difficult, as the current pushed one away from the base, and once that obstacle was surmounted one still had the challenge of climbing the rock face.

Yes, these were the thoughts in my mind as I stared at the Great Cataract of Mouleen. Of course I had begun to ponder how it might be done. If you know anything of my life, you will not be surprised.

Natalie and I discussed it, once we had retired far enough to be able to converse in more normal tones. "I expect it used to all be like that," she said, sketching out a shape with her hands. "Multiple tiers—you can still see fragments of it, apart from that major island. But the force of the water would, over time, knock down the lower tiers, leaving that one remnant as the only piece of significant size."

The geologic history of the place interested me less than the navigational opportunities it afforded. "I don't suppose there are likely to be caves behind? Perhaps it's a mystery of sorts, with a tunnel that offers safe passage. Those who pass the test are the ones who find it."

"And those that don't are the ones who die," Natalie said, with a decided lack of optimism. "It would be lovely if there were a tunnel, but somehow I don't think you will be that lucky."

I noticed her choice of pronoun. Somehow, without ever saying so directly, we had agreed that I would be the one to attempt this thing, not both of us together. There was no particularly good reason for it, and several against; indeed, others were quick to point out later that only one of us had a small dependent child at home, and that one was not Natalie. But only one of us was mad enough to try, and that one was not Natalie, either.

Because I could not look at that island, overgrown and floating in the midst of rainbows, and not want to experience the triumph of standing on it with my own two feet.

Yeyuama caught frogs and roasted them while the two of us discussed the matter in Scirling. There was no need to speak in the Moulish tongue for his benefit; he had made it clear that he would offer no advice, and he was good enough at maintaining his poise that no twitch of alarm or satisfaction would steer us in one direction or another. We were entirely on our own.

"Why is this the test?" I asked at one point, when our speculations had ground to a halt. Then I repeated myself in Moulish, for this, at least, was a question Yeyuama might answer.

But he shook his head. "You will see—or you will not."

Meaning that only those who passed the test were fit to know the answer. I ground my teeth in frustration and renewed my determination to reach that island.

We scouted the area for another two days, circling the edge of

THE WATERFALL ISLAND

the lake to view the island from different angles. It seemed likely that the best approach was from above, coming down from the rivers onto the island; without viewing the land up there it was hard to be certain, but it seemed more promising than any attempt to come at it from below. But then how to return? "If I had a long enough rope . . ." I began, then shook my head. "It would have to be absurdly long, and I have never been good at climbing."

Natalie opened her mouth to answer, then stopped.

"No, it's foolish," she said, when I looked at her inquisitively.

I laughed. "And I am, of course, the *last* person to entertain foolish notions. Out with it, my dear."

"You would break your neck," she protested.

"And I am unlikely to do so by the means we have already discussed? You have my curiosity up now, you know. There is no help for it; you will have to tell me."

She sighed. "We don't even have suitable wood, so it couldn't be done anyway. But I was thinking of those glider wings."

Her obsession back in Scirland. An untested design, though recently improved by that enthusiast in Lopperton.

A chance to *fly*.

I tried to throw a halter over the nose of my sudden, wild hope and hold it back from galloping away. It was reckless. It was impossible. Natalie was right; we did not have suitable wood.

We did, however, have something else.

EIGHTEEN

A need for dragonbone—Sketches in the air—
An angry dragon—More truth—"We have the forest"

Can you not tell me what you need them for?" Tom asked, as we waded across a shallow stream. "Even the slightest hint."

I could have told him that I didn't want to offend Yeyuama and the others; it had the virtue of being true. It was not, however my chief reason. "If I tell you, then you will try to talk me out of it."

He stopped on the bank and stared at me. "Is that supposed to set me at ease?"

Our time in the swamp had left him a scruffy thing, his clothing stained beyond repair, his hair grown shaggy and his jaw darkened by stubble. Likely my own appearance was little better (although I was at least spared the stubble). Had we wandered the streets of Falchester in this state, we would have been thought lunatics—which was, I imagined, not far off the mark. Long residence in harsh and unfamiliar conditions does strange things to the mind. You swiftly learn not to heed irritations that would be unbearable in the normal course of your affairs, and you embrace notions that would be unthinkable at home.

"It is supposed to be honest," I said. "I do not want you chiding me afterward for hiding more from you than I must."

Tom's first response to that was inarticulate. Then he said, "I have asked myself, time and again, what possible need you could have for dragonbone—*dragonbone*, when we're among a people for whom dragons are in some way sacred. You don't mean to impress them with it; that wouldn't be as dangerous as you've implied. What, then? Everything I can think of is worse than the previous idea."

He would not have thought of Natalie's wings; I was fairly certain he had no idea of her interest in the subject. I considered asking him what he *had* thought of, but decided it would only upset him further. Instead I fell back on the only recourse available to me, which was simple persuasion. "Please, Tom. If we are to proceed with our research, and fulfill our promise to the oba, I must do this. And it will go better with your help."

He sighed in frustration, but said, "I am here, am I not?"

"Yes," I admitted. "For which I thank you."

By then the others had caught up to us: Natalie and Yeyuama, Mekeesawa and Faj Rawango. The rest of our camp was not far off, but we six were making a side journey to retrieve something left behind during our earliest days in the Green Hell.

The box was still where we had buried it. Already the wood was somewhat worse off for being buried in the wet earth, and the fabric that wrapped the bones was half-eaten by insects, but the bones were still wholly preserved.

"Will it be acceptable to use this?" I asked Yeyuama, holding out an alar humerus for him to see.

He frowned at the bone. "Who killed this dragon?"

"A hunter," I said. "But not in the way that your brothers are hunters. He kills animals only for the pleasure of proving himself stronger than they, and takes trophies to prove his strength to others." Yeyuama indicated the bone, and I shook my head. "He does not know we have this, and would try to take it if he did. We kept the bones so we could understand dragons better."

Akinimanbi had explained to him our purpose in the swamp.

Her rendition had made us sound more like priests than scholars—but that was not entirely unfitting; or at least it was useful to our cause. Yeyuama said, in a cool tone masking something I could not read, "Dragon bones fall to dust. How is this one still solid?"

We had been cautious in who we shared that information with, but I had no fear of sharing the truth with him. Not because he lived far from Vystrana and would never trouble the dragons there; not because he lacked the chemical equipment to imitate our work. Those things were true, but also irrelevant. Yeyuama was pure: he would never kill a dragon for its bones. Nor would he help others do so.

I therefore told him everything, as much as my command of his language allowed. The mourning behaviour of rock-wyrms; Rossi's experimentation; Frederick Kemble's struggle to synthesize a replacement for the bones, which might be aided by Tom's efforts with the savannah snakes. Yeyuama listened in silence, and when I was done he sighed, gesturing at the bones. "You should not have done this before facing the island. But you may use it."

I wondered if the Moulish had funerary customs for their own dragons. Was that what Yeyuama meant by "touching the dragons"? Well, I would find out soon enough—if I did not break my neck.

Natalie sorted through the bones, chewing on her lower lip. "Mr. Garsell insists a curved surface is better, but still, I could wish some of these were straighter. The ribs, though, will be useful for the center of the frame, and we can make cords . . ." She trailed off, sketching in the air.

Tom had a good visual imagination. He followed the movement of her finger with narrowed eyes. Before I could divert him, his jaw sagged in disbelief. "You—Isabella, *please* tell me she isn't planning to build some kind of wing."

My mouth opened and shut a few times, while he stared at me. Then, helplessly, I said, "Would you like the truth, or a comforting lie?"

"What in God's name are you *doing?*" he demanded. We were speaking Scirling; the three Erigans looked on in interest, no doubt speculating as to what we might be saying. "Do you have to fly with the dragons to prove your right to study them? Moulish swamp-wyrms don't even *fly!*"

"They do glide, though—and I shall do the same. It's an unconventional solution to the problem I've been set . . . but Tom, I believe it will work."

He squeezed his eyes shut, hands frozen in midair as if, should he just concentrate hard enough, he could make this entire conversation not have happened. Then he opened his eyes and fixed his gaze on Yeyuama. In Moulish, he said, "I know I am not 'pure.' But please, for the love of—of whatever spirits you worship, let me help with this. If she is injured, I'll never forgive myself."

His concern touched me, all the more so because he made no reference to the consequences he would likely face in the event of my death. Jacob had once told me he would be blamed if anything happened to me in Vystrana; Tom, I suspected, now occupied the role of "man responsible for my well-being" in the eyes of society. I said to Yeyuama, "He has some knowledge of healing injuries. I hope, of course, that his skills will not be necessary, but if they are . . ."

Yeyuama sighed, looking resigned. "If I don't agree, he will probably follow us." Tom did not deny it. "Very well, Reguamin. Your brothers and sister may assist you. But they may not go all the way with you."

(At the time, it surprised me that Yeyuama agreed to let anyone else be involved. In retrospect, I think Tom was not the only one dumbfounded at my chosen approach to the problem of the island,

and Yeyuama did not want to be responsible for killing me, however indirectly. That is only speculation on my part, though.)

We bundled up the bones Natalie deemed useful and took
them with us back to camp, but we would not be with our hosts
for much longer. As I proposed to come at the Great Cataract
from above, and was bringing bulky equipment with me for the
task, it would be easier for us to make the journey along the top
edge of the swamp, rather than in its depths. So long as our paths
lay together, however, we would travel with the other members
of the camp, who were shifting to a new location.

It was by then becoming a larger group once more, as the seasonal round brought the Moulish back together, and they sang as
they walked. Natalie had been singing with the Moulish for some
time, but now Tom joined in; his voice was rough but tuneful.
"You should sing," Yeyuama prompted me; when we left the camp,
he would break off on his own to wait for me at the base of the
Great Cataract.

"Oh, no," I said hastily. "The frogs are more melodious than I."

He seemed puzzled by my protest. "Why does that matter? It
makes harmony."

The word he used, *ewele,* has the same double meaning as its
Scirling translation: not only the effect produced by music, but a
concord among people. Judging by the way he deployed it now,
he meant the latter sense—or rather, he meant the latter produced the former. Still—"I would be embarrassed to try."

But Yeyuama would not accept my refusal. Nothing would do
but that I sing. And so I did; Natalie gave me an encouraging pat
on the shoulder, and Tom did his best not to wince. But the
Moulish all smiled: however out of tune I might be, now I was
harmonious.

Our harmony, alas, did not last. It was broken by a furious,
coughing snarl, and the sound came from some distance ahead.

All singing fell silent. The hunters, who carried few burdens other than their spears and nets, dropped anything else they held and vanished into the surrounding growth. Mothers and elders boosted children into the trees, and within a few seconds I could not see them, either. Even after my time among them, I was startled at the speed with which they all concealed them-selves.

Yeyuama had gone stiff at my side. He met my gaze, and I saw him make a decision. "Dragon," he said, and I nodded. "An angry one. Come."

That seemed to be extended to all three of us—three, because Faj Rawango had gone with the hunters. Tom stepped forward, but Natalie shook her head and grabbed the bones tied to his back. "Leave these with me. I'll hide them."

As I went forward with Tom and Yeyuama, I wondered uneasily whether those bones might be the cause of the disturbance. It was the death and theft of their kin that had made the Vystrani rock-wyrms angry; we had not observed anything of the sort here, but the absence of evidence is not the evidence of absence. Moulish dragons were sullen and hostile creatures under the best of circumstances, but I had never seen one in a fury. Had we inadvertently provoked this one?

I had my answer soon enough, in the shouts and curses of men.

They were not speaking the Moulish tongue. I picked out Yembe words here and there, but the part that came through the most clearly to me was an unholy admixture of Thiessois and Eiversch. And although I had not heard that voice in months, the language of the profanity told me who the speaker must be.

M. Velloin had come into the swamp in search of newer and more exciting prey.

Yeyuama's expression hardened as I gave him this explanation in a quick, worried undertone. "We will not let him kill a dragon," he said—leaving unspoken what measures they might take to prevent him. Yeyuama himself might be pure, his hands unsullied by death, but the same was not true for the hunters.

I half-expected to hear screams before we even reached the scene. The hunters, after all, had gone before us, and must already be in place. I also expected the raging of the dragon to subside, for Velloin was assuredly armed with a good rifle, and had shown pride in the swift kill. But neither shift came, and as we crept to the edge of the scene behind Yeyuama, I saw for myself what was happening.

Five or six Yembe hunters were ranged around the dragon, spears at the ready—but it was spears they held, not rifles, and they used them only to keep the dragon at bay. Three other men were engaged at closer range, hauling with all their might on ropes that had been looped about the swamp-wyrm's limbs. Velloin stalked around this fray, protected, as the others were, by a kerchief tied over his mouth and nose in addition to a pair of goggles, to keep the noxious gas from his eyes. He held another lasso in his hands, and as I watched, he flung it over the dragon's muzzle and dragged the loop tight.

"God almighty," I whispered, staring. "They're not trying to kill the dragon. They're trying to *capture* it."

Velloin had done it before, and had said he wanted to try again. But the swamp-wyrm before us was no runt; it was a splendid beast, one of the largest I had seen. Even with four men trying to bind it, the creature still thrashed. It was difficult to imagine Velloin could drag it ten feet like that, let alone into a cage.

As it transpired, he didn't intend to. Velloin passed his rope to another man, then picked up a bow. The arrow he nocked was too light to have any chance of killing the creature, but before he put it to the string, he dipped the head in a small clay jar. Poison of some kind, I assumed. Something to weaken and slow the dragon for easier transport.

He did not get the chance to try. Yeyuama had been watching the scene with narrowed eyes; when he saw the poisoned arrow, he lifted his hands to his mouth and made a sound like a birdcall. Like, but not the same: clearly it was a signal, and just as clearly, this was what our own hunters had been waiting for.

I would have sworn my oath on the Holy Scripture that there were no Moulish in the immediate vicinity of this struggle, but on Yeyuama's call, half a dozen nets dropped from the trees to snare the men below. Spears thudding into the ground at the feet of the Yembe caused several of them to leap back. Ropes slipped free of hands, and then the dragon spun about, smashing men to the ground with its muscular tail.

What followed was chaos. Half-restrained as it was, the swamp-wyrm could not move easily, but it was determined to crush its tormentors; then Yembe spears began to stick in its hide, and it changed its intent to flight. This most of the Yembe seemed willing to let it do, but as the dragon slipped away, I saw Velloin raising a rifle.

"*No!*"

I did not even realize I was the one who had shouted until I had already flung myself forward. Then there was nothing to do but continue. "Hold your fire, sir!" I commanded, staggering across the trampled ground, coughing on the foul air.

One of the Yembe caught me. But I had caught Velloin's attention; for a moment that rifle was pointed at me. Then the hunter saw me properly, and jerked in surprise.

"Well," he said, tugging down the kerchief that covered his face. "Mrs. Camherst, I presume. My God—you still live."

"I was not aware my status was in question," I said, trying and failing to pull my arms free of my captor. "Will you tell this man to unhand me?"

Velloin grinned, not pleasantly. "I do not give orders to the son of a king, Mrs. Camherst."

Confused, I twisted to look up at the man holding me. He released one arm and uncovered his own face, revealing Okweme n Kpama Waleyim.

"Is this your scheme?" I asked him. "Or Velloin's? I have a hard time believing it is his; surely he would prefer to kill his prey, rather than snare it."

Okweme's grin was as unpleasant as Velloin's. Had I ever thought the man friendly, let alone attractive? "We are here at the request of my royal father. He will not be glad to hear that you interfered."

"It wasn't just her," Velloin said. He resettled his rifle on his shoulder. "Those nets and spears must have come from the swamp rats. Come out!" he shouted, turning to scan the trees. "We know you are there."

Tom needed no encouragement; indeed, I suspected Yeyuama must have been holding him back. Yeyuama himself followed a step behind. One might have mistaken his slow stride for relaxed, but to my eye, it had more the character of focused anger. The hunters stayed hidden, and I blessed them for it.

I had grown accustomed to measuring people according to Moulish stature, against which Tom, whose height was middling at best, seemed a giant. Facing Okweme and Velloin, Yeyuama was almost childlike in his smallness. There was nothing childlike, however, in the look he directed at the interlopers. "You are not welcome here."

"Speak Yembe," Okweme snapped.

Yeyuama merely raised his eyebrows at the man. "He doesn't know your language," I said, remembering my own experience with the Moulish tongue. "He might pick a few words out from what you say, and vice versa for you—no more."

"Then you translate," Okweme said.

However little I wanted to follow his orders, an interpreter would be necessary. "Unhand me, and I will."

Scowling, Okweme complied. I explained my position to Yeyuama, then repeated his original message and his subsequent expansion. "You have tried to harm one of the dragons. Because he is feeling merciful, he will let you go, but you must not return." (His actual phrasing had been "Because you are ignorant," but I softened it; proverbs about shooting the messenger kept dancing through my mind.)

"Harm?" Velloin said, with half a laugh. "That is rich. How many have you harmed, Mrs. Camherst, pursuing your research? Or are you still reliant on others to do your butchery for you?"

"I can learn by observation alone—and so I have," I said. Yeyuama looked to Tom for a translation, but Tom was rigid with tension, watching the rest of us. Gritting my teeth, I conveyed what Velloin had said.

Velloin saw my discomfort and pressed the advantage. "Have you stolen any eggs yet? *Eggs*," he repeated in Yeyuama's direction, very loudly, making sure he noticed the word. "Tell your friend about your own orders—that the oba sent you to take away something even more precious than a living dragon. See how he likes you, when he hears that."

He had me over a barrel. I was not good enough at lying to make up something else to say to Yeyuama; even my hesitation gave too much away. Desperate, I looked at Tom, and saw him open his mouth, perhaps to lie on my behalf.

No, I thought, very distinctly. Perhaps I was like these two, in that I had come here for the oba's gain as well as my own. I would not further compound that by trying to conceal anything. That was witchcraft, at least in the nonsupernatural sense; it was evil. And such evil must be purged with truth.

I relayed Velloin's words as faithfully as I could, then said, "It is true. The ruler of Bayembe sent me here to take eggs, though I have not done it. If these men do not shoot us, I will explain more later; but the explanation will not supercede the apology I give you now. I made my promise to the oba in foolish ignorance, without first learning what its consequences would be. I am sorry. And I am doubly sorry for not telling you sooner."

Yeyuama listened without blinking, without any hint of reaction. When I was done, he remained silent a moment longer, while my nerves wound tight. Then he said, "You will be tested. After that, we will see."

Tested? Another witchcraft ritual, perhaps. Okweme interrupted my speculations. "What did he say?"

I translated both that and Yeyuama's next words. "You are noisy—he means something more like 'disruptive'—and ignorant, and you do not care to learn. You must leave now."

Velloin snorted. "How does he think to make us leave? We have rifles."

"And we have poisoned spears," Yeyuama said, through me. "We have nets and traps. We have the forest. You are villagers, and our home will eat you. Go now."

The other Yembe heard my translation and looked uneasy. They were indeed villagers, outsiders to this place, and although they had spent this entire time looking for the hunters they *knew* must be about, they had not yet spotted a single one.

It was a fragile threat. These people could easily kill Yeyuama; the Moulish, however, could kill more than a few of them. Then the oba might send a larger force, this one hunting not dragons, but men. However well the Moulish knew the Green Hell, they were safe here largely because no one cared to face the difficulty of coming after them. If they gave the oba a reason to change his mind, they would lose.

But those were future possibilities; the present was this confrontation, and I could see that the other men were not eager to gamble their lives against the demons of the forest.

"I recommend you take his advice," I said. "The Moulish are quite fierce in defending what they hold sacred. Please assure the oba that I will have useful information for him soon; he must, however, be patient a while longer." Information, of course, was not the same thing as eggs, nor was "useful" the same thing as "encouraging." But it would, I hoped, buy us a little more time.

"Very well," Velloin said, and shot a look at Okweme that silenced whatever the prince had been about to say.

Tom spoke, for the first time since this entire affair began. "I don't recommend trying to come back at a different point. By this time tomorrow, the entire swamp will know of your hunting party, and I doubt they'll be so generous a second time." The talking drums. The Moulish were not a unified state, but at times like this, they could act in concert, and would.

I did not know whether Tom had convinced Velloin or Okweme, but it at least gave the other Yembe something else to be worried about. The two leaders might have a mutiny on their hands, if they tried to come back.

They left for the time being, at least, and I sagged in relief when they were gone. But not for long: there was still Yeyuama to deal with, and the revelation Okweme had forced upon me. As little as I wanted to return to that topic, delaying would be even worse.

But when I tried to explain further, he stopped me with the same answer as before: "You will be tested, Reguamin. Then we will see."

Ominous words. Unfortunately, I had no choice but to accept them.

NINETEEN

Given the dangers I had already faced in my short life—deadly disease, attacks by wild beasts, kidnapping, and other threats from human sources—you would not think that leaving the forest for the more open ground of the savannah should be frightening. Yet so it was.

The villagers of the Moulish border fear the forest, and when I went into the Green Hell, I experienced a taste of their fear. But the reverse side, which I have not yet mentioned, is that the Moulish themselves fear the land outside the forest. It does not quite go so far as what physicians term agoraphobia—the fear of open places and crowds—but after a life lived in the close embrace of the swamp, the savannah feels like a desiccated wasteland by comparison, one in which there is no shelter to be found. You are exposed: the sun beats down without mercy, the scattered trees providing only tiny oases of shade, and everything can *see you.*

Being not Moulish, and only a visitor to the Green Hell, my reaction was not so extreme as theirs; but I did gain a degree of sympathy for it. My months in the swamp had acclimated me to an environment never further away than my elbow. Now I felt as if I teetered atop a small and unstable perch, and might at any moment go tumbling away into the emptiness.

This feeling was all the stronger because I knew I would only be in the open air for a short while, after which I would tumble (or, one hoped, serenely glide) back into the confines of the swamp. I was not particularly eager to return to the Green Hell, but at the moment it felt familiar—and besides, I hoped, great discoveries awaited me there.

Having departed from our Moulish hosts, Tom, Natalie, Faj Rawango, and I picked our way across the broken land where the fault that created the Great Cataract began. It was not easy going, but moving out onto flatter land would bring us too near the villages, and the men who fortified and held the rivers against Ikwunde advances. We did not want their attention and their questions. In due course, however, we came to the bank of the Hembi and settled down, under Natalie's guidance, to build a pair of wings.

I would not be able to fly with them, of course, in the sense of achieving the kind of lift and maneuverability that most breeds of dragons can manage. I lacked the thoracic muscles necessary for such a thing; the best I could hope for would be to glide. Even that was the fulfillment of a girlhood dream, though, and so I threw myself into this task with goodwill.

The center of the frame was an oval shape, made by lashing ribs together, with a division where they could be pulled apart for easier transport. Two femurs reached out from this to form the leading edges of the wings, the surface itself consisting of canvas stretched over fans of alar cartilage. I painted that canvas with the sap of the rubber vine to make it airtight, while Tom helped Natalie lash the bones and cartilage together with gut and cord.

I myself would hang feet-down from the center of this affair, just behind the femurs, with a crossbar for me to grip. Natalie was going to use a fibula for the crossbar, but I had, out of nostalgia for my childhood, insisted that a wishbone be among the pieces we preserved, and it seemed too apt not to employ here. (Apt and—I must admit—superstitiously lucky. If wishbones were a thing of flight, and I wished to fly . . . an irrelevant connection, of course, as it would not be serving anything like the anatomical function of a furcula in this instance. But when one is going to fling oneself off a cliff, these little superstitions become oddly vital.)

Tom and I had spent enough time studying the mechanics of flight for me to need little instruction in the use of my glider. By leaning my weight to one side or another, I could turn; by throwing it forward or back, I could direct myself down or up. But only so far: the control offered by such a design is limited in the extreme, as enthusiasts of more advanced designs are no doubt shouting at the page even now. Furthermore, while I might not need instruction, to undertake such a thing without practice is little short of suicidal. But the art was in its infancy back then, and that meant there had been no dramatic accidents (such as the one that claimed the life of Mr. Garsell, Natalie's Lopperton friend, three years later) to instil the proper fear in me. I therefore had only enough fear to make myself terrifed—not enough to turn back.

While we did this work, Faj Rawango scouted the river. He soon returned with good news. "If you can cross the Hembi," he said, "and come at the falls along the spit of land between it and the Gaomomo, I think you will be almost directly above your island."

"That sounds ideal," I said. "I would prefer not to have to glide along the waterfall any farther than I must, as the air currents there are likely to be unpredictable." (We had, in those days, a general sense that air currents were relevant to flight; the specifics had not yet been tested with anything more complicated than a kite. If they had . . . but it is quite useless to second-guess my own actions at this late date.)

To cross the Hembi, I would need some sort of vessel. Faj Rawango accordingly went out again, and while he was gone, I held my final conference with Tom and Natalie.

FURCULA

"There's a good vantage point a mile or so back," Tom said. "We'll watch from there—though to be honest, it will make no difference one way or another."

A born gentleman would not have shown his nerves at the thought of what I faced. I was glad Thomas Wilker was not a born gentleman; it made me less ashamed about the storm of sparklings dancing in my stomach. "I will feel better for knowing you are watching," I said, and shook his hand.

Natalie embraced me. She had been all efficient concentration during the building of the glider, but with that task done, she had nothing to distract her from the situation. "I think the design is good," she said into my shoulder, "but if it is not—"

"I have every confidence," I told her. "Come, though—we must give my conveyance a name. What shall we call it?"

A dozen possibilities fluttered through my mind as I said that. I had named my son after his father, but to call a glider after them both seemed a bit much. *Greenie,* after my beloved sparkling trophy? *Ankumata,* in an attempt to flatter the oba, or alternatively *Lord Hilford? Draconean,* in honour of the ancient civilization?

Tom made a sound I had never heard from him before, which I can only call a gurgle, as if he almost swallowed his tongue laughing. "Furcula," he said.

I had related the story while we built the glider, of how I dissected a dove in my childhood to discover the purpose of a wishbone. "It *is* vital to flight," I admitted. "And if it breaks, well, that is supposed to make my wish come true. *Furcula* it shall be!"

And so it was that, with the wondrous *Furcula* in two pieces athwart my lap, I came to be rowed across the Hembi River near the border of Bayembe, for the purpose of flinging myself over a waterfall.

Faj Rawango rowed the small boat, and studied me with an unblinking gaze as he did so. "What is it?" I asked, when I could bear the silence no more.

He did not answer immediately, to the point where I thought he might not do so at all. At last he said, "You could have gotten eggs more easily than this."

"Perhaps," I said, after some reflection. "We still know nothing about dragon mating: when it happens, where eggs are laid, even how to tell a female swamp-wyrm from a male. I would have had to go searching. That would have upset the Moulish, possibly to the point of violence—which is a different sort of cost, and one I am not eager to pay. And then there are other things I would not have learned. They may not be entirely relevant to natural history; tree-bridges, for example, are not directly concerned with dragons, but rather with how humans coexist with them. That is, however, something I am interested in knowing. As is this priesthood, or whatever term I should use for it, that Yeyuama belongs to. So perhaps I pay in difficulty, but I believe I gain more than enough in return."

Faj Rawango pulled steadily on the oars, not taking his eyes off me. "You do not do this for them."

The Moulish. In all honesty, it took me a moment of thinking to understand what he meant. Some years later—after stories of my exploits aboard the *Basilisk* began to filter back home, and the outrage over my Erigan deeds had faded somewhat—there were those in Scirland who romanticized me as some kind of champion of the Moulish, nobly aiding them with no desire for my own gain. This is entirely false, and I cannot decide if its falsity is too flattering to me, or perversely insulting, to myself and the Moulish both. One could imagine that I approached my research the way I did out of respect for our hosts and their traditions, but insofar as that is true, I cannot claim credit for it. It was the accidental consequence of my true reasoning, which was concerned with how to achieve the best results with a minimum of fuss. Flinging myself off a waterfall was, in my ledger, less fuss than Velloin's approach; that is as noble as I can claim to have been.

We were nearly to the far bank of the Hembi. The Moulish had not been on my mind, not in that fashion, but now Faj Rawango had put them there, reminding me of a conversation in Vystrana years ago, about what good our expedition could do for the people of Drustanev. This time we had done better; we had not held ourselves aloof from those around us, but had assisted in their daily work, contributing where we could in repayment for their hospitality. Still, it was not as much as we might have done.

Now was hardly the time to be thinking about such matters, when I needed all my concentration for the task of not dying. I said to Faj Rawango, "I hope I have at the very least not been detrimental to our hosts. But if you know of any way I can be more beneficial to them—"

The prow of the boat scraped against the bank. Faj Rawango did not answer me. It was, I think, not his place; I was asking about the Moulish, and although they were his father's people, they were not his own. Furthermore, the point was not so much to effect a trade, wherein I gave them a particular thing in exchange for what I had received thus far, and would receive in the future. The point was to make me think about the question.

I did not intend to think about it right then, not when I had more immediately perilous concerns at hand. But as I turned to brace myself against the boat's edge and step out, I swept my gaze across the long, shallow valley where the three rivers came together, just to reassure myself the Ikwunde were not even now sneaking a raiding party across.

They were not. The waters here were too treacherous to make a good crossing, and the close spacing of the rivers meant they could too easily be caught with their forces strung out in a vulnerable line. But as those thoughts went through my mind, I remembered something I had heard Natalie say.

The Royal Engineers were planning a dam, somewhere in the west.

I knew the geography of Bayembe passably well by now. More than well enough to be certain that there was only one part of the country with a river that might usefully be dammed, and that was this western region, the border with Eremmo.

Speculation froze me where I stood, with one foot in the boat and one on the bank. They could try to dam the Hembi—but if they did so anywhere in this valley, it would spill over into the nearby Gaomomo and Girama, with very little profit to anyone.

If one were to dam all *three* rivers, though . . .

Faj Rawango said something to me, but I did not hear it. My mind was racing across the landscape, wishing desperately that I had one of those survey maps on hand, or that Natalie were there to answer a few questions. *Could* all three rivers be dammed? And what would happen if they were?

It would create an enormous, shallow lake all through this valley. One which the Ikwunde would find much more difficult to cross than these three rivers; they would need a fleet of boats, or else—if the lake stretched far enough—they would be forced up into the western hills, which offered difficulties of their own. Provided the thing could be built (which would be easier said than done, with the Ikwunde making forays into the area), it might substantially improve the defensibility of this border. Had Galinke not said something about that, when we were in the *agban?* And with the water turbines Natalie had been so excited about, it could supply power for a number of industrial purposes, which I was sure would be very useful to our commercial interests here.

But what would it do to the swamp below?

I turned, staggering a little as the boat shifted beneath my foot, and looked toward the Great Cataract. I was no engineer; some of the ideas that went through my mind then were utterly false. (The dam would not, for example, cut off all water to the Green Hell; it must perforce allow the rivers through eventually.) But I was correct in my basic assumption, which was that a dam would interfere with the flow of the water, and that would, in turn, have untold consequences for the creatures and people of Mouleen.

By then Faj Rawango had stood and reached for my arm. "Are you all right?" he said, awkward in his concern. "If you do not wish to do this . . . I'm sure there's another way."

He thought I was paralyzed by my impending doom. "No, that isn't it," I said, then belatedly added, "Thank you." I finished disembarking and bent to retrieve the pieces of the *Furcula* out of the boat; they were light enough that it was easy to carry one in each hand. "But please do me a favor. Ask Natalie whether those engineers were talking about building a dam *here*."

Whether they had admitted it to her or not, I was convinced that was their intent. If memory served, Lord Hilford had said something about an attack on the Royal Engineers in this area. This might also explain what Sir Adam had meant, the night we dined at Point Miriam; he had said something about how the Green Hell might not always defend Bayembe. Oh, he knew what this would do—I was certain of it. Certain, and seething mad, that he would dismiss the "backwater" as an unimportant casualty in pursuit of this goal.

It seemed Faj Rawango knew nothing of such plans; he frowned in puzzlement, but nodded. Then he handed me my small, waterproof bundle, which I strapped to my back. It held a notebook and pencils, a bottle of water and a few strips of dried meat, a coil of rope, a penknife, and bandages with which to strap up any joints I might sprain along the way. A few other small odds and ends. They would, I hoped, be enough.

Faj Rawango blessed me in the Yembe fashion, which I acknowledged with gratitude. They say there are no atheists in war; I tell you that pantheists abound at the edge of a cliff. I would have taken the blessing of any god I could get.

Then there was nothing left to say. I put the dam out of my mind; it should have been difficult, but preparing to risk one's life concentrates the mind wonderfully. Natalie had a letter in her pack, addressed to my son, in case I should not survive this. Jacob was too young to read it, or even to understand its meaning if someone else read it to him, but the words needed to be set down for posterity. (His posterity, not that of the world; I will not share its contents with you here.)

I hesitated: this was my last chance to turn back. Then, with what I hoped looked like a decisive nod, I left Faj Rawango and walked toward the edge of the cliff.

Rocks broke the smooth flow of the water here, making treacherous rapids no boat could approach. Now that I was atop the cliff, I could see those rocks went very near to the edge—no, all the way to it; there was a perch from which I could survey the (vertical) terrain. Leaving the wings of the *Furcula* on the ground with my bundle to pin them in place, I went to see what I faced.

From the ground, the mist of the falling water had been an exquisite thing, veiling the cataract in rainbows and mystery. From here, it veiled the ground instead—which was a mercy. I had vertigo regardless, the world reeling around me as I gazed over the cliff. But it did not reel so badly that I failed to find the island for which I aimed.

It was not so far away. In fact, from here it looked quite different: not so much hovering as dangling, as a pendant dangles from its chain. The chain on the far side was broken, inasmuch as I could see through the thunderous mist, but a rough string of rocks, some of them overgrown with vegetation, appeared to lead from my perch down to not very far above the island's surface. Was this how the Moulish made their own journey?

(In fact it was not. But I will not tell you how they did it, for I do not want hordes of curiosity-seekers to try that path for themselves. Suffice it to say that their way is far easier than my own—which accounts for Yeyuama's willingness to permit me some assistance. Fortunately, few people are reckless enough to imitate what I am about to detail.)

This presented me with an interesting choice. The intent had been to fly the *Furcula* down to the island, and then to fly a second time from the island to the swamp below. But that, of course, was to commit myself to the hazard twice, and furthermore to do so when my first jump, of necessity, must be the more difficult of the two. The wind whipped about me quite strongly, and my target was small. It seemed I had another option, however, which was to try to climb down by terrestrial means, and then to use the *Furcula* for the second, and much easier, stage.

Of course this had its own hazards. The rocks were wet with spray. I must climb with the two pieces of the glider strapped to my back, which would not be easy; they might act as a sail to carry me off. I could not even be certain that the path I thought I saw would take me all the way; it might prove more broken than it seemed from this angle.

But with a choice between those perils and the ones attendant upon flinging myself from the cliff, I found my answer was clear.

The first part of the descent was relatively easy, save that I had to watch the edges of the glider's wings, lest I damage them against the stone. (The dragonbone, of course, would survive any knock I might give it; the bindings and canvas, however, might not.) The stones were indeed slick beneath my hands, but there were also pockets of dirt and small plants; for a wonder, none of them were thorned, nor occupied by anything worse than a confused beetle or two. I had to make a sideways traverse that was worryingly narrow, and the wind was indeed tugging at my unused wings, but the difficulty grew the closer I came to the island.

I will not pretend I navigated this challenge with aplomb. My heart was racing, my hands cramping with tension, and I knew that the mist was a blessing; without it I might have seen exactly what awaited me if I fell. As it was, I kept my gaze glued to the rock no more than a few feet away. Unfortunately, I could not do so forever: there came a point where my so-called path ended, and I was not yet at the island.

From above, it had looked complete. As I had feared, however, the view had been deceptive. The path brought me *laterally* to the island, but not *vertically*. I stood above it, with no easy way to close the gap.

Evaluating this required me to look down, which promptly rendered me certain that my foot would slip, the wind would seize me, the very stone would fling me off. I clutched the cliff face as if it were the dearest thing to me in the world; indeed, at that moment no thing could have been dearer. But I could not stay there: one way or another, I had to move.

To go up would be as hazardous as coming down had been, with a flight still waiting at the end of it, and my body exhausted by this trial. Would the others see me, and send Faj Rawango back?

The alternative was no safer. I had a coil of rope wrapped about my body, and Jacob had taught me to abseil in Vystrana. Even presuming I could do so again, however, it would cost me my rope; I could not untie it once I was at the bottom. And to try abseiling with my bundle and wings strapped to my back . . .

I am a scientist, and fond of thinking matters through in a rational fashion. On some occasions, however, rational thought is not one's friend. Before I could weigh the circumstances in great detail, I edged back along my path, to a space where a larger outcropping gave me a bit of safety to move.

There I unstrapped my wings (nearly losing one to a gust of wind) and my bundle, tying them together with my belt. This achieved, I went back to the end of my pseudo-path and, hoping with all my might that I was not committing an act of abject stupidity, dropped them over the precipice. They tumbled a bit in the air, but landed on the island as I had hoped. Whether they had been damaged in the fall would remain to be seen: first I must try not to damage myself.

I had kept my coil of rope, which I fixed about a stone, blessing Tom and Mekeesawa for teaching me knots during my time in the swamp. There was no time for questioning whether the rope might slip, or my weight pull the stone loose; such questioning would only paralyze me. I wrapped the rope around my body as Jacob had taught me, and committed myself to the void.

It was not like abseiling in Vystrana. Here there was mist, which softened my hands and made the rope burn them unmercifully; here there was also an unpredictable wind that tried to spin me about like a top. I cracked not only my knees against the wall but also my shins, my hips, my shoulders, my elbows—every part of me, including my head, though fortunately that blow was glancing. I felt I had gone a hundred meters, but I was not yet at the island; I dared not let myself look down to see how much farther I had to go.

As a consequence, the ground beneath my dangling left foot took me by surprise, and I thumped onto my posterior when my grip loosened for an instant. Fortunately the rope, wrapped about my body, kept me from rolling off the nearby edge, which I might otherwise have done.

Some minutes passed before I could force my mind to work again, and more before I could persuade my body to unwrap itself and crawl away from that edge.

But I had done it—half of it, at least. I was on the island.

Not without damage. I was bruised and scraped, and my wings, when I collected them, had suffered three small ruptures in the canvas. I had needle and waxed cord with which to repair that, however, and they were (I hoped) not large enough to endanger me. I was not eager to contemplate the perils of getting *off* the island, however, not when I had only just arrived.

Instead I set myself to discover why Yeyuama had sent me here.

The island was not large. I estimated it to be no more than thirty meters across where it met the cliff face, and less than that in depth. Here and there the rocks projected through the vegetation, but much of it was thickly overgrown, and rivulets from the thin falls behind traced paths through and under the green. It was a beautiful place, and I intended to draw it before I left, but I saw nothing that looked like an answer.

So I went to the edge of the island, where it projected into the air. My gaze went first to the cliff above, to the place from which I thought Tom, Natalie, and Faj Rawango might be watching. Between the distance and the mist, however, I could not spot them. Next I looked down (with a careful grip on a stone to make certain vertigo did not send me over), but there was no hope of seeing Yeyuama. He should be watching for me, though, and we had arranged to meet by a particular large and identifiable tree.

I did, however, see something else.

There was movement in the water below that was not turbulence from the falls. It moved crossways to that turbulence, in a smooth and sinuous curve, shifting as I watched. The curve was not large relative to the lake as a whole but, measured against the bank, must have been at least ten meters long. It reminded me of nothing so much as a serpent I had seen eeling through the muddy, still waters of the swamp.

Serpent. Sea-serpent. *Dragon.*

Heedless of my lofty perch, I dropped to my knees, then to my stomach, so I could lean out in greater safety and get a better view. The movement I had been watching faded—dove deeper, perhaps?—but there was more to the south. A second disturbance. Watching, scarcely daring to blink, I counted three in all, that I could be certain were distinct from one another; there might have been more.

This, I was certain, was what Yeyuama had sent me to see. There were dragons in the lake below.

(I was glad all over again that I had not chosen to try and swim those waters in my quest for the island.)

Dragons in the lake. What might it mean? They were not swamp-wyrms; of that, I was sure. They were too large and too mobile, eschewing the stalking tactics of their downstream kin. Kin—that was an intriguing notion. How did these dragons relate to the other local breeds? Surely the lake could not support a large population. How did they propagate, with so small a number?

The chain of thoughts that followed was not, I confess, entirely scientific. My astonished mind leapt from one idea to another with the speed and unpredictability of a grasshopper, making connections and then discarding them. But the picture formed by those it did not discard *felt* right; it explained the data, albeit with some intuitive leaps along the way.

I had been asking about dragon eggs. Mekeesawa put me off. Akinimanbi told me I would get no answers so long as I was under the baleful eye of witchcraft. I duly got myself out from under it, and Yeyuama appeared. He brought me here, saying I would understand once I saw.

And our expedition, in all our observation, had not managed to record the differences between male and female swamp-wyrm anatomy.

Humans have a small degree of what we term sexual dimorphism, with males generally a bit larger than females, and slightly different in form. Other species have more. And in some insects, for example bees, the number of fertile females is extremely low, with all others being males or infertile females.

In Vystrana, I had speculated briefly about the existence of a "queen dragon." Rock-wyrms had no such thing . . . but lying full-length on that waterfall island, I became convinced that swamp-wyrms did, and they were in the lake below me.

The full shape of the thing did not become clear to me until later, when Yeyuama, satisfied by my achievement in reaching and returning from the island, shared with me the details of his calling. (Details I will, out of respect for his wishes, leave incomplete here. The biology is of concern to my audience, and that I will share; the rituals and geographic specifics will remain with the Moulish.) But my theory was correct in its general outline, which is that what lived in the lake were the females of the breed, and those we had seen until now were exclusively male. And while I might have seen that from the shore—with difficulty, on account of the turbulence in the water—this rite of passage served a multifarious purpose, not only showing me the female dragons, but testing the qualities necessary for carrying out the work of Yeyuama and his brethren.

I sat back, breathless with speculation and delight. A thousand questions wanted to burst from me, about the dragons, about how the Moulish interacted with them, and what I might do now that I understood.

Alas, the man who could answer them was a very long way below me, and I had not yet passed his test. First I had to return to the ground in one piece.

Newly energized by my excitement, I retrieved the pieces of the *Furcula* and set to work stitching closed the holes that had formed in my wings. My needlework has never been impressive, but the necessity of repairing our clothing, not to mention modifying my skirts into trousers, had made it functional, and I included patches cut from my shirt-tails to cover the seams for extra reinforcement.

When that was done, I drank some water and ate a little, surveying the island with an eye toward sketching it before I departed. It was only partially a delaying tactic, putting off the moment when I would have to test the glider; but I am glad for that delay, as it led me to notice the oddity of my surroundings.

Some of the island's stones were too regular in shape.

Not *very* regular; they had been badly weathered by the elements. But here there was something like a row, and there, a corner. Heedless of my raw palms, I began to dig at the covering growth and dirt, hacking away with my penknife when the roots and vines resisted my pulling. And I uncovered enough to confirm my suspicion.

There were ruins on this island.

Ruins of ruins: if Natalie was right, and there had once been a more continuous ledge interrupting the progress of the Great Cataract, then the rest of what once stood here had gone tumbling down with it. But there was enough for me to be certain that what I saw was not natural.

The Moulish do not build in stone. There is no reason they should; the Green Hell is not well supplied with it, except at the edges, and stone houses cannot move with their owners when the nearby food runs out. Anything they might build would be lost to the jungle by the time they came back, and so it is far easier and more sensible to simply fashion a new hut at need. The peoples of Bayembe use some stone, but much more mud brick, whose raw materials are abundant and cheap. And with these ruins so weathered and overgrown . . . it was not the work of anyone recent.

My instant thought, of course, was that the ruins were Draconean. Yeyuama had sent me up here as a rite of passage, so that I might "touch the dragons"; it seemed obvious that this should be a relic of the civilization that had once worshipped them, the civilization to which Yves de Maucheret had compared the Moulish religion. There was nothing here, however, to indicate a Draconean connection, apart from their apparent great age— and I was no archaeologist, to estimate more precisely than "thousands of years old." No great walls stood on this island, no striding statues or other characteristic pieces of Draconean art.

Nonetheless, it was intriguing enough that I felt obliged to document the remains. In several places the overgrowth was too thick for me to pursue the remnants of the walls, but I sketched as much as I could uncover, working my way methodically across the island. This systematic approach soon brought me to another suspicious regularity: an alcove in the cliff, where the water of the falls parted around the promontory of the island. It was nearly my height, and oblong in shape—almost like a door.

"I will feel like an idiot if I was right," I remarked to the air. If there truly was a tunnel to this place, and I had simply failed to find its entrance . . . but at least that would save me jumping off the island when I left.

Closer inspection told me I was not so lucky as to be an idiot (at least not where this matter was concerned). The alcove was far too overgrown and silted with dirt to be the means by which the "pure" reached this place, and my probing hand, reaching through the leaves, found stone beneath.

Smooth stone. Far too smooth to be natural.

Thrusting both hands into the greenery, I found more smoothness—indented with lines, as if it were carved.

The vines resisted my tearing them away, as they had a good foothold in the dirt along the sides. But I was stubborn, and my curiosity was up; and once I had torn enough out to see what lay behind, nothing short of the island dropping out from beneath me would have turned me from my task.

The entire back of the alcove was filled with a vertical slab of granite, much discoloured by the ages, but inscribed from top to toe, except where a gap in the middle broke the text into two portions.

I stared at it, mouth open. This was not, I felt sure, what Yeyuama had sent me to see; it was too thoroughly buried. No one had laid eyes on this in a long time. But then what *was* it? The writing in the top half reminded me of Draconean—well, truth be told, it reminded me of chicken scratches, which had been my first impression of that ancient script when I saw it as a child. But I had seen enough Draconean writing since then to know this was far more chicken-scratchy, as if a child had tried to imitate their work.

Or had been in the process of developing it. Could this place be older than the Draconean ruins we knew? I wished I were archaeologist enough to guess. Regardless of the truth, I had no idea what to make of the text in the lower half, which was quite different in appearance: little rounded blocks, which I might have thought decorative had there not been so many, in tidy lines.

I take the time to describe this stone to you, even though many of my readers have likely seen photographs (or the thing itself, in the Royal Museum or a touring exhibition), because I want you to understand what I found that day. I did not know what I was looking at, other than a puzzle. And one which, alas, I could not take with me: had the Lord Himself given me the strength of ten men, to pluck that slab from its sheltered pocket, I could not have taken it off the island. The weight would have sent the *Furcula* straight into the lake. Nor did I have any large sheet of paper with which to take a rubbing.

I briefly contemplated tearing all the blank pages from my notebook and making a kind of mosaic, but it would have taken an age, and my sunlight was rapidly vanishing. As nervous as I was about trying my wings, darkness would make that task neither easier nor safer. I must do it now, or wait until the morrow, and I did not relish the thought of a night spent up here in the thunder and the cold spray.

Were it not for that ticking clock, I do not know how long I might have dithered. Instead I set to work, slotting the two pieces of the glider together, tightening their lashings, tying my bundle to my back.

That sufficed to get me physically ready. My mind was another matter entirely.

The wind tugged at my wings as I went toward the edge of the island, though not so strongly as to risk lifting me off my feet. I almost wished it had; that would have reassured me that this contraption was indeed capable of supporting my weight. But no: like a baby bird, I must hurl myself into the air, and see only then whether or not I could fly.

(I had always thought baby birds adorable beyond words. Now I found myself admiring them for their courage.)

Have you ever stood at a precipice and felt a sudden fear, not that you will fall, but that you will fling yourself over? That the instincts which preserve our lives will fail you for that one vital moment, and in the gap, you will, for no good reason, step forward and seek your own end? I have, on more than one occasion. That afternoon in Eriga, however, I discovered that it is not so easy as your fears would have you believe. I had *reason* to step forward; flinging myself over was my purpose in being there. Yet my legs stood frozen. They might have sunk roots into the ground, so little capable was I of lifting my foot even an inch. With the harness of the *Furcula* wrapped about me—a promise that I would not die—I became convinced of my own doom, and could not move.

The wind jarred me from my paralysis. A stronger gust knocked me a little sideways, slightly off balance, and before I could regain my inertia, I ran forward and leapt from the island, into the rainbows and mist.

TWENTY

*On dragon wings—Air currents—Demise of the Furcula—
Journey downward—I spend a miserable night—Movement
in the forest—Labane—The use of a Scirling woman*

A nd I flew.

Glided, rather—but it was enough. Instead of falling to my death, I hung suspended in the air, floating on currents and the carefully measured physics of my wings.

It was a miracle.

An uncomfortable one, I must say. We have invented better harnesses since; the one I wore dug unmercifully under my arms, and I held the crossbar in a strangulation grip out of fear that I would somehow slip free. This dragged the nose of the *Furcula* downward, and I began to descend more rapidly; a hasty shove sent my nose upward once more, leveling me out. My heart pounded so hard it seemed in danger of leaping from my chest, but I was *flying.*

My panicked gyrations had not only changed my altitude; they had altered my direction. I was headed swiftly for the northwestern corner where the Green Hell met the Great Cataract and the plateau above, and while the dragonbone struts might survive the collision, my own bones would not. I attempted to turn right, over the forest, but something—a wrong shift in my weight; a trick of the air currents—fought me, so that it was easier to go left instead. I skimmed along the falls, back toward the center and the waterfall island, though too low now to make a landing where I had begun.

Landing there was not my aim regardless. I had lost sight of the tree where I was supposed to meet Yeyuama, but was more concerned with finding a safe place to alight. My original intent had been to plunge myself into the lake, in preference to crashing into a tree; now that I had seen the queen dragons, such plans seemed less wise. If I could direct myself to the edge of the lake, though, it might be safe enough.

No one, man or woman, can take into account factors they do not know in the first place. So it was with me and the behaviour of air currents.

Hot air rises. Birds take advantage of these drafts, which we now call thermals, to gain altitude. The air near the falls had been cool, owing to the mist thrown off by the water and the growing shadows of the setting sun, but over the forest proper it was the full blazing heat of a tropical afternoon.

The *Furcula* rose. I was trying to direct it downward, but my control was minimal and my skill even less; I was, even more than I had realized, at the mercy of the elements around me. Instead of settling, my glider lifted me up, up, above the shorter trees near the lake's bank, above the giants beyond. Glorious as flight might be, this was not at all what I wanted.

As before, I would have to turn myself about and head back the way I came. I threw my weight to the side . . . and lost stability altogether.

Some unexpected draft—from the Great Cataract or the slopes of the Green Hell, I do not know which—sent me veering sharply to the side. This sudden shift in my balance made my legs swing wildly, turning my course still more erratic. The attempt to bring my lower body under control caused me, by reflex, to draw my arms in; the *Furcula* tipped downward. My toes slapped a high branch. I forced my hands outward again, and the glider lifted, but by then there was no hope of regaining control.

I was going to crash.

I knew this, very clearly. I felt I had all the time in the world to know this fact, to study it, to imagine what the consequences would be. I saw the forest below me and tried to evaluate one spot or another for its desirability as a crash site. A foolish waste of time: the emerald sea that was the canopy of the Green Hell had little to offer in the way of variation, and I had not the slightest control over where I would fall. I saw the top branches approaching, and had the presence of mind (though it threw my glider off even more) to draw my legs up, so I would be less likely to catch my ankle somewhere and dislocate a joint.

Then I struck the branches, dragging through them for a short distance before the resistance grew enough to stop my forward momentum.

And then I fell.

I did not fall very far. I was strapped into a dragonbone glider; the wings were too large to pass easily through the trees, and too strong to break. But they dragged some distance through the branches before catching against a few sturdy enough to hold, and then I jolted to a halt.

I almost kept going. The *Furcula* had stopped at an angle that left me dangling from the crossbar, my weight only partially supported by the harness, and the jolt caused my grip to falter. I made an undignified noise, half yelp, half squeak, and clutched for dear life at the wishbone. My devout wish at that moment was for it *not* to break.

The bone held. But my grip would not; sooner or later it would give way. Thinking to support my weight by some other means, I glanced about, saw a nearby branch, and attempted to hook my leg over it.

This jarred my glider loose from its precarious angle. With a cracking of branches, the *Furcula* and I slid free once more. For a moment we were in relatively open air, and I, driven by terrified instinct, dragged the glider's nose down as hard as I could, lest I lose the support of the harness entirely. The *Furcula* struck another branch, nose first, and flipped entirely upside down—and there, again, it stopped.

Once my heart slowed to something like a sustainable pace, I realized that I had inadvertently improved my situation. I still sat above a lethal fall, but at least the glider was now between me and my potential demise.

Moving carefully, I persuaded my hands to let go of the wishbone, extricated my arms from their harness, and shifted myself around until I sat atop the bones that formed the central frame of the glider. The branches beneath me might give way, but the bones, at least, would hold.

There I sat for several long moments, concentrating on nothing beyond my breathing and my pounding heart. When at last I achieved a semblance of composure, I opened my eyes and looked about.

I was still in the forest canopy—a fortunate thing indeed. Beneath the level on which I sat, the branches became much more numerous, and might have speared me through the canvas. Below *that* would be a gap in which there were few branches at all; had I plunged through the understory, I would not have stopped until I reached the ground thirty meters below, and there I would have died. As it was, I had suffered nothing worse than an assortment of scrapes and bruises, and two wrenched shoulders. For an uncontrolled landing in a glider, I considered myself virtually unharmed.

Of course, I still had to reach the ground alive.

I thought longingly of my rope, left dangling above the waterfall island. I could have used its aid now. Lacking such, I faced a long and hazardous climb—one I was not at all certain I would survive.

What did I have that might serve as a rope? My clothing, if cut apart; but I did not relish the notion of climbing naked, nor surviving in the Green Hell that way afterward. I was neither as hardy nor as resistant to disease as the Moulish. The bindings on the glider frame, but they were too thin to grip, and too firmly lashed into place. The canvas of the glider wings.

That, clearly, was my best prospect—compared against the alternatives, which was not saying much. I would not call it ideal. I had to balance on the branches of the tree in which I had landed and use my penknife to cut through the tough, rubber-painted fabric. My harvest, such as I could collect without endangering myself, was not very large. But I had seen the Moulish use vines to support themselves when they climbed trees, wrapping them about the trunk like straps, while bracing their feet against the bark. Where the tree afforded no good branches, I could try the same.

My descent to the forest floor was nothing short of grueling. As I said in my description of the tree-bridges, I was not much of a climber (though I was a much better one by the time I reached the ground). I slipped often, and had to rest a dozen times along the way. I strained my fingers and my ankles, scraped my left knee raw, and was stabbed by countless thorns before I thought of wrapping a length of rubberized canvas around my palms to protect them.

The only saving grace was the chance to observe the life of the forest from this new vantage. (If you doubt that I had any care for such things when my own life was in danger, understand that it was a means of distracting myself from my peril.) Birds and insects buzzed about me, and monkeys danced through the trees. I saw a drakefly alight on a nest not ten feet away, and discovered that in addition to eating insects, they are thieves of eggs.

I would have taken notes on this, but the light was failing me. As I neared the lowest rank of branches, I was forced to consider my situation. Should I finish my descent to the ground or not?

I hardly relished the notion of spending the night in a tree. But I was exhausted in body and mind, which would make the remainder of the climb even more perilous; furthermore, this would be my first night in the Green Hell without the shelter of a tent or hut and the warning light of a fire to keep animals away. There were nocturnal predators in the swamp, some of which would certainly be bold enough to prey upon a lone, helpless woman.

No, the tree it must be. I lashed myself in place with the strips of my poor, butchered *Furcula*, and attempted to get some rest.

As you might imagine, this was easier said than done. I had grown accustomed to the sounds of the forest, but they seemed different when no wall, however flimsy, stood between me and the creatures making them. Furthermore, my bindings did nothing to convince my brain that I was not going to tumble off the branch if I so much as breathed too deeply. Nor could I help but think about my companions, who would have seen me go careering off over the swamp. They might have even seen me crash. The thought of their fear made my heart ache.

How far had I gone? I had the vague sense that my course had taken me southward and east, but beyond that, I had lost all sense of distance or direction.

My sense as a naturalist reasserted itself. I was not in the heart of the Green Hell, that wet, tangled delta. The ground beneath me was drier, which meant I must be on the slope—but not *too* far up it, as the vegetation was not the scrubby stuff we had camped in while first waiting for the Moulish. ("Scrubby" by the standards

of Mouleen; it would have been a respectable forest, albeit fan-
tastically overgrown, in Scirland.) And I had not been in the air
so long as to come anywhere near the bay. I was therefore somewhere in the southwestern quadrant of the swamp, and if I headed
west and perhaps a bit downslope, I would come once again to
the Great Cataract, which was a place my companions might
find me—if I did not come across any Moulish first.

If I did not *perish* first. I had only a little water and food; my
survival was far from assured.

Fear of my state kept me awake long into the night, but exhaustion can trump many things. I did at last snatch a bit of sleep,
and woke with a start around dawn.

My disorientation was profound. I did not know where I was, and
felt for an instant as if I were about to fall. I clutched the branches
around me, then hissed in pain at the pressure on my abused
hands. Every part of my body *ached*; I had not felt this poorly
since my bout of yellow fever. This, I realized when my heart
slowed down, was the flaw in leaving the last of the climb until
morning: my various injuries were all much the worse for a night
spent rigid and terrified in a tree.

But there was nothing to be done for it now. I worked my way
methodically through my body, easing cramped muscles and
warming stiff joints as best I could without unbinding myself from
the tree. (That, I wanted to leave for as long as I could.) This done,
I considered the food and water still tied to my back. Should I consume them now, for strength? Or conserve them for later?

Before I could decide one way or another, I saw movement
down below. My instant thought was *predator*, and I froze—but
then I saw the movement had a human origin.

I was exhausted and terrified, and did not yet have my bearings. Moreover, I had no reason to expect anyone but Moulish here, on the southern side of the Green Hell.

"Hello! You there, down below! Oh, thank heaven you're here. I was so worried I would—"

The men froze, raising their spears as if to attack. Then, far too late, I took in all the details that should have warned me.

These were not the short, slight figures of Moulish hunters. They were taller and darker of skin—nearly as dark as the Yembe. They wore fringed bands about their arms and calves, carried shields of hide stretched over a frame. And they journeyed in silence through the swamp, as the Moulish rarely do.

They were strangers, men of a people I had never seen before, and by the looks of their armament, their purpose here was not peaceful.

You may blame me for being so slow to recognize them, and I will grant that as fair. I had seen no accurate images, only the caricatures then current in Scirling news-sheets, which were exaggerated for the purpose of whipping up support for the Nsebu colony and our alliance with Bayembe.

They were Ikwunde warriors.

On the other hand—and I can laugh about it now, when the event is years behind me—it took them a comically long time to spot *me*. They had no reason to look for a woman halfway up a tree. When one of them at last turned his gaze upward, he leapt back a full pace in shock.

By then I was wishing I had untied myself, so I might at least have tried to hide. But I was still bound in place, and could not take back the unwise words that had drawn their attention to me. The one who had seen me pointed his spear, directing the others' eyes, and they began to talk in quick, low voices amongst themselves.

Their language is wholly unrelated to the Sachimbi family; I could not understand a word of it. The tone, however, and the hostile looks I received, told me their conversation was not one of pity. With fumbling fingers, I began trying to unbind myself.

They saw the movement, and it seemed to hasten their decision. One of the men yanked the spear and shield from my spotter's hands, giving what was clearly an order for him to climb the tree. I redoubled my efforts—to what end? Did I think I would escape them? But I had to try. Whatever these men were doing here, I wanted no involvement with it.

I soon discovered why my spotter had looked grumpy upon being ordered after me. Ikwunde, of course, is a nation of desert and grassland; they are a herding people—or they were, before the inkosi Othaku Zam redirected their efforts toward conquering his neighbours. My spotter was as bad a climber of trees as I. He got one of his companions to give him a boost up, but then had to contend with the parasitic tree wrapped around the base of my own, and did very poorly.

Not that I fared much better. I got myself untied at last, but nearly fell in trying to change my position. I could not go groundward, not with that man below me, nor could I leap across to another tree like a monkey. Up once more? I could not reach the stripped frame of the *Furcula*, and it would not do me any good if I did.

I was, I thought, too high for them to throw a spear at me. (I did not know how far an Ikwunde warrior can throw a spear.) Given how badly my pursuer climbed, I might simply outwait them on my branch—for surely they had pressing business elsewhere.

But I underestimated the determination and agility of the man sent after me. He drew close below me, close enough that he would have caught my skirt, had I been wearing one. Frightened, I kicked out, trying to deflect his hand or even strike his head.

I should not have tried. The attempt destroyed my precarious balance, and I fell.

My panicked grab at the branch slowed me, as did the smaller vegetation I crashed through on the way down. It was brake enough that I escaped a fracture. But I landed hard, driving all the breath from my body—and even had I not, they would have been upon me before I could flee.

The Ikwunde surrounded me. There were five of them, and very terrifying they looked, from my perspective on the ground. One barked a question at me, which of course I could not answer. He asked again, his voice growing steadily more angry, and I feared he would kill me simply for my lack of comprehension.

I held out my hands as if they could ward off such a fate. "I am unarmed. You see? I am no threat to you. I—"

They, I think, understood me no more than I did them. One seized the bundle on my back and wrenched it away, upending its contents onto the ground. Notebook, needle, thread; what remained of my scant rations. He picked up the notebook and began to page through it. "I am a scholar," I said, even though I knew the words were useless. "Surely you must see. I am only here for study."

But it mattered naught what I was there for. The fact remained that I had seen them. Ikwunde warriors, in the Green Hell, where they had no business being.

No more than they had business at the rivers, which was territory Bayembe supposedly controlled. But our soldiers were on guard for them there, and so I supposed it was inevitable that they should try their luck here, despite the lethal reputation of this place. I had heard nothing from the Moulish of previous attempts; this must be their first.

There were only five of them, though, with no sign of more. Five men might be dangerous to me, or to the Moulish, but not to

Bayembe. Not even *these* five, whose distinctive regalia I now recognized: they were Labane, some of the most elite troops the Ikwunde possessed. Chosen as young as ten, they were taken into intensive training, and lived the next twenty years in a regiment with their new brothers, according to their shared age. A Tsebane (for that is the correct form of the singular, though one never saw it in Scirling papers at the time, and rarely sees it now) cannot marry while he still serves; there is nothing in his life except loyalty to his brothers and to the inkosi, the ruler of Ikwunde. And the task to which the inkosi set him was war.

Such men had no need of a captive. I would only slow them, threaten the secrecy of whatever they sought here. I knew, as clearly as I knew my own name, that they stayed their hands only out of confusion, that a battered, trouser-clad Scirling woman should fall out of a tree at their feet; once their confusion was satisfied or grew dull, they would kill me.

What reason could I possibly give them for sparing me?

Innocence would not avail. Neither would a plea to their compassion. I seized upon the only thing I could—which was my notebook, dropped in disgust just a moment before.

When I reached out to collect it, three spears whipped down to point at me. I persevered, taking the volume in my hand and paging to a suitable sketch. This I held up for one of the Labane to see: the one I thought must be their leader, for he had ordered my pursuer up the tree. "You see this? The dragon. *Legambwa*," I added in Moulish, for there was a greater chance they would recognize that word than the Scirling one. Belatedly, I thought to switch to that tongue, and proceeded in a mixture of it and Yembe, in the hope that some fragment or other would be familiar to my captors. "They are all over this swamp. Very dangerous. They will attack you. But I—I can show you how to avoid them. How to be safe."

LABANE WARRIORS

I illustrated my words with pantomime, pointing repeatedly at the swamp-wyrm sketch, then using my hand, clawlike, to suggest a draconic attack. My palm I pressed to my heart, indicating by warm and hopeful tone that I offered a way to avoid such perils.

Perhaps someone among my captors spoke a rudimentary amount of Moulish or Yembe; perhaps my pantomime was effective. Perhaps something else passed among them, during their brief conversation. I had, as some readers may recall, been caught by strange men in a foreign country once before, but on that occasion I had been able to parse their language as a dialect of Eiversch, which made communication possible, if not easy. This was as opaque to me as Draconean, and that, as much as the warlike nature of the men who had caught me, made this incident far more terrifying. I felt as if I were in the grip of yellow fever again, the world around me making no sense, and I my next breath potentially my last.

Something persuaded them, whether it was any part of my plea or a notion of their own making. All I knew was that the one who came for me did so with a length of vine rather than a spear, and so I did not resist as he bound my hands together behind my back. Nor did I protest when he ripped apart the fabric of my bundle and used it to gag me, though I dearly wished for a drink of water before he did. I was not dead yet, and that was more than I had expected a moment ago; everything else could wait.

When they dragged me to my feet, someone worked at my wrists for a moment, and then I felt a tug on my bound arms. They had tied another length of vine to the first, making a kind of leash to prevent me from running.

As if I *could* run. You have an image, I hope, of the treacherous terrain that makes up the Green Hell; now try to imagine traversing it at speed, with your hands behind you to disrupt your balance. I would not get ten paces before I fell. I nearly fell when a Tsebane shoved me forward, but through sheer determination not to squander my reprieve, I managed to keep my feet.

They placed me in the lead, as if I were the canary whose demise would warn them of danger. I dearly wanted, once I could think straight, to lead them into just such a situation; there were predators out there, patches of sucking mud, even perilous insects that might be persuaded to attack. Unfortunately, my previous luck with such tactics notwithstanding, I could not be sure I would survive the trap myself—and besides, they did not yet trust me. Any attempt to lead them astray would result in a spear between my shoulder blades.

In order to survive, I had to prove my worth as a guide.

I therefore bent all the knowledge I had gained of the swamp to the task of impressing them. This was difficult to do, bound and gagged as I was, but I led them ostentatiously away from a thicket of underbrush whose thorns housed very unpleasant ants, then veered again, nodding my head upward, to avoid a serpent dangling from a branch.

Step by step, hazard by hazard, we proceeded into the depths of the Green Hell.

TWENTY-ONE

The safety of the Moulish—Another party—Something
in my pocket—The loss of my knife—Refuge on high

I had some hope that a friend might find me. Tom, Natalie,
and Faj Rawango had promised to watch from the plateau
above; they, unfortunately, were on the north side of the
swamp, and could not quickly reach me, the descent from
that point being more or less impassable. But Yeyuama had promised to watch from the lake. He knew this place as well as I knew
my own garden, and might even now be on his way toward me.

Which, I soon realized, might get him killed. One against five
was terrible odds, and worse when the one is sworn to nonvio-
lence. But surely his sharp eyes would spot the Ikwunde before
they saw him? And if not, I had seen for myself how easily the
Moulish could conceal themselves when they chose. Perhaps he
could gather hunters to help. They had followed his lead against
Velloin and Okweme—though I suspected that was because the
conflict there was dragon-related. Would the camps here stir
themselves to help me? We had met briefly during my first journey to the Great Cataract, but these were not the Moulish who
had been a part of my larger social world these past months.

Such were my thoughts, chasing in anxious circles like a mouse
trapped in a box. It was preferable to thinking about the alternatives.

Unfortunately, the Labane were driving me northeast: deeper
into the swamp, but away from the lake. With each step, the chances

of Yeyuama finding us decreased, and the chances of us stumbling across a Moulish camp increased. I had once likened finding them to searching for a migratory needle in a haystack, but now, with such risk attendant, I feared a needle behind every straw.

It was possible the Moulish would be safe nonetheless; they might hear the Labane before they drew near, might hide themselves before one of these warriors struck. That possibility was not one I could rely upon: to do so would be despicable, a callous abrogation of what I owed them for their shelter and aid.

I therefore had to escape.

The skill and courage of the Labane are praised even by their enemies, but they were not foolhardy enough to travel the Green Hell in darkness. When it came time to halt, I meekly advised my captors away from what I recognized as a trail nocturnal predators would follow; this I did not only for my own safety, but to convince them of my sincere aid. We camped in as secure of a location as I could find, and I was, with reluctance, ungagged long enough to consume what remained of my own water and food. Whether they would give me any of their own the next day, I could not tell.

They bound me, of course, feet as well as hands, before sitting me against a tree and tying my body to it for good measure. One of the five kept watch, too. I had expected it, but still I cursed inwardly. How could I escape, with such measures in place?

In time I had to give up that question, for exhaustion claimed me, like falling over a cliff. In the morning my captors held a conference in which they seemed to be debating my continued use; I could scarcely breathe until one came to untie me. I would live another day. But how many more would I have?

This day proceeded much like the first, except that I did my best to guess where the Moulish might be, and to guide the Labane away from such places. This made for a fair bit of wading through inhospitable muck, but my captors could scarcely fault me for that; as far as they knew, inhospitable muck was what the Green Hell was made of. At one point I smelled a foul odor clearly recognizable as the lingering effects of a swamp-wyrm's extraordinary breath, but the dragon itself—both fortunately and otherwise—was nowhere to be seen.

We did, however, find something else. And as wretched as it was to be a captive, a part of me is glad I had not escaped the previous night, for I would have missed my chance to learn more about what the Labane were doing in Mouleen.

I feared at first that we had come across Moulish hunters, or worse, a camp. But the sound and movement that made my captors go into ready crouches proved to have another source: a second group of Labane.

This was a group of three, but I saw that they carried extra equipment, and some of it was bloodstained. From this I guessed that their brothers had met with misfortune along the way. I cannot be glad for the death of men, even my enemies, but it reassured me that my captors would see my value as a guide. Indeed, I hoped that was what they were telling the second party, as the two exchanged information in low tones. By his gestures, it seemed the other leader was vastly annoyed at his men having gotten turned around in the swamp.

For my own part, I was busy thinking. Two groups: that made it likely there were more than two. Both of them small. None of them carrying guns, whose crack would advertise their presence for kilometers around. Everything about this arrangement spoke of stealth. I was certain now that these were scouts, looking for a path across the Green Hell.

I was no military strategist, but I knew that if they succeeded, it would mean dreadful things for the defense of Bayembe. It was more imperative than ever that I escape and warn someone.

The second group did not join our own, strengthening my belief that these were scouting parties. I wished them ill fortune and damnation in their search. *Our home will eat you,* Yeyuama had said. For the sake of those to the north, I prayed that it would.

We continued on. I stumbled often with exhaustion; the leader finally unbent enough to allow me more water, without which I believe I would have died. But the various scrapes I had taken were hot and tender, and my joints ached; I was not sure how much farther I could go. Only the prospect of escape gave me strength . . . but I knew that the later such escape came, the more likely I was to fail.

Oddly, it was a fall that gave me hope. I tripped over a tangled fern and landed hard on my right side—hard not only for the force of it, but for the object in my pocket that dug painfully into my hip. It was, I realized, my penknife: the same penknife I had once nicked from my brother Andrew, so many years ago, which had accompanied me faithfully ever since.

With that knife (and a bit of flexibility), I might be able to cut myself free. That was one hurdle cleared, at least potentially; and the relief of it gave me conviction that I could clear the others, too. I would need a distraction, something to divert the man keeping watch that night, and then I would need an escape route.

Both meant choosing our campsite wisely. I forced my tired mind to focus, and was rewarded with the observation that there were quite a few drakeflies about. I mentioned before that they are insectivores; from my research I knew that, for drakeflies to be present in such numbers, there must be a hive of some sort nearby, to provide a suitable concentration of potential meals.

Finding what I was looking for without being obvious about it was difficult, but at last I spotted what I had hoped for: a wasps' nest, not too high above the ground. The wasps would ordinarily be dormant at night, but I knew—from painful experience—that they were easily disturbed.

I contrived to get my knife out of my pocket while taking care of biological necessity—the one task for which my captors unbound me, as none of them wanted the job of assisting me. (They did not, however, grant me any privacy during the process.) I kept it folded in the palm of my hand while one of them re-bound me, and breathed easier when the task was done. I was, as before, tied to a tree, and then I watched as they ate their evening meal.

They carried some rations of their own, but supplemented them with hunting as the occasion arose. (Hunting only, never gathering; I cannot blame them for fearing what plants might be poisonous, nor for distrusting the advice I tried to give them.) Earlier that day I had discovered how far a Tsebane can throw a spear, when one of them skewered a duiker at a distance I would have thought impossible. It raised the very real possibility that, in my flight, I might catch a spear between the shoulders . . . but I screwed my courage tight. I *must* do this thing.

This thing, however, had to wait for them to settle in for the night. The evening before, the leader had checked my bonds before bedding down; I could not risk him noticing any change. Once the camp was silent, though, with only one man keeping watch, I unfolded the knife and set to work.

The vines binding my wrists were first, and the most difficult. I cut my hands several times, and once dropped the knife—a loss that put my heart in my mouth, for what if I could not find it again? But I did, and resumed my task, feigning exhausted sleep the whole while.

The next part posed a different set of challenges. I waited, eyes closed to slits, until the watchman looked the other direction; then I slid my right shoulder (the one farthest from him) out from under the vines. Now I must be swift, for if he looked closely, he would see that I should not be able to slump so far in my bonds. With my right hand I felt about for something I could throw: a stone, a branch, *anything.*

Nothing came to hand. There are few stones lying about in Mouleen, and fallen branches are too often tangled with whatever has grown about them. With a sinking heart, I realized I would have to throw what was, right then, my most precious possession: my knife.

Before I did that, I would need to get one more use out of it. Working quickly, trying not to pant with fear, I transferred the blade to my left hand, blessing the undergrowth that gave a tiny amount of cover to my movements. I drew my ankles up as close as I could, wincing at the sound; the guard glanced my way, but did not react. With the penknife I cut through the vines on my ankles (and also cut my calf, for I was clumsy with fear and insufficient ambidexterity).

Perhaps I made a sound. Perhaps the Tsebane was simply that wary. But he turned then, half-rising from his crouch, as if to come investigate me.

I yanked myself free of the last of the vines and threw my knife at the nest. My arm had not the range of a Tsebane's, but I had spent their entire meal calculating the arc from me to that nest, repeating to myself again and again that I *would* strike it true. And so, through blind luck, divine providence, or sheer conviction that I would succeed, I threw right on my first try.

I did not stay to see the results, though I heard them as I fled. I dodged around the tree, and knew I had chosen right when the watchman's spear thunked into the wood; then I was off, through the forest, running desperately (but not at all quietly) for the closest thing I had been able to approximate for a safe escape route.

A nearby waterway.

I dove in without a single thought for leeches, snakes, fang-fish, swamp-wyrms, or anything else. I exhaled a portion of my air, so as better to sink down, and began to push my way along the muddy bottom, trying not to shriek in fear when I felt things brush against my body. With my eyes shut, I could not see where I was going; I could only hope that by me moving underwater like this, in the darkness, the Labane would not be able to see me to throw a spear. (Or, better still, that they were too occupied with the wasps to pursue—but I could not take that risk.)

My intention was to stay underwater for as long as I could; and so I did, but that was not very long. The pounding of my heart soon drove me to the surface, where I tried to gasp in a new breath as quietly as I could—partly to keep from being heard, and partly because I wanted to listen for the Labane. I thought to hear curses and shouts from the direction of the camp, on account of the wasps. The silence that greeted me caused my muscles to clench in fear. The Labane were not ordinary soldiers; they were trained from childhood to accept pain and privation without complaint. They might die of the wasp stings, but they would not scream.

It meant I had no idea where they were.

I continued along a short distance, diving when I could, but fear kept using up my air. My progress was maddeningly slow, and when I surfaced for the fourth time, I saw movement on the bank I had left.

Whether it was a Tsebane, I cannot tell you. I believed then that it was, and did not stay to confirm my suspicion. I flung myself toward the opposite bank, not caring now how much noise I made, and plunged into the forest on that side, praying the water would delay them, praying some creature might eat them, praying for *anything* that might aid me.

What I found was a tree.

There were many trees about, but this one was of a particular sort: one of the forest giants, its trunk well wrapped in parasitic growths, standing alongside what a few months ago would, I knew, have been a flooded region. It was, in short, the kind of tree often used for tree-bridges—and that gave me an idea.

I dragged myself up with the panicked agility of a squirrel, clawing my way from one handhold to another, too driven by fear of what lay behind to even squeak when my footing slipped. The farther I went, the more apparent it became that I had chosen correctly: this tree and its parasites had been cultivated by the Moulish, which meant there was a bridge somewhere above me.

When at last I reached it, I crawled out a little distance, until I was something like halfway along the span. Here I lay, flattening myself as best I could amidst the twined branches and vines of the bridge, far away from any tree the Labane might expect to find me in.

They did not know the forest. They would not think to look for the bridge.

Or so I prayed.

My decision was rewarded when I heard a quiet voice below. Whether it had been a Tsebane on the other bank, one was here now—no, two, for I heard a response from not far away. They were indeed searching for me. And I had no doubt that if they found me, they would not take the chance they had before, that a Scirling woman was too useless to pose a threat.

But they did not find me. They searched in the area for a time; I heard them going back and forth, though they were surprisingly silent for men in darkness, in terrain totally unlike their homeland. I was well concealed by the structure of the bridge, though, and from the ground the bridge itself looked like nothing more than a particularly thick tangle of branches. One had to know what to look for to spot it, and they did not.

Nor did they know what hazards to look for. I heard a coughing roar, familiar to my ears, and knew they had woken a swampwyrm.

I heard no shouts of pain to tell me the creature had taken a bite out of a Tsebane, nor any equivalent sound from the dragon. I did catch a faint scent of its extraordinary breath, drifting up from the ground below, and was glad to be out of range. More distant sounds might be the Labane fleeing; I could not tell. But I stared into the darkness above me and blessed the forest which had cut and scratched and stung and battered me—and, ultimately, protected me.

I lay rigid and frightened for what seemed like an age before light began to filter through the green, and then lay for a time longer before I could persuade myself to move. Even then, I peered through the vines in all directions, picking off leeches while reassuring myself (insofar as I could) that the Labane had not laid a clever trap that I was about to spring.

They had not. Eventually I climbed down, aching from head to foot. But I could not permit myself the luxury of collapse: quite apart from my ravenous hunger and need for water, I had to warn the Moulish.

TWENTY-TWO

*The drums speak—Others are missing—Ikwunde plans—
Point Miriam—Politics—Wisdom and foolishness—
Moving the eggs—Fangfish*

I would not go so far as to say I found the Moulish; it would be more accurate to say they found me. I did, however, correctly read my surroundings to the extent of guessing where there might be a camp, so of that I can be proud.

My grammar, I fear, suffered terribly from my exhaustion and distress. It took far longer than it should have to explain the situation to them, while an elderly man fed and watered me. Then one of the hunters, an energetic fellow named Lumemouwin, wanted to go out with the others to look for the Labane. "They will *kill* you," I said helplessly. I knew the Moulish were perfectly capable of moving in stealth, but that did not change the fact that I would feel any deaths as if they were my fault. "Please, will you not warn the other camps—"

"We will," said one of the grandmothers, a woman called Ri-Kwilene. "But first we must know what to tell them."

She meant rather that they wanted to make sure what I said was true, before they alarmed anyone else. I suppose I did not look like the most reliable messenger, and foreigners have been known to run mad in jungles before. That did not make me any calmer as they sent hunters out to investigate.

But the men returned before long with confirmation that they had seen what few signs the Labane camp had left behind. (No bodies; it was too much for me to hope that the wasps or the dragon had done them in.) Then the elders took to the drums, pounding out the message that would soon spread from one end of Mouleen to the other.

The drums brought Yeyuama to me a few days later. As grateful as I was to see him, I immediately noted that he was alone—or rather, accompanied by two young men I did not recognize, both of them Moulish fellows. "Where are the others?" I asked, my hands twisting about one another. "Has something happened?"

Yeyuama shook his head. "I do not know. They never came down from the cliff."

My first thought was that the Labane had captured them. Then I told myself that was foolishness; the Labane were coming from the southern side of the Great Cataract, and my friends had been on the northern. Still, it did little to reassure me. (It would have done even less had I known that the Ikwunde pressed an attack along the Girama River the very day I went over the waterfall—I think to divert attention from their scouts in the swamp.)

If I would feel guilt for the deaths of any Moulish, how much more would I feel if anything happened to my companions? I bore a great deal of responsibility for their presence here in the first place. I looked from Yeyuama to Rikwilene. "Can a message be sent out, asking after them?"

She frowned and shook her head. "The villagers will wonder, if they hear too much speech from the drums." (The "villagers" in this case were the Labane scouts.) "Someone will send word if your brothers and sister are found. The other camps know you are here."

I argued, but could not budge her. Which was, I suppose, practice for what followed, when we began to discuss what to do about the Labane.

With the aid of a map laid out in sticks and leaves, I explained the larger situation: the impending war against the Ikwunde, of which the Moulish knew only a little, and what might happen if the people to the south could bring their army through the swamp. Here, however, I ran into immediate objections. "As many villagers as all the people of the forest together?" Lumemouwin said skeptically. (I had told them there were more Ikwunde than that, but they simply had no personal experience of human crowds on that scale.) "Impossible. They could never bring them through. The forest would eat them."

"The forest might eat some, yes—but even if two in every five die, it could be disastrous," I said. "For you as well as for the peoples of Bayembe; I assure you they would not hesitate to kill Moulish along the way. Though I wonder . . ." My words trailed off as I stared at my own map. Yes, the Ikwunde could march through, if they were prepared to accept such attrition. But could they do so *effectively*? I had heard military men talk about the importance of supply lines, and my own experience with the logistics of carrying equipment through the Green Hell made me doubt an army would fare well. A small, mobile group like the Labane could manage—but a small, mobile group would not be good for much more than harrying villages along the northern border. Was the aim to distract the defenders stationed along the rivers? Surely this was too much trouble for something so small. Unless they had a more valuable target . . .

My map was incomplete. I had focused on the Great Cataract and the northern and southern edges of Mouleen, but I had not paid much attention to the eastern end. With one hand I fumbled blindly for another stick, and jammed it into the soft dirt.

"Point Miriam," I whispered.

It was a fort—but one built to defend the harbor. The Ikwunde were not great seafarers; they had, however, conquered enough coastal towns that they might conceivably mount an assault on

Nsebu and Atuyem. That was why the Scirling colony had been placed there: our defense of the harbor was part of our agreement with Bayembe. We had built our walls and placed our guns, and *all* of that effort was focused on the sea, which they believed to be their only point of vulnerability.

But the eastern fringes of the Green Hell came very close to Point Miriam. And if an attack came from the fort's *landward* side . . .

How many men would they need to take it? I was not tactician enough to guess. A small force might do it, though, if they had surprise on their side; and undoubtedly it would be a great surprise if the Ikwunde appeared out of the swamp to assault the fort. My mind spun out possibilities for what would follow: an invasion force by sea, perhaps, once the harbor's main defense was gone, or perhaps an attempt to hold the fort itself. All of the possibilities were dreadful.

Swiftly I laid out for the others what I envisioned. "Can you warn the fort?" I asked when I was done. The Moulish carried out some amount of trade with the villagers along their borders; surely that was true along the bay as well.

Those around me exchanged glances. "We can tell the camps in the east," Rikwilene said. "But will the villagers listen?"

The villagers, or the Scirling officials at Point Miriam. "If the message was from me . . ." I dismissed this thought before it was even complete. "They'd have no reason to trust such a claim. Even if they believed the words came from me, they would doubt my judgment." Sir Adam would hardly be inclined to vouch for my reliability. And while I wanted to believe they would take precautions regardless, I knew they were just as likely to laugh it off. No one could assault Point Miriam through the Green Hell. No one.

If I went in person, I might have a chance of persuading them. But the scouts were already in the swamp; the army could not be that far behind. My odds of making it the length of Mouleen before they mounted their attack were even worse than my odds of Sir Adam listening to a transcribed drum message.

But there were people who *would* listen to the drums. And I had seen for myself how effective they could be, the day we found Velloin and Okweme trying to kidnap a dragon.

I looked around the circle at the gathered camp, youths and hunters and elders, with the children slipping between legs to listen. "Please," I said. "You can stop them before they even get to Point Miriam. You can save any number of lives in Bayembe. If you send a message to the camps—I have seen how strong your hunters are. You can fight the Ikwunde. Not head-on, of course, but from the shadows—"

Even before I started, I knew it was a lost cause. Heads were shaking all around, men and women drawing back in disapproval. "This is a villager fight," someone said; I did not see who.

Ikwunde against Yembe, Scirlings interfering, Satalu in the wings. What did any of that mean to the Moulish? Even if the Ikwunde conquered Bayembe, enclosing the Green Hell on three sides, it would have little consequence for the people here. Oh, perhaps someday that would rebound ill upon them—but vague fears of "someday" would persuade no one to put himself in harm's way. Indeed, from their perspective it might be better if the Ikwunde triumphed, for that would destroy or at least set back the Scirling colony, and take with it the plans for a dam above the Great Cataract.

Not that the Moulish knew of the dam . . .

"What does this mean?" Yeyuama asked, snapping his fingers.

I stared at my hand. I had not even realized I had done that, so caught up was I in my thought. "It means I've had an idea," I said slowly. "One I should perhaps share only with you—to begin with, at least. It concerns the dragons."

He nodded and beckoned the two fellows who had arrived with him to join us off to one side. "They are pure," he said, when I looked quizzical. "I brought them for the ceremony, but what you have to say comes first."

I would have been happier sharing this only with Yeyuama, who at least was familiar to me. But I was in no position to object. "It concerns what those hunters said," I told the three of them. "I needed permission to come here, from the oba of Bayembe, and he required a promise from me in return."

This tale I kept as short as I could, stressing at every point my ignorance in making that promise, and my apology for having done so. "But," I said, and then took a deep breath. "If it is not wholly blasphemous to suggest this . . . then I think, should that bargain be kept, it would help save the forest from a very great danger. One your people are not yet aware of."

Explaining the dam was both easier and more difficult than I expected, first when I told Yeyuama and the other two, then again when I repeated my words for the rest of the camp. The Moulish understood dams well enough; they created their own in certain seasons, to aid in their fishing. But a dam large enough to control the Great Cataract? Nothing in the world could be so powerful.

"I assure you it can," I said, with all the conviction I could muster. "And if this is built, it will change your forest forever. No longer will the floods rise as before; the swamp will always be in its dry season. The waterfall itself will be changed, and Yeyuama fears what the consequence of that may be for the dragons." This had not been in my original speculations, when I stood on the bank of the Hembi, for at that time I had not yet seen the queens in the lake. Yeyuama's hands had trembled when the possibility came to him. After that, he had given his full support to my plan.

I said to my assembled listeners, "If you stop the Ikwunde

from crossing the swamp and attacking Point Miriam, I will tell the oba that in gratitude for your help, he must not build this dam. It will be an agreement between his people and yours, sealed by the giving of a gift. The specifics of that gift are a matter for the pure, but I truly believe it will gain you this man's friendship. And that friendship will protect your home for generations to come."

They needed time to consider it, of course. Such a thing could not be decided on a whim. I chafed at every minute of delay, but Yeyuama took pity on me; he and the other two pure drew me aside for the ceremony acknowledging my safe return from the island, which also served as distraction.

It should have been done on the bank of the lake, but we could not spare the time to go there. They built a hut away from the camp, then put me inside it with a small fire, onto which they threw the leaves whose scent was so reminiscent of a swamp-wyrm's extraordinary breath. It was the same material used on the fire the hunters passed when leaving camp, but whereas they were only required to walk through the smoke, or perhaps scoop it onto themselves with their hands, I was left inside the hut until I nearly asphyxiated. When Yeyuama finally let me out, I was glad enough of the fresh air that I hardly minded his insistence that I strip naked (yes, in front of all three of them) and bathe myself in a quiet and predator-free part of the swamp.

"The smoke purifies us," he said when I was done and clothed once more. "Nothing can undo the harm caused by that first death, but we come as close as we can."

Yeyuama's distraction had served its purpose, with perfect timing. A boy came running up just then, summoning the four of us once more back to camp.

The other pure were drawn into conversation briefly after we returned, while I waited apart. Then I was beckoned over, and

Rikwilene delivered their answer. "You speak wisdom on some things," the old woman said, "and foolishness on others. We will not attack the Ikwunde."

My heart sank. All that hope . . . but this was too much to ask of them, and the possible reward too uncertain.

"Our hunters can be hunters of men when there is no other choice, but what you ask—for us to stop their camps so directly— that would only result in death on both sides. *But*," Rikwilene said, and my breath stopped, "we have agreed to try other ways."

On the instant, my imagination filled with new possibilities, each one madder than the last. The hunter Lumemouwin stopped me, though, with a cautionary hand. "You do not know the forest, or our people. Not well enough. We will be the ones to make these plans."

He was right. I was no tactician, nor was I Moulish; I did not know how they might be most effective. What I had to offer was information, and assistance with the world outside when this matter ended. "If it would be useful," I said, "I can tell you things about Point Miriam, and the weapons the people on both sides carry."

Yeyuama laughed. As tense as I was, it shocked me that he could be so cheerful. "We will have to think how to translate that for the drums, but yes. And you can do more than that. You are one of the pure now."

As pure as a hut full of foul smoke could make me. "Yes," I said. "The promise I made—"

"Not that," Yeyuama said, grinning. "Come. This, too, is only for a few ears."

The ears in question were those of the pure: those who had qualified themselves to "touch the dragons."

That category, you may note, does not include *your* ears, nor your eyes neither. (Unless you have undergone that test yourself and passed, in which case you will not need me to tell you what I am about to omit.) As before, I will speak only of those things which I believe are safe to be shared with others, based on the judgment of my more experienced Moulish counterparts. I may have gone to the island and returned, but that was only the barest part of what it meant to join their ranks.

"If we move the eggs now," Yeyuama said when we had drawn apart, "they will hatch early. And then they may feast upon those who come into their waters."

I received these words in wide-eyed silence. He spoke the way my parents' housekeeper in Tamshire might, suggesting that it would be advisable to shift the winter shutters into position a few weeks early. As if "moving the eggs" were a common task—just one not usually done at this time.

While the other fellows considered it, Yeyuama explained to me. And this, suitably edited, is what I learned.

The dragons I had seen in the lake were, as I have said, queen dragons, the females of a species for which I had heretofore only seen the males. Now I learned that the chief task of the pure was first to bring suitable males up to the lake for breeding, and then to disperse the eggs after they were laid, to various points around the swamp.

The ramifications of this have been laid out extensively in my more academic works; I will dwell on only one now, as many of you are no doubt anxious to leave the dusty byways of natural history and get back to the invading army. The eggs so distributed were *not*, as is common among other draconic breeds, large and few in number. They were myriad, and shockingly small: less than ten centimeters in length. I thought of swamp-wyrms and their usual habits, and asked Yeyuama how on earth newly hatched dragons could be of much use in stopping an army, however many of them there might be.

He grinned from ear to ear, as delighted as a magician pulling back the curtain to reveal his great trick. "You have seen them, and feared them. But you have called them fangfish."

The tiny, eel-like predator that had taken a bite out of my left arm back in Floris; the entirely aquatic creature we had thought at best to be a draconic cousin. In reality it was the infantile form of the great swamp-wyrm. They hatched in abundance, and were eaten in abundance not only by snakes and other creatures, but by their own, more mature kind; those who survived grew and changed, eventually becoming the full-grown dragons to which we had devoted the bulk of our attention and study.

(Despite the unsightly scar on my arm, there was a part of me that thought in delight: I've been bitten by a *dragon!*)

Then I remembered the swarms of fangfish that had roiled the waters during the flood, the avoidance of which had spurred the construction of tree-bridges. If the Ikwunde attempted to wade through on their way to Point Miriam—and they could hardly avoid it—then the consequences would be very bloody indeed.

"You will help," Yeyuama said, still grinning. "Your way of going to and from the island was madness; I have never seen anything like it. Most of us go a much easier way! We should call you Sasoumin instead."

Sasoumin—"woman who flies."

Yeyuama went on while I was considering my new appellation and fighting the urge to giggle with delight. (Even now, I believe that is the name by which I am best known in the swamps of Mouleen. It is much more flattering than some of the sobriquets I have born in the news-sheets of Scirland.) "I will show you where the eggs are, and you will help move them; that is your work now. We will use the drums to tell others to do the same."

I will, of course, not tell you where the eggs are initially laid, save to say that they are not *on* the island; the purpose of that challenge is to give a view of the queen dragons, and to test the mettle of those who will henceforth be taking their unhatched offspring from their original place of laying to new locations deeper in the swamp. This stage of the process I did not do, for it was not the correct season for newly laid eggs. Although the experience sounds hair-raising—queen dragons are decidedly unfriendly—it is one of my great regrets that I never had the chance, for my time in Mouleen was drawing to an end, and I have never been able to return for more than a few days. To come so close to one of the queens . . . I have had other breathtaking experiences in my life, some of which (others would say) surpass even that one. But one does not cease to treasure a gem simply because one owns another that is larger. I would have loved to place that in the jewelry box of my memory.

I did, however, go with Yeyuama to where the current clutches of eggs were buried, in soft swamp muck. This is where they do much of their incubation, before being shifted to the water for hatching. The history of how this process developed has been discussed at greater length by the Yembe historian Chinaka n Oforiro Dara; I advise those interested in such matters to read her work, and to consult my own monographs for analysis of its effect on draconic development.

But enough of such matters: there is an invading army to attend to.

Drums had passed the requisite messages through the Green Hell, faster than any messenger could carry them. The four of us (myself, Yeyuama, and our two companions) were not the only ones shifting eggs; indeed, ours were likely to be the least relevant, for the Ikwunde were almost certain to make their crossing farther to the east. To hatch only some of the dragons now would,

A Fangfish

however, disturb the balance of the swamp. As it was, Yeyuama admitted that the effects of this would be difficult, as it was not the season of flooding, when food would be most abundant. "I hope they get a good meal off the Ikwunde, then," I said.

He shrugged philosophically. "If necessary, we will make another queen egg next year"—and that is how I discovered that part of the egg-handling process fosters the sexual differentiation between the queen dragons in the lake and their male suitors in the swamp.

I keep diverting to matters of natural history. This is, I suppose, because what followed was akin to a large number of dominoes toppling over where I could not see them. Much of it I only learnt about afterward, or pieced together from what I was not told; altogether, the picture it made was very complex. As is only fitting, I suppose, for the chain of events that led to me being accused of treason against the Scirling crown. I shall have to give you the larger picture first, and then my humble strand within it that stitched these events together.

TWENTY-THREE

Nagoreemo's message—Tom, Natalie, and Faj Rawango—
The Ikwunde cross the swamp—Captives of war—My army

The Moulish had, as per my request, sent a messenger to the fort at Point Miriam. In their generosity, they did not even recruit a coastal villager to carry the word on their behalf; this was deemed important enough that they sent one of their own, a man who spoke Yembe, an elder named Nagoreemo.

He left the Green Hell and climbed the rocky slope up to Point Miriam, drawing many stares, I imagine, from Scirlings unaccustomed to seeing a man in nothing more than a loincloth. At the gate to the fort he was stopped by one of the soldiers on guard, and in his careful Yembe, conveyed the news that an Ikwunde force intended to pass through Mouleen and attack them from the landward side.

What words he used to explain this, I do not know. My own conjecture had been translated into the language of the drums, which is (of necessity, owing to how that language functions) both long-winded and limited in its specifics. But the Moulish are practiced at sending a message the length of the swamp without distorting it, so I have faith it arrived at the coast in much the same shape it left our own drums in the west. Once there, however, it was interpreted by the local camps, then given to Nagoreemo, who then translated it into Yembe and relayed it to soldiers whose own grasp of that tongue was, I suspect, less than fully proficient.

Small wonder that no one believed him. One of the officers at the fort, an army major by the name of Joshua Maitland, believed Nagoreemo was a defector from his own people, come to warn them about an ill-advised *Moulish* assault on the fort. Others thought him simply mad. The result was that he was turned away—with, I am ashamed to say, many jeers, and even a few blows from rifle butts. That venerable elder deserved better from us.

In the meanwhile, events at the far end of Bayembe had become quite warm, to distract all eyes from anything that might be happening along the bay. The Ikwunde mounted a series of assaults along and across the Girama, including one that nearly made it to the Hembi before our forces caught them. This, as you may imagine, raised alarms all through that region, with the consequence that our side instituted new patrols to watch for any Ikwunde advance scouts. They not only found some of those; they also found Tom, Natalie, and Faj Rawango.

Had the patrol that found them been composed of Bayembe forces, all might have been well, for Faj Rawango was experienced enough in the ways of the oba's court that he could have demanded, and likely received, a proper hearing. They were, alas, found by Scirlings—and promptly taken prisoner.

Did the lieutenant think those three were Ikwunde spies? No, of course not; only one was Erigan, and even the blindest Scirling private could see that the short, slight Faj Rawango was nothing like the tall, well-knit men in the Ikwunde army. But they were something inexplicable, and so they had to be detained. (The fact that Tom and Natalie both explained themselves to him at length did not dissuade him from this course.)

They were soon transferred into the care of a captain—but this fellow, alas, had heard complaints of their activities from the despicable Velloin, who had given a highly biased account of our meeting in the swamp. As a result, they were read a lengthy diatribe on civilized behaviour and the necessity for them to reflect well on Scirland; following this, they were summarily packed up with the wounded from the river fighting and shipped back across toward Nsebu. All three of them were somewhere in the middle of the savannah when the rest of this matter resolved.

The Ikwunde, from what we can determine, were following a plan more or less like the one I had posited, though with a great many subtle flourishes I could never have imagined and honestly cannot recall. (Those interested in such things can find an exhaustive discussion of all aspects of the Ikwunde War in Achabe n Kegweyu Gbori's ten-volume work *Expansion and Retreat of the Ikwunde*, translated into Scirling by Ezekiel Grant.) Scouts like the ones I encoutered had been sent into Mouleen all along its length in the hope of locating a waterway suitable for transporting their army by boat; needless to say, this failed. The Ikwunde therefore took the information gathered by their scouts—including, I fear, some I provided myself—and sent five companies of Labane by the shortest route possible, from Osheth on the Eremmo border to Point Miriam.

Toward Point Miriam, at least. They encountered some difficulty along the way.

I saw with my own eyes how rapidly the swamp-wyrm eggs hatched once placed in water, the "fangfish" wiggling free like the eels they resembled. They are a disturbing sight then, soft and almost helpless looking, but with mouths already full of teeth. We took great care in crossing the waterways as we traveled from egg cache to egg cache, and even more care after that task was done, when Yeyuama and I set out for the eastern edge of the Green Hell.

For although I esteemed the Moulish greatly and knew they would be of more use than I in opposing the Ikwunde, I could not bring myself to sit idly by while this matter played out. If nothing else, I needed to see enough that I could accurately inform the men at Point Miriam of what had transpired.

Which meant I was there to see one of the Labane companies—already much worse off for their travels to that point—attempt a crossing of fangfish-filled water.

They had searched for a way around it, and been thwarted by creative Moulish troublemakers; now they had no choice but to build rafts and attempt to pole across. Yeyuama had refused to try and provoke any fully grown dragons into troubling them, because these Labane carried guns, but he could not stand in the way of a swamp-wyrm's own inclination. One took great exception to the Labane trespassing upon his territory, and rammed a raft before anyone aboard it saw him there.

I had thought to feel triumph at watching the forest eat those who would trespass in it. When the moment came, I merely felt sick. There was no pleasure to be had in the screaming—for even a Tsebane will scream when a dozen infant dragons latch onto him. It is a horrible way to die, and yet those who did may well have been luckier than those who were merely bloodied, for the latter faced near-certain infection, which in many cases was only a more protracted way to go.

But I knew better than to think we could warn them off their course; these were, after all, the most dedicated troops the inkosi possessed. And when my resolve faltered, I had only to remind myself of the casualties my allies suffered. Despite warning and care, the Moulish had not been able to stay entirely safe; Labane scouts had caught some of them, and one camp was overrun as they tried to move out of the army's line of march. All in all, twenty-one Moulish died, which is a massacre for numbers as small as theirs.

Because of this, some among the western camps argued in favor of actively hunting and killing those the forest had not disposed of. But the youths brought out the *legambwa bomu*, the dragon mask, and charged around with it, reminding all that killing was what cursed humankind with mortality; and while killing for food might be a tragic necessity, killing these men was not. They therefore took the surviving Labane prisoner.

Prisoners were not something they had much experience with. The Moulish deal with their own internal problems by talking it out or walking away to a new camp, not by waging war. Tying people up was something done only when a person had run mad (or, as they would put it, was targeted by serious witchcraft). What should they do with their captives?

Had I not just spent seven months in the swamp, flung myself off a cliff, crash-landed in the trees, been a captive myself, and then run the length of the Green Hell, I might have thought my answer through more thoroughly. As it was, I asked whether they would be willing to send enough hunters with me to escort the prisoners to Point Miriam, and the Moulish, glad to be rid of them, agreed.

This is how I marched out of the jungle toward the fort with what, at first glance, might understandably be mistaken for a small invading army.

Our slow pace (limited to the speed of hobbled Labane) and general disorganization went some way toward establishing us as no threat. Soldiers, however, are apt to get nervous around armed strangers, even when the weapons in question are nets and fire-hardened sticks of wood. I placed myself prominently at the front of the group, intending to draw the eye and give the soldiers something like a familiar (by which I mean a Scirling) face to re-assure them.

This might have been more successful had I looked less a scarecrow. I had been in the same clothing since the morning I parted from Tom and Natalie, and it had seen a great deal of abuse in the interim. I was unwashed, underfed, and giddy with the success of our plan. So it was that when rifles were leveled in our direction, I waved my arms above my head, hallooed the fort, and cried out in a loud, laughing voice, "Do you believe us now?"

It was of course my luck that Major Maitland answered me from the wall (though I did not know he was the one who had misinterpreted Nagoreemo until later). He shouted down at us, "You and your army of savages can stop right there!"

"*My* army?" I looked at the Moulish with exaggerated surprise. "These do not belong to me, sir. Unless you mean our prisoners? I would not claim them if you paid me, for it was their intent to sneak up on you from a direction you did not expect—as I believe you were warned, though you did not listen. Fortunately for you, the Moulish believe in sharing what they have, and they have wit and common sense in abundance. More than enough to make up for its lack elsewhere.

"I, by contrast, am Scirling, and less well schooled in generosity. I therefore say that if you and your masters do not promise to clap these Ikwunde in irons and then reward these brave people as they deserve, then we jolly well may just let these fellows go, for they are not worth the nuisance of keeping."

(In hindsight, I can see how this may have been construed as a threat.)

Maitland went quite purple. I think he might have given the order to fire—a few warning shots to put me on better behaviour, at least—but by then Sir Adam had attained the top of the wall and seen what lay outside. "Mrs. Camherst?" he called down, shocked, and I answered, "What is left of her."

"What the devil is all of this?" he demanded, gesturing at the mass of people I stood with.

This time I answered him with more decorum, although Maitland provoked me sorely with his own interjections. Sir Adam continued to question me—how had we captured them; how many there were; what on earth did I think I was wearing—until I said, "Sir, I will answer everything to your satisfaction, but not by shouting it up at you. This is dreadfully public, and my voice will give out. Will you take the prisoners, and give your surety that the Moulish will be rewarded? They, not I, have done the work of capturing these Labane, and have killed a great many more besides, at no small risk and cost to themselves."

Maitland snorted loudly enough for me to hear it, even at that range. "You expect us to believe that your savages killed Labane warriors with—with what? Sharpened sticks?"

"No, Major," I said coolly. "They killed the Labane with dragons. As a gentlewoman and natural historian, I assure you it is true."

I suspect it was my declaration more than anything else that opened the gates of Point Miriam to us, for everyone wanted to know what I meant by *they killed the Labane with dragons.* We shuffled in, me at the front, the Moulish surrounding the hobbled prisoners, and I made sure to find a soldier with good Yembe to serve as an interpreter before I let Sir Adam take me off for questioning.

If that strikes you as a phrase that might be applied to the suspect in a crime, you are not far wrong. Sir Adam was deeply suspicious of my tale; he called in a doctor to examine me before anything else, so certain was he that I had lost my reason. (I blame the trousers.) Much tedious back-and-forth ensued after that, but the important moment came when I told Sir Adam what I intended going forward.

"In return for their work in saving this colony and Bayembe," I said, mustering what remained of my energy, "the Moulish do have a price."

"Gold?" Sir Adam asked. "Guns? Out with it, Mrs. Camherst; tell me what you have promised them."

"Nothing so mercenary, I assure you. But it is the forest known as the Green Hell that has protected Bayembe and this colony; it must be protected in return. I understand that you intend to build a dam in the west, across one or more—I presume all three—of the rivers. The plans for this must stop."

The governor shot to his feet. "Mrs. Camherst, I do not know where you have gotten your information—"

Under no circumstances was I going to name Natalie. "Do you think no one knows what your engineers are here to build? Do not fear for the defense of Bayembe, Sir Adam. Even without your lake, I assure you, this country will be safe."

I was extraordinarily lucky that he stopped me before I said anything more.

"Damn the defense," he growled. "Our soldiers can stop the Ik-wunde. There are *contracts* depending on that dam, Mrs. Camherst—blast it, what do you think the point of this colony is?"

"What do you mean?" I asked, mostly to purchase time to think.

He made a disgusted noise. "Power, of course. Of all kinds. Power from the dam, and we have contracts saying that eighty percent of it will be ours for a period of fifty years after construction is done. With that and Bayembe's iron, our profits will be enormous. Think of what the effects of *that* will be. And you expect us to throw all that away, simply because a few naked savages stopped a raid?"

My hands were shaking; I clutched them tight in my lap. "I knew nothing of this."

"Of course you didn't. You are nothing more than a reckless young woman—"

"Who just saved this colony from invasion and possible destruction." My voice wanted to shake, too; keeping it steady made my words come out loudly. "You should perhaps consider keeping the young ladies around you better informed, Sir Adam— but in this case I am glad you did not. Can you not see the headlines now? SCIRLING GENTLEWOMAN SAVES NSEBU. DARING FLIGHT REVEALS DASTARDLY PLAN. SWAMP NATIVES DEFEAT LABANE WARRIORS. HUMILIATED PRISONERS BROUGHT IN CHAINS TO FORT. And then can you imagine the response if people learn that you turned your back on those who kept Labane spears out of it?"

He did not go purple as Maitland had; he turned pale instead. "Are you threatening me, Mrs. Camherst?"

"No, Sir Adam," I said. "I am merely explaining how people back home will see this. If you hear a threat in that, it is only because you fear the inevitable consequence."

"It is *not* inevitable," he said, his voice trembling. "It is something you intend to bring down upon me. It is a threat, Mrs. Camherst, however you try to disguise it with pretty language."

I sighed. I was weary; I was filthy; I had entirely spent the energy which had sustained me on the way here, and wanted nothing more than to sleep for a month while my various wounds healed. "Very well, Sir Adam. Call it a threat if you must. I gave my word to the Moulish that I would do everything I could to assist them in this cause, and I intend to keep it. Lock me up if you wish; it will not help you, for I have already written down my tale, and made arrangements for it to be shared with friendly ears."

It was the last inspiration of my tired brain: an utter fabrication, invented on the spot to forestall the house arrest I otherwise saw in my future.

It failed.

Sir Adam strode to the door. "Find a room for Mrs. Camherst. And see that she does not leave."

TWENTY-FOUR

Royal displeasure—Eggs for the oba—Overly frank questions—
Accusations of treason—Life outside the Green Hell—
Farewells, and a reflection on sorrow

But of course I did leave in the end—courtesy of Anku-mata n Rumeme Gbori.

I do not know what precisely he said to Sir Adam, but I believe it had something to do with the promise I had made before departing for the Green Hell. He wanted to know why I had failed him, and refused to let a Scirling question me in his stead. It was not freedom; armed guards accompanied me from Point Miriam to Atuyem, and took me back again afterward, too. Still, it was the salvation I needed. Sir Adam's outburst had stopped me before I admitted that the success of my plan depended on me speaking with the oba, and so he let me go.

This time there was no public ceremony, no hangers-on. The oba preferred to express his displeasure in private. Apart from the guards who stood both outside and inside the chamber, there was only his *griot* for company, and his sister Galinke.

"The Golden One grants you what you desire," the *griot* said, "and in return, you betray him."

It was not a good sign that the *griot* spoke to me. This is a thing they do in Bayembe, to underline the exalted status of the oba; he speaks to his *griot*, and the *griot* speaks to whatever lowly soul is unworthy to receive the words directly. Mr. Wilker and I had previously been honoured by Ankumata's friendliness, but I had now lost the privilege.

Galinke sat with her hands folded and eyes downcast. This rebuke was for her as well as for myself; she had suggested me to her brother as a tool, and so she too had failed him. And I, in a sense, had failed her.

My curtsy was as deep and respectful as I could make it. "*Chele*, I thank you for bringing me here today. There is more you have not heard, but Sir Adam would not release me to tell you."

Ankumata gestured at his *griot*, who said, "Speak."

I had rehearsed the words all the way from Point Miriam. "You asked me to bring you eggs. Whether you meant me to collect them, trade for them, or steal them outright, I soon discovered that for me to do any such thing would have been a grave insult to the Moulish, and dishonourable repayment for their generosity, without which I certainly would have died in the swamp. My promise was a blind one, and I will know in the future not to repeat that mistake.

"But blind although my promise was, I have found a way to keep it."

Alert readers may recall that Yeyuama had told Okweme that he would address my intended theft of eggs after I had visited the island. I thought at the time that he was referring to my possible death in the attempt; had I perished, it might well have been seen as proper judgment upon me for my intended crime. But when we debated the possibility of stopping the Ikwunde and the dam alike, he told me his true meaning—which was not at all what I expected.

It is the privilege and responsibility of those who touch the dragons to move the eggs where they are needed. Prior to the island, any attempt on my part to interfere with that process, whether by theft or trade, would have been a blasphemy grave enough to ensure my death.

But *after* the island . . . if I wanted to move eggs somewhere, then it was my right to do so.

"The Moulish have agreed to let me offer you eggs," I said. "I do not have them with me; you will have to wait for more to be laid. But when the time comes, certain men among them will bring you eggs and instruct you in their care. When one of those dragons perishes, they will bring you another—for the ones they supply will be incapable of breeding. This is not meant as a slight against you; it is the unavoidable consequence of swamp-wyrm biology. But if you place those dragons in the rivers above the Great Cataract, you will have a defense like that which has just protected Point Miriam."

The oba listened to all of this impassively, hiding his thoughts behind the mask of a man who has survived political waters more dangerous than those the Labane tried to cross.

I swallowed and went on. "For this arrangement to work, however, the Moulish will require something in return. They have sheltered your land, at no little risk to themselves, and now offer you a treasure; moreover, what they require is a necessity for that treasure to thrive. I hope your generosity and wisdom will see the value in granting their wish."

Here I paused, until the *griot* prompted me to continue. This was the most delicate point, for if I angered Ankumata as I had Sir Adam, I might be locked up and never let out again.

But I could hardly stop now. "The dam," I said. "The one planned in the west. Its effect on the swamp would be catastrophic for the Moulish and their dragons both. If you wish for the arrangement I have described, then you must not allow the dam to be built."

Silence fell. Ankumata propped one hand against his leg brace, unblinking gaze never wavering from me. I fought not to squirm under its weight. Eighty percent of the power, Sir Adam had said;

that was the dragon's share of the benefit, and I had no doubt that most of the cost in labor and material would come from Bayembe, not Scirland. It was not a deal that favored the oba. But could he abandon it? And did he wish to?

The next words did not come from the *griot*. They came from Ankumata himself.

"There is no profit for your people in this trade."

"We have already had our profit," I said, "in the safety of those who would have died in the Labane attack." My mouth was very dry. Surely it was a good sign that he was no longer speaking through his *griot*, but his words reminded me that my peril came from multiple directions. "As for the rest . . ." I shrugged helplessly. "I can only do what I think is right, *chele*. For as many people as possible. This seems better to me than allowing the dam to be built. But perhaps my judgment was incorrect."

More silence. I do not know whether Ankumata was still thinking, or merely waiting, to make certain no one would think he rushed into his decision.

I nearly jumped out of my skin when he said, "The gift is good. There will be no dam."

Muscles I had not even known were tight suddenly relaxed. Then my traitor mouth betrayed me, saying, "Are you certain? Sir Adam, I fear, will be angry—"

Ankumata's eyes gleamed with what I think was suppressed amusement. "Your country has promised assistance in defending Bayembe. I accept the assistance you have provided on their behalf."

That was undoubtedly *not* the wording in the treaty—but if he thought he could get away with that argument, who was I to disagree? I asked, "Is that why you sent me to the swamp, instead of one of your own? Because you could call it Scirling aid? No, that cannot be it. I thought at the time that you would not mind as much if we died. Later, it occurred to me that you could more easily disavow our actions if we caused trouble. But if that were the case, you could have sent Velloin. Or both of us together, but I am sure someone has informed you of how I detest the man. I cannot think why you did not send him instead, before me, unless it is because I am Scirling and he is not."

This is why I have declined all offers of diplomatic postings. As I have grown older (and in theory more sedate), various government officials have thought to take advantage of my experience and international connections by sending me as an ambassador to one place or another. But I have at all ages been too prone to speaking my mind, and not always judicious enough in who I speak it to.

The oba of Bayembe, however, chose not to punish me for my frankness. He said, "If Velloin were a woman, he would not have gone into the *agban*."

I did not immediately parse his meaning. I looked to Galinke, who smiled; I thought of the days she and I had spent in conversation there. My seclusion had been less than entirely willing . . . but I had gone, rather than risk offense to my hosts, which might have jeopardized my ultimate purpose.

Velloin would not have bent to such concerns.

Understand: this is not the same thing as saying I was perfectly respectful of Yembe traditions, or Moulish ones, either. Romantics of various sorts over the years have painted me as a kind of human chameleon, adapting without difficulty or reservation to my social environment; this is twaddle. (Flattering twaddle, but twaddle all the same.) As I indicated during my account of the witchcraft ritual, my driving concern has always been my research. In pursuit of that, however, I have generally believed that it is more to my advantage to cooperate with those around me than to ignore them. Sometimes this has been a nuisance, and on occasion an outright mistake, but overall this philosophy has served me well.

And on this occasion, it explained why my solution to the problem had appealed to Ankumata.

I curtseyed again and said, "Thank you, *chele.*" Then one final thought occurred to me. "If—if I may ask one more thing—"

He made an exaggerated show of wariness, but gestured for me to continue.

"Have you ever killed anything? Not flies and such, but animals or humans."

His hand had come to rest again on the iron of his braces. They made him strong in some ways, including a few that healthy legs would not have, but they could not do everything. Ankumata said, "I am no hunter."

I nodded. "Only those who have never killed may do the work that will bring swamp-wyrm eggs to you. There are other requirements as well, which you cannot fulfill . . . but I think it would please the Moulish to know that they are giving their dragons to a man who is in that sense pure. You may wish to find others who have not killed and recruit them to assist." My gaze flickered briefly to Galinke. "Women as well as men."

This audience had used up more than enough of the oba's time. He dismissed me with a wave of his feather fan. "I will read your research notes before you depart."

None of the secrets Yeyuama had shared with me were written down, so agreeing was easy enough. "I will see to it that you have copies of what is printed afterward as well," I promised, and retreated from his presence with a sense of profound relief.

The natural effects of the agreement to transplant swamp-wyrm eggs into the border rivers of Bayembe did not become fully

apparent for a number of years after my departure, and so I will
not address them here; that is a matter for later volumes.

The political effects, however, played out more rapidly, as I
found myself accused of treason against the Scirling crown.

These accusations came in three distinct waves. The first was
immediate, following on the rumours that I had brought an army
to the walls of Point Miriam and threatened the soldiers there.
That, I think, prepared the soil for the later rumours; it made for
a good story, and a pleasingly scandalous counter-narrative to
the tale of Isabella Camherst, savior of Nsebu.

The second wave was a product of my argument with Sir
Adam and subsequent house arrest. He had the good sense not to
share the specifics of our conversation, but a great many people
knew I had done *something* dreadful enough to warrant being
locked up, and later marched under armed guard to see the oba.
When that selfsame oba intervened to have me released, whispers began to fly that my loyalties lay not with my own homeland, but with our colonial ally. No one could say for certain
what action I had taken on their behalf—that awaited the third
wave of accusations—but rumour supplied any number of scur-
rilous possibilities.

As for the third wave, it did not take shape immediately. Ankumata was too experienced a politician to tell Sir Adam of his
arrangement with the Moulish before he had to; I was safely back
in Scirland by the time that matter came to light. (And a good
thing, too, or I might never have escaped with my life.) But eventually it became known that there had been plans for a dam, and
that Bayembe had backed out of those plans, in favor of some
arrangement with the Moulish. This damaged the trade agree-
ments with Scirland, which led to other foreign parties taking an
interest in Bayembe, and ultimately weakened our influence in

that country. I would not say this damaged Scirland, in the sense of inflicting harm upon my own nation; but it robbed us of a profit we might otherwise have had. This was more than enough for some to declare me a traitor to my own people.

All of this was inadvertent on my own part—but it does little good to cry, "I only wanted to study dragons!" Science is not separate from politics. As much as I would like it to be a pure thing, existing only in some intellectual realm unsullied by human struggle, it will always be entangled with the world we live in.

(That is a lie, though I will leave it in. Not the entanglement— that much is true—but the notion that I would like it to be otherwise. If science were only some abstract thing, without connection to our lives, it would be both useless and boring. But there have been times when I wished that I might snip a few of the threads tying it to other matters, so they would stop tripping me as I went.)

The effect of these accusations, along with others acquired during the expedition (such as the rumours of intimacy with Tom), was to drive all interest in my scientific discoveries out of the public mind in both Bayembe and Scirland. While my companions and I recuperated from our trials—in Nsebu, for Sir Adam had refused to allow us to return to Atuyem, even after my house arrest ended—we endured endless questions, not one of which had to do with natural history. On Tom's advice, I answered as few of those as my indiscretion and the status of my inquirer would allow. The political negotiations played out with a minimum of our involvement, which was as I preferred; I devoted myself instead to making better notes of my observations in Mouleen, since swamp conditions had made proper efforts there impossible.

It was a peculiar time. If I had felt odd briefly leaving the Green Hell for the savannah during our trek to the Great Cataract, how much stranger was it to sit on a chair in a Scirling-style house, to sleep in a bed, to wear skirts once again? The air felt positively cool and dry after the oppressive humidity of the swamp, and the sky seemed impossibly huge. Things that had become routine to me these past months reasserted themselves as unthinkable: had I truly eaten *insects*? Conversely, things which had once been shocking were no longer so. When every woman one has seen for half a year, only Natalie excepted, goes about wearing nothing more than a loincloth, the Gabborid custom of leaving one breast bare seems positively modest.

Over it all hung the certainty that we would not be in Eriga for much longer. "They'll drag us home," Tom predicted, shortly after we were reunited. "The soldiers were talking on the way here; they said the government might recall all civilians from Nsebu, if the Ikwunde continue to press. Except for the trading companies, of course. And now, with what you've done . . ." He shook his head, bemused. "There will have to be an inquiry."

Natalie laughed. The recent surprises seemed to have done her in; her manner was that of a woman who had washed her hands of everything, and now was merely waiting to see what would happen next. She said, "Well, I've ruined myself thoroughly enough to avoid marriage, and if I am *very* stone-headed I may yet avoid the madhouse. I suppose I am ready to go home."

I was not. Now that I knew fangfish were immature swamp-wyrms, I wanted to study their life cycle in greater detail, perhaps get an estimate for what percentage survived that infantile stage and grew to adulthood. I wanted to see the seasonal mating of the swamp-wyrms in the lake below the Great Cataract; I wanted to watch the great queen dragons lay their eggs, and distribute them through the forest alongside Yeyuama and the others. I wanted to document how the hatchlings fared in the river environment of Bayembe (and that was *before* I knew what would happen after their transplantation).

But I have never once left the site of an expedition feeling that I have learned everything, answered every question there is to ask. My curiosity always finds new directions. Despite that, I was honestly not certain I could face the Green Hell again—not so soon. Like a man undertaking strenuous labor, I had thought myself fit enough while I was still working, but now that I had stopped, a profound weariness set in, as much psychological as physical. A mattress might feel strange beneath my back at night, but I was not eager to trade it for a damp pallet again.

Regardless, the choice was not ours to make. Tom was right: before the month was out, Sir Adam informed us that we were to return to Scirland. "Are our visas revoked?" I asked.

I meant the question politely enough, but Sir Adam was not inclined to read anything I said in a charitable light. He said, "They will be, if that's what it takes to get rid of you."

"That won't be necessary," Tom hastened to assure him, and we left his office.

We did obtain permission to return to Atuyem—under escort, of course—so that we might make our farewells there. I had already parted from Yeyuama two weeks before; the Moulish did not tarry long in Point Miriam after handing over the Labane. I sent gifts with him, as lavish as I could arrange: more iron knives, foodstuffs not found in the swamp, anything I thought the Moulish might find of use. They wear little jewelry, but I sent a carved wooden pendant for Akinimanbi, a charm made in Bayembe to protect infants from sickness. I had no belief in its supernatural efficacy, nor would Akinimanbi necessarily think much of an item that invoked a Yembe god, but it was the best gesture I could think of to express my gratitude for her aid and forbearance.

In Atuyem, I met with Galinke and clasped her hands. "Despite all the trouble and confusion that has come of it," I said, "I am still more grateful than I can say that you recommended me to your brother. I only wish there were something equally vital I might do for you in return."

She smiled broadly. "In a way, you have. The more secure Bayembe is, the less likely it is that I will be sent to the mansa as his wife."

I had not forgotten our early political discussions in the *agban*, which had played no small role in affecting my decisions. "Then I am glad to have been of service," I said.

Galinke was not the only one who benefited from our expedition. Faj Rawango had, on account of his ancestry, been appointed to a prominent role in the new contact with Mouleen. And of course Ankumata had gotten what he desired, though he did not bid us farewell in person.

When people speak of the tragedies in my life, they ordinarily mean the deaths: not only Jacob, but all those around me who have perished, whether in direct consequence of danger or simple misfortune and the passage of time after our friendship has formed. At times, though, I think these partings should be accounted as highly, if only in the ledger of my own sorrow. Akinimanbi did not die on a Labane spear, but I never saw her again after leaving for the Great Cataract; in that sense I lost her as thoroughly as if she *had* died. So it was with Yeyuama as well. I only saw Faj Rawango once more, years later, and although Galinke corresponded with me, we could not be friends the way we might have been had we dwelt in the same land. So it has been, again and again throughout my life, as I form connections with people and then lose them to distance and time. I mourn those losses, even when I know my erstwhile friends are safe and happy among their own kin.

But the only way for me to avoid such losses would be to stay home, to never journey beyond the range of easy visitation. As my life will attest, that is not a measure I am willing to take; nor would I forgo the pleasures of my transient friendships if I could.

So we made our farewells, packed our things, and boarded a steamship in the harbor of Nsebu. Much browner, thinner, and more worn than we had been when we arrived, we made our way back to Scirland.

TWENTY-FIVE

Reactions at home — A stranger to me — Conversations
and apologies — No longer a recluse — The thief —
A small bar — The cost of the world

There was indeed an inquiry, and a flood of articles in the news-sheets, and gossipmongers swirling in the social waters like so many hungry fangfish.

That I survived these things at all owes a great deal to Lord Hilford, who was my tireless champion in venues ranging from Society to the Synedrion. He defended me against Sir Adam's report, accusations of fornication, and his own son (who had not forgiven me in the least for absconding with his daughter). Natalie was disowned, and took up residence with me as my permanent companion.

She proved surprisingly able with Jacob, once she was a resident of my house rather than a visitor to it. "I would not want one of my own, I think," she said with a laugh, "but I do not mind borrowing yours for brief spans of time."

My son. Now three years old, he had grown tremendously in my absence; I might not have recognized him, had his resemblance to his father not become even stronger. He, I think, barely recognized me at all, shrinking into Mrs. Hunstin's skirts when I crouched down and held out my arms for him to come.

His diffidence struck me like a blow. It was not only his youth that made him forget me, or the fact that I had been absent for a third of his short life; it was the distance between us before that. I was, I thought wryly, as remote a figure in his world as a queen dragon was to a fangfish, dwelling far away in the clean, turbulent waters of the lake. (Of course I thought of it in those terms. My head was full of plans for the book I would publish, which I had been using as a distraction from the prospect of a Synedrion hearing. And I had begun to think about motherhood as a naturalist might—which made it much more interesting to me.)

The witchcraft ritual had purged some of the tension and pain from my thoughts, though, and on the journey home I had realized that I was eager to see my son once more. I vowed, as Mrs. Hunstin coaxed him toward me, that I would find some means of improving matters between us. I still had no desire to be the sort of mother society expected me to be; but surely I could be *some* kind of mother to him, in my particular way, to a greater extent than before.

My own mother . . . I will not go into detail regarding the conversation between us, save to say that "conversation" is an exceedingly polite name to give it. She had heard the rumours about Tom Wilker, and drawn very erroneous conclusions from them, not the least of which was the notion that I had only gone to Eriga for his sake. I took great exception to her readiness to condemn me, and after that I no longer had to ignore her letters, for she wrote me none.

Andrew I apologized to for the loss of the penknife he had given me when we were children. He listened to the tale of its demise with all the wide-eyed excitement of the eight-year-old boy he had been, and afterward clapped me on the back as if I were a man. "It fell in a noble cause," he said solemnly, and then demanded to know whether Erigan women really went bare-breasted.

I had expected to return to my life as a recluse, albeit for different reasons than before. I imagined myself rising each morning to write papers on our observations, Tom and I having agreed to bombard the Philosophers' Colloquium and other scholarly bodies with material until they were forced to acknowledge our existence and our merit. We had plans for another book as well, which ultimately turned into two: *Dragon Breeds of the Bayembe Region* and *Dragon Breeds of Mouleen*.

But I had not accounted for my celebrity, which brought a flood of mail and even some curiosity-seekers to my house in Pasterway. Natalie dealt with these, but I could not (and did not) refuse all invitations to events and house parties; if I wanted the Colloquium to acknowledge me as a scholar, it was to my benefit to present myself as such in public. (This also lent strength to my assertions that any scandals, real or imagined, associated with my time in Eriga were secondary at best to my true purpose there.) I set to work making a place for myself in Society, even if it was not the place Society intended for me.

And, one Athemer morning in early Pluvis, I sat down in Kemble's parlour with Tom, Natalie, Lord Hilford, and Frederick Kemble himself, to discuss the matter of dragonbone.

"It was Canlan," Lord Hilford said. "I have no proof of it—nothing I could take to a court, not with a marquess as the defendant—but I'm certain he is the one behind the break-in. The man I set to investigating wrote to me recently, reporting that Canlan received a very large sum of money from a company in Va Hing. A new outfit, one whose members include several chemists and industrialists."

Tom frowned, drumming his fingers on one knee. "But why sell the information, when he could profit more by exploiting it himself?"

The earl snorted. "Because he needed ready money. The Canlan estates are not what they once were; to invest in this research himself would require more funds than he can spare. And also, I suppose, because he's lazy. Gilmartin isn't a chemist himself, which means he would need to hire men who are, which means dividing his profits, and also a great deal of work I doubt he's inclined to undertake. Much easier for him to hand it off to someone more energetic."

I thought of the accusations against me, that I had betrayed Scirland by helping Bayembe do without *our* help. That had largely been inadvertent on my part, but Canlan had sold this knowledge to Va Hing with malice aforethought.

Of course, I could hardly throw stones, not when we had stolen the seeds of it from a Chiavoran working for a Bulskoi lord in Vystrana. Whatever came of this would be an international collaboration, against the will of all involved.

"What do you have for us, Mr. Kemble?" I asked.

He rose and unlocked his desk, taking from it a small oblong wrapped in canvas. Because I was the one financing his work, he handed it to me first.

My hopes were too high; I nearly dropped the thing, surprised by its heavy weight. This was not the feather-light material from which we had built the *Furcula*. I unwrapped it nevertheless, and found in my hands a solid bar the color of dragonbone, no longer than my palm.

"Chemically, it's the right substance," Kemble said. "Which is more than I had a year ago. But the structure is entirely wrong. It's too dense; it weighs more than lead. Though it's stronger than lead, for what that's worth."

His tone said he did not think it was worth much. "If it has the strength of dragonbone, surely that is of use," I said, giving Tom the bar to examine.

Kemble grunted. "Only if you could produce it in large quantities, easily and cheaply. Which, right now, you can't. Or at least I can't. I gambled on making that; it cost all the funds you gave me

for the next year. I had to know if it would work. But you might as
well build your machines out of firestones as use that for any industrial purpose."

I could not contain my wince. His funds for a *year*? I could not
fault him for the experiment, but even so . . .

Kemble proceeded to outline the method by which he had created the bar, while Tom and Lord Hilford asked intelligent questions. I followed none of it, but slouched in my chair in a most
unladylike fashion and chewed on my lower lip. It was progress,
though not success. And I was determined to follow through until
it *became* success, even if it bankrupted me—but far better, of
course, if it did not. With Natalie now a part of my household and
Jacob steadily growing, I would need a greater income.

Up to that point, my sketches had only been for private pleasure, and later for field notes and scholarly illustrations. But news
of what transpired in Eriga had ignited public interest: all the
world knew the Moulish had just defeated the mightiest warriors
of the Ikwunde with dragons. Might there not be a market for
pictures? Several news-sheets had offered me money for the
"true story" of what happened in Eriga, and while I did not trust
them to report my experiences honestly, it suggested I might
profit by selling a non-scholarly book as well. Something of more
substance than *A Journey to the Mountains of Vystrana*, but less
density than what I would present to the scholarly community.

I had more reasons than just Kemble's research and the main-
tenance of my own household to spur me. Lord Hilford had been
my patron for this expedition, but I could not depend upon his
generosity forever; he had his own financial security to consider,
and besides which, he was not a young man. By the time I was
ready to begin the project I had in mind, he might not be in a position to fund it.

The sea-snake we had seen on the voyage to Nsebu; the lack

of difference between savannah snakes and arboreal snakes; the drakeflies in Mouleen; the swamp-wyrms and their queenly kin and the fangfish I had not known were related. Wolf-drakes and sparklings and wyverns, and all the other creatures that we classed as mere cousins. I was increasingly convinced that our entire draconic taxonomy needed to be rethought—but to do that properly, much less persuade anyone to heed me, I would need a great deal more data than I had now. For all my reading, there were still woeful gaps in my knowledge, particularly where the scholarship was in another tongue; and once I had remedied that lack, I would need to undertake a much larger study than anyone, so far as I knew, had ever attempted.

Tom saw me chewing on my lip and leaned over. "Something troubling you?"

"Not troubling, precisely," I said, keeping my voice down so that I might not interrupt Kemble and Lord Hilford.

He raised one eyebrow, inviting me to elaborate.

A slow grin crept over my face, against all rationality and common sense. "How much do you suppose a voyage around the world might cost?"

THE MEMOIRS OF LADY TRENT CONTINUE IN

VOYAGE OF
THE BASILISK

AVAILABLE AT ALL
BOOKSELLERS OF REPUTE.

Lady Trent has graciously shared an excerpt from
the manuscript for your enjoyment.

ONE

Life in Falchester—Abigail Carew—A meeting of the Flying University—M. Suderac—Galinke's messenger—Skin conditions

At no point did I form the conscious intention of founding an *ad hoc* university in my sitting room. It happened, as it were, by accident.

The process began soon after Natalie Oscott became my live-in companion, having been disowned by her father for running away to Eriga. My finances could not long support the two of us in my accustomed style, especially not with my growing son to consider. I had to surrender some portion of my life as it had been until then, and since I was unwilling to surrender my scholarship, other things had to go.

What went was the house in Pasterway. Not without a pang; it had been my home for several years, even if I had spent a goodly percentage of that time in foreign countries, and I had fond memories of the place. Moreover, it was the only home little Jacob had known, and I did question for some time whether it was advisable to uproot so young a boy, much less to transplant him into the chaotic environment of a city. It was, however, far more economical for us to take up residence in Falchester, and so in the end we went.

Ordinarily, of course, city life is far more expensive than rural—even when the "rural" town in question is Pasterway, which nowadays has become a direct suburb of the capital. But much of this expense assumes that one is living in the city for the purpose of enjoying its glittering social life: concerts and operas, art exhibitions and fashion, balls and drums and sherry breakfasts. I had no interest in such matters. My concern was with intellectual commerce, and in that regard Falchester was not only superior but much cheaper.

There I could make use of the splendid Alcroft lending library, now better known as one of the foundational institutions of the Royal Libraries. This saved me a great deal of expense, as my research needs had grown immensely, and to purchase everything I required (or to send books back to helpful friends via the post) would have bankrupted me in short order. I could also attend what lectures would grant a woman entrance, without the trouble of several hours' drive; indeed, I no longer needed to maintain a carriage and all its associated equipment and personnel, but rather could hire one as necessary. The same held true for visits with friends, and here it is that the so-called "Flying University" began to take shape.

The early stages of it were driven by my need for a governess. Natalie Oscott, though a good companion to me, had no wish to take on the responsibility of raising and educating my son. I therefore cast my net for someone who would, taking pains to specify in advance that my household was not at all a usual one.

The lack of a husband was, for some applicants, a selling point. I imagine many of my readers are aware of the awkward position in which governesses often find themselves—or rather, the awkward position into which their male employers often put them, for it does no one any service to pretend this happens by some natural and inexorable process, devoid of connection with anyone's behaviour. My requirements for their qualifications, however, were off-putting to many. Mathematics were unnecessary, as Natalie was more than willing to tutor my son in arithmetic, algebra, and geometry (and would, by the time he was ready for calculus, have taught it to herself), but I insisted upon a solid grounding in literature, languages, and a variety of sciences, not to mention the history not only of Scirland but other countries as well. This made the process of reviewing applicants quite arduous. But it paid an interesting dividend: by the time I hired Abigail Carew, I had also made the acquaintance of a number of young ladies who lacked sufficient learning, yet possessed the *desire* for it in spades.

I will not pretend I founded the Flying University in order to educate unsatisfactory governess candidates. Indeed, most of those young ladies I never saw again, as they moved on in search of less stringent employers. But the experience heightened my awareness of that lack in our society, and so once I had my subscription to the Alcroft, I made the contents of my library (both owned and borrowed) available to anyone who wished to make use of it.

The result was that, by the time my sea expedition began, on any given Athemer evening you might find anywhere from two to twenty people occupying my sitting room and study. The former room was a place of quiet reading, where friends might educate themselves on any subject my library could supply. Indeed, by then its reach extended far beyond my own shelves and items borrowed from the Alcroft, as it became a trading center for those who wished to avail themselves of others' resources. Candles and lamps were one point upon which I did not scrimp, and so they could read in perfect comfort.

The study, by contrast, was a place of conversation. Here we might ask questions of one another, or debate issues on which we held differing views. Often these discussions became quite convivial, the lot of us raising one another up from the darkness of ignorance and into the light of, if not wisdom, then at least well-informed curiosity.

On other occasions, the discussions might better be termed "arguments."

"You know I love wings as much as the next woman," I said to

Miriam Farnswood—who, as a lady ornithologist, *was* the next woman, and very fond of wings. "But you are overstating their significance in this instance. Bats fly, and so do insects, and yet no one is suggesting that *they* are close relatives of birds."

"No one yet has found evidence of bats laying eggs," she said dryly. Miriam was nearly twenty years my senior, and it was only in the last six months that I had ventured to address her by her given name. Not coincidentally, the last six months had also seen the commencement of this particular debate, in which we were very much at odds. "It's your own work that persuades me, Isabella; I don't know why you resist so strenuously. The skeletal structure of dragons shows many resemblances to that of birds."

She was referring, of course, to the hollow structure of the bones. This was not often to be found in reptiles, which I championed as the nearest relation to dragons. I said impatiently, "Hollow bones may easily be evolved on separate occasions. After all, that is what seems to have happened with wings, is it not? Much *less* common to evolve a new set of forelegs, where none were before."

"You think it more plausible that reptiles suddenly evolved wings, where none had previously been?" Miriam snorted. It was not a very ladylike snort. She was the sort of woman one expected to find tramping the countryside in tweeds with a gun under her arm and a bulldog at her side, probably one of her own breeding. The delicacy with which she moved when out birding was nothing short of startling. "Please, Isabella. By that reasoning, you *should* be arguing for their relation to insects. At least those have more than four limbs."

The reference to insects diverted me from what I had been about to say. "Sparklings do complicate the picture," I admitted. "I really am persuaded that they are an extremely dwarfish breed of dragon—though I am at a loss to explain how such a reduction in size might come about. Even those tiny dogs they have in Coyahuac are not so much smaller than the largest breed of hound."

My comment brought a quiet chuckle from a few feet away. Tom Wilker had been in conversation with the suffragette Lucy Devere, discussing the politics of the Synedrion, but their talk had momentarily flagged, and he had overheard me. It was not the first time he had been subjected to my thoughts on sparklings, which were an endless conundrum to me in matters of taxonomy.

We could hardly avoid eavesdropping on one another's words. My Hart Square townhouse was not so large as to give us much in the way of elbow room. And indeed, I often preferred it that way, for it encouraged us to wander from topic to topic and group to group, rather than separating off into little clusters for the duration of the evening. Tabitha Small and Peter Landenbury had been sharing their thoughts on a recent work of history, but as usual, Lucy had drawn them into her orbit. With Elizabeth Hardy rounding out their set, there were seven of us in my study, which more or less filled it to capacity.

Miriam's eyebrows had gone up at my digression from the point. I shook my head to clear it and said, "Be that as it may. I think you are reading too much into the fact that the quetzalcoatls of Coyahuac have feathers. They are not true dragons, by Edgeworth's definition—"

"Oh, come now, Isabella," she said. "You can hardly use Edgeworth as your defense, when you yourself have led the charge in questioning his entire theory."

"I have not yet reached any conclusions," I said firmly. "Ask me again when this expedition is done. With any luck, I will observe a feathered serpent with my own eyes, and then I will be able to say with more certainty where they fit in the draconic family."

The door opened quietly, and Abby Carew slipped through. She looked tired, even in the forgiving candlelight. Jake had been running her ragged lately. The prospect of going on a sea voyage had so fired his imagination that he could hardly be made to sit at his lessons.

The notion of bringing my son along had come to me about two years previously. When I first conceived the notion of a trip around the world, to study dragons in all the places they might be found, Jake had been a mere toddler—far too young to accompany me. But such a expedition is not organized overnight, nor even in a single year. By the time I was certain the expedition would happen, let alone had prepared myself for it, Jake was already seven. Boys have gone to war at sea that young. Why should one not go in the name of science?

I had not forgotten the opprobrium I faced when I went to Eriga, leaving my son behind. It seemed to me that the clear solution to this problem was not to stay forever at home, but rather to bring him with me the next time. I saw it as a splendid educational opportunity for a boy of nine. Others, of course, saw it as more of my characteristic madness.

I excused myself to Miriam Farnswood and crossed the room to meet Abby. She said, "Natalie sent me to tell you—"

"Oh dear," I sighed, before she could finish. A guilty look at the clock confirmed my suspicion. "It has gotten late, hasn't it?"

Abby was kind enough not to belabor the point. The truth was, I did not want to show my guests to the door. This was to be our last gathering before I left—or rather I should say *my* last gathering, since Natalie would continue to host them in my absence. As much as the upcoming voyage excited me, I would miss these evenings, where I could expand my mind and test its strengths against people whose intelligence dwarfed mine. Thanks to them, my understanding of the world had grown far beyond its early, naive beginnings. And I, for my part, had done what I could to share my knowledge in return, especially with those individuals, male or female, whose opportunities had not been as great as mine.

I write in the past tense now; I caught myself *thinking* in the past tense then, and shook myself. I was going on a voyage, not relocating to the other side of the world forever. What had started in my sitting room was not ending tonight. My part in it was merely pausing.

They went without a fuss, though with a great many good wishes for safe travels and great discoveries. The farewells took more than a half hour in all. The last to depart was Tom Wilker, who had no need to say farewell; we would be going on the voyage together, for I could not imagine trying to conduct research without his assistance.

"Did I overhear you promising specimens to Mrs. Farnswood?" he asked, when it was just him, myself, and Natalie in the foyer.

"Yes, of birds," I said. "She will pay for them, or sell those she does not wish to keep for herself. It will be another source of funds, and a welcome one."

He nodded, though his smile was rueful. "I don't know when we'll find the time to sleep. Or rather, when *you* will find the time. I'm not the one who has promised regular reports to the *Winfield Courier*."

"I will sleep at night," I said, very reasonably. "Writing by lamplight is a terrible waste of oil, and there are not so many species of nocturnal birds as to keep me busy *every* night."

It got a laugh from him, as I had intended. "Sleep well, Isabella. You'll need your rest."

Natalie came out into the hall in time to bid him goodnight. When the door was shut behind him, she turned to face me. "Are you very tired, or can you spare a few moments?"

I was far too awake to sleep just yet, and would only read if I tried to go to bed. "Does it have to do with the arrangements for my absence?"

Natalie shook her head. We had been over those matters enough times already: my will, in case I should die; the transfer of my townhouse to her temporary stewardship; how to contact me once I was abroad; all the logistical hedges that must be leapt before I could depart. She said, "I spoke with Mr. Kemble again today."

I sighed. "Come to my study. I shall want to sit for this, I think."

My worn old chair was some comfort to me while pondering a topic that was not comfortable at all. Once ensconced in its embrace, I said to Natalie, "He wants me to make a deal with the Thiessois."

"He is at a standstill," Natalie said. "He has been for more than a year. The fine structure of dragonbone continues to elude him, and so long as it does, you do not have synthesis. M. Suderac's aeration process may be what we need."

The mere mention of this topic made me want to beat my head against my desk. Only the knowledge that Frederick Kemble had been beating his head against something far less yielding for nearly a decade now restrained me. Tom and I had hired him to create a synthetic replacement for preserved dragonbone, so that human society might enjoy the benefits of that substance without having to slaughter dragons to obtain it. Kemble had re-created its chemical composition, but the airy lattice of its structure, which reduced the already-slight weight without sacrificing strength, had proven less tractable.

Natalie was correct: the aeration process devised by M. Suderac might indeed help. I, however, could not abide the man—to the point where the mere thought of partnering with him for such a venture made me ill. He was a handsome Thiessois fellow, and clearly thought his good looks ought to earn him more than mere friendliness from me. After all, I was a widow, and if not as young as I had once been, I had not gathered so very much dust on the shelf yet. It was not marriage M. Suderac wanted from me; he had a wife, and even if he did not, I offered very little in the way of property to tempt him. He merely wanted unfettered access to my person. To say that I was disinclined to grant it to him is a howling understatement.

And yet, if financial partnership would save the lives of countless dragons . . .

The secret of preserving dragonbone was out in the world. That particular cat had escaped its bag before I went to Eriga, when thieves employed by the Marquess of Canlan broke into Kemble's laboratory and stole his notes, and Canlan subsequently sold them to a Yelangese company, the Va Ren Shipping Association. The fellows there seemed to have kept a relatively tight lid on their information, for it had not become common knowledge yet, but I knew it was spreading. Which meant the need for a synthetic substitute was urgent.

I weighed these factors, until my heart sat like lead in my chest. "I do not trust him," I said at last to Natalie. "I *cannot*. He is the sort of man who sees a thing and wants it, and thinks that alone entitles him to have it. I truly would not put it past him to crack the problem at last, but then keep the results for his own profit. And while I might forego my own stake if it meant having the answer, I cannot allow Kemble and the others to be robbed in such fashion."

Natalie dropped her head against the back of the chair, staring in resignation at the ceiling. "Well, I tried. You are not wrong about Suderac, I think—but I do not know how else we will make it happen."

"Perhaps *I* should try hiring thieves. They could break in and steal the secrets of the aeration process."

"Thank God you're about to get on board a ship," Natalie said. "Otherwise, I think you might honestly follow through."

She exaggerated—but not by much. For the sake of dragons, there was very little I would not do.

The next morning's post brought a number of letters, some of them from people who had not noticed that I was about to be gone from home for an extended period of time and would not have much chance to answer them. One, however, caught my eye.

The handwriting on the outside of the envelope was unfamiliar to me. It was not merely that I did not recognize the hand; the entire style of it was strange, as if written by a foreigner. And yet it reminded me of something, but I could not say what.

Curious, I slit the flap with my knife. The note inside was written on excellent paper, again in that strange hand. It was an invitation to join one Wademi n Oforiro Dara for lunch at the Salburn that day, if I was not already engaged.

Now I knew what the handwriting had evoked. I was still in occasional contact with Galinke n Oforiro Dara, the half-sister of the oba of Bayembe. This man's script showed traces of the same style, though in his case much fainter. From this I deduced that he was more accustomed to writing in Scirling than Galinke was.

Oforiro Dara. He was of the same lineage as Galinke. A brother? No, I was fairly certain she had no brothers born to the same mother, and the Yembe inherit their lineage names through the maternal line. He might be anything from Galinke's mother's sister's son to a far more distant cousin than that. But the connection was enough to make me dash off a quick acceptance and send it to the man's hotel. My alternative plans for lunch involved a quick meal gulped down while packing; this promised to be far more interesting.

In those days, I did not often dine at the Salburn—which is my polite way of saying that I could not really afford it. I minded very little; I have never been a gourmand. But it meant that Wademi n Oforiro Dara was either a wealthy man or well-funded by someone else, as lunch for two there was not a thing to undertake lightly.

I had no difficulty spotting him in the lobby. He was Yembe and dark, and dressed after their fashion in a wrapped and folded cloth, though he made concession to Scirland's cooler climate and stricter sense of propriety with a mantle over his upper body. The coloration was almost Scirling-sober, too: black and gold in a simple geometric pattern. He was already on his feet when I entered, and approached me immediately.

We exchanged Yembe greetings, which served to show me just how badly my accent and grammar had deteriorated. When he shifted to my native tongue, I apologized to him for it. "I'm afraid my command of Yembe has atrophied terribly for lack of use—and it was not good to begin with. Galinke and I correspond in Scirling."

His own Scirling was accented but fluent. "You should come for a visit! I hear that you are about to set off on a journey. Will you be stopping in Bayembe?"

"Would that I could go *everywhere*," I said. "But I'm afraid that my research requires me to expand my knowledge in breadth, rather than depth. I must devote my time to new areas and new species."

This was true, but not the entire story. I could not tell this man about my conversation with a certain member of the Synedrion (who shall remain nameless, though he is dead now and cannot be harmed by the gossip), wherein he made it clear to me that the government would not look kindly on my ever returning to Bayembe. What precisely they feared, I cannot say; I only ever knew the one state secret about our affairs there, and it was long since out of the bag. But having thus erred once, I could not be trusted not to err again.

To my surprise, Wademi and I did not dine in the main room. He had acquired one of the private rooms for us—perhaps because that way we attracted less attention, the Yembe man and the woman once accused of betraying her country for his. The mystery of how he could afford such a thing was soon cleared up, for it transpired that he was indeed the son of Galinke's mother's sister. Anyone so closely linked with the oba of Bayembe, even through a lesser wife, could easily purchase me and my entire household without so much as a blink.

We passed the starter course with pleasantries, but after the main course arrived, I discovered that he had another reason for arranging this private room.

"What have you heard of the dragons?" he asked, once the waiter was gone.

"The dragons?" I echoed. My mind was so full of various draconic species that it took me longer than it should have to see his meaning. "Do you mean the ones the Moulish have given to Bayembe?"

It was not that I had forgotten them. One does not easily forget about deals one has helped broker between two foreign peoples, especially when that assistance has caused one to be accused of treason. But my interest in dragons was biological, not political; the fact that there were now Moulish swamp-wyrms in Bayembe rivers was not at the forefront of my thoughts.

Wademi nodded, and I spread my hands. "I have heard very little, really. Galinke mentioned that the eggs had been brought as promised, and then had hatched—I believe she said the total was somewhat poor, though. There were arrangements to make sure the fangfish were sufficiently fed. But nothing since then." Which, now that I thought of it, was peculiar. Granted, the dragons in the rivers of Bayembe were intended as a defense for that country's border, and as such might be a protected secret. But Galinke would know very well that I wanted to hear more of their progress, and could have found some way to tell me *something*. Instead, her infrequent letters had diverted me with other matters.

It seemed that she had indeed found a way to tell me something, and his name was Wademi n Oforiro Dara. "The situation has become . . . odd," he said, "and we are hoping you can make sense of it."

This, of course, piqued my curiosity like nothing else. "What do you mean, 'odd'?"

He spoke slowly, in between bites of his food. I reminded myself to eat my own, though I fear the best efforts of the Salburn chefs were entirely wasted on me that day.

Wademi said, "At first it was the eggs, which did not hatch in the quantities hoped. But the Moulish brought more the next year, so we have enough now. The fangfish ate one another, and those who survived grew—some of them. Many were runts. But even those which grew are not like the dragons in the swamp. They are more slender."

"Juveniles," I said. "Have you asked the Moulish? They would know how long it takes to reach full maturation."

He shook his head. "They should be fully grown now. And their hide is different; their scales are more fine."

I could not stop myself from asking, "Are you certain it is not a skin condition?"

By way of reply, he reached beneath his mantle and brought out a small box, which he laid on the table between us. When I opened it, a strong smell of formaldehyde marred the air. The box contained a scrap of skin, which I pinched gently between my fingernails and lifted for a better view.

It was not a skin condition. I had often observed the rough, crocodilian hides of swamp-wyrms, and while they were vulnerable to disease, what illness would *refine* their integument? What I held in my hand was more like the skin of a fish.

Or a savannah snake. "They cannot have bred with the dragons of Bayembe," I said. Although some of that species ventured into the fringes of the Moulish jungle, they did not go far enough in to encounter swamp-wyrms. And even if they did—and succeeded in producing viable eggs—the Moulish would not have given those eggs to the oba. They had a very rigorous process for breeding their dragons, which involved taking the males of the swamp proper to the lake where the queens swam.

My fingernails pinched tighter on the skin. The queens . . .

I had not learned as much about swamp-wyrm biology as I would have liked. I knew that the Moulish took the eggs after their laying and distributed them about the swamp, and I knew that the different incubation of the eggs encouraged some to develop into queens, while the rest remained male. (At the time I suspected, but had not had a chance to prove, that some of the "males" were either neuter or infertile females. Neuter sex was known in other draconic types, and I had a sense that only some of the wyrms in the swamp were eligible to breed with the queens. But I had not gotten to examine enough dragons at sufficiently close range to be certain.)

My head was awhirl with these thoughts and others, various theories and observations colliding in untidy ways. What emerged from the scrum was this: what if the transplantation of the eggs to the rivers of Bayembe had produced queens instead of males?

My observations of the queen dragons had all been at *quite* a distance, so I was only speculating that their hides featured such fine, overlapping scales. It made sense, though. They swam in the turbulent waters of the lake below the Great Cataract, where they would benefit from a more streamlined surface.

But if that were the case, why had the Moulish not said anything to the Yembe?

Because they did not want the existence of the queens known. The oba would certainly try to trade for one, and if that failed, he might well try to take one by stealth or force. Or, if he learned enough of the incubation procedures, try to mimic them so that he might breed his own dragons, without needing to rely on the Moulish.

Which left me in rather a pickle. If my theory could be correct, then I desperately wanted confirmation. Moreover, Wademi—and through him, Galinke and all her people, half-brother included— were looking to me for aid. But it would not very well repay my Moulish friends if I spilled a secret they were trying to keep.

I laid the skin back in its box. "I am not certain what to say. It may be a response to the cleaner, fresher environment of the rivers; swamp water is very full of silt and organic matter, which I imagine is quite an irritant to the skin of the young dragons." Certainly it had been an irritant to my own hide. "Do your dragons seem healthy?"

"For the most part," Wademi said.

"I should like to know if they keep growing," I said. "Some fishes change size according to their environment; it is possible that your dragons will grow larger than those in the swamp, because of the more open waters." If they grew to more than four meters in length, that would tell me a great deal. The queens, from what I had seen of them, were much larger than the males.

Wademi made the humming noise that, among the Yembe, stood in for the refusal it would be rude to state directly. I thought about our private room, and Galinke's reticence in her letters. He had invited me to lunch so as to convey information they did not want committed to paper. (It did not occur to me until some months later that someone in Scirland might even be reading my mail. If they did not want me going to Bayembe, they might have an interest in the letters I sent to and received from there. To this day, I do not know if it was so.)

My thoughts were not on such matters that day, but even then I knew it might be difficult to keep me informed. I sighed, saying, "It will be difficult to write to me regardless, as I shall be rather peripatetic for a while."

"But what of the dragons?"

Even had I possessed the courage to defy that unnamed gentleman of the Synedrion, I could not change our itinerary now. Although there was room for diversion in it—as this account will demonstrate—we could not divert all the way to Bayembe, just so I could look in on the dragons in the rivers. "I'm afraid there is very little I can do from where I am, sir. If they are healthy, then surely that is enough."

He looked dissatisfied. Had I given the Yembe such a high opinion of my knowledge that they believed I could resolve this question over lunch in a distant country? Or had they expected me to come to their aid in person? If so, it pained me to disappoint them. But there was nothing for it: too many things prevented me from going.

As a sop to Wademi, I said, "I anticipate a great expansion in my knowledge of dragons, thanks to this expedition. It is possible I will learn something of use to you."

Which, as it happened, was true—albeit in a roundabout way. But that was no comfort to him at the time, and so we both left our meeting in less than good spirits.

ABOUT THE AUTHOR

MARIE BRENNAN habitually pillages her background in anthropology, archaeology, and folklore for fictional purposes. She is the author of the Onyx Court series, the Doppelganger duology of *Warrior* and *Witch*, and the urban fantasy *Lies and Prophecy*, as well as more than forty short stories. Learn more at www.swantower.com.